THE BLUE MOON EROTIC READER III

THE BLUE MOON EROTIC READER III

BLUE MOON BOOKS
NEW YORK

The Blue Moon Erotic Reader III

Published by
Blue Moon Books
An Imprint of Avalon Publishing Group Incorporated
161 William St., 16th Floor
New York, NY 10038

ISBN 1-56201-315-7

9 8 7 6 5 4 3 2 1

Printed in the United States of America
Distributed by Publishers Group West

Contents

from

Tropic of Lust

by Michele de Saint-Exupery

1

Michele was taking the plane from London to Bangkok. All that she could perceive on her first glimpse at the inside of the plane was the odor of new leather, the thickness and the silence of the carpets, and the lighting of another world.

She couldn't understand what the smiling man who was guiding her had said, but she wasn't worried. Perhaps her heart was beating more quickly, but it was not out of apprehension or bewilderment. The blue uniforms, the signs of attentiveness, and the authority of the personnel charged with welcoming and initiating her all gave her a feeling of security and euphoria. As for the rites she had to go through at the various counters—whose mysteries she had not even tried to understand—she knew that their object was to give her access to a universe that would belong to her for twelve hours of her life: a universe with laws that were restricting but delectable. This structure of winged metal would soon be sealed and the freedom of the outside world would give way to the leisure and quietude of the flight.

They pointed out her compartment. It was uniformly covered and had no holes. The traveler could see nothing beyond that silky wall. What difference did it make? Michele wanted nothing more than to give herself up to the softness of those deep armchairs, to be numbed between their soft arms, to lean against their shoulders and on their long siren's legs.

She didn't dare stretch out yet as the steward had invited her to do, showing her the controls that made the back go down. He pressed a button and a lilliputian beam of light traced a bright ellipse over her knees.

A hostess walked by with her hands flying, placing the light honey-colored leather bag which Michele had brought over her seat in a little compartment. The hostess spoke French and the feeling of dizziness that Michele had been experiencing for two days in a foreign country went away.

The young girl leaned over her and her blondness made Michele's long hair seem even darker. They were both dressed almost identically: blue skirt, white blouse and shantung jacket. But as light as the English girl's bra was it deprived her silhouette of the mobility which Michele's naked chest disclosed. And, while the rules of the company forced the stewardess to button her blouse up to her neck, Michele's blouse was open in such a way that an attentive spectator could make out the profile of a breast either by chance or with the complicity of a sudden air current.

Michele was happy that the hostess was young and that her eyes were like her own—dark with tiny chips of gold.

Her compartment, she heard the girl say, was the last in the plane and the closest to the tail. This would insulate Michele from all the jolts that the other parts of the plane would experience (and here the young girl's voice filled with pride); on board this plane the comfort was not the same everywhere, because obviously the passengers in the tourist class would not benefit from as much space around them nor from such soft seats or the privacy of the velvet curtains between each row of chairs.

Michele wasn't ashamed of these privileges nor of the fortune she had to spend to procure them. On the contrary, she experienced an almost physical pleasure at the thought of the excess of attention of which she was the object.

Now the hostess was boasting about the management of the rest rooms, which she would let her passengers visit as soon as the flight had begun. There were a sufficient number on either side of the plane so that Michele wouldn't have to worry about walking a great distance. If she desired, she would only have to come in contact with the three people who were sharing her compartment. But if, on the contrary, she preferred a little company, then it would be easy for her to become acquainted with the other passengers by walking along the aisles or sitting down at the bar. Did she wish something to read?

"No," said Michele, "no thank you. You are very sweet. I don't want to read at the moment."

She wondered what she could do to please the hostess. Should she show interest in the plane? What speed were they flying at?

"Over seven hundred miles an hour with only one intermediary stop." Michele's trip would thus take no more than half a day. But, since she was going to lose time turning in the same direction as the earth, she would not arrive in Bangkok before nine o'clock the next morning, local time. Therefore, she would barely have time to have dinner, get some sleep, and get dressed.

Two children, a boy and a girl, so identical that they could only have been twins, parted the curtain. Michele noticed their conventional and ungraceful behavior, indicative of

English schoolchildren, their almost Russian blondness, their expressions of affected coldness, and the arrogance with which they spoke in short phrases that they spit from their lips to the company employees. Although it seemed that they were no more than twelve or thirteen, the sureness of their gestures assured a distance between them and the employees which the stewardess would not have dreamed of attempting to breach. They placed themselves squarely in their seats which were separated from Michele by an aisle. Before she had a chance to examine them in detail, the last of the four passengers for whom the compartment had been reserved entered and the young woman's attention turned to him.

He was over a head taller than she, with a resolute chin and nose, black hair and mustache. He smiled at Michele, leaning over her a little to place a dark leather briefcase in the compartment over the seats. Michele liked his amber suit and white shirt. She thought he was elegant and well-bred which are, after all, the essential qualities that one expects from a neighboring traveler.

She tried to guess his age—forty, fifty? He must have lived well because of those little lines of indulgence around his eyes. His presence was more agreeable, she thought, than that of those pretentious little brats. But she immediately laughed at herself for this hasty aversion. It was useless—they would only be together for one night! She fell back into indifference.

Or rather, she forgot the children and the man. As she relaxed, the sensation of irritation which had been floating between the waters of her mind for a moment left her and was no longer spoiling the pleasure of her departure. The hostess, profiting by the commotion that the arrival of the new passengers had created, had left their compartment and through the gap in the curtains, Michele noticed her blue hips pressed against an invisible voyager. She hated herself for her jealousy and tried to turn her eyes away. A phrase from somewhere ran through her mind like a sad chant: "In solitude and in abandonment." She shook off the feeling, her black hair whipping her cheeks and flowing over her face. The hostess, finished with her duties for the moment, returned to the back of the plane, appearing between the draperies whose lazy legs she parted with her hands. She went over to Michele.

"Would you like me to introduce you to your traveling companions?" she asked and, without waiting for an answer, she announced the man's name.

Michele thought she heard "Eisenhower" which amused her and made her miss the twins' names.

Now the man was speaking to her. What could she say to him? The hostess saw Michele's embarrassment and questioned her compatriots, laughing and uncovering the tip of her tongue.

"What a shame," she said. "None of your companions knows any French. What a marvelous opportunity for you to refresh your English!"

Michele tried to protest, but the young girl had already turned, moving her fingers in a hermetic and gracious sign to the passengers. Then she was gone. Michele was alone. She wanted to sulk, to be disinterested in everything.

Her neighbor persevered and tried to articulate sentences whose fruitless good will made her smile. She made an apologetic expression and confessed in a childish voice: "I don't understand!" He resigned himself and was silent.

Just then a loudspeaker came on. After the English announcer had finished, Michele recognized the stewardess' voice slightly altered by the amplifier and speaking French (*for me,* she told herself). She welcomed her passengers, gave the time, the list of the crew members, notified them that the takeoff would be in a few minutes, that their seatbelts should be buckled (a steward came up to adjust Michele's himself), and that the passengers were requested not to move as long as the red light was on.

Hardly more than a murmur, a shiver of the soundproof compartments, gave away the sound of the motors being started. Michele didn't even notice that the plane was rolling along the runway. It took her a long time to realize that she was flying.

She only guessed it when the red signal went out and the man got up and offered to hang up her suit jacket which she had kept on her knees. She let him. He smiled again, opened a book and didn't look up again. A waiter appeared, carrying a tray of glasses. Michele chose a cocktail whose color she thought she recognized, but it wasn't what she had expected. It was much stronger.

What must have been an afternoon beyond the silk walls passed without Michele having time to do anything else but eat pastries, drink tea, and leaf through a magazine that the hostess had given her (she refused a second one so as not to be distracted from the novelty of flying).

A little later, they put a small table in front of her and they served her numerous dishes. A quart of champagne accompanied the meal which seemed to Michele to last for hours. But she was in no hurry as this game was beginning to please her. There were many desserts and coffee and liqueurs in immense glasses. When they came to take the table away, Michele was certain she was going to enjoy her adventure and began to savor the sweetness of life.

She felt light and a little sleepy. She noticed that she had even lost her dislike for the twins. The hostess came and went, never failing to say something nice to her in passing.

She wondered how late it was and if it was time to sleep.

But in truth, wasn't she free to sleep any time she wished? Having reached that part of space in which there were no more winds or clouds, Michele could no longer even be sure whether it was day or night.

Michele's knees were naked under the gold lights. Her skirt had uncovered them and the man's eyes were now glued to them.

She was conscious that she was lifting her knees so that he could take his pleasure. But would she make herself look ridiculous by covering them? Anyway, how could she do it? She couldn't stretch her skirt any further. And why was she suddenly ashamed of her knees? She loved to have as much of her legs showing as possible below her skirts. She knew the excitement they would cause. As she contemplated the beauty of her body, she felt her temples beating more quickly and she closed her eyes. Now Michele no longer saw herself partially, but completely naked, giving in to the temptation of this narcissistic contemplation before which she knew that she would once again be defenseless.

She resisted, but only to better taste, by degrees, the delights of abandonment. This was announced by a diffuse languor, a sort of warm awareness of her whole body, a desire for relaxation and opening without any precise thoughts or identifiable emotions; nothing which was very different from the physical satisfaction that she would have experienced from stretching out in the sun on a warm beach. Then, gradually, at the same time as the surface of her lips became more brilliant, as her breasts began to swell, she stretched her legs out, attentive to the slightest contact, and her brain began to cry out images, at first almost formless but sufficient to moisten her membranes and arch her back.

Half imperceptibly, but steadily, the cushioned vibrations of the metal cocoon harmonized with Michele and blended with the rhythm of her body. A wave rose along her legs, leaving her knees, echoing inexorably on the surface of her thighs, higher and higher, making her shiver.

From then on her fantasies took flight obsessively: lips resting on her skin, male and female organs against her face, cocks touching her, rubbing against her, making a passage between her knees, forcing her legs apart, opening her cunt, penetrating her with a force that would overwhelm her. One after another they entered Michele's body, never finding an end to their voyage, traveling indefinitely inside her, taking their fill of her flesh and finally relieving themselves of their juices inside her.

The hostess thought Michele was asleep and she carefully lowered the chair, transforming it into a couch. She stretched a cashmere blanket over her long legs which the lowering of the chair had uncovered to mid-thigh. The man got up then and made the same maneuver which placed his seat next to his neighbor's. The children were asleep. The hostess said good-night and turned out the overhead lights. Only two violet night-lights prevented the objects and people from losing all form.

Michele had abandoned herself to the care the girl was taking without opening her eyes. Her dream had not lost its intensity or its urgency during the course of these movements. Her right hand was now running over her abdomen very slowly, holding back, finally reaching the level of her cunt under the light blanket which her movement was causing to undulate. But, in this darkness, who would see? With the tips of her fingers she explored herself, and crushed the supple silk of her skirt whose tightness was opposing what her legs were half-opening: they were stretching the material in their effort to part; they finally succeeded enough so that her fingers could feel through the thinness of the material the tip of erectile flesh which they sought and on which they pressed tenderly.

For several seconds, Michele let the waves subside in her body. She was trying to hold back her orgasm. But soon, no longer holding back, she began with a stifled moan to give her middle fingers the tiny and gentle impulse that would bring her orgasm. Almost immediately, the man's hand rested on hers.

Breathless, Michele felt her muscles and her nerves tense, as if a flood of icy water had been thrown at her. She remained immobile, not empty of sensations but with all sensations and all thoughts stopped in the way a film is stopped without obscuring the image. She was not afraid nor was she really restricted. She didn't have the feeling of being caught at anything either. In truth, she was not at that moment capable of formulating a judgment about the movement or the man or her own conduct. She had registered the event, then her mind had become fixed. Now, from all evidence, she was awaiting what was going to succeed her own thought.

The man's hand did not move, yet it wasn't inactive. Just by its weight it was exercising a pressure on her clitoris, on which Michele's hand was resting. Nothing else happened for a long time.

Then Michele noticed that another hand was lifting the covers and pushing them away to be able to seize one of her knees and touch it in detail. Soon it rose in a low motion along her thigh, moving over the top of her stockings.

When the hand reached her naked skin for the first time, Michele jumped and tried to escape. But, partly because she didn't know exactly what she wanted to accomplish, and partly because the man's two hands seemed too strong for her to have the least chance of escaping their grasp, she scarcely lifted her head and shoulders, brought her free hand to her abdomen as if to protect it and turned over on her side. She realized that it would have been as simple and more efficacious to press her legs together without being able to explain why this movement seemed suddenly so laughable that she didn't dare do it. Finally, she renounced control over a situation that was overwhelming her, letting herself be overcome again by the paralysis that she had only succeeded in surmounting for a brief instant.

As if they intended to teach Michele a lesson for her vain revolt, the man's hands abandoned her suddenly. She didn't have time to wonder what this sudden withdrawal meant because they were on her again already, this time at waist level—sure, rapid, undoing the zipper in her skirt, pulling the material over her hips down to her knees. Then they rose again. One hand penetrated Michele's panties, which were thin and transparent like all the underwear which she usually wore—garterbelt, sometimes panties, but never a bra or girdle. In the shops where she bought her lingerie, however, she often tried on innumerable models of strapless bras, long-lines, girdles, or all-in-ones with one or another of the blonde, brunette, beautiful half-real salesgirls who would get on their knees at her feet, uncovering their long legs and moving their long, graceful fingers over her breasts or thighs and caressing her patiently with repeated, supple movements until Michele's eyes closed and she gently bent her knees, resting on the ground strewn with nylon and opened, warm, giving up to the perfect and intoxicating skill of the hands and lips.

Michele's body fell back into the position from which her show of resistance had momentarily moved her. The man caressed her flat and muscular abdomen just above the swelling of her pussy, as one strokes the neck and shoulders of a thoroughbred. His fingers ran along the folds of her groin, then above her mound, tracing the sides of the triangle. The interior angle of it was very open, a rare enough quality which Greek sculptors have nonetheless perpetuated.

When the hand that was running over Michele's abdomen

had satiated itself with proportions, it forced her thighs to separate more, but her skirt around her knees was restricting their movements. They gave however, opening as much as they could. The hand caught the warm and swollen sex in its palm, caressing it as if to calm it, without haste, in a movement that followed the trail of the lips, plunging—at first lightly—between them, to pass over the erect clitoris and to come to rest on the thick pubic curls. Then, with each new passage between her legs, which were separating more and more, the man's fingers would move further, pushing more deeply between the humid moisture, slowing their progression, seeming to hesitate, as Michele's tension increased. Biting her lips to dam up the sob that was rising in her throat, arching her back, she was panting from the desire for the spasm which the man seemed to want to bring her to without ever letting her attain it.

With only one hand he was playing a rhythm and melody on her body according to his desires, disdaining her breasts and her mouth, seeming disinterested in kissing or embracing, nonchalant and distant. Michele was tossing her head from right to left and letting out a series of stifled moans, sounds which resembled a prayer. She half-opened her eyes and sought the man's face. There were tears in her eyes.

Then the hand stopped, holding on to the part of Michele's body that it had inflamed. The man leaned a little toward the passenger and took one of her hands with his other hand which he drew toward him and introduced inside his clothing. He helped her move over his rigid cock and guided her movements, regulating their amplitude and rhythm according to his desires, slowing her down or accelerating her according to the degree of his excitation, until he was sure that he could rely upon her intuition and desire.

Michele moved a little so that her arm could better serve the man and he in turn moved closer so that she could be sprinkled with the sperm that he felt forming in his glands. Yet he succeeded in holding back for a long time while Michele moved her fingers up and down, growing less and less timid, no longer restricting herself to an elementary coming-and-going motion but suddenly becoming expert, sliding along the big swollen vein, over the cock's arch, plunging as low as possible (imperceptibly scratching the skin with her long nails)—as close to his balls as the tightness of his pants permitted, then returning with lascivious torsion, until the folds in the supple skin in the hollow of her moist palm had covered the tip of the member, which she never seemed to reach as it continued to grow. Then, squeezing very hard again, the hand left for the bottom of the staff again, holding the foreskin, again and again strangling the tumescent flesh or relaxing its grip, rubbing the membrane or tormenting it, massaging with great wrist movements or with little merciless jabs. The gland, doubling its size, seemed closer to bursting at each instant. Then, at last, it came.

With a strange exaltation, Michele received the long white and odoriferous spurts which the satisfied cock finally released. It fell on her arms, her naked abdomen, her breasts, her face, her mouth, and in her hair. There seemed to be no end to it. She thought she could feel it flowing down her throat, as though she were drinking it . . . A strange pleasure came over her, a shameless ecstasy. When she let her arm fall, the man seized Michele's clitoris with the tips of his fingers and made her come.

A rumbling noise indicated that the loudspeaker was going to be used. The hostess' voice, intentionally stifled so that the passengers would not be too suddenly awakened, announced that the plane would rest at Bahrein for about twenty minutes. They would board at midnight, local time. A snack would be served at the airport.

The lights gradually came back on in the compartment, imitating the slowness of the rising sun. Michele used her blanket (which had slid to her feet) to sponge off the sperm that had covered her. She adjusted her skirt, covering her hips again. When the hostess came in, Michele, sitting up on the couch whose back she had not lifted, was still trying to fix herself up.

"Did you sleep well?" the young girl asked gaily.

Michele finished zipping up her skirt. "My blouse is all wrinkled," she said. She looked at the wet spots that were showing around her neck. She turned the collar out and the tip of one of her breasts appeared. The blouse remained opened like that and the eyes of the passengers were riveted to the bursting profile of the naked breast.

"Don't you have anything to change into?" asked the hostess.

"No," said Michele.

She made a face that seemed to be holding back a laugh. The two women's eyes met and recognized their complicity; their concern was the same. The man was observing them. There wasn't a single wrinkle in his suit, his shirt was as clean as at the departure, his tie wasn't changed.

"Come with me," said the hostess.

Michele got up, walked by her neighbor, and followed the young English girl into the powder room, all mirrored, with ottomans and white leather trimmings and little tables filled with lotions and other bottles.

"Wait for me!"

The hostess disappeared and came back a few minutes later, carrying a small valise. She opened it and took out a pullover that was the color of fall leaves, made of orlon, silk, and wool and so soft that you could crumple it up in your hand. When she shook it, it seemed to suddenly swell up like a rubber balloon and Michele, astounded, clapped her hands.

"You'll loan it to me?" she asked.

"No, it's a gift. I'm sure it will suit you. It's your type."

"But . . . "

The hostess placed a finger over her lips which rounded out as if to protest their embarrassment. Her tender eyes were twinkling. Michele couldn't stop looking at them. She moved toward her but the hostess had already turned around and was holding out some perfume:

"Put some of this on, it's wonderful!"

Michele washed her arms and neck and plunged the cotton pad she had impregnated with the perfume between her breasts. Then, changing her mind, she quickly undid the last buttons on her blouse.

Throwing her arms back, she lowered her silk blouse to the white carpet and took a deep breath, suddenly giddy from her half-nudity. She turned toward the hostess and looked at her with candid jubilation. The stewardess bent down to pick up the chiffon blouse. She pressed it against her face

"Oh! It smells so good!" she cried, laughing maliciously.

Michele was losing her self-control. The incredible scene of the preceding hour seemed irrelevant at the moment. The sole thought that kept turning around in her head as if in a cage, was to get rid of her skirt and stockings, to be completely naked for this beautiful girl. Her fingers played with the zipper on her skirt.

"Your hair is so thick and black!" the hostess said ecstatically, enjoying sliding a brush through Michele's curls which fell down her naked back. "It's so shiny and silky! I'd love to have such beautiful hair."

"But I love yours!" protested Michele.

Oh! if only her companion wanted to undress too! She desired it so much that her voice was hoarse. She begged:

"Can you take a bath on the plane?"

"Of course. But it would be better to wait. The bathrooms at the airport are even more comfortable. And, anyway, you wouldn't have time. We're going to land in five minutes."

Michele couldn't resign herself. Her lips were trembling. She pulled on her skirt zipper.

"Hurry up and put on my sweater," said the young English girl, holding out the woolen garment to Michele.

She helped her put her head through the tight neck. The stretch-sweater fit so well that her nipples stood out in relief as visible as if, instead of having been dressed in a sweater, they had simply been painted on. The hostess seemed to notice them for the first time.

"You're so seductive!" she exclaimed.

And she laughingly rested her index finger on one of the pointed breasts—a little like she might have pressed a doorbell. Michele's eyes sparkled.

"Is it true," she asked, "that airline stewardesses are all virgins?"

The young girl let out the laugh of a singing bird then, before Michele had time to act, she opened the door, beckoning to her passenger.

"Quick, take your seat. The red light is on. We're going to land."

But Michele looked sullen. She didn't have the least desire on top of everything to be side by side with her cabin partner again.

The landing seemed like a nuisance to her. What good would it be to know you are in the Arab desert if you couldn't see anything? The airport, aseptic and chromium-plated, strangely resembled the inside of the artificial satellite that at that very moment was showing the television programs on the screen in the waiting room where the guests were taken. Michele bathed sullenly. She drank tea, and quietly ate some sandwiches with five or six other passengers among whom were her own companions.

She looked at the man with astonishment, trying to understand what had happened between them an hour earlier. That episode didn't go with the rest of Michele's past. Was she even sure that it had really happened? Oh, how complicated it was to think about it. Too risky besides. The simplest and most prudent thing was to refuse to think about it anymore. She tried to form a vacuum in that part of her brain that persisted in posing such questions.

By the time the movement of the others, rather than the incomprehensible voice of the loudspeaker, told her that they were going to reboard the plane, she had succeeded in no longer being certain about what it was that she had taken so much trouble to forget.

When the passengers were on the plane again, they saw that it had been cleaned, put in order, and ventilated. A fresh perfume had been sprayed in the cabins. The chairs were covered with new blankets. Pillows that were shiny white and puffy made the dark blue velvet they were resting on seem even prettier. The steward came to ask if anyone wanted drinks. No? Very well! Good-night! The hostess brought her wishes for a good-night in turn. All this ceremony delighted Michele. She felt herself growing happy again in a positive manner, with certitude. She wanted the world to be exactly what it was. Everything on earth was definitely good.

She stretched out on her back. She wasn't afraid of showing her legs this time. She wanted to move them. She lifted them one by one, bending her knees, making her thigh muscles flex, rubbing her ankles against one another with a sweet rustling of her nylons. She enjoyed the physical sensation that this exercise of her legs gave her with great pleasure. In order to be able to move better, she deliberately lifted her skirt even higher without hiding anything, pulling the material with both hands.

"After all," she thought, "it's not just my knees that deserve to be looked at, but my entire legs. You have to admit that they're really pretty. They're like two little rivers covered with dry leaves and all brimming with bad spirits which amuse themselves by jumping over one another. And that's not all I have to offer. I also love my skin that gets golden in the sun like a grain of corn but never burns; and I also love my buttocks. And also the little raspberries at the tips of my breasts with their little collars of red sugar. I would love to be able to lick them!"

The lights went out and, with a sigh of well being, she pulled the cover over her that was impregnated with a scent of pine needles which the airline company offered to protect her dreams.

When there were no lights except the night-lights, she turned on her side and tried to distinguish her cabin companion, whom she had not dared to really look at since she had again found herself stretched out next to him. To her surprise, she found the man staring at her and his eyes seemed to reach her despite the almost total darkness. They remained that way for some time with their eyes on each other in an expression of perfect tranquility. Michele recognized the sparkle of affection that was a little amused, a little protective, which she had noticed the moment they had met for the first time (when exactly? Was it only seven hours earlier?) and she thought to herself that it was this that she liked best about him.

She smiled, closing her eyes because this voyage had become so agreeable to her in such an unexpected way. She desired something vaguely—but she didn't know what. She found no other distraction than that of beginning to enjoy her beauty again: her own image danced in her head like a favorite refrain. Her heart beating, she sought in her imagination the invisible crack which she knew hid under her promontory of black herbs, at the junction of the two rivers: she felt the current coming to lick their border. When the man lifted himself on his elbow and leaned toward her, she opened her eyes and let him kiss her. The taste of lips on lips had the freshness and the saltiness of the sea about it.

She raised herself and lifted her arms in order to help him when he tried to take off her sweater. She savored the feeling of seeing her breasts jump out of the red wool which the darkness made appear even rounder and more voluptuous than during the day. To leave him the complete pleasure of undressing her, she didn't help him when he tried to find the button on her skirt. However, she lifted her hips so that he would be able to slide the zipper down without any difficulty. This time, the narrow skirt did not remain twisted around her knees: she was completely freed from it.

The man's active hands relieved her of her miniscule panties. After he had also removed her garterbelt, Michele herself rolled her stockings down and threw them down with her skirt and sweater to the foot of the couch.

Only when she was entirely undressed did he press her against him and begin to caress her from head to foot, neglecting nothing. She wanted to make love so much now that her heart was hurting her and her throat was choked—she thought she would never be able to breathe again. She was afraid, she would have liked to call out, but the man was holding her too tightly, one hand in the furrow of her buttocks, caressing the little trembling crevice, one finger completely swallowed up. At the same time, he was kissing her avidly, licking her tongue, drinking her saliva.

She moaned, little moans, without knowing exactly why

she felt this pain. Was it the finger that was foraging so far into her, or the mouth that was taking nourishment from her, swallowing each breath, each sob? Was it the torment of desire or the shame of her lust? The memory of the long arched form which she had held in the palm of her hand haunted her, magnificent and stiff, hard, red, burning unbearably. She moaned so loudly that the man took pity: she finally felt his naked member, as strong as she had expected, being placed on her abdomen, and she pressed herself against him with all the softness of her body.

They held each other like this for a long moment, without moving. Then the man, seeming to suddenly make up his mind, lifted her in his arms and put her underneath him, so that she was now stretched out on the couch which was beside the aisle. Less than a few feet separated them from the English children.

She had almost completely forgotten that they existed. She suddenly realized that they were not sleeping and that they were watching her. The boy was the closest, but the girl was pushing against him to be able to see better. Immobile and holding their breaths, they were staring at Michele with their enlarged pupils from which she could read nothing but a fascinated curiosity. At the thought of being possessed before their eyes, of giving herself to this excess of debauchery, she experienced a kind of vertigo. But, at the same time, she was in a hurry to do it and for them to be able to see everything.

She was lying on her right side, her thighs and knees bent, her body offered. The man was holding her buttocks. He slid his leg between hers and introduced himself into her with an irresistible thrust which facilitated the absolute rigidity of his cock as well as the humidity of Michele's body. It was only after having reached the deepest point of her vagina and stopping for time to catch his breath that he began to move his member in large regular coming and going blows.

Michele, delivered from her anguish, panting, became moist and warm with each of the thrusts of his phallus. As if it was feeding off her, it augmented its size, its movements, and its amplitude. Through the haze of her pleasure, she succeeded in being amazed that the length of his cock could be so deep inside her. She amused herself by thinking that her organs hadn't seemed to have atrophied during so many months that they had not been stimulated by a masculine tool. This rediscovered desire made her want to profit as completely and as long as possible.

The man didn't appear close to tiring of foraging in Michele's body. She would have loved to know at a given moment how long he had been in her, but no point of respite permitted her to judge.

She held back her orgasm without it costing her either effort or frustration. She had trained herself from infancy to prolong the pleasure of waiting and she appreciated even more for the spasm to have that deep sensitivity, that extreme tension which she knew marvelously well how to give herself.

She was used to refusing to give in to the supplication of her own body, until finally the pressure of her sensuality would carry her away, escaping in frightening tornadoes like the convulsions of the dead, but from which Michele would immediately recover more alert and cheerful.

She looked at the children. Their faces had lost their morgue-like expressions. They had become almost human. Not exciting, not sneering, but attentive and almost respectful. She tried to imagine what was going through their minds, the confusion which the event they were witnessing must have caused them, but the thoughts died in her. Her brain was filled with stars and she was too happy to really care about the others.

When, from the acceleration of his movements, and from a

certain stiffness of his hands that were grasping her buttocks and also, from a sudden swelling and pulsating in his organ, she realized that her partner was going to ejaculate, she let herself go. The flood of sperm carried her pleasure to its paroxysm. During the time he was emptying himself into her, the man held himself very deep inside her, fitting perfectly in this respect to the neck of her womb and even in the midst of her spasm Michele had enough imagination to enjoy the picture of the gland pouring out its creamy fluid—which the oblong opening of her uterus was swallowing, furtively and greedily like a hungry mouth.

The man finished his orgasm and Michele calmed down in turn, overcome by a feeling of well being that was without remorse, to which every small detail contributed: the sliding out of the male who was withdrawing, the contact of the blanket which she smelled all around her, the comfort of the couch and the warm darkness of the sleep that was coming over her.

The plane had crossed the night like a bridge, blind to the deserts of India, to the gulfs, the streams, the rice-mills. When Michele opened her eyes at dawn she couldn't see because the inside of the cabin was completely shut off from the time of day that was coloring the world outside.

The white blanket had fallen off the couch and Michele was stretched out naked on her left side, curled up like a child. Her conqueror was sleeping.

Michele regained consciousness by degrees and remained immobile. Nothing that she might have been thinking could be read on her face. At the end of a long time, she slowly stretched out her legs and turned over on her back, starting to cover herself with her hands. But her hands remained suspended: a man, standing in the aisle, was looking at her.

The stranger, in the position which he occupied with respect to her, appeared like a gigantic statue and the young woman thought that he was unbelievably handsome. It was no doubt this beauty that made her forget her nudity, or at least which didn't embarrass her. She thought: it's a Greek statue. Such a work of art couldn't be alive. A fragment of a poem came to her that was not Greek: "Deity of the temple ruins . . . " She would have liked primroses, faded herbs, in abundance at the god's feet, foliage around his pedestal, and a breeze moving the short soft hair that curled over his ears and forehead. Michele's eyes moved down the straight edge of his nose, rested on his full lips, on the marble chin. Two firm tendons sculptured the line from his neck to his shirt that was half-opened on a hairless chest. The woman's eyes pursued their study. Close to Michele's face a huge swelling was pushing out his white flannel pants.

The apparition leaned forward and took the skirt and sweater that were on the floor. It also picked up the panties and garterbelt, and the stockings and then standing up said:

"Come."

Michele sat up on the couch, placed her feet on the ground, and took the hand that was stretched out to her. Then rising with a supple effort, she moved forward, naked, as if she had changed worlds in the altitude and the night.

The stranger led her into the dressing room she had already seen with the hostess. He leaned against the silk-covered door. He placed Michele so that she was facing him. She let out a cry when she saw the Herculean reptile that was standing up in front of her out of his golden bush. Because she was much shorter than the man, the huge gland stood up right between her breasts.

The hero seized Michele by the waist and lifted her without difficulty. The young woman crossed her fingers around the masculine neck whose muscles she could feel hardening in her palms, and she separated her legs so that the scarlet member which her assailant had pushed against her could penetrate her. Tears ran down her cheeks while the man entered her carefully, tearing her despite the slowness of the assault. Michele, leaning her knees against the wall and on her partner's buttocks, helped the fabulous serpent as best she could. She writhed, scratching the neck she was clinging to, sobbing, crying out unintelligible words. She wasn't even conscious that the man was coming, and when he did it was with a thrust that was so savage that he really seemed to be trying to open a path through her right up to her heart. When he withdrew, his face calmed, he kept her standing up pressed against him. His moist phallus was refreshing to Michele's stinging skin.

"Did you like it?" he asked.

Michele placed her cheek on the Greek god's chest. She could feel his semen moving inside her.

"I love you," she murmured.

Then: "Do you want to take me again?"

He smiled. "Soon," he said. "I'll come back. Get dressed now."

He leaned over, and placed such a chaste kiss on her head that she didn't dare say anything. Before she had even realized that he was leaving her, she was alone again.

With slow movements, as if there was a ceremony involved (or because she had not completely regained consciousness), she turned on the shower, covered her body with soap, rinsed herself a minute, then rubbed her skin with warm, sweet-smelling towels. She then sprayed a perfume on her neck and chest, under her arms and on her pubic hair, which evoked the greenness of an underwood. Then she brushed her hair. Her reflection returned to her from three sides by way of the long mirrors; it seemed to her that she had never been so fresh or resplendent. Would the stranger return as he had promised?

She waited until the loudspeaker announced the approach of Bangkok. Then, with an expression of anger, her heart on fire, she dressed, went back to the cabin, took down her bag and her coat and placed them on her knees as she sat down in the chair. Her neighbor, at whom she tossed an absentminded glance, looked surprised.

"But . . . aren't you going on to Tokyo?" he asked in English, with a shade of disappointment in his voice.

Michele guessed quite easily what he had wanted to say and shook her head negatively. The man's face fell visibly. He asked another question which she did not understand and which she didn't have the energy to answer anyway. She looked straight ahead of her with an expression of grief.

The traveler had taken out a notebook and he held it out to Michele, making a sign for her to write in it. No doubt he wanted her to leave her name or an address where he could find her. But she refused with another shake of her head. She wondered if the godlike stranger, the fantastic genie of the temple ruins would also leave the plane at Bangkok, or if he would fly on to Japan. In that case, she would see him at least on the stairs . . .

She looked for him among the passengers who, having descended the plane, were waiting under its wings to be led to the cement and glass buildings whose futuristic silhouettes stood out on the sky that was already white with heat. But she did not recognize anyone that had either his figure or his hair. The hostess smiled at her: she could hardly see her. They were already pushing her toward customs. Someone crossed a barrier, showed a pass, and called Michele. She ran forward and, with a cry of joy, threw herself into the outstretched arms of her husband.

How Cute Is That?

by Eve Howard

from *Best of Shadow Lane*

Even though he had been teaching at Hollywood High for twelve years, and had been robbed so often that he now held a gun permit, David Lawrence had not lost his optimism. He was an amiable, youthful thirty-seven, amusing and well liked by his associates, especially the female ones.

Living in the *Blade Runner* world of modern Los Angeles, he accepted his grim wages, the fact that his marriage had failed and the continuous dangers of his thankless profession without repining. Blessed by nature with wit, remarkably good looks, a cheerful disposition and a propensity for indulging his senses, David found ways to enjoy himself every day.

Meeting women was not a problem, but finding a girl who shared his interest in *spanking* was. It wasn't enough just to find a woman who would take a spanking. What he really craved was a female counterpart, a fabulous fetishist, who thought about spanking as much as he did.

"It wouldn't have to be someone like Babydoll," he mused, looking out his classroom window, three stories above the intersection of Sunset and Highland, where every day at 3:45, for the last week, the most heavenly little blonde with wavy hair to her waist in a halter top and snug knee pants, on rollerblades, flew down Sunset on the south side of the street, urgently transporting a bag of take-out food.

On day five David made it his business to be out on the street at 3:45. Sure enough, Babydoll passed, this time carrying her take-out in a glossy shopping bag with Clark Gable's photograph on the side. She gave David a quick, little smile as she skated past him, and actually said, "How cute are you?" An instant later, she blushed as she realized that she hadn't meant to say that aloud.

Meanwhile, David was bowled over by his first closeup look at Babydoll. First of all, she was a radiantly beautiful young lady, in her early to middle twenties, whose only business on Sunset Boulevard ought to have been in decorating a billboard. She was in fact, astonishingly beautiful as she turned the corner at La Brea and disappeared.

"I must have imagined I heard that," David mused as he strolled to his favorite coffee bar. He chose a window booth and opened a copy of the *L.A. Free Press* inside of his *L.A. Weekly* in order to daydream about visiting one of the B&D salons that advertised in the former.

David didn't bother to go up to the counter and order because Brooke Neuman began to prepare his regular double cappuccino as soon as he sat down.

Brooke was the brightest student in David's World Literature class. Her single parent was a subsistence-level stand-up comic and Brooke had to maintain several part-time jobs in order to supply herself with an allowance. David had conversed with her many times and found her both original and charming.

Brooke's graceful form, fine complexion and dark, silky hair barely registered on David because he never thought about his students in that way, although he couldn't fail to notice that she was perhaps the only student at Hollywood High who wasn't either radically pierced or in some way tattooed, and whose hair was all one color.

Brooke's boyfriend, a sardonic German boy named Willie Kronenberg, was the only other brilliant student in the class, but David didn't care for Willie's captious personality and wondered what Brooke saw in him besides his good looks and outstanding grade point average.

Sublimely unaware of the magnitude of crush Brooke had on him, David didn't even bother to close the adult newspaper when she brought his coffee over. He couldn't have closed it at that moment if he wanted to, for he had just seen a photograph that riveted him. In the middle of a two-page spread on a well-bred B&D club called The Keep, there was Babydoll! The girl he had seen on the in-line skates just minutes before and had watched from his window for a week, was billed as a *submissive* and displayed in a leather halter dress, perched naughtily on a bench with a paddle close by. David's heart leapt so high he nearly choked.

Babydoll available for sessions! His Babydoll. Right here in Hollywood. The ad called her Hope and as both a student of language and a dreamer he took note.

"I can't wait until *I'm* old enough to work in a B&D club," Brooke remarked to her mentor casually. David gave her a look and smiled, used to her cynical humor. "And that one in particular," she added, beginning to shock him. "I've been staring at their ads for two years."

"Why this one?" he returned off-handedly, wondering whether she was as intuitive as she was precocious.

"The mistress of course," said Brooke. "I love the way she never takes her glasses off. I've written her several letters, but she's firm that I can't even come and visit until I'm eighteen."

"Brooke, you astonish me," David nearly gasped at her temerity. Meanwhile, he thought to himself, "That does it, I'm visiting The Keep today!"

Brooke left him to wait on another customer while David smoked and looked out the window. Finally he got up and went to the phone in the back of the cafe and dialed the number of The Keep. The phone was answered on the first ring.

"Hello!" a euphonious female voice replied.

"Hello," he replied, in his own dulcet tones. "I've been looking at your ad in the *Free Press* and was wondering what was involved in a visit?"

"Well, what exactly are you looking for?"

"A spanking session."

"Giving or receiving?"

"Giving."

"Well, a half hour session is a hundred, an hour one sixty. Today we have Cherry and Hope available for spankings."

"I'd like to see Hope if I may," said David, throbbing with excitement at his perfect luck.

"She's free right now," the young woman said pleasantly.

"Where are you located?"

The mistress of the house gave David a residential street address not four blocks from where he stood. David promised to arrive within fifteen minutes and went to the counter to pay his bill.

Brooke, who had seemed to be busy the whole time he was on the phone, had none the less noted his every expression and attached great significance to the fact that he had left his paper open to the spread on The Keep before making his call. On his way out he scooped up both his newspapers and departed with an urgency she'd not observed before.

Rushing back to the phone she inserted a quarter in the slot and pressed the redial button. The same mellifluous voice answered, causing Brooke to hesitate a moment before replying, "Mistress Hildegarde?"

"Yes." The voice grew even warmer.

"It's me, Brooke Neuman. Remember? The girl who wrote you the letters?"

"Of course I remember, darling. But do you remember that I told you I couldn't even talk to you until you turned eighteen?" Hildegarde sounded only mildly annoyed.

"I'm sorry," Brooke meekly replied and immediately hung up. Then she ran outside to see whether Mr. Lawrence was still on the street. Luck was with Brooke and she spotted her teacher across the street at an ATM. "Wow, he's really doing it!" she said to herself, racing back inside to tell her boss, Oscar, that she needed an hour to take care of an errand. Then grabbing her camcorder, which she never went anywhere important without, she ran out the door.

Mr. Lawrence had just begun to walk briskly up Sunset. Brooke followed at a distance, filming kids on the street as she went. She had decided to be a filmmaker at age 11 and since then had devoted every leisure moment to watching films, shooting footage and writing scripts.

Mr. Lawrence was easily tracked to the quiet, shabby-genteel side street on which the white wooden house that lodged The Keep was situated. She was even able to video Mr. Lawrence knocking on the door and being given admittance by a gloriously beautiful blonde.

In the office of the club, the tobacco-marinated bouncer Rusty watched the closed circuit television monitors which pictured the street with mounting unease. As soon as Mistress Hildegarde came out of session he intended to make her aware of the girl who was taping everyone going in and out of the club.

Meanwhile, David had been taken by Hope up to the blue dungeon.

Since returning to the club and being told that a spanking session was on his way, Hope had changed into a gauzy white party dress and put her hair in a ponytail with a blue satin bow. The dress was new and matched to white pumps.

"We can pretend I'm Carol Linley, circa 1959," she said, when he admired her outfit, for her hobby was the history of glamour and she enjoyed identifying with various periods and looks.

"What's that?" he asked, regarding a form on a clipboard she was preparing to fill out.

"Just your membership application," she explained, handing it to him. "We'll just need you to write your name and address in the blank spaces there."

"Must I? I'm a high school teacher and I'd really rather not."

"You can make up a name, you know. And don't you have a P.O. Box?"

"As a matter of fact, I do."

"I'm sure!" Hope laughed, then observed cleverly, "How else could you receive naughty things through the mail?" Then she looked at him closely. "Do I know you?"

"I work in the neighborhood. Perhaps we've eaten in the same restaurants," he ventured, delighted that she remembered him from their brief eye contact on the street earlier.

"If I'd had teachers as handsome as you I never would have dropped out of college," she confided flirtatiously.

"Dropped out of college, did you?"

"I suppose you don't approve of that."

"You bet I don't."

"Would you like to give me the allowance now so I can take it downstairs and have them start us?"

"Certainly."

David handed her the money and watched her slip out of the room. While she was gone he noticed that someone had placed a paddle, a hair brush, a strap and a small flogger on a leather padded bench. The thought of Hope collecting these items for use on her own (no doubt) flawless bottom was sheer heaven.

But oddly, just before she returned to him, the image of Brooke Neuman flashed into his mind. Why would a quiet, thoughtful girl like Brooke dream of working in a place like this?

He paced the room, examined the equipment, lit a cigarette, then pulled the heavy velvet drapes aside to look out the window. What he saw on the street below caused his heart to lurch painfully. There was Brooke Neuman, on the sidewalk opposite The Keep, with her camcorder on her shoulder, blithely taping as she walked up and down. He let the curtain fall back into place and rushed for the door. Then he forced himself to pause and wait for Hope's return.

When Hope came back with a serene smile on her face he allowed himself one moment to appreciate her loveliness before panicking.

"Come here," he said, pulling back the curtain slightly. "Look out there. Do you see anyone across the street?"

"Yes, there's a girl with a camcorder on her shoulder. God, is she taping our front door?" Hope looked at David in alarm.

"That's my favorite student. She must have followed me over here."

"Does she know what kind of place this is?"

"Does she! She wants to work here."

"Oh! Well, she's certainly gorgeous," Hope breathed sincere admiration. "She'd make a fortune."

"She's only seventeen at the moment."

"Ooops. But why is she taping the house?"

"She tapes everything. She wants to make movies."

"I admire her initiative, but we'd better get her to stop filming, before she alarms everyone in the house," Hope said sensibly. "Do you want to go out there and talk to her?"

"Me? God, no!" David protested. "I could probably lose my job for talking to her under these circumstances."

"Is that really true?"

"I have no idea and I don't think I'll ask."

"I'd better go and explain the situation to Mistress. Just wait here. And don't worry."

After Hope's departure David continued to monitor Brooke out the window. In a moment craggy old Rusty crossed the street to confront Brooke, never taking his cigarette out of his mouth or his hands out of his jeans' pockets. No more than two sentences were exchanged before Brooke quickly marched away. Rusty then ambled back to the house and Hope returned to the dungeon.

"It's all taken care of," she reported sunnily.

"What did that man say to her?" David asked with some concern.

"Just that you need a permit to film on the streets of Hollywood."

"Smart!" David was all admiration for Rusty.

"I hope this hasn't put you off playing."

"Oh, no," he replied candidly, hanging his jacket on a peg. Hope gasped as he turned to see the reflection of his gun and shoulder holster in the mirrored wall opposite.

"I thought you said you were a teacher!" she cried with some alarm. "Are you a vice cop? Was that chick your back-up? Is this a bust?"

"Not at all. And do calm down. Honestly, I'm just a high school teacher who's been beaten up enough times that they finally gave me a permit to carry a gun." David showed her the permit, his driver's license and teachers' union card. Hope was still skeptical and looked as though she might burst into tears of frustration, for she had been looking forward to playing with him. "Take these to your Mistress," he said with a sigh, thrusting his I.D.s into her hands. "I'll be here."

Hope disappeared yet again, only to return a few moments later, wreathed in smiles. "Hildegarde says I should ask you some questions to make sure you're on the level."

"Oh? What kind of questions?"

"You say you're into spanking, right?"

"Why, yes."

"Prove it."

"How do you mean, prove it?"

"Tell me some things about spanking that you like." Hope sat beside him on the leather covered bondage bed, stretching out her legs to admire the white grosgrain bows that tied across the insteps of her shoes.

"That would take some time," he smiled.

"You haven't proven anything yet."

"Say, how old are you anyway?" he asked her suddenly.

"How old do you think I am?" she laughed.

"Twenty?"

"Thanks! If you are a cop, you're a gallant one. I'm twenty-five."

"That's a relief anyway."

"Oh? You wouldn't rather be spanking your adorable pet with the camera?"

"I'm not interested in my students."

"If that really was your student, I'm sure she has a giant crush on you."

"That's true, girls do get crushes on me from time to time. But she has more common sense than that."

"Then why follow you here?"

"Oh, we had a conversation in the cafe where she works

about an hour ago during which she revealed that she's been dreaming about working at this very club for two years. I was indiscreet about telephoning and she was smart enough to follow me."

"So she's brilliant, beautiful, has a crush on her dominant male teacher, and wants to work in B&D. How cute is that?"

"I think one of the things we're going to discuss if we ever do get to play is this NewSpeak you kids talk. You, for example, seem smart enough to form more original expressions."

"Now I know you're a teacher!" Hope declared, with an irrepressible grin. Then she hit the intercom button and told Rusty to call them in a half hour.

Except for the nagging sensation of impending doom which set in every time he allowed himself to ponder the notion of Brooke and what she now knew about him, David felt divinely satisfied by his first trip to The Keep.

Spanking the vivacious yet compliant Hope had surpassed all his expectations of sublime erotic pleasure. The way she ground against his lap, the way her alabaster skin had pinkened under his hand, the delicious little gasps she gave as he stroked her in between smacks, all confirmed his long held theory that some women did really enjoy being paddled.

Hope had been all high spirits and ingenuity. She seemed as interested in him as he was in her and made such incisive comments on his favorite subject that he felt as though he was out on the most agreeable date of his life.

When the session ended she had sat on his lap the right way around and given him a tremendous hug, telling him she hoped that he would visit her often. He vowed he would never visit anyone else and pressed a twenty dollar tip into her hand, wishing it could be more.

Toward Brooke, David's feelings were a mixture of resentment, distrust and uneasy admiration. He felt in his heart of hearts that Brooke would do nothing to hurt him. Not even if he gave her the spanking she deserved for following him to The Keep and setting everyone's nerves ajangle! But given the current climate, he wondered if instead he ought to consult a lawyer before even talking to his student again.

Brooke suffered torments all weekend, wondering whether Mr. Lawrence had been informed by the walking tobacco stick that she'd been outside The Keep with her camera. World Lit was her Monday second period class and the moment he walked in and slammed his briefcase down on the desk she no longer had to wonder.

Normally, Brooke was the first person her instructor smiled at. Today he never glanced her way unless he had to. Of course he had to eventually, because she always raised her hand. Even today, when she wanted very badly not to, pride forced her to do so. They were reading *Madame Bovary* and she was full of opinions on it.

Willie, who sat directly behind Brooke and noticed everything which pertained to that young lady, marked a difference in their teacher's attitude toward his girlfriend which puzzled the observant boy.

As they left class he demanded an explanation in his usual overbearing style. "How come Mr. Lawrence was ignoring you today?"

"Mr. Lawrence called on me several times," Brooke pointed out, unwilling to be roused from her bittersweet meditations on her idol by her tiresome contemporary.

"Yes, but he didn't commend your responses with his usual enthusiasm. In short, he seemed much less than charmed with you today. What's going on?"

"I don't know. Maybe he's gone off me."

"Aren't you concerned?"

"Why should I be concerned?"

"Weren't you counting on him for your college references?"

"I'm sure he'll give me the references I deserve."

"You know more than you're letting on," Willie accused. But the commencement of their third period American History class cut short the conversation.

Brooke had been going out with Willie since their sophomore year. He was her first lover and she his. Early on she had confessed her spanking fetish. Being a German male, naturally dominant and sexually playful, Willie had given Brooke a spanking on their first date.

They had driven up to the restaurant Yamashiro, which sat atop a Hollywood hill. Brooke had attempted to order wine with dinner, though she had only just turned 16. Willie told her, "Behave, or I'll spank you," in front of the waiter.

"They weren't going to proof us," Brooke protested, for it was her birthday and this was her first real restaurant date.

"You need a spanking anyway," Willie told her firmly, causing Brooke to fall instantly in love.

After dinner, while they were waiting for the car to be brought up, they leaned over the parapet to view the magnificent city lights stretching below.

"That reminds me," said Willie, locking one arm around her waist, "you needed a spanking." And briskly he brought his hand down on the seat of her skirt six or eight times, letting her up the very instant the valet drove up with the car.

Brooke shuddered with excitement all the way home. Since it was a night when her father was emceeing at The Star Strip until three a.m., she invited Willie in and her first love affair was begun.

As it later turned out, Willie spanked more out of an innate feeling of male superiority than a desire to arouse her, and this was not an attitude that Brooke was prepared to tolerate much beyond graduation.

David now avoided the coffee bar where Brooke worked. He never addressed a remark to her that wasn't relevant to a lesson or walked with her down the hall chatting. In short, an arctic floe separated them until graduation and well beyond.

Of course David wrote outstanding recommendations for Brooke. By early spring she'd received all her acceptances. She might have gone to Yale if she'd chosen to do so. Instead she picked the U.C.L.A. film school and decided to save on expenses by living at home. She had more than one reason for selecting this option.

Towards the end of the school year, when everyone was discussing their college plans, David's resolve never to speak to Brooke again began to weaken. Some months had passed since the incident at The Keep and David was virtually positive that Brooke did not intend to expose him. But there was still the problem of her being underage dynamite. He couldn't risk igniting her with so much as a smile. Even on graduation day, David remained remote.

Brooke felt that she was being cruelly punished, but the firmness of her handsome teacher thrilled her.

Meanwhile, David went to visit Hope once a week, whether or not he could afford it. She was an exquisite addiction.

Then, one Friday afternoon in late September, David arrived at The Keep for his usual appointment and was told that Hope had quit!

"She's going to do lots and lots of movies," Hildegarde informed the stunned David. "Don't despair, darling, she was determined that I give you and you alone her number," the pretty mistress told him, writing down the number. "She said she couldn't live without her favorite spanker." David's heart contracted at these soothing words.

"I don't suppose you'll ever find another sub of her quality," he mused.

"I wouldn't be too sure," Hildegarde smiled. "I've got a

brilliant little college girl coming to me in October, as soon as she turns eighteen."

"You're not talking about my Brooke?" he snapped back at once.

"Is she your Brooke already?" Hildegarde shook her head with disapproval.

"No, certainly not. In fact, I haven't even talked to her since that incident back in March."

"Neither have I, but I feel certain we'll be welcoming her shortly. In fact, if I were you, I wouldn't miss our Halloween party. October 31st is her birthday."

Not even a large earthquake could have kept David away from The Keep on Halloween. He arrived at eight, in a medium grey pin-striped suit, bearing a large bouquet of red and white autumn roses, which he had cut from the bushes outside his tiny cottage in Laurel Canyon. Hildegarde was gratified but not surprised by the perfect buds. David's funds were limited but his thoughtfulness was not. In the short time she had known him, he did her many kindnesses, from driving girls home to editing her advertising copy.

Hildegarde was pouring David a glass of wine in the kitchen when Hope arrived, in a black velvet gown and cape. The blonde girl put one arm around David's waist as she held out her wine glass to be filled.

"Darling, I'm so glad you came," said Hildegarde, who was exactly the same age as her ex-employee and had missed her favorite this last month. "Are you going to play?"

"I think I should. Don't you?" Hope grinned at David, for she knew that he rather enjoyed spanking her after she'd already been spanked hard. "Is she here yet?" asked Hope.

"Not yet," Hildegarde replied.

"She probably forgot all about it by now," David stated with conviction.

"Darling, a girl who's been dreaming B&D for years and who lives ten minutes away from me, is not going to forget about it," Hildegarde declared as the bell rang. "Excuse me," she said, kissing Hope's white throat as she exited.

"What are you going to do and say?" Hope demanded, smiling up at him.

"What do you mean?"

"When she comes in?"

"She isn't coming. But if she does, I don't know."

"You've never been at a loss for words with me," Hope teased him.

A glance upward at the kitchen security camera monitor showed them a leggy young brunette in a black PVC slip dress.

"That's her," David breathed. Hope squeezed his hand.

Brooke was conscious only of a blur of faces as Hildegarde ushered her into the main parlor and relocated a gentleman or two so that they might sit down together on a sofa.

"Mistress Hildegarde, I'm the girl who wrote you those letters this summer," Brooke confided, momentarily riveted by the milky perfection of the club owner's bosom, displayed in a midnight blue velvet bustier gown. "I hope it's all right that I came by tonight," Brooke continued, producing her driver's license and passport for inspection.

"I've been expecting you," Hildegarde told her, handing her identification papers back with a smile. "And so has someone else."

"You mean he's here?" Brooke looked around with a sudden thrill and saw David in the doorway. She thought him more striking than ever and felt her face grow warm as his gaze fell upon her lissome body in the shiny cocktail dress. He approached her with a smile too faint to please her and she wondered whether David was still angry with her for taping him going into the club the previous spring.

“Hello, Brooke. How are you?”

“Is that all you can say to me on the occasion of my eighteenth birthday and my first visit to The Keep?” Brooke jumped up and impulsively kissed David on the lips. “Please forgive me, Mr. Lawrence, but I’ve been wanting to do that for several years now,” Brooke explained, intoxicated with joy at the coincidence of him being at The Keep on this of all nights.

“Really, Brooke, I would have thought you had more common sense,” David scolded, while inwardly aglow. Normally he wasn’t attracted to college girls, but Brooke was so sophisticated for her age. The very fact that the little go-getter didn’t seem to need him to accomplish her fantasies raised her to a level of experience he’d not met in women twice her age. Now that it was legal to admire Brooke, he did, though he wasn’t about to let her know it.

“Mr. Lawrence, may I ask you a question I’ve been dying to know the answer to ever since that day I followed you here?”

“You certainly may not,” he growled, but then smiled as Hope brought him a glass of wine.

“Hello,” said Brooke to Hope.

“Hi. How cute are you?” Hope complimented Brooke.

“Hope, what did I tell you about that mindless incantation?” David demanded with real annoyance.

Hope looked at David with surprise, then, in her usual quick way, realized that David’s most intelligent ex-student might not think too well of Valspeak. Now Hope blushed deeply as only a natural blonde can, for she was in love with David herself and wanted always to be thought well of by him.

“I’d better escape while I can then.” Hope smiled with perfect grace at Brooke and avoided David’s eyes entirely as she slipped out of the room and ran upstairs to join a friend in a dungeon.

Meanwhile, Brooke had mentally recorded the little scene for all eternity and was moved almost to tears by the pathos of her ravishing rival's humiliation. So this was David's favorite, a heavenly creature as sensitive as she was kind. But David didn't value her, thought Brooke, not nearly as he should.

Brooke was aflame with excitement. Everything was glamorous tonight. To think that the male she worshiped had his own fairy creature to punish and pet was past exotic. She had never seriously thought Mr. Lawrence submissive, but there was always the possibility. Until now, when he had made his attitude so clearly known. Whether in the classroom or the dungeon, Mr. Lawrence remained the instructor.

"Now see here, young lady, you don't seriously mean to come work here?" They sat down in the parlor.

"Why not? It seems to have the nicest clientele," Brooke teased.

"Does your father know you're here?"

"My father knows and approves of everything I do," she returned haughtily, which gave David a start and caused Hildegarde to beam. "You don't think he wants me to graduate college sixty thousand dollars in debt, do you?" the eighteen-year-old replied sensibly.

"Well, no but—" David stammered.

"My job at the cafe paid seven dollars an hour."

"But a girl like you in a place like this?"

"Don't be disrespectful, Mr. Lawrence," Brooke replied, "after all, Mistress Hildegarde is here."

"Yes, well I'm sure she agrees with me that there are better places for you than in a dungeon," David said with a conviction Hildegarde didn't share.

"David," Hildegarde said, "one of my best girlfriends put herself through law school working for me."

"I never realized you were so stuffy, Mr. Lawrence,"

Brooke baited him, while looking around the room for the first time at the waiting clients.

"Let's go somewhere and talk," said David impatiently.

"You mean leave now?"

"I do."

"But I just got here."

"Surely you didn't intend to start working tonight?"

"David may have a point, darling," said Hildegarde, cognizant of the hostile looks being tossed in Brooke's direction by several of her other girls. "I've got a full house tonight of both staff and clients and it's unlikely I'll be able to give you a complete tour."

"But I was counting on at least one birthday spanking," said Brooke.

"Is it your birthday?" a plain, conservative looking, fifty-year-old male asked with some excitement from a nearby loveseat.

"Yes. I turned eighteen today," Brooke replied.

"God, I'd love to do a session with you," the gentleman vowed. "What's your name?"

"Yes, darling, what is your *play* name?" Hildegarde ignored David's glower to murmur.

"Do I have to have one?"

"Everyone does."

"I've always liked the name Alison."

"Excellent. Well, Alison, may I present Paul, who is very much into spanking. Why don't you let him know what days you'll be coming to us and he can plan his next visit accordingly," suggested Hildegarde pleasantly.

"Friday and Saturday nights for sure," mused Brooke, upsetting David. "And probably a weekday afternoon or two as well."

"I'll definitely be in," Paul promised.

"Meanwhile, Cherry is here and I have Hope visiting for the

entire night," Hildegarde consoled the spanker before jumping up to answer the door.

"Can we go now?" David demanded, causing a shudder to run through Brooke.

"Are you going to buy me dinner?"

"Dinner? Sure. Of course." He was taken aback by her complete lack of embarrassment at the entire situation and found himself continually readjusting his attitude toward his ex-student.

"And what about my birthday spanking?" she asked as he led her out the door.

"Don't worry about that!" David promised.

Because he hadn't spent any money at the club David took Brooke to an expensive French restaurant, where she was served wine without question. With her tall, elegant carriage, sophisticated dress and high heels, she might have passed for twenty-one.

Brooke was as happy as love, success and promise could make a girl. Her guiltless exuberance was attractive yet frightening to David.

"Tell me about you and that fairy princess at the club," Brooke demanded over dessert.

"If I give you my cake, can I avoid answering that question?" David asked, pushing a chocolate lacquered pyramid across the table to her.

"I want to know about my rival."

"Your what?"

"My competitor."

"Brooke, what's gotten into you?"

"Nothing. I'm just staking my claim."

"That wine must be going to your head," he declared, amazed at her boldness.

"What's the matter, Mr. Lawrence, don't you want Betty and Veronica fighting over you?"

"Certainly not."

"We don't have to fight. We can do a split shift."

"You're talking out of turn, young lady," he growled, both shocked and aroused by her self-confidence.

"Oh, yeah? What are you going to do about it?"

"I think there's only one thing to do—take you home and spank you."

Brooke had not the slightest hesitation about being alone with her ex-teacher, who took her home to a pleasant guest house on Amor Drive. In fact, she longed to surrender to him as soon as possible. But as he locked the door, adjusted the lights and gave her a long, cool look, she suddenly remembered the remarks she had made at dinner and wondered if he thought her very rude.

"I suppose I did speak out of turn," she confessed shyly.

"Having second thoughts about coming?"

"Oh, no. Never. You must have figured out how much I care."

"I did nothing of the sort. You think I sit around day-dreaming about my students?"

"No, but after the incident last Spring . . ."

"Oh, that. I see your point. Well, yes, I admit I did think about you quite a bit after that, but only in the context of my job being jeopardized by your infernal snooping and video taping."

"Oh, I see, you're too pure and noble to ever think about a girl student, is that it?"

"No, that is not it, you fresh brat. I never claimed to be either pure or noble. Far from it. I'm just not attracted to teenaged girls. Now, I know that may come as a shock to you, but it happens to be a very good trait in a high school teacher."

"I see. I have to get older before I can become interesting to you."

"I didn't say that. You may be the exception." David smiled. "You certainly don't act like any teenaged girl I've ever met before."

"Thanks!"

David's house was decorated in the pastel-hued, spare, uncomfortable Southwestern style. Thus, Brooke was led into a nook with peach washed walls, which contained a distressed plank table and four sturdy, wooden chairs. One of these was pulled out and David sat. He then pulled her down across his lap.

"Tell me what kind of spanking you've been thinking about," he demanded, smoothing her short, shiny skirt down and running his palm across her slim, upper thighs.

"The silver screen kind."

"You mean, just over your skirt?"

"For starters."

"How many smacks?"

"You're asking me?"

"How hard?"

"You decide."

"I don't want to hurt you."

"You won't."

"Oh? You mean someone has done this before?"

"Willie has spanked me," she admitted.

"Willie!" David didn't have to pretend indignation. "You granted that callous youth the divine privilege of turning you over his knee?" Smack! David's hand came down. Smack! Now on the other cheek. "I'm appalled," he added, unleashing a stinging volley of spanks that caused Brooke to yip.

"But, he was my boyfriend," Brooke pointed out. "Ouch! You have a hard hand, Mr. Lawrence," she added, without rancor. When she reached back to rub he caught it and pinned it to her side before continuing the spanking.

"If you want to work for Hildegarde you're going to have to learn to take much harder spankings than this without making a fuss," he informed her, rapidly warming the back of her skirt with sharp, measured smacks.

"I wasn't complaining," she hastened to explain.

"You'd better not complain, after the anxiety you've put me through!" Now David began to fully express his resentment against Brooke for tracking him down at The Keep seven months before. He pulled up her PVC skirt, carefully tugged down her expensive seamed pantyhose and snapped the black satin G-string she had on underneath. "Lesson #1," he told her, slapping her hard after every remark for emphasis, once on each cheek, "you don't go out to play with a spanking person in pantyhose and a G-string!"

"But this skirt is too short for a garter belt," she confessed after catching her breath, for his hand felt much harder on her bare bottom. Now he yanked her G-string down and spanked her several dozen times more.

"Then the skirt is too short to go out in," he declared. "You want to be mistaken for a hooker?"

"I got this jumper at the hottest shop on Melrose," she protested, wriggling on his lap.

"I say the dress is too short. Are you arguing with me?" he demanded.

"No," she replied.

"And wear regular panties next time," he ordered.

"Is there going to be a next time?"

"I mean next time you go out with a spanking person," he replied coolly.

"Oh."

"That reminds me." He renewed his grip on her waist and

brought his hand down hard on her already pinkened, peaches and creamy bottom, "I didn't like that fresh remark you made about staking your claim." Now he spanked her even more emphatically. Brooke took it as long as she could, but finally burst into sobs.

"What are you doing?" He stopped spanking her and looked at her face. He'd never spanked a girl to tears before and it gave him a terrible thrill.

"I'm not sorry I did that," he told her, lifting her off his lap and helping her to set her clothes to rights. "You had a real one coming for all sorts of reasons."

"I know," she replied, as meekly as it was possible for her to be.

"Naturally, I never meant to make you cry," he added, searching her face for a clue to her real state of mind.

She merely rubbed her bottom and returned his gaze wide-eyed.

"You see how disagreeable I can be when someone irritates me," David tossed off casually as he lit a cigarette.

"I don't blame you," she told him.

"No?"

"Oh, no. You have every right to be annoyed with me. Because I'm such an egotist, I never considered the fact that you might be truly indifferent to me. I apologize."

"Come off it, Brooke, I hate false humility. I've never been indifferent to you for a second and you know it."

"Then how do you feel about me?"

"You scare the hell out of me."

"I'm really harmless," she assured him with a smile.

"Yeah?" he laughed.

"May I have a cigarette?"

"You don't smoke."

"I started."

"You ought to know better," he observed, lighting her a cigarette.

"So, are we going to play again?" she asked shyly.

"I don't know. I want to talk to a lawyer first."

"But I'm eighteen now."

"You're also a recent ex-student of mine, which could damage my reputation, and possibly lead to my dismissal. And what kind of references could I expect if I were fired under those circumstances?"

"I see that I'm getting the brush-off," she commented.

"Honey, it's not like that. But a man in my position has to be more careful than the average player in the scene."

"I see. The man I worshiped has no backbone!" Brooke said angrily.

"You must want another spanking," he replied, unruffled.

"I might as well, since it's the last time I'll be seeing you."

"Look," he told her, taking her by her forearm and pulling her against him, "you'll see me whenever I tell you to come over here. Understand?" Then he kissed her.

The next day was Saturday and as on most recent Saturdays, David's first order of business was calling on Hope at her tiny, fifth floor apartment on Franklin Street, Hollywood, to see if she needed help with any errands. He found her in her favorite position, in front of her mirror, planning her morning outfit. She was in a robe of white merino wool, her small feet thrust into matching slippers with embroidered toes. Next to her was fresh ground coffee. Propped up against the mirror was *Elle*. Laid out on a nearby chair was a short denim jumper and white T-shirt. It was a warm day for November and Hope planned to do some shopping. She was deciding between well behaved flats and open-toed, sling back, 4" pumps when David entered with his usual offering of rose buds.

"I didn't expect to see you for some time!" Hope cried, jumping up to throw her arms around his neck.

"Why not?" He looked puzzled.

"Well, you did leave with Brooke last night," Hope pouted.

"Well, it was her birthday."

"And I suppose she got her birthday spanking?"

"Yes."

"And what else?"

"A kiss. She's only eighteen, you know."

"Whereas I'm all of twenty-five," Hope said, sitting on his lap and nuzzling his ear. "You need have no reservations with me, my darling."

"Thanks," he tightened his arms around her waist.

"You know, we haven't played since I left The Keep," she reminded him, squirming on his lap in a way that aroused him acutely.

"I know. But I did bring allowance today," he told her.

"That's nice, but not necessary. In fact, I'd almost rather hand you money now and then, you dear, underpaid public servant. "

"That arrangement wouldn't suit me, my little working girl," he told her firmly, divesting himself of his jacket and moving a good armless chair into the center of her studio.

David took Hope over his knee and spanked her as he always did at The Keep. He began over her robe and gave her a good warm up, then pulled it up to discover that she had nothing on underneath.

As usual, her silken skin colored quickly under his hand. And as usual, fifteen minutes into the session, Hope began to reveal her accessibility and excitement. But as usual, when she arched to his hand, he ignored the invitation, refusing to touch her intimately. And with her usual frustration, Hope wondered why.

"David?"

"Yes, dear?" He paused to rub away the sting.

"Don't you like girls?'

"What?"

"Don't you like me?"

"What a question. You're one of my favorite things in life."

"Then why do you always spank me so prudishly?" Hope sprang off his lap. "Are you not into sex?"

David flushed. "Of course I'm into sex. But not with someone I'm paying for a session."

First she gasped with indignation, then hot tears filled her eyes. Drawing herself up to her full five feet and five inches of lithe femininity, Hope deliberately slapped him, albeit very lightly, across the face.

"Is that all you think of me?" she cried.

"I think the world of you, that's why I wouldn't insult you by expecting your favors for a hundred bucks," he replied angrily, for he also had a quick temper and disliked being slapped, even lightly.

"Insult me? Don't you think you insult me every time I invite you to touch me and you ignore me?"

"I was attempting to behave respectfully," David frostily replied.

"It's a safe sex thing, isn't it? You think I'm some sort of high risk slut, don't you?"

"Certainly not. Everyone knows you're a princess."

"They do?" Hope smiled briefly with relief.

"I'm probably a lot more of a slut than you are," David tantalized her. "Anyway, I always use a rubber, so that's not the point."

"Well, what is? You're not in love with Brooke, are you?"

"Of course not. She's even less suitable than you are."

"Don't tell me you only go out with other academics," Hope protested.

"Not exactly."

"You don't think I'm smart enough for you!"

"You're plenty smart, but you're also a B&D call girl. You think I want my girlfriend running out at all hours to do sessions with strange men? Or making fetish videos?"

Hope began to cheer up when she realized he had given this some consideration before deciding to act like an idiot.

"Why not? You often told me at the club that you liked to spank me after two or three other men had warmed me up. Now you're playing the Puritan," she reminded him.

"That's a good point," he granted.

"If you wanted to keep things impersonal between us, you shouldn't have begun coming to see me like this. Why, the way you're always offering to perform chores and do favors for me, is it any wonder I got the wrong idea about your intentions?" she demanded haughtily, shrewdly targeting the one area in which he was genuinely culpable.

"Look, isn't there some way we could still be friends and play without getting involved? I mean, I thought that was the beauty of doing sessions," he protested weakly.

"Oh, you make me sick. Get out. And don't come back!" she ordered, throwing the allowance at him. "You stupid, conventional, hung-up, impotent, high school teacher!"

David stared at her for a moment, more impressed by her ability to tell him off so succinctly than hurt by her accusations.

"All right," he snapped, "you asked for it. Get over here!" He took her in his arms and kissed her on the mouth for the first time. She went limp, then clung to him, astonished at the depth of his kiss.

Then David pulled her robe off and looked at her completely nude body for the first time. "Slap my face, will you?" He gave her a shake, wound his hand in her hair and kissed her again. Then, because she weighed nearly nothing, he picked her up and carried her to the day bed.

"Face down," he told her, taking off his belt. "You're getting six of the best for that smack in the face."

"You deserved it," she replied defiantly.

"I said face down."

Hope obeyed with a pout. The belt came down hard and fast across her bare bottom six times. She hardly had a chance to gasp between each whack. Number three brought tears to her eyes and by six she was sobbing. When he was finished he threw his belt aside and pulled her around to face him.

"I've got a better way to punish you for that crack about impotence," he told her coolly, but wiped her face dry with his handkerchief. Then he took her over to a green leather spanking horse, which was the only piece of B&D equipment in the tiny flat, and bent her over one end.

She turned to him and asked, "Are you telling me you have a rubber in your pocket this instant?"

"Worried?" he asked insolently, pushing her head back down. "Just behave yourself like the submissive you're supposed to be."

Hope gave a murmur of surrender at the new tone in his voice. She turned to see a zipper come down, a large cock emerge and a rubber come out. Once the truncheon was properly sheathed, he let it rest between her cheeks and reached around to capture and lightly squeeze her breast. She ground back against him with her bottom and arched her sex up.

"Since you're so impatient . . ." he spread her and nudged into her lightly, but she was extremely small and he pulled away. "You're not nearly wet enough," he told her, spanking her bottom and fingering her pussy until she was. He had never touched her like this before and she could only whimper and pant her encouragement. "How aggressive you were today," he scolded. "My little Princess demanding sex!" He slapped her inner thighs until she squirmed. "Is that the way a perfect submissive is supposed to behave?"

"I suppose not," she conceded. Her soft response was rewarded by five or six light, sharp smacks on her parted sex. She arched up a little more to show him how agreeable this felt. He went around to one side of her, tucked one arm under her waist, lifted her off the horse an inch or two and spanked her damp pubic mound and labia even more firmly.

"You couldn't wait for our romance to take its course and for me to approach you in the proper way at the proper time, could you?"

"I'm sorry," she murmured as he let her back down and went around behind her again.

"Did it ever occur to you that you may have opened Pandora's Box?" he suggested, penetrating her slowly, with his hands fastened to her waist.

"What do you mean?" She gasped as he thoroughly filled her.

"Now that I've had you like this, do you think I'm going to be satisfied just to spank you and lace your corsets?"

"I hope not, my darling," she breathed.

"Got any lube?"

"What for?" she turned her head.

"What do you think?"

"Isn't this a little sudden?" she squeaked, barely able to accommodate him in the proper place.

"Not to me; I've been daydreaming about sodomizing you for six months," he confessed, spreading and examining her bottom.

"Can't I have six months to dream about it too?"

"You can have six minutes," he told her, withdrawing to abandon her and search for the lube. "And don't move, unless you want the strap again," he warned her.

Upon his return he found her pacing and nervously smoking one of his cigarettes. He relieved her of it with a smile. "Worried?" Now he bent her back over the horse and went to work with the lube, fingering her deeply in both places until she sighed and ground against the leather. Then he only fingered her bottom and slapped it in the middle of it. "Your six minutes are up, bad girl." When Hope only whimpered in reply he spread her and took her, like an expert in the tricky art of sodomy, giving them both an orgasm in a matter of a few short minutes.

"You brute," she whimpered, for form's sake. "No one's ever done that to me before."

"Really?"

As she turned to see him smile there came a knock on the door.

"You expecting some one?" He unceremoniously extracted his still throbbing cock from her tighter than ever sheath and disappeared into the bathroom to dispose of the evidence and put himself back together.

"Only Brooke," Hope replied, pulling her robe back on and answering the door without concern.

"Brooke! What are you doing here?" David demanded as Hope let her in.

"We're going shopping on Melrose. Didn't I tell you?" Hope linked arms with the willowy brunette, who smiled down at her and then across at David.

"So you're going through with this, are you?" David frowned at his ex-student.

"Through with what?" Brooke replied.

"The Betty and Veronica thing."

"Nonsense, Mr. Lawrence, we've simply realized how much we have in common," Brooke explained.

"And think of the impact we'll make as a tag team," Hope suggested blithely, squeezing Brooke's long waist. David did and it made him shudder.

"I'll just jump into these," Hope reported, taking her pre-selected outfit into the bathroom to dress.

Alone with David, Brooke wasn't quite so cocky and indeed avoided his gaze.

"I still say you're too young for any of this," he grouched.

"And I still say I'm into B&D and always have been."

"Well, if something awful happens, don't say I didn't warn you."

"Something awful could have happened to you when I discovered your secret life. But it didn't."

"Your point being?"

"My point being, preach what you practice, Mr. Lawrence."

"Don't be smart," he snapped and Brooke had the grace to blush. Still annoyed at the interruption of his first sexual tryst with Hope, he frowned at Hildegarde's newest protégée. Then he put his jacket on and crammed his grey fedora down on his head. "I'll be going now," he announced as Hope emerged fully dressed.

"You don't want to take us to brunch?" Hope asked, astonished at his eagerness to deprive himself of their company.

"No, I do not want to take you to brunch," he returned, with an edge to his voice that made the girls stare at each other. "Good-bye!" was his final word to them before clattering down the five flights of stairs.

"What did we do?" Hope wondered.

"Maybe it's a sensory overload thing," Brooke speculated as they leaned over the railing to follow the descending fedora.

"You're probably right," Hope agreed. "In the past twenty-four hours he's spanked you for the first time, had me for the first time and now he's just found out we're determined to be friends. No wonder he's confused."

"He seemed more hostile than confused," Brooke observed.

"Well, that's to his credit. Could you respect a man who wasn't slightly unnerved by a situation like this?"

"Still, he might at least have offered us a ride to Melrose."

"Never mind, he brought me plenty of allowance. We can take cabs, have lunch and even buy stockings."

"And let's not forget a present for Mr. Lawrence," Brooke suggested, training her video lens on Hope's radiance for the first time.

"Mr. Lawrence doesn't accept presents from ladies," Hope declared, establishing an immediate relationship with Brooke's camera.

"Nor apparently does he take them to brunch."

"It's better this way," said Hope, "we can talk about him all afternoon." They ran downstairs and followed David out into the brilliant sunlight.

Animal Sex Animal Sex

by Eva Morris

from *RoadBabe!*

I sat next to a California cowboy in a Florida diner who told me, over coffee, a few interesting things about women; gee, you'd think I'd have known them, being one. He told me that, When they tell you to stop, that they've come now and had enough, honey, so you can stop now, "Don't stop" he said. "Keep up your pace and give them another orgasm. When they *can't* say stop is when you stop," he said.

I'd like to meet a man like that, I thought.

The point is *not* to rush an orgasm; he told me how he'd bring a woman close, and then bring her away from it, not letting her have that orgasm, instead of trying to get her to have one fast, for his own score-keeping benefit, really. "I'd be slow and strong and bring her close to it again," he said slowly. My, it was hot in that diner. I changed my drink to an iced tea.

"A man shouldn't go for her orgasm, first and *fast*. He should build it up and then take it." I felt myself getting slippery and knew he was right.

* * *

In Memphis I accepted a dance with a full-lipped, flashing-eyed, compact, full-bodied Mexican man, for one of those long, mindless Mexican songs. With my arm on his shoulder, we danced well together. Within the range of our small footsteps, it was the same movement over and over, my body softened, my hand in his hand, and his eyes on my eyes. After twenty minutes of this, he winked at me with the devil's own smile, and said, "I think you should try a Mexican man."

Hmmm, I thought. I know I need to try *something*.

Lately, when I get in bed with a male, he enters me when he feels the first good opportunity, pumps his hips strongly, and fidgets with my more obvious body parts until he comes. Sometimes I come first, then he comes immediately after. Then the action stops. I curl up in his big strong arms, and think "blah."

I want to get fucked. For the kind of fucking I want, I believe I need to get to know a different kind of critter than the kind I've known so far. I want a man to not overpower me with his body's size; I want a man who believes he can out-endure me. I want to be "worked," made to break a sweat, made to moan from deep inside myself, made dirty, made crazy from the heat.

So far as I can see it, I need the Mexicans' unwavering pace, a true deviant, an animal, and a very dirty mind.

A Sexy Texan told me all about cows.

"Jersey milk cows are light tan in color, and are a small cow. It's because a man can fall for those big, brown eyes they have that this happens. She won't think anything, absolutely nothing about a man being behind her. But, hers is a different kind of pussy. It's a meaty pussy, and you'd have to stand up on something to get your dick into it. A bucket.

"The cow won't move, believe me, she won't. Jersey milk cows are very loving animals. I imagine it feels real well. I know, from pulling a calf out, that that it's a hot cunt. It's hotter than a woman's, because cows run a higher temperature than a woman does. If you are really kinky, you can grab the udders, milk them, and squirt warm milk all over your cock. That warm milk—I think it's sexy as shit to get milk from a woman's tits after she's pregnant, or nursing. A woman can nurse for three years, if she wants to. That warm milk—it just feels so good.

"She wants to compare her cunt to the Jersey milk cow's. I do it. The Jersey milk cow turns her head back and looks at me with those deep, deep brown eyes."

I asked another friendly hick to take me to wherever they breed horses. I'd heard from my friend Paul they have what they call "breeding hobble"; the mare goes in there, gets sedated, and then gets a stiff cock. "All right!" I said, thinking I'd get one, too; sure, I could have lived without the heavy sedation, but why skimp? I wanted to shoot the works!

It was the wrong season, he said.

I've fantasied two or three times about something else I could never admit: being the victim of "warm necrophilia," as my (dog's) vet explained the threat, hardly knowing he was turning me on. "Just watch out, because the drug is only now controlled; it's colorless, odorless, tasteless, and if someone puts it in your drink, you'll be out for hours. Surely, some guy will then offer to walk you out to your car, so no matter what, don't do it! No matter what, stay in the bar!" (As a funny aside, soon after I heard this, in fact, *the same day*, I was at a bar and suddenly believed I felt "light-headed, confused, and disoriented." Meaning absolutely no harm, some guy offered to walk me out to his car so that I could lie down. You should have seen the look I gave him. Poor guy.) I'd like a delicate white powder stirred into a swank-sounding drink of mine, at a disco, I think, and I want to feel what I'd feel the minute I went down and at the same moment realized, "The gig's up!" What kind of fear thrill would *that* be! Maybe I'll ask someone I know to do it for me. Steve would. Come to think of it, a lot of guys I know would. "Hey! Put this in my drink, carry a quiet and well-behaved me home, and fuck my brains out. You can do whatever you want to me; I don't care, and I won't find out about it anyway." God, can you imagine? *They'd line up.*

This from upstate New York:

A hot summer Saturday. Beautiful blonde girl goes for a drive in the country with her dog. Horse country. Car is a convertible. Sun begins to beat down on girl and dog. They grow hot and thirsty. Turn down a quiet back road, pass beneath some shade trees, and see a handsome farmhouse and stables, with a man sitting on the porch. Girl pulls car over, waves at man, asks for water for the dog. Man invites both onto porch, supplies bowl and water for dog, offers girl an iced tea. She accepts.

Man is very strong and handsome, late forties, steel-gray hair at temples. Says he's a retired racehorse vet. Even on the porch, the heat is still very strong; the girl feels dreamy. Man offers to show her the stables. Her dog is asleep, and the girl thinks, If the dog can sleep here, then it's okay. Whole scene very dreamlike.

They enter stables: dark, warm, horsey smells, lots of leather tack, several horses in the pasture beyond. Man opens up the last stall. Remarks that the property was once a famous breeding operation and was world renowned for its stud service. Explains this was where the breeding took place. Stall contains a large, padded apparatus. A kind of tilted table with padded leather straps.

Sound of cicadas outside are echoing inside the girl's head. Thrumming in the heat. Man puts his strong arms around girl, saying, "Let me show you how this works." Girl, feeling safe and sleepy, leans over the apparatus, rests her body on the tilted tabletop, immediately feels comfortable and secure there. Man talks hypnotically, words thrumming in girl's head, and she feels him fix a leather strap across the small of her back. Then, her hands are guided into padded rests and strong straps buckled across her wrists and her upper arms. Finally, her legs are parted, panties removed, and more straps affixed to hold them open, in place. She is completely immobilized now, but the heat and the drugs in the iced tea keep her dreamy.

She is comfortable, unconcerned. Finally, the man opens a small tack box, takes out a short, soft bridle with a bit, and pulling the girl's long blonde hair back, straps it onto her head, gently working the bit into her mouth. She feels like a warm and protected mare as he lifts up her dress and works down her panties. His voice is gentle and soothing, and she sees him open a jar filled with sweet-smelling salve, which he uses to gently lubricate her mons Venus. It mixes with her own oozing juices and she feels her nipples and vulva swelling. The straps hold her fully exposed. She feels the man's strong hands cupping her muscular, round buttocks, kneading them, and she begins to feel herself slipping into readiness.

The hard, smooth head of his member feels like a third thumb rubbing against her until she feels him fit himself into her wet, swollen vagina, slowly thrusting, pushing aside her muscles until she is completely filled with him, and now the restraints keep her from budging at all as he rocks back and forth into her. Her mind is whirling now, abandoning any sense of reason, and animal noises rise up in her throat. Little pants at first, then grunts, then moans, then finally, as she begins to peak, shuddering orgasmic cries. She comes again and again and again, as he steadily pumps her, puts his whole hand up into her; straining against the breeding hobble, she is unable to stop him, unable to stop the waves of pleasure wracking her body. In a great hot flash she feels the man explode in orgasm, the warm tickling of his come down her sex drives her into another orgasm. His semen fills her, and more; then, she goes limp, she hears the thrumming of the cicadas get louder, then softer; she drifts into a drugged unconsciousness.

When she wakes, her dog is licking her hand. She's sitting at the wheel of her car, in the shade of a tree, on a quiet back road. Behind her she sees a handsome farmhouse and stables. The porch is empty.

THE GIRL: ME THE MAN: PAUL THE DREAM: HIS

"Come here, Tyler," A sweet Southern accent camouflaging the dirtiest of thoughts.

In Memphis I met a man so foxy, so fucking hot-looking; with a rugged, wild appearance coming from a world other than my own; sporting a big, wide, snug-fitting, good-looking cowboy hat, creased, starched tight jeans that held a basket, a veritable basket, of eggs, or so it looked to me. A tight ass like I've never seen before, or after. Round and up and tight, without being overly muscular. Sleek hips and buttocks almost female in their sloping, beautiful lines. "An ass like a horse has, when it bucks," I thought, and started to get excited, thinking about the buck in him. He'd gotten out of his big, brand-new, white truck at a truckstop, checked something quickly, and jumped back in. It was enough for me to see I had to have it. I used my CB radio. It didn't take much effort to get him to stop. Not after I pulled up alongside him and he had a chance to take a good look at me. We went to another channel, (16), and I asked him where he lived. The outskirts of Memphis.

My second question was, "Do you have livestock?"

He turned from his steering wheel and looked flatly across the road at me.

He must have reasoned I was a Northerner, *or something,* "Whatever," I saw his mind say.

"Yes, ma'am. I ride bulls for a living. So I keep them," he answered, all the while thinking, but not saying; Why do you ask?

"Hey, can I go see them? Now? Are they close by?"

"Yeah, twenty minutes or so," drawling and skating in the sexy cowboy's way of speaking in spurts, fast thoughts dripping out of tight jaws. "Why ask why?" he must have figured. "This babe wants to come look at my cows? So what? Who knows? Maybe I'll get lucky."

"Come here, Tyler," I cooed.

I laid myself across the top fence post. I was supported by my elbows leaning up against a tall wooden fence post and shook my ass at him, my beautiful, peach-comparable, sweet, ripe size 3 of an ass. Temptation: Like I have the black blood in me. I shook it again. I knew exactly what I wanted out of this. I'd had a whole trip to think about getting it.

Now was the moment. My prey was in range. I turned and smiled at him.

His eyes locked into mine. He saw the whole plan, all laid out, like I was laid out, and He saw that it was no coincidence. He saw the open-to-anything-that-even-smells-like-sex look in my eyes, however much I tried to disguise it with a simple sexy look. I think he saw I meant business. No man likes to be told what to do.

He set back into his heels, stood tall, and looked incredibly, wildly, give-up-the-boat sexy to me; I'd have given anything to have him right there and then. He knew that, too. "Damn it," I thought. On to plan B. I undid my Levi's, slid my tight jeans over my tomboy hips and down my long legs. I had slim red Justin boots on. The jeans dropped down to my ankles. Ass naked, I leaned myself over the fence to the corral, supported by it. He sucked in his breath and walked up to me. Oh, I wanted it. Stick a hard thick one in me, my mind begged whoever was in control. "Oh, God, please . . ." I wagged my ass in the air like a sweaty mutt just dying for it.

"Damn, woman, you look good," he said. I thought, "Could you say that and unzip your pants at the same time? Please? Thank you." He brought his outstretched hand close to the mound of my ass, warm in the Tennessee sun, but he didn't lay it down on me. It was a technique; he held it there, to calm me. Well, it calmed his calf. I didn't move. But neither did he.

"Fuck," I thought. "What the fuck? Unzip those fucking jeans!" I made a slow circle with my ass. He couldn't take his eyes off of it. His gorgeous green eyes. God, this man was good-looking. Unfucking believable. He could have rammed anything into me and I'd have been happy, but what I really wanted was to get fucked in a superior way by this sexy, mustached stud who walked like a King with ten-pound balls. "Give it to me, give it to me," I moaned audibly, which was a mistake.

"Don't tell me how to fuck you." From there on in, the trip was completely driven by him.

He stood there for a minute: 5'10, a body of steel, cream-colored flannel cowboy shirt with the silver snaps, big—huge!—belt buckle, massive balls, and a salami for a cock, it looked to me; no underwear, thank God, those tight jeans, tight hips, tight ass, and foxy cowboy boots. He glided on his feet. He would be a fabulous dancer, I thought. His voice could melt butter; it melted me. Jesus! LOOK AT ME! *Up against a fence like a whore against a car, for Christ's sake,* and why aren't I getting fucked yet? I turned to look at him, feeling like a cow looking over her shoulder at the man approaching her from the rear. My neck stretched prettily and my eyes looked from down to up at him. I smiled. He smiled. His look said that he knew what I wanted and that he was going to give it to me. His worldly and experienced look said he knew just how wild a woman's fantasies ran. He knew, and I knew he knew. He knew I knew. But did he know? I thought, Did he *really* know?

"Wait here a minute," he said, turning and heading over to his barn. All of a sudden, I saw the implications of my being here. Anything could happen. I felt fear. Kind of. I felt something. My body shook. I knew he wasn't about to play by the rules. And he was in control at this point. Trust me, this was no passive man. He had a look in his eyes of evil ideas, stuff I wouldn't want to know about. The wind blew its breath at me, and the wet, exposed areas of my pussy jumped and puckered. I was so hot to fuck, so excited by the prospect of not just what that bulging package of his would look like, but how masculine his eyes were, and how he obviously was preparing to do something to me that was . . . how can I say it? Deviant? Dirty? Evil? Secret? Illegal? Sweaty? Sick? He'd had his chance to do me already: still, here I was, all lips swelling a little, my back swaying and curved, my ass thrown up in the air, and my pussy right here, looking like the sexual equipment on an animal, for Christ's sake.

An animal? I thought. Hmmm. Isn't that how all this started, with my wanting to see his animals? Were real animals going to get involved here? My mind blew a fuse, I think, and I didn't hear him walk up to me. He put his rough hand gently on my back.

He must be good with animals, I thought dumbly; with that reassuring touch he could probably treat them and care for them and even clip their nails without a fight. Animals? Why am I thinking about animals? My mind, thrown, was down on the floor, trying to clear its head and get up when here it came again, the thought of animals. "I'm not into doing animals," I told myself, at the same time realizing that, in all probability, he was, and it didn't matter what I was into, now.

While I thought this, he rubbed a white powder on two of his fingers and hooked them into my mouth. I fought it, because it tasted mediciny. Then I thought it was coke, and why would I fight that? But it wasn't, I could tell right away. I stumbled, got my balance, leaned up against the fence, then stumbled again, that's how I knew. This wasn't a new way to do coke. I was being drugged.

Forget fucking animals, I thought, I'm about to become someone's warm necrophilia! He wiped the powder off his hands, onto his black jeans, careful not to touch it himself.

I felt very, very stoned. I couldn't have stood up without falling down, but, with my jeans around my ankles, how far would I go and where would I go to? I sensed everything with great perception, however: I still felt the wind at my pussy. I was naked, sloppy, my head running in circles, treating this fence like a lifeboat. He was rolling his large hands in something, like a salve. He was lubing his hands with it. He stepped closer to me. I was petrified, but unable to feel it, if that makes sense. I was awake. I wonder if, to the outside eye, it looked as if I was asleep. I wondered if he's just missed giving me enough to drop me. My body, at this point, now ten minutes afterwards, was as manipulative as it would get. My head did fast circles; I felt drunk, then I felt his hands, both of them, part my thighs, from behind. His hands were heavy and smelly with whatever jelly he had all over them. At first, it chilled my skin like Bio-Freeze. He put his palms together, pushed them into the backs of my thighs, setting apart my legs; his large, rough, tough, and experienced (with cows) open hands held down and steadied my pussy while his right hand worked into me. It wasn't how you'd touch a woman; it was, very certainly, how you'd get your hand into a cow. His hand went all the way to the end of me, deep, inside, and to places uncharted—no delicate feeling, that. Despite the thick petroleum-based anesthesia and his having done something similar to this before, albeit on another species, it was still, very painful, and my mind reeled again, as if I'd been slow-punched. Thank God I was drugged with whatever tranquilizer he'd given me, and lubed with the bad-smelling jelly. Still, I screamed. He covered my mouth.

It took me about four or five of the slow "cattle-probe" thrusts of his arm for me to catch my breath. He used his whole hand, twisting it and pushing it. In a fast summary, I was being fistfucked. He was getting his huge hand—slowly—in, changing the hand hold, and out and in—slowly; you'd better believe it, his hands were huge. My eyes closed and rolled back a few times, from the drug or the exertion. I don't know if it was pleasurable, or painful, after a point. It was sore. I blacked out. I was still up against the fence.

He changed my position, throwing my upper body over one side of the fence, leaving my legs hanging down on the other. My head lolled. My legs were spread and he was kneeling down between them, behind me. My mind was drunk, my body was flaccid. He knelt down behind me, doing something to me with his hands. I couldn't figure it out. He was doing the same move, slowly, again and again; he was putting his hand inside me, hooking it and bringing something, some part of me, out toward my opening. He was pulling me inside out. In a steady, working pace. He was turning my pussy out, like I've heard a love-hungry cow does. A sweat had risen on my body, from the strong manipulations. He was engorging me, pulling me down and out, my labia hung down, thick, red, and swollen, down like small balls.

If a man needed a reason to "work" an animal, to work, with his strong hands, a part of an animal's body, forget *why* . . . if he *could*, and wanted to, he'd be doing what this man who obviously got off on getting a body to move this way and that way, was doing to me. He was squatting behind me, looking up, working on me like a mechanic under a low car.

He slid his hand out, leaned back, stood up, and rearranged me. I was pushed up against the fence in a new way, forming a right angle. My back was straight across, my arms hung down on one side of the wood, and my legs kept my back end propped up. He came up behind me, stepping into the space between my two spread legs to where my huge engorged, hot, sex-ready, raw cunt hung down and low and smelled of the mediciny salve, which stung, and of a heavy, sensuous musk. His hands had worked me so hard I was now the keeper of another type of pussy, one not mine. It had been pulled and stretched, it was raw and open. My muscles had been pushed so far I'd lost the ability to clench. I was swollen everywhere and would wake up in the morning feeling as if I'd been hit by a train.

Oddly recognizable—from watching football?—he came up behind me, appraised the two sweaty, trembling cheeks of my ass, twisted his head a little to the side, and looked down at a pussy, which was in a place it usually isn't in. It stuck out from behind me. He could look down at it.

He started to take off his belt buckle with one hand, then he zipped down his jeans, pulling them down from his hips, so he could move more freely. I had the strength to bring my head up. Maybe I'd been there for 45 minutes to an hour, while he worked this deviant hand work on me. I lifted my head and my arms, crossed them, and laid my head back down, on them. I felt sleepy, but wasn't. He cocked an eye at that movement, then looked back down at my pussy, a few inches from his groin. He had a hand on either side of me, holding my waist like he was going to ride me. He spread his legs a little wider, for balance.

Don't tell me how to be fucked, I thought, out of nowhere.

He was going to pull it out, ram it into me, pump it back and forth for however long it took to come, and I'd be right back where I started, with boring sex. Sure, it hadn't been normal so far, I was truly exhausted, my throat ached, and I wondered if I'd moaned or cried while I'd been knocked out. And now I was going to get fucked just like I'd get fucked by any other guy! "Blah" I thought.

The man at the diner had told me that if I was ever with a man whom I suspected of having been wild with a horse, or cow, that my most powerful tool was my own pee. "Drink a lot of water and then, when he's arrived at the top of his cliff, let it gush, turn yourself on, have the warmth trickle down the back of your legs, in the sun, and get it all over yourself."

"You're kidding!" I'd said then. Well, I don't question that anymore.

I started to pee, moistening my mound and then letting my secret weapon run down my spread legs. It was very sexy-smelling, especially at first. His head jerked up; his nostrils flared open. There was a steamy quality to it. It was the smell of sex. I could smell it myself, from where my nose was. That the scent of the strong, different than I've ever smelled it, the rank of my wet slickened red and raw pussy, set him on fire.

He inhaled deeply and moaned; he moaned with such force. "Oh, girl, oh, Christ, God, girl," gasping and taking in deep breaths like he'd just had a scare. My sweet pussy was golden, musky, inflamed. That smell did it; he smelled the farm and sex and animals and the end point of my struggle. I knew he'd come immediately.

Mixed with my own wetness, the smell combined with that of the animal salve, the pheromones were alive and jumping. In his mind he called me a cow's name, "Betty," he quivered, and then shot his load. What a shame. There went nine inches and a good man.

I shook my long hair, it whipped my lower back, tickled my ass, and it said something to him. I don't think he liked what it said. Without the trace of an accent it said, "Blah."

Co-operations

by Martin Pyx

from *Tutor's Bride*

4

The brightest spot in any day, seeing you, Lady Morgan." A florid-faced Englishman with heavy dundreary whiskers, Colonel Andrew S.F.X. Sandemarche bowed her into his office. The major seated before his desk prudently slipped away through a side door, his sheaf of papers in hand.

"Courtly as ever, Sandy. Lady Morgan, indeed!" She laughed in a trilling peal. "Not bad for Molly Morgan Mulcreavy, the convent orphan."

"And finest proprietess ever to preside over a house of assignation." He seated her and went around the desk to his own chair. "Assuredly. Your aunt commanded all our love, of course—"

"She'd peel your hide with her oaths and piss on your skinned remains." Lady Bisque-Hardy perched her parasol by her side. She unlaced her bonnet.

"That too, that too. You should have known her before the sickroom days." He shuddered. "I've seen guardsmen verging on tears at her rages. No cavalry sergeant ever had her command of the Devil's language."

"I seem to recall some of that fired in my direction," she admitted. "You'll be up to dine with us Friday, with your lovely wife? The Hunters will join us in our recreations, after."

His thick whiskers quivered in astonishment. "You don't say!"

"I promised the tutor a good look at how a woman keeps discipline in her household. Magenta and those two spratlings should provide an educational display, indeed." A smile played on her lips. "He has his own plans, too. I'll say no more, but . . . there should always be an element of the uncertain about a public performance, don't you believe?"

"Too true. Though I am by vocation consecrated to the most exacting detail in planning, yet I reserve the right to the spontaneous in a campaign. My aides find that disconcerting. It worked well enough against our friend the Zulu to earn me this sinecure in our drowsing second Eden."

"You underrate your importance to the island."

"Whom do we guard against? The French? The Germans? Dutch spice traders from Guiana? Is there cause to fear revolt?" He leaned forward. "I'll be candid. I'd fear more for my regiment in Dublin than here in St. Louis le Prophète."

"As well you should, knowing my countrymen."

"May I offer some tea," his hand gripped a bell, "laced, perhaps, with rum, as in the old days."

"No, I've a favor to ask, and I must be on my way. I wish to make my darling sister a present of a visit to one of Sir George's private assizes."

"Ah . . . ah. An opportune time." He glanced about on his desk. "I have a request for an escort—yes, tomorrow. You shall be my guests, assuredly, you and Mrs. Reardon. May I hope for Sir Polkinghorn's company, as well?"

"Polo has gone into the hills to see about extending cultivation. He prefers to make a slow journey and rest over in the labor camp. I believe the hardships give him pleasant evocations of his hunting days."

"A famous sportsman, yes; a pity the chase finally bored him."

"I have no such regrets, though I first met him on one of his tramps through the underbrush, you may know." She picked up her bonnet and her parasol. "Tomorrow, then."

"Shall we meet at the Barracks at 2:00? Will that interfere with your sister's duties at the schoolhouse?"

"She shall adapt her schedule, I'm sure; she has proctors."

"Perhaps some rum-sweetened tea afterward?"

"You're too tempting. The Serpent himself couldn't refuse such an invitation." She smiled with white, long teeth.

"Done, then."

She left and he fell to pleasant recollections of St. John's Wood rambles, in particular to August Mulcreavy's house of resort. A carnal Heaven for a man wearied of killing and the false gallantries of warfare. Molly Mulcreavy had been her aunt's faithful protege, young at the procuring trade though she'd been. Refined conversation refreshed visitors in the sitting rooms; utter, whorish abandon slaked the stormy flesh in the fucking rooms.

Reluctantly, he put aside thoughts of England and summoned his aide.

"It is, I suppose, expected." Sir Polkinghorn Bisque-Hardy surveyed the three opulently naked black virgins awaiting his attentions.

"Without the ceremony, the planting cannot begin," the labor gang foreman assured him. "The Yemoja must be placated. Unless they cool and control Ifa, his terrible neglect can shrivel the crops before they mature."

"I know, I know. Nutmeg is a chancy creature at best; why anger the weather spirits before you begin, eh?"

Before her respiring bosom, each sable-skinned maiden bore the *abede,* a cowrie shell-ornamented fan emblematic of the riverain goddess she served. In her left hand, each held the naked sword associated with her female society's militant witchcraft. He recognized the blades as British Navy sabers bound in *rafia* fiber, hung with river flowers.

Accommodatingly, he surrendered his trousers and shirt to the foreman. The turned earth felt warm, embracing under his spine. He raised his knees and opened them.

Her bottom still dully smarting from a flogging three days before, Magenta made a second stroll past the small parlor her father had transformed into a schoolroom. Her ear strained to hear something besides chanted conjugations of *amo, auras, amat.* She lingered in hope by the closed door.

Who cared to know what an "equilateral triangle" was? The silly question and answer examinations she sometimes heard held no interest. She had studied accomplishments at her school, one of the finest in England—which meant the world. Dancing, the piano, elegant embroidery—those were a young lady's learning. Who was there to dance with on this miserable island, where they only knew country hopping and strutting? Father's piano had fallen out of tune within weeks of their arrival. Embroidery—elegance in this wild, primeval place?

She caught raised voices through the door panel. Boyish anger. Mr. Hunter's sonorous scolding. Perhaps . . . she glanced up and down the corridor. No servants spying. She settled her ear snugly against the door.

" . . . will *not* read . . . "

" . . . as I determine . . . "

" . . . mother calls it indecent . . . "

Footsteps approached from within the room. She started, hands grasping her skirts. She began to walk away briskly.

"Oh. Miss Bisque-Hardy." Hunter spoke from the doorway. "Is your—is Lady Bisque-Hardy unoccupied at the moment, do you know?"

"She has gone to visit Colonel Sandemarche, sir, but I am sure we shall see her at tea."

"Pity." He turned inside. "A moment. You may be able to assist me. I do regret that unfortunate incident at tea yesterday."

A bit of Chinese lacquer set on a tiny, narrow table occupied her gaze. "Thank you, Mr. Hunter."

"I assure you, I have forgotten all details, save one—you are experienced in applying corporal correction?"

A warmth seeped through her bosom, rising to congest her throat. "Yes. I am."

"The tawse, you've applied it to . . . male fundaments?"

"I have."

"Successfully, I do not doubt. Would you consent to do me a considerable service?"

She found strength to meet his level stare with a look of gracious assent.

"I have a lad here who balks at punishment in front of girls. I mean that he shall feel it, and an appropriate humiliation for such contumacy would be correction by your fair hand. If you do not find the task indelicate, it would be much more appropriate than if performed by Lady Bisque-Hardy."

"I shall endeavor to merit your confidence."

"Please come in, then."

She had never seen the room occupied. Seven scholar's desks, four boys to her left, three girls to her right. They stood as she entered.

Syndon and Auberon glowered, having to rise for *her.* Ravenna Aubusson, Lydia Temple, Elise St. Remy looked like children in their short dresses. She felt her long, womanly skirts swish about her. Her London bearing wrapped her as in a mantle. Mr. Hunter had requested her assistance in his little kingdom . . . she stood at the fore, facing them as his equal.

"A bright lad, but stubborn. We have a disagreement on France's Revolution. I propose Carlyle as a text for study. He denies the authority of any but French authors."

She recognized Gerard Cloutier, a large-nosed, squint-eyed boy. He had teased all the girls stupidly at a gathering at Colonel Sandemarche's, even molesting her with his nonsense. His father had some notoriety as a smuggler—or at least his ships were skilled at evading import duties in Jamaica, Barbados, and other ports.

"Carlyle." She spoke clearly, against a pounding heart. "Such a noble writer."

She dimly recalled her father reading some tedium about Frederick of Prussia aloud over several interminable evenings. That was Carlyle, she thought, almost assuredly.

"I should think the biographer of Frederick would know something of the upheavals in France." She gazed at the boy disparagingly.

"Ah, you see, young Master Cloutier, you may not know Carlyle's greatness, but this educated lady certainly is familiar with him."

"He is an Englishman," the boy muttered passionately.

Magenta remembered something further. Her father comically affected a most horrible Highland burr when reading certain passages. Her success emboldened her to venture, "He was, I think, a Scotsman."

"Brava, Miss Bisque-Hardy!" Hunter had moved to the other side of the lad's desk. "You have disarmed him utterly. Do you see the importance of acquiring learning, young Master Cloutier, rather than acting the fool in educated society?"

His hands sprung and seized the boy. The tutor bent the squalling lad across the desktop.

"You will find a reliable three-fingered tawse on the rack behind my desk, Miss Bisque-Hardy. If you would be so good . . . "

He doubled the youth's right arm behind him, easily fending off the flapping other hand. Hunter pulled the boy's school jacket high and attacked the buttons holding his braces.

Magenta rounded the tutor's large desk and faced the wooden rack. It spoke stern volumes, with its aspish, varnished canes and equally shining brown and black straps, smelling of fresh wax.

She lifted the requested tawse from its hook. A full two feet of sturdy leather ran from the doubled handle to the broad fingers. The steer's hide had been cut deeply to form three tails, each well over half an inch across.

She touched it on the way back to the struggling, foolish Gerard. The fire-hardened fingers felt like iron. Worse, far worse than the light tawse her stepmother had allowed her to use on Auberon.

The boy's short trousers had fallen in defeat. His narrow backside poked into the air, paler than his face and legs, but still showing the dark Southern French coloration. She had read her Dumas and found it strange to realize that D'Artagnan the Gascon had been as swart.

"Five for resisting scholastic authority," Hunter sentenced crisply. "Five for continued resistance. Five, I think, for refusal to accept proper punishment."

Hunter controlled the boy easily. Gerard trembled in anger, but his threshing had stopped.

"Do you wish to take this side, Miss Bisque-Hardy?" Hunter indicated where he stood.

Magenta's blood rushed to her ears, like a river. "I believe that a descending backhand blow is more telling than a descending forehand one, where no run is permitted."

"True, true. I bow to your experience, demoiselle."

She still found that island address strange, but she knew it meant respect and recognized station.

She raised the heavy tawse in her right hand, carrying it back over to fall behind her left shoulder. Praying for true aim, she swung a full-strengthed diagonal stroke. It exploded onto his curved buttocks.

The boy grunted, like the pig he was.

She pulled the strap away, watching the hot coloration begin. Her own muscles ached from the violent strain.

Still, in under half a minute she caught him equally hard across his impudent hinds. The whipped muscles bunched.

She tried to aim, but wound up hitting him at random. Still, her strokes covered his rebellious behind. At ten he gave up a moist, reluctant sob.

At twelve he raised his head, bloodless and drawn. "Please, sir!"

"Beg clemency from Miss Bisque-Hardy; she is correcting you."

He ducked his face, teeth grinding.

She used all her strength on those final three. By some gift they struck the most claret-hued, sorest marks.

She stood back. Hunter released the boy. He cradled his face in both his arms.

"Button up your braces. You wouldn't wish to scandalize the girls now, would you?" Hunter mocked.

Gerard reached back, face averted. His fingers could lift his trousers, covering his scalded behind, but he couldn't work the buttons. He simply sat, head reared, lips stretched over his teeth.

Exultation swam through her.

"Thank you, Miss Bisque-Hardy." Hunter extended his hand, taking the tawse from her. He placed it on the desk before the boy. "That is a reminder for the rest of the day."

The tutor bowed, taking and kissing her tingling fingers.

"May I call upon your generosity should a like occasion arise?"

"Pray do, Mr. Hunter. I shall always be pleased to aid your work with these children."

She paraded out in triumph, past Syndon and Auberon, past the big-eyed island girls.

"Yemoja, the mighty wind that gyres in strength upon the land!

Yemoja, whose watery rage brings low the river-vaulting bridge!

"Oh, Mary most-Virgin, whose heel defies the lurking fangs!

"Ever-purest bride whose monthly flow refreshes a parched land's fruit!

"Yemoja, sisters of Blessed Mary, show her loving mercy to your land!

"Accept as your love the lord of this land, who serves you now and always!

"Protect his acres and his crops; accept the service of his body and his brain!"

All three nubile ebony witches danced with flagrant eroticism, now fanning Sir Polkinghorn's risen member, now touching swordpoints and revolving in a scythe-edged pinwheel about him. He lay patiently upon the ground.

The first held her blade intimidatingly across his throat while she settled over his ripe and ready peggo. She supported herself on her elbows with her saber menacing his windpipe and her other hand fanning his brow lustily. The naked maidens spread her narrow, sable lips and nuzzled his blunt member into place.

With a wild, devotional look, she plunged her hips against his. The sword edge nicked his flesh. Blood started from both as she emitted a woman's cry. She lifted the saber blade higher and he began the necessary labors.

The ritual proved stenuous work, no denying. He had his hands overly full, tickling, tantalizing, and titilating her sweetly molded body into the requisite climactic paroxysm. She shrilled and bounded happily, her eager, clutching vulva fairly savaging his rigid fellow.

When she rose, it was only to have the next African pythoness mount his blood-greased staff.

Damn those busybodies who sharpen ceremonial swords, he thought. He felt the fresh cuts on his Adam's apple as he bucked and cuddled, lithely muscled thighs in a rapturous death-grip about his loins. Bountiful buttock-moons weaved their ancient magic beneath his kneading hands.

As stern ritual prescribed, none of the three women performed any volitional act beyond her depucellation. He built the amorous frenzy within each one; her bottom began its wigglings of satisfaction in instinctive response to his manipulations; her breasts crept up his chest to his mouth of their own apparent will. He nibbled at inky, hard nipples.

He wondered if the solemn merchants strolling the 'Change in London ever appreciated the tribulations of the provincial planter. He doubted it.

The last ecstatic deflowered maiden actually trapped his fingers in her gyrating, clenched bottomcleft. The dusky witch rode him with a ferocious chanting of unassuageable, inarticulate lust. Always the last one, he marveled.

Teeth set, he strove to avert the discourtesy of a masculine eruption. One couldn't afford to play favorites among the three Yemoja whose votaries had claimed their initiation into womanhood on his strained, weeping affair.

She dismounted, doe-eyed and spraddle-legged with pleasure.

All right, John Thomas, he thought, now for the final effort.

He felt the three swordpoints lift his swollen glans, smirched with female blood and outpourings. The fans began their fluttering cooling. Their breeze tickled his engorged thing.

Sir Polkinghorn thought of Nanny Trent, whose Sunday treat had been a brisk chaffing for his youthful wand between her Midlothian peasant bosoms until he "poured his cream on my puddings." He remembered the shy investigations his hands made into his sister's drawers as she stood in the forboding study's corner, her nose pressed to a ha'penny, after punishment; the fugitive fondling of her hot welts practically merited the half-crown she bargained him into giving her . . .

He felt the near rush of his tribute, but it receded. He concentrated on Magenta's mother in her fine, apple-cheeked fury as she burst into the hunting lodge on that Irish holiday, to find him on the rush-stuffed mattress with a convent girl, her uniform rucked about her moist armpits; he remembered dew-tipped young Molly Morgan Mulcreavy, shrieking her piquant cries as Lady Betty chased her about the room and out into the night, hunting whip cracking repeatedly across the girl's chubby, spritely bottom . . . *Ah!*

The spermatozoic offering to the riverain goddesses' potency foamed high and long. The blades whisked through the pulsing jet, scattering gouted drops over the turned earth. The fans kept their agitation until the mighty monster had been thoroughly tamed back into a wet, pale worm.

Polite applause rewarded him as he stood, swatting the clinging loam from his backside. This was truly warm work, he reflected, fucking on a hot day. He longed for a bracing pint, drawn from the deep stone cistern of a hospitable pub. Yet, he had foregone such pleasantries when permanently locating himself on Mardi Blanc.

He had donned his clothing when Father de la Charrette, carefully absent during the pagan portion of the proceedings, arrived with his censer and sanctified water to bless the field and the work crew.

The round-faced, awl-nosed French priest had talked quite freely with him about the relations between the religions in the Caribbean islands. The discussion had certainly eased the yoke of Catholicism upon Sir Polkinghorn's shoulders. He had, however, no inclination to discuss such philosophies with his wife. It would be unprincipled to disturb her contentment with the faith of her childhood.

from

DRAMA

by Michael Hemmingson

5

The night Kristine suggests that Jonathan come live with her so they can be together all the time and make love and drink beer and talk and be happy, he is on acid. Again. It's one of those days: he goes to the beach, he drops acid. He has a key to her place now and after the beach, the acid wearing off, he goes over to the cottage to take a shower and wait for her to come home. Inside, there is a giant brown moth on the light on the ceiling. It is the biggest moth he has ever seen. It must be a foot long. It's very brown and has an intricate design on its wings. It looks so majestic. Jonathan just stares at the moth. He sits down and thinks he has a connection to the moth. There is, he knows, a great reason why this moth is here. And how did it get in here? He sees that Kristine left the backdoor open, probably to let air circulate. It's strange, because while he was on the beach tripping on acid, he felt a great sense of doom, but it was an odd happy-go-lucky kind of doom. He felt that something tremendous and terrifying would be revealed to him. Jonathan knows, from past experience, that LSD has a way of allowing the mind to manifest things in the real world. He knows that this moth is an extension of his acid brain. He is in love with the moth.

"I'm going to take a shower now," he tells the moth.

The moth flutters its long wings, as if to say okay.

He closes the back door. He doesn't want the moth to leave.

In the shower he masturbates, thinking of the moth. He fantasizes about fucking the moth, shoving his dick way up the moth and becoming all the more one with the creature.

When he comes out of the shower, the moth is gone. He looks around for it. He can't find the moth. He starts feeling anxious.

"Mothra," he sings, and images of Godzilla fill his head.

Kristine comes home; he starts rambling on about a giant moth. She looks at him like she doesn't know what to think. She looks at his dilated eyes and says, "You dropped acid today, didn't you?"

"Yeah."

She laughs. "And you want me to believe this giant moth is real?"

"It wasn't a hallucination!" he cries. "This was a real live in color in the flesh GIANT MOTH!"

"Yeah, right," she laughs. "Okay, I need a shower now."

She showers, he lies on the futon, yearning for moths. He wants to cry. He feels frightened. It must be the acid. He knows he wasn't seeing things. He never hallucinates on acid, that's just a myth, or a condition of people with weak minds.

He hears Kristine leave the bathroom and go to the kitchen. She screams. He runs to her.

She's pointing at the wall. She's naked and dripping wet with water. "The giant moth!"

It's there, on the wall.

"I told you it was real," he says, relieved. "I told you so."

"I've never seen a moth," she says, "so huge."

"It is weird," he says.

"Where did it come from?"

"My mind."

"What?"

"There's a reason why it's here."

"It's so beautiful," Kristine says dreamily.

The big brown moth *is* beautiful. They both gawk like children at the wellspring of wonders. The moth flaps its wings and flies. They both jump back, Kristine and Jonathan. The moth returns to the living room.

"Wow," Kristine says.

They have to go now. They're meeting some people at a bar. They say goodbye to the moth.

"I wonder if it'll be here when we get back," Jonathan says.

"Where would it go," Kristine says, "the doors and windows are closed."

Kristine drives her big old car. Jonathan feels something dreadful again. She gets on the freeway. She says the wheel feels funny. She takes an off-ramp. The wheels screech, the car wobbles, Kristine makes a sound, it seems like she's losing control. Jonathan has a vision of the car turning over, he and Kristine injured or dead. The vision, for some strange reason, makes him sexually aroused. It's like something out of a J.G. Ballard novel.

Kristine pulls the car over. "Oh my God. I thought we were going to crash."

She can't drive. He gets behind the wheel. He doesn't really want to drive, not in his condition. Kristine takes a cigarette out of her purse and lights it.

"I didn't know you smoked," he says.

"Sometimes now and then I have one," she says. "I used to smoke a lot. I really need this cigarette right now."

He drives. There is something wrong with the car—the steering wheel pulls, the tires don't feel right. He thinks the tires are unbalanced and the alignment and axle are messed up, not to mention the suspension. This is a crappy car. She should get rid of it. He asks her why she bought it.

"Kyle got it for me, when we separated," she tells him. "He took our car, the little Honda, and I told him he had to buy me a car. So he got this car."

"What did he pay?"

"A thousand."

"A rip-off," he says.

"I know."

They get to the bar, hang out with the people they came to meet, and leave. Halfway there, Jonathan begins to have the heebee-jeebies. They pass cop cars and he gets paranoid. He thinks the cops have an LSD radar and know he's coming off the drug and will pull him over and haul him off to jail. He stops the car and tells her he can't drive, he says it's the acid, plus he had about five beers at the bar. Kristine, smoking, drives the rest of the way to her home. She takes the backstreets, not the freeway. It takes longer to get home, but it's safe.

"The moth protected us," Jonathan announces.

"What?"

"We also died on that off-ramp in an alternate, parallel universe. We could've in this universe. The car could've flipped over. But I felt the moth protect us. It spread its wings of love and protected us—in this universe."

"Maybe you're right."

"You feel it too?"

"Sure." He wonders if she's humoring him. He can't stop thinking of their dead counterparts in the alternate universe. He mourns for those two dead people, and becomes more frightened for the two live people that are in the here and now.

The moth is gone when they go inside. They look everywhere for it and can't find it. It's a mystery. Jonathan feels like he's going to have a nervous breakdown. They go to bed. She wants to make love. He can't even kiss her. He starts to cry.

"What's wrong?" she says, holding his head to her chest.

"I don't know," he says, his body shaking, "we could've died."

"We didn't. We're alive."

"*Are* we alive?"

"Of course we are."

"I don't know what's wrong."

"It's the acid," she says. "Ssssh."

"It's not just the acid. It's something else."

"It's okay."

"Plus, my sublet ends in two weeks. I don't know what to do. Where should I move?"

"Move here," she says.

"Here?"

"Here with me."

"Live here with you?"

"Why not?"

"You think that'd be a good idea?" he says.

"I don't know."

"It might not be a good idea," he says.

"You can stay here until you figure out what to do," she says. "I'd like that, actually."

He still can't stop crying. She rocks him in her bosom, in the darkness of the quiet bedroom.

She says, "It's okay, it's okay."

"It's okay."

She says, "Do you want to know something?"

"What?"

"Do you really want to know something?"

"What?"

"I'm in love with you."

6

Kristine wakes up in the middle of the night, her head spinning from the alcohol. She's having a hard time sleeping. Jonathan is next to her, his back against the wall, a pillow between his legs. She adores him. She does love him. She knows now that she never did, in fact, love Kyle, because she never felt this way about Kyle. She's felt this way twice in her life, when she was a teenager.

Her first love was Randy. He wanted to have sex but she wasn't ready, not yet, and in those early years she entertained an ideal notion of waiting until she was married before she would do such a thing. It's not that she was afraid of sex, or a prude about it (even though her adopted parents were quite conservative), she wanted it to be special and glorious. Sex had been on her mind since she was twelve, and she wondered if she'd be able to wait for marriage.

Looking at Jonathan sleeping, she wonders who his first young loves were, if he had any; what his first sexual experience was like, and with whom.

Her first sexual experience was oral sex and it was with Randy. If she wasn't going to let him fuck her, maybe she would give him a blowjob. She gave this some thought. She talked about it with her best friend, Jannine, who'd been giving blowjobs to guys for a year now. Jannine told Kristine to go ahead and do it, it was no big deal, even fun, it'd make Randy happy. "Just don't swallow the sperm," Jannine said, "it's gooey and tastes like junk." At a party at someone's house, Jannine talked Kristine into believing now was the time—she and Randy could go to this bedroom to be alone, and Kristine could suck Randy's dick just like Jannine told her how.

Kristine didn't know that Jannine had set this whole situation up for the sake of some of the people at the party. Jannine lived next door, and from her bedroom window next door, one could see into the bedroom where Kristine and Randy went. So when Kristine gave Randy head, a dozen kids from the party were across the street watching.

She was nervous, but determined. Randy sat on the edge of the bed, his pants and underwear pulled down to his ankles. His glasses slid down his nose. She thought he looked vulnerable and cute, sitting there with an expectant red penis sticking in the air like a proud solider. She got on her knees in front of him and went to it. She wasn't sure if she'd be repulsed and stop. She was surprised to discover she liked it—she liked the feel and taste of his flesh: rigid and pulsating; she liked how he moaned as she slid the penis in and out of her mouth. She was excited, and reached between her legs and made herself come twice, silently and quickly. When Randy shot his semen into her mouth, she didn't pull away or spit it out. She liked the bittersweet and salty taste, the way it felt going down the back of her throat. (She'd read enough about oral sex in books to have a general idea what to expect.)

They left the bedroom, Randy was happy, and Kristine was appalled by the group—who applauded. She figured it out, before she was told. She felt angry and betrayed, but Jannine assured her that this happened at these parties all the time. (Later, she too would sit in Jannine's room and see various sex acts performed by her schoolmates and friends.)

So began her escapades into giving head, which she gave to Randy almost every time they got together, and sometimes he'd do the same for her. After she broke up with him, when he was in love with a girl who put out her pussy, Kristine would give blowjobs to the boys she dated. Kristine thinks she may have been known as the Blowjob Queen in the boys' locker room, because she must've, during the rest of high school, gone down on over a dozen guys. (She went on one date with a football player who said, "I hear you love sucking dick and you're good at it." She wondered where he heard that. She *didn't* suck his dick.)

Kristine graduated high school and she was a virgin and getting ready for college and she decided she didn't want to be a virgin anymore. She didn't want to wait for marriage, but she wanted to be in love. None of the guys she was casually dating were material to be in love with. She had to find someone to love.

She decided Jannine's brother, Travis, would be the one.

She didn't know why she'd never thought of him before. He was twenty-five, he'd just finished graduate school, he was back home and wondering if he should get a Ph.D or a job. She saw him playing tennis at the local courts one day, admired his body and maturity, and said to herself: *I will make him fall in love with me and I will lose my virginity to him.* The problem was, she knew he didn't see her that way—she was just a little girl, his sister's best friend. She was determined; she planned and schemed. She talked him into teaching her how to play tennis. She said it was her dream to play tennis, although she really, secretly, didn't care for the sport. Three afternoons a week, he conceded to give her lessons. The tennis handsome, as it were. At first, he didn't want to. Jannine goaded him into it. (Kristine hadn't told her best friend her plan, but Jannine was quick enough to figure it out.)

After several weeks, Kristine was certain that Travis was looking at her more than a girl, that there was interest. She was nearly bending over backwards to flirt and give him signals. Then there was the afternoon that he was showing her a serve technique, his body behind hers, close to flesh, and she could feel his semi-erect penis against her butt, and when their skin touched, there was electricity, and she turned, and he kissed her, and it started.

First, the kissing; then, the petting. His hand in her underwear, bringing her to orgasm, her hand on his cock, semen flowing over her wrist. When she showed him her expert technique at blowjobs, he was delighted. He said most of the girls he dated never wanted to get their mouths anywhere close to a cock.

"They don't know what they're missing," Kristine said.

She didn't tell him she was a virgin. She couldn't. She wanted to, and almost did several times, but she was afraid he might treat her differently, that he might not want to go that far with her. She was in love with him, and this was good enough. The time came when they were in the bathroom at his house—the upstairs bathroom, to be exact, his parents' bathroom, which she'd never seen. They were alone in the house and why they didn't go to bed, she didn't know. The bathroom was white. It was the most white bathroom she'd ever seen. White walls, thick white carpet, white towels, white porcelain tub, basin, and toilet. He lifted her skirt and tried entering her from behind. She was leaning against the basin. She stared at their reflection in the mirror. She kept her mouth shut, she didn't want him to know how uncomfortable she was, how much it hurt as he kept trying to get inside her. His cock just wasn't going in.

"This always happens," he said apologetically, "I'm too big."

He did have a pretty large penis, now that she thinks of it. She'd never compared sizes before, and she did usually have to stretch her mouth wide to suck him. It wouldn't be until years later, and some men later, that she'd understand that Travis was among the minority of well-endowed men. His cock was ten inches long, two inches thick, and had a mushroom bulb of a head.

Travis wasn't about to give up. He asked if she still wanted to go on and she said yes. He opened the mirror cabinet, and took out a jar of petroleum jelly. He applied the jelly all over his cock and on her, and with a few more tries, he was inside her.

It didn't hurt as bad as she preconceived. Well, she thought, I'm not a virgin anymore.

It was quick, and when he pulled himself out of her, he said, "Uh-oh."

He pointed to the floor. There was a spot of blood, and it'd come from her. The blood stood out in this white bathroom like a Nordic blonde in a sea of Japanese businessmen.

"Did I hurt you?" he said.

"No," she said, "it's my period."

7

DeeDee is an actress who has done a few shows at The Jarry, has slept with David the artistic director on a number of occasions, and wants to have sex with Kristine.

This is what Kristine tells Jonathan.

"Really?" says Jonathan.

"What she really said was that she'd like to have a threesome with me. I think she had in mind me, her, and David."

"Would you do it?"

"Subtract David, I wouldn't mind."

"What about me?"

"You could join in," she says, "if DeeDee wanted you to join in. Otherwise you might just have to watch."

A week later, at a big party, Jonathan is drunk enough to approach DeeDee about this; so is DeeDee. They are both leaning against a wall in the house where the party is; they're drinking beers and Jonathan says, "So I hear you want to do a threesome with my girlfriend."

DeeDee smiles and says, "Your girlfriend has a big mouth."

"Oh, it's a *good* mouth."

"Does it take your big cock in well?"

"Who says I have a big cock?"

"Do you have a big cock?"

"So you *do* want to have sex with my girlfriend."

"I said I wanted to do a threesome with her," DeeDee goes, "but I'm in for fucking her."

"Could I join?"

"If you're a good boy."

They look for Kristine at the party. Kristine is also drunk.

Jonathan says, "Let's go home and go have us a threesome."

"Okay," Kristine says.

Back in the cottage, they don't waste any time and there's no second thoughts or bashfulness. They get naked and jump on the bed and have a fun time kissing, licking, sucking, fucking, you name it.

DeeDee kisses them both; she moves from Jonathan to Kristine with the slick and wet ease of an experienced bi-sexual slut. When she kisses Kristine, Jonathan touches both their bodies, running his hand over backs and stomaches, squeezing and cupping asses and tits. DeeDee is tall and slender, her body rippled with muscles—a dancer, an actress, a runner who runs five miles a day. DeeDee also doesn't have any pubic hair, which both Jonathan and Kristine like. When DeeDee kisses Jonathan, Kristine takes his cock into her mouth. He's so excited that he immediately comes in Kristine's mouth. She holds the sperm in, doesn't swallow, and when she kisses DeeDee, she spits Jonathan's semen into DeeDee's mouth. DeeDee is surprised, she makes a sound, moves back. She licks at the semen. She goes back to kissing Kristine. Then they both kiss Jonathan, two mouths on his, making him taste himself.

DeeDee says she wants to go down on Kristine. "I want to

taste your cunt," she says, and Kristine lies down on the bed and spreads her legs. DeeDee spreads Kristine's pussy lips and says, "How nice," and works her tongue into that cunt.

Jonathan watches.

He likes watching this.

He likes it when Kristine puts her mouth to DeeDee's shaved cunt.

"I want you to fuck her," Kristine says, and she says to DeeDee, "Can he fuck you?"

"If you want him to fuck me, yes," DeeDee says.

"What do you want?"

"No, it's all about what *you* want," DeeDee says.

Jonathan doesn't care what either wants. He moves on top of DeeDee and gets inside her. Her cunt is a little loose. She's probably fucked everyone in the theater community, or so he has heard.

"You slut," he says, "you dirty slut."

"That's me," breathes DeeDee, "I'm a dirty little *fuck.*"

8

Kristine likes women sometimes; she tells Jonathan that she likes the taste of pussy. "That's why I like sucking your cock right out of my cunt," she says; "I like the taste of it on your dick."

Jonathan wants to explore this more. The night with DeeDee was good for both of them.

The first time Kristine ate pussy was with a friend from high school, Laura. It didn't happen until they were both twenty-one; she was with her boyfriend at the time and Laura was with this guy and one night the four of them got drunk and stoned and someone introduced the idea of a foursome. Kristine was all for trying anything at least once.

"I always wondered what it would be like to go down on you," Laura said.

"Have you ever?" Kristine asked her friend.

"No. Have you?"

"No."

"But you want to?"

"Oh yes."

Their boyfriends were happy to watch them go at each other's cunts, and then take turns fucking them during and after.

"After that first taste," Kristine says to Jonathan, "I have always loved pussy."

"Let's hunt for pussy," Kristine says one night.

"Together?" Jonathan says.

"We can be like Simone de Beauvoir and Jean-Paul Sartre," she says. "She had a theater group, he was a writer, they both enjoyed young females. She even wrote a book about it. I have it somewhere." Kristine checks her bookshelves. "Here it is." She hands him a copy of Beauvoir's *She Came to Stay.*

"I didn't know Sartre was so kinky," he says.

"He was. They were."

Jonathan wonders what kind of kinky things Camus was up to in the last century.

"So I'm Sartre," he says, "and you're de Beauvoir?"

"Yeah."

"Okay."

The hunt for pussy around the The Alfred Jarry Theater proves to be a little more difficult than fantasy or theory would have it. Jonathan tries to approach several actresses, making lewd suggestions. The actresses don't know if he's kidding or if they should be disgusted, offended, etc.

It seems to be a better idea that Kristine approaches the nubile young actresses first. She has a more delicious and exact seductive approach.

Jonathan watches her in action at an after-show party one night and admires her moves. He wishes he were as smooth as Kristine.

That night, they take home a twenty-year-old petite and reddish-blonde actress named Sumi. She's a little drunk and a lot excited. She says she's only done this sort of thing once.

"And how did you like it?" Jonathan asks.

"It was cool," Sumi says.

In their bedroom, Jonathan and Kristine undress Sumi and run their four hands all over her small, hard body. Sumi shudders and closes her eyes and smiles.

"Suck his dick," Kristine tells Sumi, "I want to see you suck his dick."

"Yummy," Sumi says, and gets on her knees to blow Jonathan. She has a small mouth and has trouble getting his cock in her mouth. Kristine pushes on Sumi's head.

Sumi coughs and pulls back. "I'm going to lose my lunch," she says. "You don't want me to hurl on your pee-pee, do you?"

Kristine pushes the small actress onto the bed and sits on the girl's face. "You won't lose your lunch on this," Kristine says.

Jonathan is amazed at how aggressive Kristine is.

Kristine is simply excited about what they're doing. She calls him "John" but he knows in her mind he is Jean-Paul Sartre and she is Simone and Sumi is just one of their conquests in a time far and gone and best left to erotic literary fantasies.

He slides his cock into Sumi while Kristine is still sitting on Sumi's face. He and Kristine both come at the same time—he fills Sumi's pussy with his seed and Kristine squirts into Sumi's mouth and it's all very nice and tasty and fun.

* * *

There's the actresses, and there's the lesbians. Just two and a half blocks away from Kristine and Jonathan's cottage is a well-known lesbian bar/club. Jonathan has been there before on Boy's Night.

"Before we met," Kristine says, "I went there one night and was picked up. We came back here and fucked."

"What was her name?"

"Wendy, I think."

"What did she look like?"

"She looked like me."

"No."

"She did," Kristine says.

"Did she spend the night?" Jonathan says.

"She left after, but I wanted her to spend the night."

"I think you need to go back there and get picked up again," he says.

"Or do some picking up," Kristine says.

The first lesbian she comes back with doesn't mind Jonathan watching, but she doesn't want to have anything to do with Jonathan. When she's done with Kristine, she says, "Your girlfriend is all yours now," and leaves.

The second lesbian is bi and she doesn't mind Jonathan joining in, but she's drunk and doesn't seem to be too much into it.

The third lesbian says she'll leave if Jonathan is anywhere near. Apparently she hates men. "You didn't say you'd have a man here," she goes.

"Yes I did," Kristine goes.

"I thought you meant a roommate, not a boyfriend."

"I didn't think you'd mind."

"I do. Maybe I'll leave."

"Don't leave." Kristine has the hots for this woman.

"He leaves, or I leave," the woman says.

"Well," Jonathan says, "I'll leave."

He walks down to a local bar. He has a few tall beers, watches TV, ignores the people around him. He thinks it'd be nice if he could find a woman here and go home with her. None of the women in the bar seem to know he's even there. He goes to the payphone and calls home. Kristine says they're still at it, come home in an hour. He drinks more beer. He's tired. He calls home an hour later. "She's gone," Kristine says.

"Was it good?"

"It was great."

She's asleep when he gets home. Their bedroom smells like pussy.

He can't sleep. He's convinced aliens might come in and abduct him.

Jonathan thinks he might be going crazy.

Aliens!

But they seem so very real—

9

It starts off, sort of, as a sensation of being watched. Or observed.

It could be that he's been listening to the Art Bell radio program too much. Still, Jonathan has always had a fascination with aliens and UFOs. When he was nine years old, he'd go into the backyard at night, look at the sky, and say, "Come to me, space brothers!" He wanted to be an alien abductee and he's starting to wonder, now, if he is; and if he's always been.

He tells Kristine about his suspicions and she nods her head and goes, "Um-hm," and he's not sure if she takes him seriously or not. He wants her to do a Tarot card reading. "What's your question?" Kristine says.

"Whether or not aliens are abducting me," he says.

She looks at the configuration of the cards and says, "Well, maybe they are."

His body tingles. "What do you mean?"

"Something has been in contact with you, is trying to teach you something."

"Aliens?"

"I don't know. Spirits, your higher self, maybe God. But it's something."

"What are they trying to teach me?"

"That's for you to find out."

"I wonder if they make me have sex with them," he says, not serious but serious enough; "I've heard about people being forced to have sex with aliens."

"That'd be kinky."

He doesn't know why the aliens have to be so clandestine. After they fuck, before they go to sleep, he says, "You don't believe me, do you? About aliens?"

"I think you're listening to Art Bell too much," Kristine says.

"You think I'm insane."

"I think you're looking for something. Maybe answers. Good night," and a kiss, and she closes her eyes—

He can't sleep. He's afraid to sleep. He knows that they come when he's asleep. The cottage fills up with blue and pale red light and they enter the house, these aliens, and they take him away. He gets up and turns on the radio. Art Bell is on. Art Bell is a late night talk radio show that covers such topics as aliens, UFOs, Men in Black, time travel, government conspiracies, and all sorts of other paranormal topics. Jonathan thinks the show is great. He feels at ease hearing people talk about the same sensations that he's going through.

It's not easy feeling as if you're being watched. It makes you jumpy, it makes you afraid of shadows, it makes you double-check that all doors and windows are securely locked, and the blinds and curtains are drawn so they can't peer in on you.

Jonathan knows this is ridiculous.

Still—

Raymond at the Circus

by Anne Marie Villefranche

from *Folies D'Amour*

There are those who will go to extraordinary lengths to acquire a reputation as a joker and usually it is those who have little else to commend them. One such was Georges Bonfils, a person whose predatory business practices might well have made him an outcast from decent society, except that his talent for devising the most elaborate farces somewhat softened the opinion of him which those who had dealings with him would otherwise have formed.

Knowing the man's reputation, Raymond was not astonished when he received from him a handsomely engraved invitation requesting the pleasure of his company at a performance of the Circus Émile. The formality of the wording on the card made him chuckle. Clearly it was one of Bonfils' jokes, something to astound and amuse those invited, something they would talk about for weeks afterwards. Undoubtedly the company would be small and carefully selected, that being Bonfils' style. As with all of these things, there would be a secret purpose—something to Bonfils' own advantage—but no one would mind that. Raymond wrote a formal note of acceptance and then asked around among his friends to discover who else had received an invitation. Quite a few had, the others looked at him enviously and said that their own invitations must surely be held up in the mail and would arrive shortly.

On the day specified, Raymond set out by car after lunch to arrive before three, the time on the card. It was no easy matter to locate the scene of the proposed entertainment. The Circus Émile was not one of the large international circuses which toured the major towns and cities. Far from it, it was a small and down-at-heel venture which had pitched its threadbare tents on a piece of wasteland in a remote eastern suburb of Paris. That was only to be expected, Raymond reflected as he drove through dismal and depressing streets, for how otherwise could Bonfils have hired the facilities of the circus for whatever entertainment he proposed to stage?

When at last, in this unknown territory, he found the spot, Raymond saw that the main tent was small and shabby, the banner carrying its name was so weather-worn and battered that it was almost unreadable. The site was bounded on one side by a railway line along which a freight train rattled asthmatically, and the ground itself was strewn with rubbish that no one had troubled themselves to clear away. A bankrupt enterprise this, Raymond thought, a few families all related and banded together to make a poor living. It was doubtful whether Bonfils had paid them very much for the use of their facilities for an afternoon, yet however little it was, it was probably more than they would make in a week of their regular performances in so poor a neighbourhood.

The main entrance to the big tent was closed off by a flap of stained canvas, in front of which stood a muscular man with a big moustache. He was wearing a striped jersey and shapeless trousers and looked strong enough to cope single-handed with any sort of trouble which could conceivably arise. Not a person a sensible man would choose to quarrel with, Raymond said to himself as he parked his new Renault a few yards from the tent and walked across the littered ground. There were seven or eight big cars parked there already—evidently he was not the first to arrive.

The bruiser favoured him with a hard stare. Raymond responded by nodding pleasantly and handing him the engraved invitation card. The wording of it was formal in the extreme:

'Monsieur Georges Bonfils, a Commander of the Legion of Honour, requests the pleasure of the company of Monsieur Raymond Provost at a private performance of the Circus . . . ' and so on. The man in the striped jersey—perhaps he was Émile himself—took it from him and glared at it briefly. The thought crossed Raymond's mind that it was improbable that striped-jersey was sufficiently literate to read what was printed on the card. Whether he was or not, he at least recognised it as the correct passport for the afternoon. He lifted the canvas flap and gestured Raymond through with a slight inclination of his head.

Inside it was stuffy. There were benches round the sides that would seat not more than a hundred and fifty spectators packed closely together. The sawdust-strewn ring in the centre was large enough for only the most modest of performances—a juggler or two, perhaps, a fire-eater, a dancing-bear with a ring through his nose, a knife-thrower with his board and unattractive wife as living target—the usual banalities. None of which would be presented today, of course, Bonfils must surely have made special arrangements for the entertainment of his guests.

The stuffiness in the tent was partly due to the lighting—

hissing gas-flares from containers set in the corners. But the atmosphere was already convivial—about twenty well-dressed men were assembled on one side of the tent, chatting away, glasses in their hands. Two or three servants were busy with the refreshment—champagne bottles cooling in a row of dented zinc buckets and tubs filled with ice and water. The buckets at least looked as if they were circus property, the long-stemmed glasses the servants were handing round obviously were not.

Bonfils detached himself from the little crowd and came forward to shake Raymond's hand and welcome him. He was dressed very formally in a long and elegant morning-coat, cravat and black silk top hat. The monocle he affected was dangling on its thin gold chain against his white waistcoat. The whole attire, Raymond decided, was itself a part of the joke. Perhaps he should have dressed formally himself, but another glance at the other guests reassured him. They wore normal suits, though of mainly dark hues.

'How very pleased I am that you can be with us,' Bonfils exclaimed. 'You missed my last little circus entertainment, as I recall. It was so popular with everyone that I felt I had to arrange another. Come and have a drink. I think you know everyone here.'

'It was kind of you to invite me,' Raymond replied. 'Yes, I know many of your other guests.'

'Good, then there is no need for introductions.'

Raymond had already recognised a number of business associates, a few acquaintances from the Stock Exchange, a couple of important politicians, even a famous author he had once met at someone's reception—a man who had made a surprising amount of money from his boring sagas of tormented family life in the provinces. Glancing round the conservatively-dressed group of men, all wearing hats, Raymond smiled as he thought for a moment that the gathering could almost have been for a deceased colleague's funeral. The only jarring note was a vivid green tie worn by the writer, presumably as a sign of his creative ability.

Glass of champagne in hand, Raymond plunged into the throng, shaking hands, exchanging greetings, on easy terms with everyone there.

'Were you at Bonfils' last circus performance?' asked a friend, Xavier de Margeville, whom Raymond had known would be there. 'I can't remember.'

'I was away from Paris at the time and missed it. I've heard about it, of course.'

'It was the talk of Paris for a month afterwards. It inflated Georges' notoriety enormously.'

'But it didn't do him any harm, as I understand it,' said Raymond.

'Of course not! His invitations are so sought after that the most unlikely people do him favours in the hope of being added to the list, but he is very selective. Why, I was told just before you came in that Georges has disappointed a Minister of State today because he didn't regard him as useful enough. But that may be no more than one of Georges' own rumours to make himself more important. The gossip last year was that he had turned away a certain Eminence of the Church who wanted to be present, on the grounds that dignitaries of the Church knew so much about these things that he would find it boring.'

Raymond laughed and emptied his glass. At once a servant was at his side to refill it.

'On the other hand,' he said cheerfully, 'both tales might well be true, Xavier. Is today's performance to be a repetition of what I was told took place last autumn?'

'No, Georges has promised us something entirely different.'

The drinks flowed freely, the conversation became more animated and the gestures more expansive. Eventually the clanging of a handbell silenced the party. It was Bonfils, standing in the middle of the sawdust ring, his tall hat pushed to the back of his head.

'Gentlemen!' he bawled, 'your attention, please! You are about to witness the most amusing, the most daring, the most original circus performance ever to be presented in Paris—or anywhere else!'

'Since last year, you mean!' someone called out.

'No previous performance can possibly equal what you are to see today, you have my assurances,' Bonfils replied at once, greatly enjoying his role of ringmaster. 'This is the genuine, the unique, the once-in-a-lifetime performance, brought to you regardless of expense and trouble. Take your seats, if you please! The attendants will circulate among you with refreshments during the performance.'

With late arrivals the company now numbered about thirty. Everyone wanted to sit on the front row, of course, and the benches were rapidly filled round the edge of the sawdust ring.

Bonfils resumed his comical introduction when they were quiet again.

'Gentlemen, it is possible that in a gathering of important persons so distinguished in the fields of finance, commerce, politics—and the arts—there might possibly be one or two who have visited certain establishments in this city. Entirely for the purposes of study and observation, I need hardly say. In such establishments there is a remote possibility that you have been compelled to witness actions of a particular nature performed for the instruction of those present.'

'Shameful!' said someone who sounded very far from ashamed at this thought.

'Shameful indeed!' Bonfils continued. 'For I must inform you that these acts to which I refer are faked. They are fraudulent. They are deceptions! But today there will be no deception—you will be privileged to observe the real thing. Gentlemen, I give you, I proudly give you . . . Bonfils' *cirque erotique!*'

He paused and bowed to acknowledge the applause from his audience.

'Thank you, gentlemen—your appreciation is the only reward I seek. And now—for your entertainment, for your amazement, for your delectation, the Circus Bonfils—for one performance only—proudly presents . . . '

He clanged his handbell loudly, a threadbare curtain strung across one end of the tent was pulled aside by an unseen hand, while all eyes turned to catch the first glimpse of what was to be presented.

'Mademoiselle Marie!' Bonfils bawled.

Amid cries of emotion from the small audience a totally naked woman rode into the sawdust arena on an ordinary bicycle. She was in her twenties and reasonably pretty. Her breasts jumped up and down as she drove the pedals round energetically with her bare feet.

'Mademoiselle Jeanne!' Bonfils announced when the first rider was part way round the ring, and another equally naked young woman rode in, smiling and waving with one hand to the admiring little crowd on the benches. 'Mademoiselle Marianne!'

A third rider joined them, this one standing on the pedals and so giving a clear view of the patch of dark hair between her legs.

'Mademoiselle Sophie!'

There were four of them cycling round the small ring, smiling and acknowledging the applause, keeping their distance from each other. They were all about the same age and averagely attractive.

'Four of the most outstanding beauties of Paris for your delight!' Bonfils announced with gross exaggeration. 'Observe them as they ride, consider their merits. Estimate as best you can their strength and fortitude. And then, when the contest starts, pick your favourite and give her your whole-hearted support! Whichever of these lovelies you fancy—urge her on, encourage her! And in addition to your moral support, place a bet when the action becomes hot.'

'Surely they're not going to fight each other!' exclaimed Raymond, aghast.

'Of course not—that would be too brutal,' said de Margeville, 'something far more amusing. You'll see.'

'Are you ready, ladies?' Bonfils enquired loudly of the women circling him on their bicycles.

'Ready!' they chorused.

'Then prepare for the signal to begin. The prize to the winner is a bottle of the finest champagne—and five thousand francs!'

All the women squealed pleasurably at that as they pedalled solemnly round in their circle.

'Go!' Bonfils called abruptly, clanging his bell again.

To Raymond's surprise they did not increase their speed at all—rather the opposite. Knowing that it was a contest between them, he had assumed that it was some sort of race. He turned to de Margeville, sitting next to him, to ask how the winner would be decided.

'Why, the winner will be the last one to remain on her bicycle.'

'An endurance test? Surely not—we'd be here all day and that would be excessively boring. Or are they allowed to knock each other off their bicycles?'

'No, they must not touch each other—that would bring disqualification. It is an endurance test of another kind. The saddles of those bicycles have been very well greased—see how the riders tend to slide a little on them with each thrust of their legs against the pedals.'

'What follows?' asked Raymond, still puzzled.

'My dear fellow—the intimate parts of our pretty bicyclists are being subjected to constant and rhythmic massage by the exertion of pedalling fast enough to stay upright. What do you suppose will be the result?

'Heavens!' Raymond exclaimed in sudden understanding. 'You mean that the action of riding round will bring on the physical crisis more usually induced in a woman by her lover!'

'Exactly! Now you understand the amusement which Bonfils has arranged for us. As these women ride around under our close scrutiny, we shall observe the signs of their arousal. This one passing us now, for example—she is already pink of face. In a while you will see her little nipples become firm, her legs tremble! At the critical moment, each woman in turn will topple from the saddle, unable to continue to ride in her spasms of pleasure.'

'Until only one is left to claim Bonfils' prize! But what if there is cheating—if one of them should try to raise herself just off the saddle without being observed?

'There is no chance of that going undetected. All four are watching each other closely to make sure no one wins the prize by cheating. And Bonfils is observing them—see how he stares at each as she passes in front of him! And finally, all of us here have the right to act as judges, to ensure that the rules are followed.'

'Champagne, Monsieur?' said a discreet voice at Raymond's elbow.

He turned to find one of Bonfils' servants behind him with a bottle to refill his glass.

'Bonfils is the most salacious person I know,' said Raymond, sipping at the cold wine.

'Oh yes, but always in an original and interesting way,' de Margeville agreed, 'Look at this little beauty!'

It was Mademoiselle Marianne pedalling slowly past them. She was perhaps twenty-two or -three years old, somewhat broad-shouldered for her slender body. Her little breasts were set high, their buds a dark red that was almost crimson in intensity.

'See—she's well on the way,' Xavier de Margeville observed, 'and they've been round no more than three or four times. I shall not bet on her.'

'You intend to bet on this contest? I thought that Bonfils was joking when he said that.'

'It is part of the entertainment. Bonfils will accept all bets, however large, at the odds set by him. While there are four riders, the odds are three to one. Pick the winner and you may win a considerable sum.'

'One thousand francs on Mademoiselle Sophie!' a voice called from somewhere to Raymond's left.

He craned his neck to see who it was and recognised a well-known banker.

Bonfils, his handbell on the ground beside him, now held an open notebook and a thin gold pen. He scribbled the name of the banker, the amount and the name of the woman.

'Well done, dear friend!' he cried so that everyone would hear him. 'She seems a good choice to me—amateur that I am in such matters! One thousand francs is bet on Mademoiselle Sophie. Place your bets, gentlemen, while the odds are still three to one in your favour.'

'I understand,' said Raymond, 'the odds will shorten as we lose contestants.'

'Exactly. I do not think that Mademoiselle Sophie is my choice—look at the generous width of her bottom. In bed that would be a great advantage, but not here. She has that much weight bearing her down on the saddle and it must take its toll before long. No, I shall choose between Mademoiselle Jeanne and Mademoiselle Marianne. But which?'

'Where does Bonfils get the girls from?' Raymond enquired, 'They're too pretty and too clean to be part of the genuine circus.'

'I suppose he hires them from one of the better houses of pleasure.'

'You are wrong there,' said the man on Raymond's other side, 'I am well acquainted with the best houses in the ten years I have been a widower. These young women are unknown to me. Perhaps they are artists' models.'

'No one else is betting,' Raymond observed.

'They are studying form,' said de Margeville.

The most unusual spectacle of four young women riding round on bicycles and displaying their bodies had a certain, piquancy, Raymond found. There were some interesting comparisons to make—the relative size and shape of breasts and bottoms— and their respective elasticity as they jiggled and bounced to their owners' movements. The relative length and meatiness or otherwise of all those thighs pumping up and down to turn the pedals! The colour and texture of the hair revealed by the action of those thighs . . . but above all, the interest lay in the expressions on the faces of the riders—that was truly fascinating.

All four had ridden into the arena smiling broadly to make the first lap—smiles that acknowledged the spontaneous applause and welcomed it. After all, these were women, whatever their profession, who experienced not the least embarrassment in displaying their naked bodies—on the contrary, they thrived on the admiration of men.

After a turn or two of the ring the smiles were still there on all four pretty faces—but they were becoming more like fixed grins as important and distracting sensations started to make themselves felt between the riders' legs. One by one even the grins disappeared as these sensations were intensified by the constant rubbing of the slippery saddles. Mademoiselle Marianne, for example, rode past with her mouth hanging open loosely and a faraway look in her eyes as she struggled against the crisis which threatened her.

'Heavens!' said de Margeville as he observed her, 'she won't last more than another time or two round the ring. This is the last opportunity of getting odds of three to one.'

He called out hurriedly to Bonfils in the middle of the arena.

'Five thousand on Mademoiselle Jeanne!'

Bonfils raised a finger in acknowledgment and scribbled in his notebook.

Raymond had also made up his mind by then. 'Ten thousand on Mademoiselle Sophie!' Plump-bottomed Sophie, hearing her name, glanced over her shoulder and smiled vaguely in Raymond's direction. Her face was very flushed and Raymond wondered if he had made an expensive mistake. Xavier de Margeville certainly thought so.

'Not a hope,' he declared, 'not with that splendid bottom. Go for the thinnest, that's my advice.'

'And also mine,' the man on Raymond's other side agreed and surprised him by betting fifty thousand francs on Mademoiselle Jeanne.

'Fifty thousand bet by Barras!' Bonfils announced loudly. 'That's more like it. He'll be able to pay his shareholders an extra dividend out of his winnings! Come along now, gentlemen—get your bets down while there's still time.'

At once several voices called out and kept Bonfils busy writing for a while, though no one approached or surpassed Barras' fifty thousand. In so far as Raymond could judge in the confusion of voices, most of the money was going on Mademoiselle Jeanne and Mademoiselle Marie and it was

Mademoiselle Jeanne who was the favourite. He heard only one other wager placed on Mademoiselle Sophie, a circumstance which did not inspire him with confidence in her.

'Ah, look at Marianne!' de Margeville exclaimed, tapping Raymond on the knee, 'in a few more moments . . . '

Marianne on the far side of the sawdust ring was riding very slowly now, the front wheel of her bicycle wobbling. She was breathing quickly through her open mouth and her tiny breasts rose and fell with the heaving of her chest.

'She's cheating!' one of the other riders shouted shrilly, pointing at Marianne, 'she's off the saddle!'

Bonfils strode across to Mademoiselle Marianne and delivered a good-natured smack with his open hand on her bare bottom.

'Sit on the saddle properly,' he cried, 'no cheating allowed here!'

Marianne wobbled on, her course becoming more and more erratic. As she approached the bench where Raymond was sitting her head went slowly backwards until she was staring up at the shabby roof of the tent. She uttered a high-pitched squeal and toppled over sideways. There was a long gasp from the audience and many rose to their feet as Marianne rolled in the sawdust and lay on her side, both hands pressed between her legs, her knees drawn up and jerking in the throes of her climactic moments.

'Mademoiselle Marianne withdraws from the contest,' Bonfils announced formally.

He raised his top hat in salute to the fallen competitor, then assisted her to her feet and gave her a friendly pat on the rump as she picked up her bicycle and wheeled it away.

All eyes were on the three women left in the ring as they circled slowly, each bright pink with emotion. The men who had not yet placed a bet were emboldened to do so now that the field had thinned out, though the odds were now at two to one only.

'Did anyone put money on Mademoiselle Marianne?' Raymond asked his friend.

'I think that Foucault over there had a few thousand francs on her. For the wrong reasons, alas. He knows nothing about betting, but he adores women with pointed little breasts like hers.'

'Who doesn't?' said Raymond, shrugging.

A groan of dismay arose from the benches as Mademoiselle Marie veered off course, her eyes closed and her belly shaking—to be followed by a shout of delight as she collided with a bench laden with spectators. The abrupt halting of her machine sent her sailing head-first over the handlebars into the laps of the onlookers—with such force that the bench tipped over backwards, depositing them all on the ground. Then a roar of laughter filled the tent as Marie writhed in ecstasy on top of two or three dark-clad businessmen who lay on the grass with their legs waving in the air.

When he could make himself heard, Bonfils announced that Mademoiselle Marie had withdrawn from the contest and that the odds had shortened to evens.

'That Sophie has more endurance than I gave her credit for,' said de Margeville, watching the two finalists pedalling slowly round, 'but mine will beat her—see how Sophie's thighs are trembling, while Jeanne's are steady and firm.'

In truth, Mademoiselle Sophie looked as if she was very close to the end of her ride. The flush of her face extended right down her neck and chest and her entire body gleamed with perspiration.

'Perhaps you are right, my dear fellow,' said Raymond doubtfully, 'but I retain my faith in her.'

'You will lose your money—and I shall win a hundred and fifty thousand francs from Bonfils!'

'You sound very confident,' Raymond responded, 'does your confidence extend to another ten thousand francs?'

'A side bet between you and me? But of course! Ten thousand from you to me when my woman wins—that will be very satisfactory.'

'Or vice-versa,' Raymond reminded him.

The vanquished Marie had not left the tent, Raymond noted. She was sitting on the bench between two of the men she had knocked over. Each had an arm round her naked waist and one of them—a banker named Weber who was nearer to his sixtieth birthday than his fiftieth—was whispering into her ear as he eyed her bare bosom. Mademoiselle Marie may have lost the prize money, Raymond concluded, but she will not return home empty-handed. Looking round the benches, he further observed that Mademoiselle Marianne, the first to be eliminated, had returned without her bicycle and was sitting bare-bottomed on the lap of the man who had wagered on her and lost.

With only two riders left in the arena, the contest must surely end very soon, for both of them appeared to be *in extremis.*

'One thousand francs on Mademoiselle Jeanne!' a voice called out, breaking the silent concentration of the spectators.

All heads turned to see who it was that had waited until the final moments before committing himself at short odds. It was the famous author of novels for good Catholics.

'What a cautious fellow he must be!' said Raymond with a grin.

'There goes your girl!' de Margeville exclaimed in triumph, 'hand over the money!'

Mademoiselle Sophie was swaying dangerously from side to side on her slow-moving bicycle, her eyes closed to mere slits and a rapt expression on her red face. With bated breath the audience watched the last moments of the contest as the two women struggled to cling to the last shreds of self-control.

There was a long wail—and Mademoiselle Jeanne clapped a hand to the wet thatch between her legs! Her front wheel turned sideways and she slid to the sawdust and rolled onto her back, her legs kicking in the air as her climactic tension released itself. A long-drawn sigh from the audience acknowledged her defeat.

'Mademoiselle Jeanne withdraws from the contest!' Bonfils cried, 'The winner is Mademoiselle Sophie!'

'Well done, Mademoiselle Sophie!' Raymond called out to her, 'I have a bonus for you!'

He wasn't sure that she heard him because Bonfils' announcement was followed by prolonged applause for the victor. She managed another quarter lap, her swaying more pronounced, then dismounted quickly and sat in the sawdust, her knees drawn up and her arms round them, shaking violently.

Bonfils snapped his fingers and one of his servants hurried to him with a new bottle of champagne. When Mademoiselle Sophie's quivering had stopped, Bonfils tapped her on the shoulder and, as her head came up, he up-ended the bottle. She opened her mouth wide to catch the stream of champagne, swallowing as fast as she could, until she could drink no more. Bonfils poured the rest of the bottle over her bare breasts and belly to cool her off and she grinned.

During this interesting little interlude the spectators were clapping and cheering, all in exceptionally good humour at what they had witnessed in the arena, however the betting had gone. Bonfils had to ring his handbell for a long time to silence them and summon the four contestants to him. Weber seemed reluctant to free Mademoiselle Marie from his grasp.

'Let go of her!' Bonfils cried, laughing at him, 'you can have her back after the prize-giving, you naughty old banker!'

'I don't believe it,' Xavier de Margeville complained, handing Raymond ten thousand francs, 'I was absolutely certain that the one I bet on would last longest. In logic it could be no other way. Why did you bet on Sophie? She looked the least likely of them all.'

'Intuition,' said Raymond with a shrug, 'no more than that.'

Meanwhile the four naked young women arranged themselves before Bonfils in a row. Mademoiselle Sophie took a step forward and Bonfils congratulated her in the most grandiloquent manner on her triumph and presented the prize-money to her with a great flourish, a bow and a raising of his black top hat. For the others he had words of consolation. Not one of them looked disconsolate, from which Raymond deduced that they had established contacts that promised to more than compensate for what they had lost.

As soon as the women left the ring to dress themselves, Raymond went forward to claim his winnings from Bonfils, thinking that he was the only winner. He had forgotten that Desmoines had also wagered on Sophie, though a smaller amount. Bonfils counted out thirty thousand francs for Raymond and handed it to him with a grin.

'Congratulations—you are a shrewd judge of women, my dear fellow.'

'My congratulations to you,' said Raymond dryly, 'By my reckoning you must have made at least a quarter of a million francs.'

Bonfils winked at him.

'Ah, you must not overlook my expenses in arranging this little contest,' he answered, 'and you must agree that everyone has been greatly entertained. Just look—they're all trying to get their money back by drinking my champagne as if it were water. Take my advice—get a glass before it's all gone. I have the pleasant task of collecting all the money due to me before our friends begin to slip away, so you must excuse me.'

Raymond need not have feared that his offer of a bonus to Mademoiselle Sophie had gone unheard. He was standing among his friends, glass in hand, discussing the finer points of the contest they had witnessed—and she appeared at his elbow. She was wearing a plain black skirt and over it a long jumper that came down below her hips and had a zigzag pattern knitted into it.

'M'sieu,' she said, smiling at him.

Her bosom was fuller than was considered fashionable and her jumper emphasised it. But for the first time Raymond found himself looking at her face properly—it was round and pleasant, though her nose was perhaps a trifle broad. Her expression was one of good-nature, not the false friendliness of the professional.

'Ah, Mademoiselle Sophie! Permit me to congratulate you on a magnificent victory against very serious adversaries. I was inspired to bet on you and you did not disappoint my hopes. I feel that it is no more than justice to share my winnings with you—if you will do me the honour to accept this little gift.'

She smiled at him as he handed her five thousand francs of his winnings and—to his delight—she raised her black skirt and tucked the folded bank-notes into her garter.

Perhaps it was the wine he had drunk, perhaps it was the emotional impact of having seen four naked young women in the throes of passion—perhaps it was both—but Raymond at that moment found Mademoiselle Sophie very desirable.

'I have a car outside,' he murmured, 'it would give me great pleasure to offer you a ride back into the city.'

'You are very kind,' she said at once, 'perhaps you could drop me off where I live.'

The offer and the acceptance implied much more than a ride in his car, as they both understood completely. After another glass of Bonfils' rapidly diminishing stock of champagne they took their leave, while that enterprising person was still working his way through the crowd, notebook in hand and his pockets stuffed with bank-notes. Once in the car and on the way, formality vanished quickly. Raymond called her Sophie, told her his own name and drove with one hand, the other on her thigh above her garter—the one which did not hold her money. He was not acquainted with the district where she lived and they were driving back towards the city centre from a direction that was equally unfamiliar to him. After a longer drive than was probably necessary, he found the rue d'Alésia and followed it westwards until Sophie was able to direct him.

The building she indicated eventually was unprepossessing, but that was of no consequence. Her room was on the very top floor, as he had guessed it would be, and that too was of no consequence. Raymond was on fire from the long contact of his hand on Sophie's bare thigh under her skirt, his apparatus was fully extended and uncomfortable inside his clothes. Sophie too was quite ready—she was breathing even more quickly than the long climb up the stairs could be held responsible for.

The meagreness of her room and its poor furnishing made no impression whatsoever on Raymond, for no sooner were they inside than Sophie's hand was thrust urgently down the front of his trousers to give her a grip on the twin dependents below his upstanding part. At another time he might have found the grip a little too forcible for comfort, but in his heightened frame of mind her squeezing of those tender objects merely served to arouse him further.

'I'm dying for it!' she gasped. 'Do it to me!'

Raymond was exceptionally eager to oblige her. Bonfils' *cirque erotique* and the car ride afterwards had exacerbated his emotions to an impossible degree—and if that were not enough, the clasp of Sophie's hand brought his throbbing stiffness to almost the instant of explosion. He pushed her down onto the untidy bed, not at all gently, his hands clenched on her breasts through her jumper while she wriggled her bottom and pulled her skirt up to her waist—for her need and his were too demanding to waste time undressing. She groped between her parted thighs to rip open the buttons of her cami-knickers, while Raymond was treating his trouser buttons to the same violence.

He threw himself on her, catching one brief glimpse of the hair between her legs still plastered flat to her skin with the vaseline which had been spread liberally on the bicycle saddles. His distended member found her slippery channel of its own accord and slid inside. Sophie screamed in ecstatic release at once and thrashed about beneath him, her loins lifting to force him in further. For Raymond the sensation of that smooth penetration was too much—he made three short and rapid thrusts and fountained his release into her, amazed, delighted and dismayed—all at once—at the speed of his response.

'My God, I needed that,' said Sophie when he lay still on her at last. 'Now we can take our time and do it properly. How about getting undressed?'

Raymond slid from her embrace and together they removed their clothes.

'What a sight!' Sophie exclaimed, staring at her wispy patch of hair, darkened and stuck flat, 'I must do something about that.'

She left him lying on the bed while she made preparations to wash herself.

The facilities afforded by her room were rudimentary—she took a large porcelain wash-basin from a rickety dressing table, set it on the floor and poured water into it from a jug. Raymond rolled onto his side to watch her at her toilet. She straddled the basin and crouched down to wash between her thighs.

'If this doesn't cool me down, nothing will,' she joked.

'God forbid,' said Raymond, 'it all happened so quickly that I feel that I have been cheated. But if that little plaything between your legs becomes chilled from the water, it will be a pleasure for me to warm it up again.'

'There's no fear of it going off the boil,' she assured him, 'when I get started, I can't stop—not even with all that riding round the circus for Monsieur Bonfils.'

She stood up and reached for a towel to dry herself.

'The speed with which it happened to us both is proof enough that the bicycle contest aroused you considerably,' said Raymond. 'It brought on a little crisis, for I saw you trembling and panting as you sat on the ground after you had won the prize.'

'Yes, I couldn't control myself that time,' said Sophie, 'though I managed to stay on the saddle through the others.'

She threw the towel aside carelessly and stood naked for him to see her, hands on her hips and a smile on her face. She was younger than Raymond had first thought, certainly not much more than twenty, but already her full breasts had lost some of their tautness and were a little slack. The slight loss in aesthetic appeal was more than compensated for, in Raymond's opinion, by the gain in sensual appeal, for a man could fondle them endlessly and find the experience rewarding—even hide his face between them—not to mention another part of his body! But without doubt her most fascinating feature was the plump mound between her thighs. Under its covering of thin brown hair the lips were permanently separated by the overdeveloped inner lips pushing through.

'It is obvious why you are hot-natured,' Raymond commented affectionately. 'In fact, I am surprised that you were able to endure the ride so long. What do you mean by *the others?* Are you saying that it happened to you while you were riding round the arena?'

'Five or six times,' she replied, getting back onto the bed with him, 'but as I had agreed to win it was necessary to continue.'

'Agreed to win? But what do you mean?'

Sophie grinned at him in a conspiratorial way as she stroked his belly.

'I'm giving away a secret when I shouldn't,' she said, 'but I like you, Raymond. The truth is that Monsieur Bonfils knows about my nature—how I have to go on when I've started. It's like waves on the sea—you must have seen it—the waves come rolling in, quite small ones, and then about every seventh wave is a much bigger one. At least, that's what I've been told. Well, that's how it is with me. I get aroused with a man and these little waves roll over me, one after the other, until the big one arrives.'

'That was when you were sitting in the sawdust?'

'No, of course not—that was a few minutes ago with you.'

Raymond was flattered that it should have been so.

'So there was an agreement between you and Bonfils to win the five thousand francs he offered as prize.'

Sophie winked at him, her hand sliding lower on his belly towards his most important asset.

'I trust you,' she said. 'The little agreement I had with Monsieur Bonfils was that I should receive ten thousand francs to enter and win.'

'But why?'

She shrugged impatiently at his slowness of comprehension and took hold of his awakening part to encourage its growth.

'Who did everyone bet on?' she asked. 'Monsieur Bonfils did very well for himself today, but I liked you straight off because you put your money on me. What made you do that—you weren't supposed to.'

Raymond chuckled at the thought of Bonfils' duplicity, now revealed to him. What a rogue the man was—yet with what entertaining cunning he brought off the coups which gave him his reputation!

'I liked the look of your bottom when you first rode past me on your bicycle,' he said, 'you have those round soft cheeks which indicate an amorous nature, not the tight little bottom of Mademoiselle Jeanne.'

'You think I've got a big bottom, do you?' Sophie asked, her hand sliding up and down his stiff part.

'A generous bottom, not a big one. Your centre of gravity is well down your body, which means that you are more at ease lying on your back than standing up—am I not right? And then those round soft breasts attracted my attention. One of the contestants had little pointed breasts set high on her chest—modish, of course, but disappointing when you have them in your hands. Yours, on first sight, were of a size and texture to please a man.'

He suited the action to the word by taking them in his hands and playing with them.

'Ah, I understand,' she said, 'you bet on me because you wanted to go to bed with me, not because you thought I could win the contest! I knew you were a sympathetic person as soon as I heard your voice calling out "Ten thousand francs on Mademoiselle Sophie"!'

'Now,' said Raymond, 'I wish to observe this interesting aspect of your nature you have described to me.'

His hand moved down her body to touch the soft and permanently pouting lips between her thighs.

'You won't collapse on me halfway through, will you?' she murmured, 'I can't stand it when that happens.'

'You may have every confidence in me,' said Raymond. 'My desire to see the little waves rolling in to the shore is so strong that I shall continue until the big wave breaks over us together.'

'Yes,' she said, 'get me started, Raymond chéri! I'll let you know when the big wave is on its way.'

VOLUME TWO

by Anonymous

from *"Frank" and I*

9

DIFFERENT STYLES OF ENJOYMENT.—"EN LEVRETTE."—FRESH ARRANGEMENTS.—LUCY'S LIPS AND HOW SHE USED THEM.—HOW THE HOUSEMAID GOT WHAT SHE WANTED AND A LITTLE MORE.—MAUD'S APPROACHING MARRIAGE.—BIRCHING FUN AND THE USUAL SEQUEL.—JEALOUSY.—THE DEPARTMURE TO LONDON.—MAUD AND FRANCES.—A COY SCOTCH LASS.

A couple of months passed over rapidly. Frances now always called me "Charley,"—my name is Charles Beaumont—and as I had expected, she turned out to be a most voluptuous girl, becoming the most charming bedfellow I had ever come across. She insisted on sleeping with me every night,—I never objected—but she always went back to her room to bed early in the morning, and so no suspicion was ever aroused among the servants. I taught her practically, much to her astonishment and amusement, all the various positions in which a man can enjoy a woman; and she was always ready for a poke, either by night, or by day. Often on a rainy afternoon, when we were sitting in the drawing-room, not knowing what to do with ourselves, I would make her lean over the back of an easy-chair, so that I could "have" her "en levrette" as the French call it. But I must say it was rather absurd to see what was apparently a young man in his shirt sleeves, bending well over the back of a chair, with his trousers down to his heels, displaying a big, white, feminine bottom.

She liked being poked "en levrette," for she said I always seemed to get deeper into her in that position than in any other.

It was all very pleasant, but I had begun to think that I should be obliged to make some other arrangements with regard to my sweetheart, for I was afraid that sooner or later she would betray herself. She had let her hair grow much longer than was befitting a "man"; moreover, since she had become a warm, loving woman, she did not keep such a strict guard upon herself as she had hitherto done; and I was in constant dread that the servants would notice her manner towards me.

I was rather bothered too, just at that time, by Lucy; who was still in my service, and who was plumper than ever. As I had as much poking as ever I wanted with Frances, I entirely neglected my buxom housemaid, whom I had formerly poked pretty regularly, and who was, I think, fond of me. She could not understand why I had suddenly given her up: so she used frequently to come to my room on some pretence or other, when she knew I was there. On those occasions, I always had a little talk with her, and sometimes gave her a kiss, but nothing else; so, when she saw that I was not going to "have" her, she would go away, looking very disappointed. However, she was a persevering woman, and one day, she regularly forced me to satisfy her desire.

I had gone up to my room shortly after breakfast to change

my coat, and having done so, I sat down in an easy-chair to read a letter which I had received that morning from Maud. She wrote telling me that she was going to be married in a month's time; and she asked me to come and see her as soon as possible, so that we might settle all our little affairs. I was not surprised at the news; for she had before hinted that she was thinking of leaving me.

I had just finished reading the letter, when Lucy came into the room; looking, as usual, very nice in her neat print frock, white apron, and cap with long streamers. She went through the form of arranging the things on the dressing-table; then coming to where I was sitting, she looked at me wistfully with her big hazel eyes, and said: "You never give me a proper kiss now. Have I offended you?"

"No, Lucy, you have not," said I, stroking her plump cheek, but not kissing her, as I did not feel the least inclined to make love of any sort at that moment, owing to my having poked Frances several times during the night and morning.

'Why, you haven't even kissed me!" she said, pouting her full red lips and holding her face up invitingly. I smiled, but did not touch her.

"Well, I'll kiss *you,* till you give me a proper kiss." So saying, she dropped on her knees in front of me, and to my astonishment,— for she had never done such a thing to me before—she unbuttoned my trousers, took out my tool, and began manipulating it with a skilful touch, saying with a laugh, as she noticed its very limp condition: "Oh! how miserable and flabby it looks; but I'll soon make it stiff." Then, bending down her head, she took into her mouth my drooping prick, and began tickling the tip of it with her hot tongue, and drawing the foreskin backwards and forwards over the nut with her lips; soon causing the member to spring up in full erection, and giving me an intense sensation of lascivious pleasure: so much so, that I felt the premonitory symptoms of the discharge. I exclaimed hurriedly: "Stop! Stop, Lucy! or you will make me go off in your mouth. Put it in the right place. Quick!" She let it go, and jumped up, with flushed cheeks, and sparkling eyes, laughing gaily; and at once pulled all her clothes up above her waist; and as she was wearing no drawers, I had a full view, for a moment, of her massive thighs, her big legs, and the forest of curly, brown hair which hid her cunt. Then she turned round, and striding over me backwards, as I sat in the chair, she put her hand between her legs, and taking hold of my prick, guided it into its proper place: then she gradually lowered herself down till every inch of the stiff column of flesh was buried in her cunt, and her naked bottom rested on my thighs. I then unfastened the whole front of her dress; and as she had no stays on, her luxuriant bubbies were only covered by her chemise, which I soon pushed down out of the way; then holding one of her big titties in each hand, I said: "Now Lucy, you must do all the work."

"All right," she replied, giggling. Then she began moving herself up and down on the points of her toes; at one moment raising her bottom till only the nut of my tool was left between the lips of her cunt, then at the next moment letting herself down with a flop upon my thighs; each time driving the weapon up to the hilt in the sheath; while I sat still, enjoying the exquisite sensation, and playing with her large, red nipples. Up and down went her bottom, her movements gradually becoming more rapid, and when she felt the "moment" was at hand, she worked with increased vigour, her titties undulating like the waves of the sea. In another instant I "spent," and the spasm seized her: I could feel a thrill pass over her body; her nipples seemed to stiffen in my fingers, her thighs gripped mine tightly, and she wriggled on the dart that was impaling her, till all was over. Then she leant back against my breast, the pressure of her thighs relaxed, my limp prick dropped out of its place, and the thick, white stuff trickled out of the orifice, down between the cheeks of her bottom as she sat straddled on my lap. She burst out laughing, and said: "I thought I could make you do it to me!" I also laughed, remarking: "I did not do it to you. You did it to me, you naughty young woman. In fact you have committed an indecent assault upon me, and I am going to give you a good spanking for your misconduct." Then I placed her in position to receive the punishment.

"Spank away. I like having my bottom warmed," she said, pulling her chemise and petticoats well up out of the way, and settling herself down across my knees.

It always delighted me to feel my hand rebounding from her fat buttocks; and as she had said she liked having her bottom warmed, I determined to spank her in right smart fashion.

Raising my hand high in the air, I laid on the hot slaps in quick succession all over the broad expanse of white skin, which first became pink, then red, and then crimson: her flesh twitched involuntarily under the resounding smacks of my hand; but for a time she bore the smart, which must have been sharp, without moving, or uttering a sound. At last, however, she could stand it no longer; and turning her head, she looked at me, with an expression of pain on her face, saying, in a quavering voice: "Oh, stop! Stop! I can't bear any more. My bottom is too sore."

It must indeed have been sore, for my hand was tingling! I let her get up, and she heaved a sigh of relief; the tears were standing in her eyes and she looked at me rather reproachfully, saying: "You *have* warmed my bottom. That was the hardest spanking you have ever given me." She added, with a little laugh: "You have made me pay dearly for my kiss."

Then she put her cap straight, gave herself a shake, and left the room. After I had washed, and made myself comfortable, I sat down and read Maud's letter again; and while thinking over her communication, the idea came into my head that I might send Frances to live with Maud. As that young lady was going to leave my protection of her own accord, I thought she would probably be willing to take charge of Frances, and get her rigged out in the garments of her sex. Then, when Maud had married and left the villa, I could settle Frances in it, and go and live with her for a time. It was just the very thing. So I resolved to go up to London next day and arrange it all with Maud.

I then went down to lunch, and as I felt a little languid after all my various excitements, I had a bottle of champagne opened, which Frances and I soon disposed of. I told her that I had to go to London on business the following day, but I did not enter into particulars.

Next morning, as soon as breakfast was over, I drove to Winchester, caught the morning train to town, and went at once to Maud, whom I had not seen for some time. She was looking very well, and she had assumed a demure expression, as befitting a lady engaged to be married. She did not kiss me, so I laughingly took the little woman up in my arms; refusing to put her down until she had given me a proper salute. She soon gave me a kiss, and then we proceeded to business.

She told me all about her affairs, and informed me that her fiancé was a well-to-do young tradesman in the neighbourhood.

When she had finished, I related to her Frances' story, giving full details of everything that had occurred at Oakhurst since the first day the girl had come to the house. Then I asked her to let Frances live with her for a time, and I also asked her to get the girl proper attire.

Maud was greatly interested in the romantic story; and she laughed heartily at my description of the way I had discovered

Frances' true sex. She was a good-hearted woman; she had always professed to be fond of me, and she was grateful to me, as I had always treated her well; so she at once agreed to take charge of Frances, and to look after her in every way, and she also promised to see that the girl was properly fitted out with everything necessary.

Then she remarked, with a sly smile: "I fancy you must have taken Frances across your knees oftener than was necessary. I know how fond you are of whipping a bottom."

"Oh, no. I assure you I never spanked her unless she was naughty. She will tell you so herself," I said, laughing.

"I suppose you will put her here in my place when I go away to be married?"

"Yes," I replied. "I have the lease of the house for some years to come; and I will take over your servants, and buy all your furniture as it stands." I had originally given her the furniture.

"Oh, that will be most convenient. It will save me the bother of having an auction here, as I had intended. My furniture would not have quite suited the establishment of my future husband." Then she added, with a grave face, but with a twinkle in her eyes: "You must not come near me after I am married. I am going to be very proper."

"No doubt you will be," I observed, laughing. "But you are not married yet, so come upstairs, and let me give you one last little touch of the rod."

"Oh, but if you birch me, you will want to poke me as well; and I don't think I ought to allow you to do that now," she said, with affected coyness.

"Come along," I said, taking her by the hand, and leading her up to the bedroom; where she at once took off everything, except her chemise, stockings and boots; then she got out the rod, and handed it to me, saying:

"Don't whip me too hard."

I made her lean over the side of the bed; then I threw her chemise up over her head, and admired her pretty little figure, naked to her garters. It was a long time since I had used the rod, and I grasped it with the feeling of pleasure that always comes over a lover of flagellation when he is about to redden a plump, white bottom.

I should have liked to birch her smartly, but I restrained my desire, and only gave her a dozen strokes, with just sufficient force to raise a bright pink blush on the cheeks of her bottom. She winced slightly at each cut, but did not remonstrate; and by the time I had finished whipping her I had a splendid cock-stand; so I laid her at full length on the bed, and poked her with great gusto. She was a nice little woman, and a good poke; but she was not in her first youth; and I fancy she had been embraced by many a man; therefore she was not to be compared in any way with my fresh, young Frances. While Maud was dressing herself, I told her that I would bring Frances up to town in a few days. Then I gave her a cheque to cover all expenses; and after giving her a final kiss, I went away.

I got back to Oakhurst in time for dinner, and when it was over, and I had lighted a cigar, I told Frances that I had something serious to say to her. She looked very much surprised, but without asking a question, she drew a stool up beside me, and sat down to listen. I pointed out to her that we could not go on any longer living together at Oakhurst; as we were sure to be found out, and then there would be a great scandal, which I particularly wished to avoid.

I added that I was longing to see her dressed in her proper attire; and that I intended taking her, in a couple of days, to a lady friend of mine in London, who could see that she was fitted out in first-rate style, and with whom she could live until she had got accustomed to wearing petticoats again.

She listened, with a very sorrowful face, to all I had to say, and when I had finished, tears came into her eyes, and she said, heaving a deep sigh: "You are right. I am afraid we should get found out some day; so I had better go and live with your friend. Have you spoken to her about me?"

"Yes. I went up to London today on purpose to speak to her; and we settled everything. I was with her all day."

A frown wrinkled her brow, she pouted her lips, and she glanced at me with a look such as I had never seen in her eyes before—she was evidently jealous of my "lady friend."

"I suppose the lady is a sweetheart of yours?" she snapped out suddenly, in an aggrieved tone of voice.

"She was my sweetheart before I ever saw you; and she is going to be married in a month; so you needn't be jealous, you little goose," I replied, smiling.

"I believe you love her more than you love me. I'm sure I shall hate her!" she exclaimed angrily; then, with feminine inconsistency, she began to cry. I felt annoyed, and spoke sternly: "Don't be so silly, Frances. I have a great mind to give you a sound spanking for showing such ill-temper."

"I don't care if you do spank me," she replied sobbing. Then she added fiercely: "I tell you I hate her!"

"You will make me very angry if you go on like that. I have already told you that she was my sweetheart before I knew you. She is nothing to me now. Do be a sensible girl. You will like her, I am sure. She has excellent taste in dress, and you will want some one to help you when you are getting your trousseau."

Her brow cleared, she wiped her eyes and smiled; all the woman in her was stirred at the thought of buying dresses.

"Oh, how funny I shall feel when I put on petticoats again. And long ones too! The last petticoats I wore,—the ones Mrs. Leslie turned up—were short, only reaching half-way between my knees and ankles."

"You will soon get used to petticoats; and I shall be delighted to see you in a toilette from some fashionable dress-maker's. I am sure you will look charming. You know I shall often see you."

She laughed gleefully, got on to my knees, and kissed me, saying: "It will cost you a lot of money to dress me out, for I shall want to have everything of the very best description."

"So you shall. And after the lady has married, and gone away, you shall live in the house, and I will go and stay with you."

"Oh, you darling!" she exclaimed, kissing and hugging me. "I am so sorry I was cross just now; but I am so fond of you that I can't bear the idea of your being with another woman."

Then she asked me a number of questions about the lady; and I answered as truthfully as was possible under the circumstances. However, she appeared to be satisfied with what I told her, as she did not show any more signs of jealousy, and by the time she had heard all I chose to tell her, it was late, so we went to bed.

Next day, we both began to make preparations for leaving Oakhurst; as it was my intention, as soon as I had seen Frances safely settled with Maud, to go up to Scotland to stay with a friend who had invited me to shoot grouse with him. The servants were told that "Mr. Francis" was going away for good; and in a couple of days, when everything was in readiness for our departure, I wrote to Maud, telling her that we should be with her next day in time for lunch.

The morning came, and after an early breakfast, the dog-cart was brought to the door; our luggage was put in; Frances, with rather a shaky voice, bade good bye to the servants, all of whom had assembled on the terrace, apparently sorry that "Mr. Francis" was going away. Then we climbed into the trap, and I drove off.

The groom had gone on before us, so we were alone in the dog-cart, and as soon as we had got out of the avenue on to the road, Frances burst into a flood of tears, saying: "Oh, I am so sorry to leave the dear old house."

"Never mind, Frances," I said. "You will soon have a prettily-furnished little house of your own: we shall be together very often, and have lots of fun in London; and by and by I will take you abroad."

She smiled, nestled close up to me, and soon recovered her spirits. In due course, we reached London, and arrived at the villa in St. John's Wood, about one o'clock.

Maud greeted Frances in a most friendly manner, and kissed her; then, after looking at her for a moment or two, said heartily, and without the least sign of jealousy: "Well dear, I must say you make a very good-looking young man; but when you are dressed in your proper attire, you will be a very pretty girl."

Frances laughed, looking pleased with the evidently sincere compliment. Then we sat down to a nice little lunch with champagne; and though Frances was a little shy at first, she brightened up under the influence of a glass of wine, added to Maud's cheerful talk and kindly manner; and in a short time she was chatting away perfectly at her ease.

After lunch, while I was smoking my cigar, the two young women sat together in a corner of the room, conversing in low tones and laughing merrily every now and then as they glanced at me, their eyes sparkling with fun. No doubt they were comparing notes on the various whippings and pokings they had received from me.

However, I was glad to see that they had taken to each other, and I felt sure that Maud would be kind to the young girl, for my sake.

I finished my cigar, and then I thought I had better tell

Frances at once that I was going to Scotland for a short time. I said to her: "You know that Maud is going to be married in less than a month. I am going away to Scotland for three weeks, and by the time I come back you will have got your 'trousseau,' and also have learnt how to wear the garments of your sex in a graceful manner; therefore you will appear to me in a new and charming light. I shall feel that you are my sweetheart in reality then."

My communication took her completely by surprise; she gazed at me for a moment, and then began to cry, saying: "Oh, I thought you were going to stay here with me."

"Well, so I am, when I come back. In the meantime, you will have plenty of amusement in buying all the pretty things you want; and Maud will take you out driving every day. You'll find that the three weeks will soon pass." She smiled sorrowfully; and Maud said, kindly: "Cheer up, Frances. We shall have a jolly time together, with no man to bother us."

There was nothing more to be said or done; so I sent for a hansom, and when it came, my portmanteau and gun case were put in. I gave Maud a kiss, and bade her good bye; and she promised to take the greatest care of Frances in every way. The girl clung round my neck, sobbing; I kissed her tenderly, left the villa, and drove off to King's Cross station, quite confident that my sweetheart would be true to me during my absence.

I had a long tiresome journey; as my friend lived in the wilds of Argyllshire, twenty miles from a railway station; and consequently I did not arrive at his place until late the following day.

My friend was a bachelor, and the house was merely a shooting-lodge, so the accommodation was rather rough. I need not enter into details of what happened during my stay in the North; for one day was exactly like another; though I will just remark that I had good sport with the grouse, but no sport of any kind with a woman. In fact the only female I spoke to, was a bare-legged, but good-looking Highland lass whom I met on the moor one evening when I was walking home alone. She had not "much English," as she quaintly expressed it; but we managed to talk a little, and she allowed me to kiss her pretty face several times; but when I took hold of her round the waist, and tried to put my hand up her short petticoats, she gave me a box on the ear, and scolded me volubly in Gaelic. I let her go!

10

IN SILK ATTIRE.—THE OLD LOVE AND THE NEW.—
A JOLLY DAY AND A GOOD DINNER.—
RETROSPECTIVE BIRCHING RECOLLECTIONS.—"DO IT AGAIN!"—
A GLORIOUS NIGHT'S WORK.

I got back to London early one afternoon, having been away just three weeks, to a day; and I drove off at once to the villa, where I knew Frances would be waiting to receive me, for we had corresponded regularly, and I had written to tell her when she was to expect me. During the long drive from King's Cross, I kept wondering how Frances would look in her woman's clothes, and I felt as excited as if I had been a young bridegroom going to meet his bride. On my arrival at the house, I was ushered into the drawing-room, where I was received by a lovely young lady, who threw her arms round my neck, and who kissed me, and fondled me, and cooed to me with all sorts of endearing terms.

It was Frances, but I should never have recognized her had I met her in the street: she appeared so much taller in her sweeping draperies, and she was far more handsome than I had ever expected. She was beautifully and tastefully dressed in a frock that set off to perfection all the rounded contours of her splendid figure; there were ribbons on various parts of the dress, and there was creamy lace round her throat and wrists. Her hair had grown longer, covering her well-shaped head with a wealth of little, silky, golden curls, which came low down upon her broad, white forehead, but did not hide her pretty shell-like ears. Her blue eyes seemed to be larger, and more limpid than ever; her complexion was like milk and roses; and the excitement had raised a pink flush on her peach-like cheeks.

Her first transports of pleasure over, she sank gracefully down upon a chair; her trim ankles and tiny feet, in smart patent leather high-heeled shoes, showed under the hem of her dainty, lace petticoat; and she held in her small, white hand, a filmy handkerchief scented with some delicate perfume.

Looking at me, with a languishing glance in her beautiful eyes, and with a smile curving her cherry lips, she said: "Well, Charley, how do you think I am looking?"

I was quite dazzled by the unexpected beauty of the girl, and I gazed at her for a short time without answering; thinking to myself, with intense delight, that she was all my own: no other man had ever touched the sweet, delicious, young creature. I lifted her up in my arms and pressing her to my breast, kissed her rapturously on the eyes, cheeks, and lips, while the subtle perfume of her hair, flesh, and clothes excited in me a dreamy, sensuous feeling.

She lay quietly in my arms perfectly unmindful of her crushed and tumbled draperies; at last I answered her question: "You are looking most charming. I always thought you were pretty when you were dressed as a man; but now that I see you in your proper dress, I consider you beautiful."

She laughed a long low laugh of happiness. She said: "Oh,

I am delighted to hear you say you admire me! And I am so glad to have you with me again. I have been pining for you. I am longing to be in bed with you again. Oh, my sweetheart! My love!" kissing me boldly, over and over again.

I sat down on an easy-chair, holding her on my knees with my arm round her waist; then I lifted up her skirts and admired her shapely legs, cased in pale blue silk stockings, held up by black satin garters; then, putting my hand up her petticoats, I opened the slit of her drawers, played with the silky hair on the lower part of her belly, and felt the cool, firm flesh of her bottom. I had a most tremendous cockstand, and I longed to poke her at that moment, as she sat on my knees; but I curbed my desire; thinking it would be better to wait till we got to bed, and then I should be quite fresh for a long night of pleasure.

So I took away my hand from the tempting "spot," rather to the surprise and disappointment of Frances, who, thinking I was going to give her a "sitting poke" had straddled out her legs so that I might be able to get my prick between her thighs. She glanced at me, with a yearning look in her great blue eyes which were moist and glistening, but she made no remark. I gave her a kiss, saying: "Let us wait till we are in bed, and then we shall enjoy our fun all the more."

Then I asked: "How have you been getting on with Maud?"

"Very well indeed. She has been most good, and kind to me in every way. I like her very much," she added, diffidently. "But she is not very well educated, and I don't think she is quite a lady, though she has very good taste in dress."

I laughed heartily, remarking: "You are a very observant young lady Maud is certainly not well-read, and I don't think her parents were what are called 'gentlefolks.' She herself started in life as a chorus girl."

A few moments after we had finished speaking, Maud came

into the room and greeted me cordially. Then, looking waggishly at us, she said: "I see you two turtledoves are billing and cooing already. I hope I have not disturbed you. Shall I go away again?" she asked, with a sly smile. Frances jumped off my knees, laughing and blushing a little, and went up to Maud, who put her arm round the girl's waist in an affectionate way, saying to me: "Haven't I dressed her nicely? Isn't she a pretty girl?"

I answered both questions in the affirmative; taking a good look at my old and my new sweetheart as they stood side by side. Frances was a couple of inches the tallest of the two; and though Maud was tastefully dressed, and was pretty, and ladylike; she was not nearly so pretty, nor had she the air of distinction possessed by Frances, who looked what she was: a refined, well-bred young lady.

Maud rang the bell, and the servant brought in a tray with a pretty tea service, which she set out on a little bamboo table near Frances; who looked very charming as she busied herself in the essentially feminine task of making and pouring out the tea.

We had a long chat, and I was glad to see that my two sweethearts were on very friendly terms; there was not the least constraint between them, and they had evidently made confidantes of each other.

After a time I told them to go and dress, as I intended taking them to dine at a restaurant. They were delighted, and ran off at once to get ready, returning in about half-an-hour, charmingly attired. I never can describe a woman's dress, but I know that both my sweethearts looked very nice; though I think Frances was the more tastefully dressed of the two. We packed ourselves into a hansom, and drove to the Café Royal where we had an excellent dinner, and we drank a couple of bottles of champagne.

We were very merry, talking and laughing without cessation during the dinner. Frances was in one of her most lively moods, and her influence made Maud more talkative than usual: for, as a rule, she had not much to say for herself.

She was to be married in four days; and she informed us that her future husband was rather a slow-going fellow, and though she liked him fairly well, she did not love him. Then she said, laughing:

"I do not suppose he has the faintest idea of what men call the 'pleasures of the rod'; but even if he has, I do not intend to let him birch me."

Turning to me, and making a little grimace, she added: "I have had quite enough whipping from you, to last me my lifetime. No other man shall ever lay a rod across my bottom."

We laughed; and Frances said: "Charley is very fond of whipping, I know, and he has made me fond of it too; but I have never had a chance of whipping anyone except one little boy, years ago. I told you all about it, Maud, and also how I liked doing it."

"Yes," replied Maud, laughing. "You told me all about it; and you also told me that the boy's mother complained to Charley, and that he gave you a smart birching. But you did not tell me you liked that."

Frances laughed, saying: "I did not like it at all. I hated it It was very painful. Charley gave me twelve hard cuts."

"Yes," I said, with a smile. "And you most certainly did not like them, judging from the way you kicked and squealed."

She made a little face at me, and then went on: "Although I do not like being whipped myself, I must say that I should very much like to whip a pretty little boy, or a big, bouncing girl."

I laughed, and Maud remarked: "It is a funny task. I have never felt the least inclination to whip, or to be whipped."

We lingered over dessert, with coffee and liqueurs, until it got late, then we drove back to the villa, where we sat in the drawing-room for a short time while I smoked a cigar. Then Maud bade us good night, and as she left the room, said to me, with a little laugh: "Let the girl have *some* sleep to-night."

Taking Frances by the hand, I led her upstairs to the "nuptial chamber," which was the largest room in the house. It was very prettily furnished, and well-lit by a soft-shaded lamp; the bed was a fine big one, in which I had many a time poked Maud; and across which I had many a time birched her.

I sat down on a chair and looked at Frances undressing herself, and I felt much more pleasure in watching the pretty creature discard her dainty, feminine garments, than I had ever felt while watching her taking off her male attire. Standing near the bed, she removed her pretty frock; then she unlaced, and took off her blue satin stays; next, sitting on a chair, she pulled off her little shoes, and then, unbuckling her garters, she drew off her tightly-fitting silk stockings; then, standing up again, she untied the strings of her drawers and petticoats, letting the garments fall to the floor; finally, she let her chemise slip from her polished shoulders, over her swelling bubbies and broad hips, down to her feet. Then, stepping clear of the pile of snowy draperies, she stood for a moment or two perfectly naked, smiling at me in a most enticing manner; but she soon hid her ravishing beauties under a pretty lace-trimmed nightdress, and got into bed. My cock was like a bar of iron; I had not had a woman for nearly a month; and I said to myself; "that it would cast her a groaning" to take the edge off me. I tore off my clothes as quickly as possible, but I did not put out the light, and in an another moment I was in bed beside the lovely girl, who at once cuddled up close to me. Pulling up her nightdress to her neck, I clasped my arms round her yielding body, feeling it all over from head to foot, and I thought that her delicate skin was softer and smoother; and that her titties were rounder and firmer; and her bottom bigger and plumper; and that altogether she was more delicious in every way than when I last had her naked body in my arms.

She twined her legs round mine, and put her soft hand on my rampant prick, saying in a low tone of delight: "Oh, Charley! Isn't it delicious to be in each other's arms again?" Then she added, squeezing my tool, and speaking with an affectation of fear: "Oh, how big it is to-night: I am quite afraid of it."

I pressed my lips to hers, and thrusting my tongue into her mouth, I kissed her that way; much to her astonishment, as I had never saluted her so before. "How do you like being kissed in that fashion?" I asked. Her breath had been taken away by the ardour of my kisses; but as soon as she could speak, she said: "I liked it very much. I will kiss you the same way now." Then she put her velvety, hot little tongue, as far as it would go, into my mouth.

Half frantic with desire, I laid her on her back, and pulled the bed-clothes down to her feet, while she at once stretched out her legs widely, and slightly arched her loins, so that I might be able to get into her with as little difficulty as possible. Putting my hands under her, I clasped the cheeks of her bottom, and extended myself on her naked bosom; her round, firm titties feeling like small elastic cushions under my breast; then pressing my lips to hers, I thrust my tongue again deeply into her fragrant mouth; at the same time forcing my prick up to the roots in her tight cunt with a few powerful movements of my loins. Then I began to fuck her slowly, but strongly; she put her arms round my neck, clasped her legs round my loins; her soft, warm thighs pressing my sides closely, and bucked up in splendid style: her whole body quivering from the violence of my thrusts. She panted, and groaned, and occasionally uttered a little squeak, as she heaved up her bottom, and bounded under me in voluptuous ecstacy, gasping out in broken accents: "Oh—Charley!—Oh—my—love! My—love!" I poked away vigorously, my strokes gradually increasing in rapidity; while she plunged and bounced so violently, that my prick was nearly jerked out of its place; but, grasping the cheeks of her bottom tightly, I held her in position, and soon was giving her the short digs. "Oh—h—h! it—is—coming! Oh—do—it—quick! —Quicker! Oh—h—h—h!"

The supreme moment arrived. I "spent" profusely; and she gasped, sighed, wriggled, and squirmed in a most lascivious manner; the lips of her cunt tightly clipping my half-stiff prick; and as each hot jet of sperm spurted up her vagina, I could feel the flesh of her bottom quiver and twitch in my hands; and when she had drained me dry, and had stopped sighing and wriggling; she exclaimed in a tone of rapture: "Oh, that was most delicious!"

I withdrew, and lay beside her, and she pressed her naked body against mine, lying quietly for a short time. Then, raising her head, she looked in my face with a smile curving her moist red lips, and a sensuous gleam in her big blue eyes; coolly saying: "Do it again."

I laughed; but as not more than ten minutes had passed since I had taken my tool out of her cunt, I was not in a condition to go to work again.

"You know very well I can't do it again so soon. Feel how limp 'it' is at this moment," I said, pinching her bottom. She put her hand on my member, and felt it, saying with a laugh: "It certainly could not get into me now."

Then we had a little talking; she all the time keeping her hand on my prick, and as soon as she felt it stiffening, she began to squeeze it, and to draw the foreskin backwards and forwards over the nut, so that in a short time the weapon was again fit for use. "There," she said, triumphantly, "it is quite ready; and so am I. Put it in."

I turned her on to her side; and lying close behind her with my belly against the warm cushions of her bottom, I put my prick between her thighs into her wet cunt; then, holding her in my arms, and placing my hands on her swelling bubbies, I poked her in the side position, which was a favourite one with us both. Shortly afterwards we fell asleep; but whenever I woke in the night, I always found Frances lying close to me with her soft legs thrown over mine. Then I would poke her, and go to sleep again. And once or twice, she happened to wake when I was asleep; but she soon woke me by gently pulling my tool; and then we again made "the beast with two backs." So that altogether we passed nearly the whole night in a succession of delicious amorous combats in various positions; and when morning came, I was pretty well played out, though Frances seemed to be nearly as fresh as ever.

At half-past ten o'clock we got up, had our baths, and dressed; Frances putting on a very pretty morning frock in which she looked most charming; then we went down to breakfast.

Maud received us with a smile, saying: "Well, you two have had a fine, long night of it. I suppose he did not let you have much sleep, Frances?"

She smiled, but made no reply; and I remarked: "Frances would not let me sleep when I wanted to do so; she can't reproach me for keeping her awake."

"I am not going to reproach you," she said, laughing. "I think we were both equally to blame."

Laughing merrily, the three of us sat down to a very good breakfast, to which Frances, and I, did full justice, for we stood greatly in need of refreshment after our labours.

When the meal was over, Maud went off to meet her lover; and after I had smoked a cigar, I took Frances out for a stroll in Regent's Park.

from

Venus in Paris

by Florentine Vaudrez

3

Not long after Dorothy had surprised her mistress and Madame Vaudrez in the latter's bedroom where she had screwed her mistress with a dildo, Madam Lucy gave one of her famous, intimate soirees. Julia and Florentine were lucky enough to be invited; they both went under assumed names: Pomegranate Flower and Miss Evergreen. Although it was against the rules of Madam Lucy's establishment, Dorothy had explained to her former employer that both ladies had plans for the future where these names might become very important. They only would visit Madam Lucy's establishment once, because in matters of sex both ladies were very inexperienced. Madam Lucy was flattered, and allowed the house rules to be broken, just this once.

Her small, select parties to which only a lucky few—mainly the very rich, the very important and the titled—are admitted, enjoyed among the highest circles a remarkable, or rather extremely curious, reputation. The secrecy which surrounded these gatherings had made them notorious throughout Paris, and everyone who was anyone desperately tried to get an invitation.

Dorothy, of course, belonged to the small group of friends of this hospitable lady, and she had really kept her word to wrangle an invitation out of Madam Lucy. She did not hide the fact from her mistress and Madame Vaudrez that getting the invitation had been exceedingly difficult. She also had some misgivings.

"My dearest ladies," the devoted maid said, "you may have to count on the possibility that as newcomers you may become highly involved, and I am almost afraid . . . what I mean is, once you are in Madam Lucy's salon, anything goes, and it is impossible to refuse anything. Won't you reconsider while there is still time?"

"Ah, rubbish, my dear Dorothy," Julia said. "I am not such a prude when I happen to be in the proper company, and neither is my sister. And besides, now you have really aroused our curiosity!"

Julia was not just curious but truly eager for an introduction to the home of Madam Lucy. When she was still the mistress of Count Saski she had picked up enough allusions to this famous establishment, and under no circumstances did she want to pass up the chance to see for herself what was going on. She knew full well that the happenings in Madam Lucy's house were incredibly licentious, and ladies from the finest families in Paris fought for the honor to be admitted to the odd entertainment of the intimate little groups that gathered there.

Two very important rules had to be followed strictly, exactly as laid down by the Madam of the house. In the first place, utter discretion was a must, and in the second place, everyone—without exception—had to accept the rules of whatever games were played at the particular party. If one could agree to these two stipulations, an evening of incredible delights was held out as a proper reward.

And Dorothy had told the sisters what Julia already had guessed, that whatever happened at the home of Madam Lucy was not exactly commonplace.

Madam Lucy was a widow of about forty years old, although she looked no more than thirty. She had a sister, Laura, who lived with her, and who appeared to be a few years younger. Laura was about to divorce her husband and, as far as the sisters could gather, this man lived in the colonies and made only very infrequent, short visits to Paris. Rumor had it that he lived with a Negress in Africa. Anyhow, he was very rich, and his charming wife had a considerable income.

When the two sisters, together with Dorothy, entered the salon of the beautiful Madam Lucy, they met a small gathering of about ten persons.

There was the old Count de Paliseul, a very interesting gentleman "in between the two ages," with graying temples and a tendency to become corpulent; an Officer of the General Staff, Baron Maxim de Berny, tall, blond and muscular and—as one could expect—the spoiled lover of all the courtesans and respectable women in Paris. Then there was Dorothy, well dressed and very ladylike, blonde and stately, with an enormous bosom and wide hips. Miss Elinor D. MacPherson was from the United States. She was a redhead, a real Irish devil with sea-green eyes, a wicked mouth with an incredible amount of lipstick and very beautiful pointed breasts. It was impossible to overlook this detail, if detail is the correct word. These huge things were truly remarkable, especially since the gown of this lady had the lowest plunging neckline Paris had ever seen. There was a banker, Monsieur de Lyncent, and a very pale, fragile-looking woman from Andalusia. She was Senora Padilla, who was at the party with her husband, a small, lean gentleman with pitch-black hair that seemed to be pasted down on his skull. He was the Consul from Spain. Finally there were

John and Molly Teeler, brother and sister, young, very young, so much so that the sisters were beginning to doubt whether the soiree would take the course they had expected.

But then they were told that the latter two were performers; he an accomplished musician and she a so-called "plastic dancer"—one of those girls who sprinkle themselves with bronze powder and then portray all the females inhabiting Mount Olympus. They were then satisfied that the evening would fulfill their expectations.

Besides, a small speech of the gracious hostess enlightened everyone completely, and there was no doubt left in anyone's mind as to what was about to take place during the course of the coming evening.

"Ladies and gentlemen," Madam Lucy said in a low tone of voice—shortly before her little speech all the lights in the house had been doused, except for a few hidden ones which spread a discreet glow—"you want, as far as I understand from your own words or those of your friends who were kind enough to introduce you to me, to taste with me the delights which are so frequently denied to us. You and I have now gathered in this small group. All have the same thoughts about this particular subject, and it is therefore that we shall be able to enjoy our desires without undesirable results and, above all, without restraint. I have seen to it that my servants, as usual, have the night off. There will be absolutely no unwanted witnesses to the proceedings. I fervently hope they will soon start, and I beg you to use your unbridled imaginations, and to throw off all your inhibitions. After all, we have gathered here with a delightful idea in mind and I beg you not to forget this, no matter in what situation you might find yourself."

A softly murmured "Bravo" interrupted the smiling Madam Lucy.

"Now, please allow me to repeat the few most important

rules of our little get together. There are actually only three. Number one: Shame is a plebian attitude. Number two: Everyone is for everyone. Number three: The ratio is three to one which means that the ladies are allowed to reach a certain delight three times. I presume that I do not have to go into detail. The gentleman can enjoy the same ecstasy only once. For further proceedings the ratio may become six to two, and so on . . . let your imaginations work, give them free rein. It is a ratio at which I arrived after many delicious experiences, and I hope that the gentlemen can be trusted upon their word of honor."

The last reminder, obviously, was only meant for the men present. It seemed that the official part of the little soiree was over, and Dorothy whispered a few little explanations, telling Julia and Florentine that everyone was expected to follow the instructions of the hostess, and that moreover the rules of the game were of the greatest benefit to the ladies.

They were gathered in a rather large living room. There was no lack of a place to sit—or rather, to lie down. The rug in the middle of the room was free of any furniture, though grouped around it were four large, oversized couches. There were several sofas in the corners of the room, and many love seats and over-stuffed easy chairs. Several small tables throughout the room were loaded with bottles and plates, filled with all sorts of delicious snacks. Various exits led into smaller rooms which were discreetly lit and tastefully decorated.

The guests walked around, inspecting the various rooms, getting acquainted with one another, and slowly pairing off in small groups. If it had not been for the words of the hostess, no one would ever have thought they were amidst a rather special gathering of people.

But then came the voice of Madam Lucy again. "Gentlemen, would you care to dance? Mister Teeler, please start the music."

And the next moment, soft music filled the room and soon several couples danced to the exotic music. Maxim de Berny walked over to Florentine and invited her to dance with him. She accepted, and his strong arms embraced her passionately. He was a very good dancer.

Julia was asked by Senator Junoy. After a few dances they remained standing together and then sank down upon one of the couches.

"Did you get a little bit warm, my dears?" Again it was the voice of Lucy, clear but husky. "I believe the gentlemen should be allowed to take off their coats. And I also think that the ladies should be permitted to unbutton their partner's flies . . . "

The two sisters were speechless. That is what one might call speeding up the proceedings! Hastily, the gentlemen, led by the Senator, that wicked creature, took off their coats.

"Well, Monsieur de Berny? And what about your tunic. That uniform must be extremely uncomfortable. And please, Madame," Lucy said to Florentine, "you will have to struggle with that hermetically sealed uniform fly!"

Florentine noticed that her partner's face reddened. "How funny," she thought, "and this is only the beginning!" But at the same time she looked around for Julia. There was her sister, sitting on the next couch, together with the little Spaniard. Madam Lucy was standing next to them, obviously repeating her invitation. It seemed that the couple needed some urging, but finally her sister stretched her hand toward the pants of Senor Padilla.

Florentine had already put her hands between the legs of her escort, and what she found there exceeded her greatest expectations.

One great sigh seemed to drift through the room. All the couples were now standing, or sitting, in a big circle. The gentlemen's behavior was still correct, though all of them were now dressed in their shirt sleeves. The ladies had their right hands extended and encircling the hardening members of their partners of that moment.

But Madam Lucy was watching carefully, and she was in full control of the entire affair.

"Well, my darlings," she said pleasantly but firmly, "I believe that the first introductions are over and done with, and I assume that you don't need my instructions any longer. I am very sure that all the gentlemen are now more than ready to pay slight compliments to their ladies. Please, gentlemen, don't hesitate. We women would love to get thoroughly acquainted with that which interests us most. Come to think of it, I would assume it to be very entertaining if the gentlemen would now take a firm hold of whatever is of greatest interest to them. Now, please, let's do it all at the same time. Grab firmly whatever charm it was that attracted you first to your female partner."

What followed was positively hilarious.

Madam Lucy's suggestions were followed to the letter. Though the women had obeyed Madam Lucy's instructions rather hesitantly and shyly, the gentlemen were more direct and firm.

Florentine looked over at Julia and Senor Padilla. And, indeed, the little Spaniard had already taken a firm hold of those charms of her sister which had undoubtedly intrigued him most, namely her perfect, delicious breasts. His brown, strong hands fingered around in Julia's low-cut gown, and he quickly succeeded in freeing one of Julia's full, well-formed breasts.

Somewhat further were the banker, de Lyncent, and the wife of the Spanish consul. Florentine could not exactly see where he had his hands, but it was easy to see that he was kissing the languishing Andalusian upon the mouth, trying to wriggle his tongue between her teeth.

"Our friend de Lyncent is a saint," a gentleman remarked.

He looked like one of Ruben's fauns, with his little, twinkling eyes, his reddish face, and his full white beard. "A chaste little kiss satisfies him completely."

This remark surely did not describe the gentleman's own desires, because he had just taken a firm hold of the charms of the silver-blonde Molly Teeler who looked, with her light blonde tousled hair and big light blue eyes, like an appetizing little doll. One hand was energetically kept busy with her well-formed, obviously firm and hard bosom, and the other hand had crawled under the pretty young girl's dress. The gentleman did not even take the trouble, once he had reached his goal, to rearrange his partner's skirt, so that her marble-white upper thighs were completely uncovered. He had put his faun-like head slightly down, and was nuzzling under her armpits. It seemed to tickle her, and she burst out in a loud giggle.

"Ooh, I can't stand that . . . please . . . please . . . Oh, sir, you're tickling me too much . . . no, please, no . . . aaaah."

The slightly tortured-sounding giggle had stopped, because Count de Paliseul had let go of his partner's armpit and had begun to nibble upon her strawberry nipples which were smiling at him from her half-opened gown.

Without a doubt, one of the gentlemen, Monsieur de Laigle, knew his manners, because he was entertaining both ladies of the house.

Each one was sitting on one side of him. Laura, who had opened his fly, was softly playing with his stiffening scepter, and he was tenderly stroking her full behind. At the same time his legs encircled the thighs of Madam Lucy, and it was obvious that his hand had already reached that spot which is covered with a tuft of hair.

The talented young Johnny Teeler—he could not have been more than nineteen or twenty years old—did not interrupt his soft musical playing. Nevertheless his hands no longer played waltzes, but they magically performed known and unknown singing melodies which increased the enchanted mood that now permeated the room.

And when Julia looked carefully at the dimly lit corner where he was playing, she noticed that he executed his paraphrases and melodies with only one hand. True, it was done with such virtuosity that nobody seemed to notice this. The only one who knew for sure was the American Miss Elinor because his left hand had taken a firm hold of one of her incredibly pointed breasts. She had taken it out of her dress and offered it to the piano player, holding it in both hands which made this pointed pear appear even larger. It was enchanting to behold this fascinating woman. Her well-filled yet slim figure rested upon a pair of firm, long-stemmed, gorgeous legs for which the American women are so justly famous. She had an unusual piquant face which was framed by fire red—one could almost call it indecent red—hair which contrasted strangely with her nymph-green, incredibly large eyes. It was not surprising at all that the young musician, whose fly was open like those of all the other gentlemen, showed an enormous hard-on.

Maxim de Berny, too, had taken the charming cue of the hostess without any hesitation. He had become an entirely different person ever since Florentine had liberated his enormous manhood out of its uncomfortable position. Florentine loved to caress this gigantic, swollen, stiff prick. She was dreaming about how it would fit into a certain pink-colored sheath.

His military reserve had made way for a zealous kindness. And, when the gentlemen had been asked to take possession of the charms that attracted them to their ladies, he had become more than just zealous and kind. He immediately grabbed a very firm hold of Florentine's legs.

"My dear and precious lady," his hot breath whispered into her ears, "I . . . I . . . have only seen you tonight for the first time. Oh, I am sure that you did not even notice me . . . there were so many other interesting people present . . . but ever since I saw you tonight, I have been haunted by a wild desire . . . I have dreamed passionate dreams . . . and I hope fervently that they will come true. My thoughts have been possessed by only one desire . . . to touch your legs . . . those beautiful, gorgeous, long legs. They seem to be sculptured out of marble . . .

His strong hands firmly underscored his words, confirming that he meant what he said. But he seemed not only interested in Florentine's legs, since his hands were also very busy with her thighs and the tuft of hair in between. He paid homage to her fleece that left no doubt as to his intentions. However, it did not disturb Florentine in the least. After all, that was what she was here for, and she fully intended to make up for her years of widowhood and her years with a rather impotent husband. She felt terribly passionate and could not have cared less if the blond giant had taken immediate possession of her. In fact, she would have welcomed it. But he was still playing with her legs, her thighs, her breasts and her slowly moistening hole. When enjoyed in the proper manner, erotic delights can be continued endlessly. The passion, after all, is always there. It is only a matter of the right place and plenty of time and a willing partner. Of course, Florentine knew that a brutal, quick embrace can have its own particular charm. One can even do it standing on a front porch, while the husband is occupied with opening the door, or in a men's room of a station when one's lover is about to depart for a prolonged time, and hastily requires a last parting favor. It can even be done, she knew, in a public park, where one is protected by the impenetrable branches of the bushes.

The large room in which the thirteen people were gathered was now filled with the most unusual sounds. One could hear a peculiar soft smacking, the rustling of the silken gowns of the ladies and the starched shirts of the gentlemen. There were the loving grunts and groans of the men, and the giggling and soft moans of the women. Breathless moaning, and the panting and the gasping which left no doubt as to what was going on. Added to this was the typical, very exciting creaking of the furniture caused by the movements of the bodies that occupied them.

But the soft, enchanting music of John Teeler had stopped. In its place an occasional note was heard whenever Miss Elinor's elbows hit a key of the piano against which she was leaning while she straddled with widespread legs the lap of the young, blond piano player. In this strange position she went with him through all the motions that people usually perform when they are firmly pinned down on a mattress.

And they were not the only couple busily engaged in this particular delight. The skinny Spaniard had succeeded in inducing Dorothy to stretch out on the couch, and he was kneeling between her powerful legs. He was working a little bit too fast for Dorothy's taste, pushing his lance with such enervating speed against the girl's belly that she finally took his prick in her hands, forcing him to slow down. Her full breasts served as supports for the nervous Spaniard's outstretched arms and his skinny brown fingers voluptuously kneaded these enormous snow-white balls.

Monsieur de Laigle had put Lucy's sister in front of him. She offered her full, white buttocks up to his throbbing spear and he took possession of her behind with a certain nonchalance. Even while he penetrated her from behind, dog fashion, he refused to take his cigar out of his mouth. It was a curious sight. He fucked her, puffing his cigar, giving her enormous jolts. Laura kept very still, but breathed passionately and deeply every time the huge shaft of her partner disappeared up to the hilt into her wide open cleft.

The hostess had not yet actively joined one of the many couples. She wandered from one little group to another, now cheering them on with a witty remark, then removing a piece of clothing which might be in the way, occasionally fondling a buttock, a breast or a pair of balls, whenever such a part was uncovered.

"Well, Monsieur de Berny, I am sure that Miss Evergreen is ready for you. Don't you want to honor the lady with your, as I can observe, more than ready sword?"

At that particular moment the couple did not need these doubtlessly well-meant encouragements, because without any further ado the strong, muscular officer had pushed Florentine down upon the couch and . . .

The girl did not think that she had ever experienced such powerful thrusts ever before in her life. The blond officer had mounted her as if he were a wild stallion, and he worked her over with tremendous force while he raised her legs high. He raved madly against Florentine's belly, his balls slamming hard against her buttocks. In a very short time she felt pains as she had never before endured. But strangely enough, the pain became pleasant, and her hips started wildly gyrating, her cleft wide open, as if she was about to swallow the whole man.

His breathing was rattling, but strangely enough, though it seemed that he could hardly get enough air, he kept exclaiming exciting words. Their monotony was, at first, strange and frightening, but ultimately Florentine became as hot and passionate as she had never been.

"Aaaaah . . . finally, finally . . . now can I fuck between those legs . . . between those legs . . . I am fucking between those beautiful legs . . . between the legs of a most beautiful woman . . . aaah . . . and what have you got between those sweet, beautiful legs? A cunt . . . a cunt . . . aaaah . . . how I have longed for that little hairy honey pot of yours . . . right between your legs . . . oooh!

Your legs, your legs . . . and I am fucking you right between those gorgeous legs! Ooooh . . . aaaah . . . let me die fucking between those legs . . . the legs of an angel . . . I will never take my prick out of this cunt again . . . I want to stay between your legs . . . my hard prick in your hairy cunt . . . aaah . . . how delicious to fuck that cunt between your legs . . . "

It was by now quite obvious to Florentine that her partner was particularly fascinated by her legs. It was also possible that their perfect line and form exceeded his wildest secret dreams. Anyhow, the muscular lover became wilder and wilder.

"Sweet . . . oh, how sweet . . . the way you raise those legs and spread your thighs . . . those legs . . . so that I can fuck between them . . . can you feel my balls slam against your ass? Oooh, I am fucking between the most divine legs . . . legs that seem to be praying for a harder and wilder fuck . . . I will give it to you, my love . . . I fuck that cunt . . . between your marvelous legs . . . and now you are spreading them so wide that I can put my prick in all the way . . . ooh, don't you like it, this big dong between your divine legs . . . oooh, feel how it rubs . . . oooh, my prick is at home at last . . . I am fucking you between your legs . . . I never want to stop . . . I want to fuck between your legs forever and ever . . . oooh, divine one, I am fucking you . . . between your legs . . . oooh, please, allow me to die between your legs . . ."

Florentine had to admit that it was a rather novel experience to have her legs honored in such a peculiar way, while she, as a person, did not seem particularly attracted to the officer. But, she told herself, she did not come to find eternal love; sex was enough. And as far as that was concerned, their coupling was extremely satisfactory, and they rammed their bellies voluptuously together.

The behavior of her partner reminded Florentine of a famous composer, a friend of her late husband, who had enticed his mistress—a divinely talented singer—to submit to him while she was singing a well-known, very difficult aria. And ever since that day he was unable to listen to her singing without being over-powered by the wild desire to possess her while the beautiful tones ran from her lips. To make this technically possible, the couple had agreed that he would rest on his back and have his mistress with the golden throat settle down upon him so that she would be able to sing her beautiful aria while he was pushing wildly under her, listening to her enchanting voice. Occasionally he would reach a certain height which would cause in her a sour note. But, on the whole, the arrangement worked perfectly for both people.

Julia, too, was literally drowning in passion. She had come twice already, though she had masterfully succeeded in hiding this. She wanted to enjoy the precisely measured, powerful jolts of Senor Padilla to the utmost. He worked without letting up, and his powerfully swollen muscle of love penetrated deeper and deeper into her longing body with every ramrod jolt.

Dorothy kept her partner working on her incessantly while she was crying out, "Oh God, I am coming . . . I am . . . coming . . . oh, my God . . . how I . . . am coming . . . again . . . again . . . oh, God . . . I am . . . coming . . . you screw so marvelously . . . I . . . am . . . coming . . . again . . . ooh, it's fantastic . . . I am so . . . horny . . . you fuck like . . . a bull . . . aaah . . . I am . . . coming all over . . . again . . . aaaah . . . aaaah!"

It was really very enjoyable to watch all these happy people. The big, blonde woman had turned slightly sideways. One of her extremely strong and powerful long legs, covered with a blue silk stocking, was held high up in the air by her partner, who held on to it as if it were a main mast of a sailboat, tossing in the wild seas. His lower body pushed rapidly with speedy thrusts against the widely opened cleft of his partner. He almost squatted between her full thighs, straddling the one under him with his skinny legs as if he were riding a wild pony.

Dorothy was resting upon her mighty hips, showing a full view of her large and imposing behind. The gigantic cheeks shimmered milk white in the subdued light of the room. They jerked and palpitated continuously, pushing violently backwards against the belly of her partner, who kept pushing against her with short, very rapid little strokes. His peter must have sealed off her twat almost hermetically, and Julia decided to try out this obviously very satisfying position as soon as she had the opportunity.

The wife of the thus busily engaged Spaniard was about to enjoy special delights herself. She had been selected by the hot-blooded Count de Paliseul. It appeared that he was more attracted to her than to the silver-blonde Molly, and maybe he had reached his goal quicker than expected. He was now about to experience new delights.

He was zealously bearing down upon the tender, completely disappearing wife of the fiery Senor Padilla. The speed of the good gentle man was surely much slower than she was used to, but the force of his thrusts must have been incredibly more powerful than those of the skinny Spaniard. The Senora was whimpering quietly, but it could have been because of incredible delight which was forcing this soft meowing out of her throat.

"Aaaaah, Monsieur, aaaah, so good you are doing it to me . . ." she almost sobbed. "It is soooo good . . . aaaah . . . aaaah . . . more, more . . . please . . . please . . . aaaah . . . ooooh . . . you satisfy me much . . . you are so much better than my husband . . . ooooh, how delicious . . . no, please, don't stop . . . it feels so good . . . more, more . . . aaaah . . .

Her partner was as red as a boiled lobster. It was obvious that he was driving his shaft into her with his last remaining force, but it was equally as obvious that this task was not an unpleasant one for him. In fact, he was enjoying himself tremendously. This pale Andalusian woman, with her exotic beauty, had beautiful, graceful, finely chiseled legs and incredibly gorgeous, slender thighs. The panting, gasping fawn had put both legs across his shoulders and his heavy, fleshy hands gripped her small but muscular buttocks firmly, pressing them with a slow but regular rhythm against his own belly. This small woman was incredibly voluptuous, because every muscle in her small body shook and vibrated. She pushed herself against the huge man on top of her with such fervor and passion that it seemed as if her frail body consisted of one heavily tensed muscle.

The blonde beauty, the sister of the pianist, was now possessed by the horny banker. But it was not the normal position in which all the other couples were engaged. Either because of weakness, or because of perversity, the banker was busily engaged in an entirely different way. His gray haired head disappeared almost completely between the widely opened white thighs of Molly, who languidly stretched out on one of the sofas.

One could almost say that the young girl was an extraordinary beauty. Most interesting was the radiance of her appearance. Every thing on her contributed to making her look like an angel. Her hair had the color of finely spun gold. The skin of her body and face was almost translucent. It was impossible to make out whether the snow of her bosom or the lilies of her thighs were whiter.

The form-fitting black silken gown, which did not hide anything on her perfect figure, was pushed up high above her waist by the horny old goat who was about to shove his facial duster into her small mother-of-pearl boudoir. It gave everyone present a peculiar feeling of tension to watch the balding gray head of the banker mix with the shimmering pubic hairs of this beautiful, innocent young girl. The zealous money lender had also pushed the gown of his willing beauty down her shoulders, thus exposing both of her full, pointed, yet very innocent looking breasts. He took this opportunity to grab them both with lustful hands, playing around with them as if they were rubber balls. From time to time he rubbed both divinely red strawberries between thumb and forefinger—the same way a lieutenant of the guards twirls his moustache—eliciting excited groans from his beautiful partner.

The beautifully formed legs of this gorgeous creature rested upon the shoulders of the old man who was kneeling before her. It was incredibly obscene and shameless. Her legs were held up high and bent backwards. The high heels of her black lacquered, piquant shoes pierced deeply into the back of the totally absorbed man, slowly pushing him closer toward her. There was actually no need for her to do so, because the head of the insatiable banker had almost completely disappeared into her widely opened cleft, and he looked for all the world like an animal trainer, sticking his head into the widely opened, hungry jaws of a lion.

Truly, the night afforded so much variety, and it was so exciting, that the sisters could not, with the best will in the world, recall every single detail. They also had no recollection how, after a certain time, the four enormous couches that formed a circle around the rug in the middle of the room were suddenly transformed into a gigantic resting place. Upon this enormous area, the couples sought and found one another. The watchful hostess saw to it that her guests' activities did not degenerate into selfish single acts, which would have robbed the people present of their sense of belonging, and which would have prevented the mutual orgy which now followed.

The bodies of the participants at this sensational soiree soon formed an incredibly complete whole. They all formed one huge body with an enormous amount of arms, thighs, legs; a great, living thing—breathing, panting, moaning, groaning and sighing out of its many lungs. It offered breasts in all shapes—huge one, pendulous ones, pear-shaped and melon-shaped, dark-skinned and milk white globes, with an equal variety of nipples—from tiny strawberry-red ones to big, jutting firm ones, inviting to be sucked and bitten. Buttocks, cunts, mouths, pricks, and balls in delightful opulence invited the many groping hands and eager mouths. The people who had become this huge thing moving on the enormous bed seemed to consist entirely of semen-filled cunts and mouths, throbbing pricks and slamming bellies. Now rule number two achieved its full, wonderful result. "Everyone for everyone" took on its true meaning.

It would have been impossible not to follow this rule, once caught up in this indescribably wonderful mass of naked and almost naked bodies. It was impossible for any of the participants to avoid the embrace of the nearest neighbor, or to escape from a throbbing prick, a yawning cunt, or the voluptuously grabbing hands of someone.

But then, nobody had the slightest intention of doing such a thing. They did everything in their power to pull as much flesh as they possibly could, to hold as many hands as was bearable and to kiss eagerly the many hungry mouths and tongues. The smell of sweat and semen worked like a powerful aphrodisiac. The groans and cries of the others seemed to spur flagging powers to even greater deeds. The two sisters found themselves now on top and then under many bodies. Sometimes they were pressed against one another and, then again, against another partner. They were in one continual hot embrace, completely entangled. It was a mystery how the various couples, or rather groups, always succeeded in getting loose from each other only to form new connections, new couplings with new partners, trying new and different techniques. They did things, and enjoyed them, which they had hitherto never thought possible.

The most incredible combinations were formed by all these steaming hot bodies! The permeating smells of come, perfume, body odors from armpits, cunts and pricks were unbearably exciting.

Everything was mixed, from the most primitive wild grabs to the most refined techniques. And each deed caused ripples of delight, running the complete gamut from voluptuous desire to gasping climax . . . over and over again. The hot spark would fly from body to body, jumping through the entire group, using the nerves of these people as if they were one single medium.

Whenever on one end of the enormous bed a female body jerked in the spasms of an incredible climax, shuddering as if tortured with unbearable pains, the next moment a body on the other side would groan and jerk, coming equally as ecstatically, as if an electric jolt had passed through the entire mass of bodies in the short span of a single second.

Florentine was no longer pinned down and fucked by the massive, muscular body of Maxim de Berny, and Julia had long since lost Senor Padilla who had had his delights both with her and Dorothy. It seemed that all the male participants of this peculiar soiree at one time or another had deposited their seed in the more than willing laps of Florentine and Julia. The two sisters, who had, so far, lived a chaste life, were reluctant to ever get off their backs.

In the wild group which the guests of Madam Lucy now formed, it was next to impossible to recognize even the most intimate partner of the moment, though the girls tried to identify some of them. But how should they know whose mighty member was pushing and jolting from the back against their sopping cunts? They were thrown across the heaving belly of another, like helpless booty slung across the back of a wild stallion, while at the same time they were trying to swallow someone's throbbing manhood that was trying to impale their widely opened mouths. Julia thought that it must have been young Teeler who was stretched out next to the officer, but her hands were caught, left and right, between their wildly banging bodies, so she could hardly be sure.

And who was working her over with such vehemence? Judging by the technique, and the words he muttered, it must have been Maxim de Berny, who had spent the earlier part of that evening ripping her sister Florentine apart. On the other hand, she suspected that it could be Dorothy who had strapped on her dildo.

There . . . oooh . . . just now . . . Julia had just started to climax and already the jolting prick had squirted into her and was about to pull out of her hotly desiring quim. She was just beginning to feel sorry for herself when suddenly two powerful arms pulled her thighs even wider apart and another throbbing prick penetrated her hospitably moistened grotto . . . how delicious! Her new lover, with renewed vigor, continued the task of replacement, jolting and jarring her wildly shivering insides. She was drowning, floating in voluptuous delights she had never known before. Her wild desire temporarily quieted down with the regular thrusts. Suddenly she felt a pair of hot lips take possession of her tickler, and the head below her formed an exciting buffer for another partner who was giving it to her from behind.

Florentine, on the other side of the bed, stretched out one hand which was just released by one of her partners. There! Wasn't that the heavy club of our insatiable faun? Yes, indeed! And before she fully realized what was happening, it had already pushed itself halfway between her lips. Then, suddenly, Florentine began to bob her head wildly, trying to swallow it all, wanting to have this gorgeous throbbing member deep in her throat. She sucked some precious drops from it and then someone else pushed her greedy mouth aside.

The heavy cylinder, which for a short moment lay there like an orphan upon his belly, disappeared into a wide, very moist opening, barely needing the help of someone's guiding hand. And now, in the place of the soft mouth of Florentine, another, even softer pair of lips encircled the throbbing flesh pole of the elderly gentleman, speeding up and down without stopping.

Florentine was incredibly fascinated to be allowed to witness this variation of coupling, and she tried to give both the heavy prick as well as the encircling lips as much pleasure as she could.

It is impossible to describe the heady atmosphere that ruled the orgy room. The air seemed to boil satanically. Continuous, almost frightening gasps, shrill screams, and tortured sighs filled the air. The silence which now and then fell was even more sinister. And then, suddenly, a thumping rhythm would set in whenever several couples started to hump and fuck each other again. Accompanied by the creaking of the furniture, one could hear fanatical hands slap naked flesh, the rubbing of nude bodies slamming together, and the slurping of voluptuous lips. Now and then could be heard the characteristic sound of a softening penis slipping out of a vagina, or someone's hardened nipples slipping out of puckering lips.

Most characteristic, and also most exciting, were the spontaneous exclamations. Sometimes they were involuntary, while others were said with the specific purpose of giving vent to the wild urge of having everybody take part in the enjoyment of a particular act. Even the rather reticent wife of the Spaniard called out her feelings without shame. While she was busily engaged upon this jolting and shuddering altar of lust and passion, she chanced to come upon her husband. He was just about to attack Laura, the sister of the hostess who herself was engaged in a battle to take on the enormous prick of the blond officer.

The Senora called out in wild ecstasy, "Miguel . . . he screws me delightfully . . . I tell you, his prick is as heavy as the spear of Saint Isidore . . . aaah . . . aaah, darling Miguel, I love it sooo much . . . aaaaah . . . aaaah . . . you, Miguel . . . Miguel . . . I have to . . . please, quick . . . quick! Tell me, darling, are you getting fucked as heavenly as I? Quick . . . quick . . . it . . . is . . . so . . . " Since she started to come at that moment the rest of her confessions stuck in her gurgling throat.

Some of them were less lyrical with their expressions. The redheaded Elinor was positively obscene. Her true character showed itself when she tried to spur her partner, or rather partners, to ever greater efforts.

"Why don't you fuck me harder . . . come on, let me feel that you have a goddamn hard-on in my cunt! I said harder, you dirty son of-a-bitch! Come on, I want to be screwed . . . put it in deeper, harder . . . ball me as if your worthless life depends on it . . . stick it in deeper . . . is, it in? Jesus, I can't even feel your balls slam against my ass . . . faster . . . deeper and quicker. Come on, who can give me a real good fuck? I want to be raped as if you were a bunch of horny cossacks who haven't seen a cunt in years! I don't want you to shove it in like a gentleman . . . ram it up my cunt like a cowboy . . . "

She veritably screamed, foaming at the mouth, "I am horny, so goddamned horny! Isn't there a prick among this damned bunch that knows how to fuck well? Come here with it . . . I'll stick it into my cunt myself . . . quick . . . quicker! Can't you hurry it, come on, fuck me . . . my cunt is burning up . . . Give me that hot dong . . . screw me to pieces . . . shove it up my cunt harder . . . deeper!"

And the raving redhead snatched furiously at the dripping prick of the Spaniard who had just pulled it out of Laura.

"Haaaah . . . here's one that just came . . . boy, did that one come! That's how I want to be screwed . . . come on, you bastards . . . I'm horny, and I want to get fucked . . . by all of you! One prick after the other . . . stick in your dong . . . dammit . . . yeah, that's it . . . one after the other . . . I want to be laid by every goddamned prick in the house . . . deep . . . hard . . . and quick! Hurry, hurry . . . that's it . . . work it in deeper . . . a little bit faster . . . deeper . . . aaaaah, that feels good. Finally I'm beginning to feel good . . . this one fucks me even better . . . come on . . . I . . . want . . . to . . . harder, dammit, deeper . . . a little more . . . aaaah . . . aaaah . . . ooooh! Eeeeek!"

Her voice suddenly gave out, but not because this terribly horny creature had reached a climax, or even found some satisfaction. One of the gentlemen had suddenly put his swollen penis into her opened mouth, penetrating deeply into her throat. This cork effectively stopped this wellspring of Anglo-Saxon lechery.

Days of Thorned Bliss

by M. Orlando

from *The Sleeping Palace*

2

All of the girls were conveyed to their individual bedrooms on the third floor. These chambers had either white plaster walls or were wallpapered with moss green-willow leaf pattern. They had a single bed, chair, washstand, and toilet basin. Each room had one door which could be opened only from the hallway. Soon after Madame Mazan's inspection, the damsels were ordered to strip off their street clothes and scrub themselves clean in the large lavatory. As might be expected, Drosera supervised the entire operation. Their soiled garments were replaced by much finer frocks from Paris and London. Upon returning to their appointed bedchambers, a simple meal and several hours' rest awaited. Drosera reminded them of how obliged they should be to their new mistress for such luxurious provisions. All of this was being done to assure the girls' necessary freshness for receiving their first visitors. In return, excellent behavior and compliance to all that would be asked of them was to be expected if they were to earn the lady's favor.

The first of the luscious nymphs to learn this would be Manuela.

It must have been about mid-afternoon when Drosera directed the olive-skinned beauty to the conservatory on the second floor. A serving tray and tea things had already been arranged neatly on a small table near an oversized wicker chair. She was to serve the dainty repast to a caller who would be arriving in just a moment. While she waited unattended, Manuela admired the stunning marble floor decorated with a mosaic of undulating water lilies. Sunlight beamed softly through the heavy glass of the conservatory's expansive windows to illuminate a collection of unusual plants. Some sprouted ruby leaves in the shape of salt spoons or inkpots, while others had trumpetlike yellow flowers still damp with moisture. Just as Manuela was about to examine another, crowned with a veined purple hood, Drosera led the guest into the room.

The stranger was introduced as Madame Kessels. She was the well-fed, smartly kept wife of a prominent steel tycoon who had grown tired of his marriage. Unknown to her, the rogue husband happened to be a client of the house as well. It was comical how this quarrelsome pair shared the same taste for young feminine backsides in their private moments apart from one another. Sometimes they instinctively selected the very same girl for an hour's delectation! The couple's visits had been carefully arranged never to coincide in order to maintain the double deceit. Before taking her leave, Drosera presented Manuela as a newly trained maid who would instantly fulfill any request given by the older woman. A barely restrained glimmer of lewdness lit Madame Kessels's eyes before she took her place upon the wicker chair.

As soon as the curtained double doors of the conservatory were secured, Manuela was ordered to pour the tea. She froze for a moment before moving haltingly toward the steaming pot. A life of libertine pleasure had certainly not prepared the wanton for this simple task. Luckily, Manuela did quite well and managed to fill the delicate cup with the hot liquid without disaster. But then Madame Kessels called for the three-tiered tray of dainty sandwiches and petits fours. This time Fate was not with Manuela. She stumbled slightly, accidentally flinging one of the small cakes directly onto the marble floor at the matron's feet.

Blushing, Manuela knelt to retrieve the smashed confection. While she was scooping up the cake, she felt Madame Kessels stroke the length of her ebony hair. Rearing back in alarm, she almost dropped the entire tea tray. The feverish glow had now returned to the woman's eyes as she grimaced and commanded Manuela to compose herself and stand at attention. Obeying this demand, the nymph waited anxiously for what she guessed would follow.

The blunt hands of Madame Kessels began a thorough examination of her voluptuous prey. They smoothed the blouson so taut that the ruddy tips of the girl's breasts could be seen through the fabric. Moaning softly, the woman suckled each one until they became hardened points of wine velvet. Madame Kessels decided that the interfering garment should no longer imprison such lovely charms, so Manuela was told to remove it. The sight of the exposed buds incited the woman to seize them between her teeth once more. Manuela gasped as her sensitized nipples were vexed almost beyond endurance by the relentless tongue-twiddling and nipping. As the famished woman nursed one of the salty orbs, she fondled the other incessantly. This went on for some time before Madame Kessels fell back into the creaking chair. After catching her breath and taking a sip of tea, she ordered Manuela to take off the rest of her outfit.

Getting into the spirit of the scene, the Spanish wanton slithered out of her skirt and low boots with deliberate ease. This sultry performance quickened the heart of the lecherous gentlewoman, who licked her lips in appreciation. Grasping the minx before her, Madame Kessels pulled the girl's nude hips in for a closer view of their thatched vortex. Then she impaled the tight opening with an extended digit. The gentle frigging raised an itch in the girl's belly in no time. Manuela's eyelids began to flutter and she bit her lower lip as the chafing became more insistent. Now the frigging became an infernal assault, peppered with fierce tugs and pinches of her inflamed cuntspur. Finally, Manuela cried out as she reached her crisis on the well-greased fingers of her captor. But there would not be any collapsing in sweet relief allowed here! For as soon as the pangs of bliss expired, Manuela was pushed to the floor and made to kneel before the wicker chair.

With an obscene grin, Madame Kessels raised her heavy skirts before the girl. Manuela was startled to discover that so dignified a lady wore no knickers at all. Then in very direct terms, the woman told her that she must perform the same act just done to her. But instead of a probing finger, Manuela must insert her tongue.

Manuela leaned forward on all fours as the society wife spread her legs wider. For a woman of her age, Madame Kessels still possessed a succulent vagina, which she scented heavily with eau de cologne. A further surprise came when the skirts were thrown back over the crouching girl's head once she was in the proper position. With a mouth well-exercised on more youthful morsels, Manuela was able to manage an expert licking and tickling of the glossy-haired slit. The lustful matron ground herself harder into the lapping maw until she sighed deeply in ecstasy.

Believing her duties at an end, Manuela retreated from

beneath the tented loins. But instead, Madame Kessels had her clear the tray from the small table and put herself in its place. Her arms and legs were to hang downward so her trim belly would remain pressed atop the flat surface. Manuela was shifted slightly forward, causing the tensed rounds of her backside to split that much farther apart. Then Madame Kessels knelt on one knee and wrapped an arm around the girl's waist to steady her on the table.

Now the grand lady had finally found her paradise at the fleshy gateway of the girl's stretched anus. Stooping precariously in her elegant finery, the woman's pallid lips quivered against the cool bottomflesh during this memorable teatime dalliance. With her other hand, she carefully delved into the tender buttocks—fingering, teasing, and trifling with the humid gap. Then she found and tickled its most hidden, pinkish nub. Manuela groaned beneath this depraved scrutiny as the length of her ebony hair swept the marble floor back and forth. Insane with desire, Madame Kessels whispered mad protestations of undying devotion to the vertical cleft, beseeching the ivory sphinx to give up its mystical secrets. This went on until her stinging tears splashed the unblemished opening.

Suddenly—without warning—the delirious woman retrieved one of the cone-shaped pastries from the nearby tray and forced it into the snug hole. Manuela tried to twist her head around to see what was being done to her. At least she was wise enough not to attempt escape.

But just then, Manuela's wriggling and the vigorousness of the bumwise feeding caused the cake to expel its lemon cream. Of course, this was the exact plan of the libidinous gourmand. Madame Kessels bent to the challenge of this delightful epicurean task. With the point of her tongue, she rapturously cleansed the arse of every trace of the sugary confection. And the demanding woman did not declare herself fully satisfied until she lingered quite awhile between its pert globes.

The woman returned to the chair, allowing the disheveled lass to fetch her a finger bowl of scented water. The girl looked on as Madame Kessels proceeded to neaten herself as if she had partaken in nothing more unconventional than the ritual of afternoon tea. With impeccable timing, Drosera appeared to escort the lady from the conservatory. The moment she left, Omar entered from a side doorway leading to the service staircase built behind the grand stairwell. He laughed heartily at the obvious cause of Manuela's unkempt state. Now it was his turn to sit in the wicker chair. He had noted the pretty ring upon Manuela's finger—the one given her by the strange lady in the café. He pried it from her finger at once. For the good part of the next hour, the girl had to suckle his thickly veined phallus before she was locked in her chamber again.

As Drosera led the bottom-fancier from the conservatory, they met Madame Mazan and a distinguished gentleman on the massive stairway of the main hall. As their paths crossed, the arse-loving matron and the dapper man nodded politely to one another in silent recognition. Monsieur Du Mortier was an extremely wealthy lace manufacturer and a highly respected figure in the city. As a rule, it was uncommon to see Madame Mazan at all, but rarer still to witness her grinning with such lighthearted abandon. Du Mortier must have been an old acquaintance because they ascended arm in arm to the fourth-floor seclusion of her private residence. A congratulatory snippet was overheard in which she commended the steely-haired rake for having a handsome son. Not missing an opportunity, the man proclaimed the lady was lovelier still than at the time of their first meeting. Just below the cobalt and ruby glass dome, a set of gleaming cypre[illegible] The couple could be heard no [illegible] chamber on a lower level had alrea[illegible] Within were Du Mortier's anxious boy a[illegible] ready to induct him into the mysteries of the [illegible]

Gerard's initiation was about to take place [illegible] roundings. Gauzy green draperies fell to the floo[illegible] large bow window, affording the lovers privacy duri[illegible] intimate ceremony. At first, the eager buck thought himself alone as the door was shut behind him. Once his searching eyes adjusted to the half-light, they discovered a vision of alluring fascination several paces before him. At his request, the lad had been promised a novice equally inexperienced in the art of pleasure. But, wisely, his father had decided upon Colette. The little harlot could play the part of the guileless waif while still teaching the boy something of lasting usefulness. From beneath a crop of auburn hair, she blinked cautiously up at him from the edge of a chaise longue in the center of the room. Gerard straightened his tie and coughed once into a clenched fist. The two stared at each other for several interminable minutes before Colette patted the striped cushion next to her.

Of course, Gerard had previous experience with several girls before this arranged visit. But these brief unsatisfactory gropings had resulted in nothing more successful than torn bodices and stained trousers. Finally accepting the invitation, he sat next to Colette and gathered enough courage to place a slightly shaking hand onto her knee. The coy nymph was more than attractive, garbed in a chemise with a faded blossom design and matching slippers of rosy silk. Shrewdly, she covered his hand with her own and pressed downward. Immediately, the stiffness between Gerard's legs leaped a bit as he sensed the heat of her slender body yearning for him.

[illegible] her suitor to turn and kiss her full on the [illegible] the process, he knocked his teeth against Colette's, [illegible] this clumsy effort did little to deter his rising passion. In no time, his tongue found a receptive mate as his hands encircled her tiny waist Their swirling kisses were accompanied by mutual squeezings and rubbings until Colette firmly gripped his straining prick through the coarse fabric of his pants.

Until this moment, Gerard had been unaccustomed to such a fearless advance. He gasped for air and almost drew back when Colette stood before him. Panicking she might halt in her rousing progress, he reached for the girl as she took one step farther away. Then a sly smile formed on her pouty lips as she reached behind to untie the flowered chemise. Gerard's face blushed crimson as the gossamer folds spilled about her delicate feet.

The faux Venus posed in her pale nudity before her wide-eyed paramour. Ever so slowly, Colette's hands fluttered about her tight breasts and began to tweak their pink nipples until they became swollen points. Then one hand abandoned a teat to find its way down along her slender belly to the thin track of reddish split-fleece below. Gerard was now in a state of such fervid wonder that it would take but a warm sigh upon his near-bursting organ to set its white honey gushing forth. But the clever imp had other plans for the threatening release.

Colette drew her legs apart and spread back the dewy slit with two fingers. Now with her other hand, she began to brush the opening with a gentle, rhythmic frigging. The lad broke a sweat and began to open and close his parched mouth as he watched in dumb amazement Then without warning, Colette began to cry out as she reached her first crisis by exasperating the inflamed spur of her cunt. Without even knowing it, Gerard had been moaning aloud in sympathy with her all the while. Now the cunning trollop dropped to her knees before the breathless boy. As Colette busied herself at his crotch, his damp palms supported him as he leaned back upon the striped cushion.

In a flash, the bone-hard prick sprang from its prison and into the smooth wetness of the girl's mouth. To be sure, Gerard was beyond questioning his sweetheart's naïveté as her lips ran up and down his throbbing root. But to any observant voyeur who might be enjoying the scene from the chamber's several peepholes, the young bitch had worked on more than a few tools in her time. In fact, she knew just when to withdraw the dripping member before it was too late. For the next few moments, she did not dare touch it. Instead, she anointed his down-covered balls with sweet kisses before sucking each one in turn. After subduing Gerard's urgency in this way several times, she stood and allowed his greedy mouth to toy with her breasts and their raised nipples.

Now he was ready for the next phase of his ravishment.

Before Gerard knew what was happening, Colette straddled him on the chaise longue. At the same time, she managed to embed his still-rigid penis between the lips of her sex. The boy almost swooned when he realized just where his cock was firmly nestled. Fortunately, he had followed Colette's example by wrapping his arms around his teacher. Now the capable seductress began to raise and lower herself ever so slowly on her mount. Gerard's eyes closed in ecstasy as he defiled a cunt other than the ones haunting his daydreams. The vigorous ride went on until Colette sensed they were near the breaking point of his passion. Only then did she pull herself off the frenzied lad.

Imagine Gerard's dismay at losing the game so close to its conclusion. But his anger changed to delighted confusion when the nymph turned her back on him, reached between her legs for the tensed phallus, and slid herself down upon it! The boy grunted as his penis was engulfed in the unexpected tightness of her tailhole. Thrilled by this novel sensation, he clapped his hands to Colette's hips and took command of the furious buggery himself. In fact, Gerard met the challenge with such instinctive ease that he kept the girl impaled in this way for longer than even she thought him able to hold out. Then with a loud howl, his burning seed shot upward into her adorable arse. Gerard would not let Colette off her post until her bottom pulled every last droplet of lust from him.

Since this intimate idyll had taken such an obscene turn for the lad, he quickly neatened himself by the washstand in hurried silence. Never having had the opportunity to thank a young lady for the vigorous use of her posterior, he was simply lost for words. Instead, he nodded politely, adjusted his tie once more, and knocked on the door as he had been instructed to do when he had finished with the lesson. He gazed at the locked entrance, shifting from one foot to the other, until Drosera saved him from further embarrassment. Later, the boy was collected by his smiling father in the conservatory. Du Mortier embraced his son proudly as the two were led down to the great beechwood doors with their lily-shaped lock. Now it was on to the Hotel Belle Vue for a congratulatory dinner and then for a game of billiards.

It was while their four-wheeled carriage was traveling up the avenue Louise that Du Mortier imparted a curious tidbit to the still-flushed lad. The older man was damnably perplexed at how Madame Mazan had not really changed at all in so many years. But his son hardly cared or listened to the hushed tones of the confounded man. For visions of pert bottoms, crying out for his hardened rod, floated before the boy's dreamy eyes.

from

MAN WITH A MAID

by Anonymous

7

I produced a large bottle of champagne, and pretending that the opener was in my alcove I went there—but my real objective was to satisfy in Fanny the raging concupiscence which my torturing of Alice and then Connie had so fiercely aroused in me.

I found her shivering with unsatisfied hot lust. I threw myself into a chair, placed my bottom on the edge and pointed to my prick in glorious erection. Instantly Fanny straddled across me, brought her excited cunt to bear on my tool and impaled herself on it with deliciously voluptuous movements, sinking down on it till she rested on my thighs, her arms round my neck, mine round her warm body, our lips against each other's; then working herself divinely up and down on my prick, she soon brought on the blessed relief we both were thirsting for—and in exquisite rapture we spent madly.

"Oh! Sir! Wasn't it lovely!" she whispered as soon as she could speak.

"Which, Fanny?" I asked mischievously. "This!—or that!" pointing to the room.

She blushed prettily, then whispered saucily: "Both, Sir!" as she passionately kissed me.

I begged of her to sponge me while I opened the champagne, which she did sweetly, kissing my flaccid prick lovingly, as soon as she had removed all traces of our bout of fucking from it. I poured out four large glasses and made her drink one (which she did with great enjoyment)—then took the other three out with me to the girls.

I found them still in each other's arms and coiled together in the large arm-chair, Alice half-sitting on Connie's thighs and half resting on Connie's breasts, a lovely sight. I touched her, she started up, while Connie slowly opened her eyes.

"Drink, it will pull you together!" I said, handing each a tumbler. They did so, and the generous wine seemed to have an immediate good effect and to put new life into them. I eyed them with satisfaction, then raising my glass said: "To your good healths, dears—and a delicious consummation of Connie's charming and most sporting suggestion!" then gravely emptied my tumbler. Both girls turned scarlet, Connie almost angrily—they glanced tentatively at each other but neither spoke.

To terminate their embarrassment, I pointed to a settee close by, and soon we arranged ourselves on it, I in the centre, Alice on my right, and Connie on my left, their heads resting on my shoulders, their faces turned towards each other and within easy kissing distance, my arms clasping them to me, my hands being just able to command the outer breast of each! Both girls seemed ill at ease; I think Connie was really so, as she evidently dreaded having to be fucked by me, but with Alice it was only a pretense.

"A penny for your thoughts, dear!" I said to her chafingly, curious to know what she would say.

"I was thinking how lovely Connie is, naked!" she murmured softly, blushing prettily. I felt a quiver run through Connie.

"Before to-day, how much of each other have you seen?" I asked interestedly. Silently both girls pointed to just above their breasts.

"Then stand up, Connie dear, and let us have a good look at you," I said, "and Alice shall afterwards return the compliment by showing you herself! Stand naturally, with your hands behind you."

With evident unwillingness she complied, and with pretty bashfulness she faced us, a naked blue-eyed daughter of the gods, tall, slender, golden-haired, exquisite—blushing as she noted in our eyes the pleasure the contemplation of her naked charms was giving us!

"Now in profile, dear!"

Obediently she turned. We delightedly noted her exquisite outline from chin to thigh, her proud little breasts, her gently curving belly, its wealth of golden-brown hair, standing out like a bush at its junction with her thighs, the sweep of her haunches and bottom, and her shapely legs!

"Thanks, darling," I said appreciatively. "Now Alice!" And drawing Connie onto my knees, I kissed her lovingly.

Blushingly Alice complied, and with hands clasped behind her back she faced us, a piquant, provoking, demure, brown-eyed, dark-haired little English lassie, plump, juicy, appetising. She smiled mischievously at me as she watched Connie's eyes wander approvingly over her delicious little figure!

"Now in profile, please!"

She turned, and now we realized the subtle voluptuousness of Alice's naked figure, how her exquisitely full and luscious breasts were matched, in turn being balanced by her glorious fleshy bottom and her fat thighs, the comparative shortness of her legs only adding piquancy to the whole; while her unusually conspicuous Mont Venus, with its tousle of dark, clustering, silky hairs, proudly proclaiming itself as the delightful centre of her attractions!

"Thanks, darling!" we both exclaimed admiringly as we drew her to us and lovingly kissed her, to her evident delight and gratification.

"Now, Connie darling!" I said. "I want you to lie down on that couch!" And I removed my arm from her waist to allow her to rise.

"No, Jack!" she begged piteously and imploringly, her lovely eyes not far from tears, "*please,* Jack! . . . Don't insist!"

"You must do it, darling!" I said kindly but firmly as I raised her to her feet. "Come, dear!" and I led her to the couch and made her lie down.

"I must put the straps on you, Connie, dear," I said, "not that I doubt your promise, but because I am sure you won't be able to lie still! Don't be frightened, dear!" I added, as I saw a look of terror come over her face, "you are not going to be tortured, or tickled, or hurt, but will be treated most sweetly!"

Reluctantly Connie yielded. Quickly Alice attached the straps to her wrists, while I secured the other pair to her ankles; we set the machinery to work and soon she was lying flat on her back, her hands and feet secured to the four corners—the dark-brown upholstery throwing into high relief her lovely figure and dazzling fair hair and skin! I then blindfolded her very carefully in such a way that she could not get rid of the bandage by rubbing her head against the couch; and now that Connie was at our mercy, I signalled to Fanny, who gleefully rushed to us noiselessly and hugged her mistress with silent delight.

"Now, Alice, dear!" I said, "make love to Connie!"

"Oh-h!" cried Connie in shocked surprise, blushing so hotly that even her bosom was suffused with colour. But Alice was already on her knees by Connie's side and was passionately kissing her protesting mouth in the exuberance of her delight at the arrival at last of the much desired opportunity to satisfy on Connie's lovely person, cunt against cunt, her lascivious desires and concupiscence.

I slipped into a chair and took Fanny on my knees, and in sweet companionship, we settled ourselves down comfortably to watch Alice make love to Connie! My left arm was round Fanny's waist, the hand toying with the breasts which it could just command—while my right hand played lovingly with her cunt.

After Alice had relieved her excited feelings by showering her kisses on Connie's lips with whispered fond endearments, she raised her head and contemplated, with an expression of intense delight, the naked figure of her friend which I had placed at her disposal! Then she proceeded to pass her hands lightly over Connie's flesh. Shakespeare sings (substituting the feminine pronoun for the masculine one he uses):

> To win her heart she touched her here and there,
> Touches so soft that conquer chastity!

This is what Alice was doing! With lightly poised hands, she touched Connie on the most susceptible parts of herself—her armpits, navel, belly, and especially the soft tender insides of her thighs—evidently reserving for special attention her breasts and cunt. Soon the effect on Connie became apparent—her bosom began to palpitate in sweet agitation, while significant tremors ran through her limbs. "Is it so nice then, darling?" cooed Alice, her eyes dancing with delight as she watched the effect of her operations on Connie's now quivering person; then she rested her lips on Connie's and gently took hold of her breasts!

"Oh, Alice!" cried Connie—but Alice closed her lips with her own, half choking her friend with her passionate kisses.

Then raising her head again, she eagerly and delightedly inspected the delicious morsels of Connie's flesh that were imprisoned in her hands. "Oh, you darlings!" she exclaimed as she squeezed them. "You sweet things!" as she kissed them rapturously. "Oh, what dear little nipples!" she cried, taking them in turn into her mouth, her hands all the while squeezing and caressing Connie's lovely breasts till she faintly murmured: "Oh, stop, darling!"

"Oh, my love! Was I hurting you, darling?" cried Alice with gleaming eyes, as with a smile full of mischief towards us, she reluctantly released Connie's breasts. For a moment she hesitated as if uncertain what to do next—then her eyes rested on Connie's cunt, so sweetly defenceless; an idea seemed to seize her—with a look of delicious anticipation, she slipped her left arm under Connie's shoulders so as to embrace her, placed her lips on Connie's mouth, extended her right arm—and without giving Connie the least hint as to her intentions, she placed her hand on Connie's cunt, her slender forefinger resting on the orifice itself!

"Oh-h, Alice!" cried Connie, taken completely by surprise and wriggling voluptuously. "Oh-h-h, Connie!" rapturously murmured Alice, between the hot kisses she was now raining on Connie's mouth—her forefinger beginning to agitate itself inquisitively but lovingly! "Oh, darling! Your cunny is sweet! Sweet!" she murmured as her hand wandered all over Connie's private parts, now stroking and pressing her delicate Mont Venus, now twisting and pulling her hairs, now gently compressing the soft, springy flesh between her thumb and forefinger, now passing along the delicate shell pink lips, and finally gently inserting her finger between them into the pouting orifice! "I must! . . . I must look at it!" Quickly she withdrew her arm from under Connie's shoulders, gave her a long, clinging kiss, then shifted her position by Connie's side, till her head commanded Connie's private parts; then she squared her arms, rested herself on Connie's belly, and with both hands proceeded to examine and study Connie's cunt, her eyes sparkling with delight.

Again she submitted Connie's delicious organ of sex to a most searching and merciless examination, one hand on each side of the now slightly gaping slit, stroking, squeezing, pressing, touching! Then with fingers poised gently but firmly on each side of the slit, Alice gently drew the lips apart and peered curiously into the shell-pink cavity of Connie's cunt—and after a prolonged inspection, she shifted her finger rather higher, again parted the lips and with rapt attention she gazed at Connie's clitoris which was now beginning to show signs of sexual excitement, Connie all this time quivering and wriggling under the touches of Alice's fingers.

Her curiosity apparently satisfied for the time, Alice raised her head and looked strangely and interrogatively at me. Comprehending her mute enquiry, I smiled and nodded. She smiled back, then dropping her head, she looked intently at Connie's cunt, and imprinted a long clinging kiss in its very centre.

Connie squirmed violently. "Oh-h-h!" she ejaculated in a half-strangled voice. With a smile of intense, delight, Alice repeated her kiss, then again and again, Connie at each repetition squirming and wriggling in the most delicious way, her vehement plunging telling Alice what flames her hot kisses had aroused in Connie.

Again she opened Connie's cunt, and keeping its tender lips wide apart she deposited between them and right inside the orifice itself a long lingering kiss which seemed to set Connie's blood on fire, for she began to plunge wildly with furious upward jerks and jogs of her hips and bottom, nearly dislodging Alice. She glanced merrily at us, her eyes brimming with mischief and delight, then straddled across Connie and arranged herself on her, so that her mouth commanded Connie's cunt, while her stomach rested on Connie's breasts and her cunt lay poised over Connie's mouth, but not touching it. Her legs now lay parallel to Connie's arms and outside them.

Utterly taken aback by Alice's tactics, and in her innocence not recognizing the significance of the position Alice had assumed on her, she cried, "Oh, Alice! What are you doing?" Alice grinned delightedly at us, then lowered her head, ran her tongue lightly half a dozen times along the lips of Connie's cunt and then set to work to gamahuche her!

"Oh-h-h!" shrieked Connie, her voice almost strangled by the violence of the wave of lust that swept over her at the first touch of Alice's tongue. "Oh-h-h! . . . Oh-h-h . . ." she ejaculated in her utter bewilderment and confusion as she abandoned herself to strangely intoxicating and thrilling sensations hitherto unknown to her, jerking herself upwards as if to meet Alice's tongue, her face in her agitated movements coming against Alice's cunt, before it dawned on her confused senses what the warm, moist, quivering hairy object could be! In wild excitement Alice thoroughly searched Connie's cunt with her active fingers, darting deeply in it, playing delicately on the quivering lips, sucking and tickling her clitoris—and sending Connie into such a state of lust that I thought it wise to intervene.

"Stop, dear!" I called out to Alice, who at once desisted, looking interrogatively at me. "You are trying her too much! Get off her now, dear, and let her recover herself a little—or you'll finish her, which we don't want yet!" Quickly comprehending the danger, Alice rolled off Connie, turned round, contemplated for a moment Connie's naked wriggling figure, then got onto her again, only this time lips to lips, bubbies against bubbies, and cunt against cunt; she clasped Connie closely to her as she arranged herself, murmuring passionately: "Oh, Connie! . . . At last! . . . At last! . . ." then commenced to rub her cunt sweetly on Connie's.

"Oh-h-h, Alice!" breathed Connie rapturously as she responded to Alice's efforts by heaving and jogging herself upwards: "Oh-h-h . . . darling!!" she panted brokenly, evidently feeling her ecstasy approaching by the voluptuous wriggles and agitated movements, as Alice now was rubbing herself vigorously against her cunt with riotous down-strokes of her luscious bottom. Quicker and quicker, faster and faster, wilder and wilder became the movements of both girls, Connie now plunging madly upwards, while Alice rammed herself down on her with fiercer and fiercer thrusts of her raging hips and buttocks—till the delicious crisis arrived! "Connie! . . . Connie!" gasped Alice, as the indescribable spasm of spending thrilled voluptuously through her. "Ah-h-h . . . ah-h-h! . . . AH-H-H! . . ." ejaculated Connie rapturously, as she spent madly in exquisite convulsions! dead to everything but the delirious rapture that was thrilling through her as she lay tightly clasped in Alice's clinging arms!

The sight was too much for Fanny! With the intensest interest, she had watched the whole of this exciting scene, parting her legs the better to accommodate my hand which now was actually grasping her cunt, my forefinger buried in her up to the knuckle, while my thumb rested on her clitoris—and she had already spent once deliciously. But the spectacle of the lascivious transports of her mistress on Connie set her blood on fire again: she recollected her similar experience in Alice's arms, the sensations that Alice's cunt communicated to hers, the delicious ecstasy of her discharge—and as the two girls neared their bliss, she began to agitate herself voluptuously on my knees, on my now active finger, keeping pace with them—till with an inarticulate murmur of, "Oh! . . . Oh-h, Sir-r," she inundated my hand with her love-juice, spending simultaneously with her mistress and her mistress's friend.

As soon as she emerged from her ecstatic trance, I whispered to her inaudibly: "Bring the sponge and towel, dear!"

Noiselessly she darted off, sponged herself, then returned with a bowl of water, a sponge, and a towel just as Alice slowly raised herself off Connie, with eyes still humid with lust and her cunt bedewed with love-juice. I took her fondly in my arms and kissed her tenderly, while Fanny quickly removed all traces of her discharge from her hairs, then proceeded to pay the same delicate attention to Connie, whose cunt she now touched for the first time.

Presently we heard Connie murmur: "Mayn't I get up now, Jack?"

"Not yet, darling!" I replied lovingly as I stooped and kissed her. "You have to make me happy now!"

"No, Jack! Please," she whispered, but Alice intervened. "Yes, darling, you must let Jack have you! You must taste again the real article," she cooed. "Let me work you into condition again!" And she signalled to Fanny, who instantly knelt by Connie and began playing with her dainty little breasts and feeling her cunt, her eyes sparkling with delight at thus being permitted to handle Connie—who not noting the difference of touch (as Fanny's ministrations to her cunt had accustomed Connie to her fingers) lay still in happy ignorance of the change of operator!

Soon Fanny's fingers began to bring about the desired recovery; Connie's breasts began to stiffen and grow tense, her body began to tremble in gentle agitation. She was ready—and so was I!

Without a word I slipped onto her. "Oh, Jack!" she murmured as I took her into my arms, holding up her lips to be kissed—no reluctance now! My rampant prick found her sweet hole and gently effected an entrance; she was terribly tight, but her discharge had well-lubricated the sweet passage into her interior, and inch by inch, I forced myself into her till my prick was buried in her cunt, she trembling and quivering in my clasp, her involuntary flinchings and sighs confessing the pain attending her penetration! But once she had admitted me into her and I began the sweet up-and-down movement, she went into transports of delight, accommodating herself deliciously to me as, with lips closely against each other, we exchanged hot kisses! Then I set to work to fuck Connie in earnest. Straining her to me, till her breasts were flattened against my chest and I could feel every flutter of her sweet body, I let myself go, ramming into her faster and faster, more and more wildly—till unable any longer to restrain myself, I surrendered to love's delicious ecstasy and spent madly into Connie just as she flooded my prick in rapturous bliss, quivering under me in the most voluptuous way!

We lay closely clasped together, till our mutual ecstatic trance slowly died away, then with a sign I bade Fanny disappear. As soon as she had vanished, Alice removed the bandage from Connie's eyes. As they met mine, bashfully and shamefacedly, blushing deeply at thus finding herself naked in my arms, Connie timidly held up her mouth to me—instantly my lips were on hers and we exchanged long lingering kisses till we panted for breath. Gently I released her from my clasp and rose off her and with Alice's help unfastened her, and Alice gently led her away to her alcove where she sedulously attended to her, while Fanny silently but delightedly did the same for me.

It was now four o'clock only—we had a good hour before us. There was now no possible doubt that Connie had surrendered herself to the pleasures of Tribadism and Lesbian love as far as Alice was concerned. So when the girls rejoined me,

Connie with a tender look on her face, and we had refreshed ourselves and recovered our sexual appetites and powers, I said to Connie: "Now, dear, you are entitled to take your revenge on Alice—will you . . . ?"

She cast a look of love at Alice, who blushed sweetly, then turning to me she murmured, "Please, Jack!" at the same time giving me a delicious kiss.

"Come along, Alice!" I said as we all rose, and I led her to the couch—the veritable Altar of Venus. "How will you have her, Connie?" I asked, as Alice stood nervously awaiting the disposal of her sweet person.

Connie blushed, then with a glance at Alice, she replied: "Tie her down, Jack, just as you did me!"

Blushingly Alice lay down, and soon Connie and I had her fastened down in the desired position.

"Will you have her blindfolded, dear?" I enquired.

Connie hesitated, looking oddly at Alice—then replied, "No, Jack! I want to see her eyes!" so significantly that Alice involuntarily quivered as she coloured hotly again.

"May I do just whatever I like to Alice, Jack?" asked Connie almost hesitatingly with a fresh access of colour. "Anything in reason, dear!" I replied with a smile. "You mustn't bite her bubbies off, or stitch up her cunt, for instance." Alice quivered while Connie laughed. "And you must leave her alive, for I am to follow you!" ("Oh, Jack!" exclaimed Alice at this intimation, blushing prettily.)

Connie turned eagerly to me. "Are you going to fuck her?" she asked with sparkling eyes. I nodded, smiling at her eagerness.

"And may I watch you?" she demanded.

"Why, certainly, dear—and perhaps help me! Now what are you going to do to Alice? See how impatiently she is waiting!"

Both girls laughed, Alice a trifle uneasily. Connie looked

intently at her for a moment, then seating herself by Alice's side, she began playing with Alice's breasts, keeping her eyes steadily fixed on Alice's.

"Your bubbies are too big for my hands, darling!" she said presently, as she stooped to kiss her. "But they are lovely!" And she squeezed them tenderly for a while—then she deserted them, shifting her position and began to feel Alice's cunt, which she lovingly stroked and caressed.

"Your cunny is fat, darling!" she exclaimed presently with heightened colour as she held Alice's cunt compressed between her finger and thumb and gently squeezed the soft springy flesh, while Alice squirmed involuntarily.

Suddenly Connie leant forward, took Alice's face in her hands and whispered: "Darling, I'm going to fuck you twice, eh?" and lovingly kissed her while Alice's eyes sought mine shamefully.

Quickly Connie got onto Alice, took her into her arms, then keeping her hand raised so as to look right into Alice's eyes, she began to rub her cunt against Alice's, gently and slowly at first with a circular grinding sort of movement; presently her action quickened, then became more and more irregular. Soon Connie was rubbing herself up and down Alice's cunt, with quick agitated strokes of her bottom, all the while intently watching Alice's eyes as if to gauge her friend's sensations. Soon both girls began to plunge and heave riotously, Alice especially, as they both felt crisis approaching—then came a veritable storm of confused heavings, thrustings, and plungings. "Kiss . . . me . . . darling?" ejaculated Alice, now on the verge of spending. But Connie only shook her head with a loving smile, rammed her cunt against Alice's fiercely, intent on Alice's now humid eyes, and apparently restraining her own discharge! A frantic heave from Alice—"Ah-h-h, darling," she gasped as her eyes half closed in ecstasy—then she spent with delicious quivering. Immediately Connie glued her lips to Alice's, agitated herself rapidly against Alice's cunt. "Al-ice!" she breathed in her delirious frenzy, a spasm thrilled through her, and Alice's cunt received her love-juice as she spent ecstatically.

For some moments the girls lay silent, only half conscious, motionless save for the involuntary thrills that shot through them. Then Connie raised her head and with the smile of the victor surveyed Alice, whose eyes now began to open languidly. She blushed deliciously as she met Connie's glances and raised her mouth as if inviting a kiss. Instantly Connie complied with passionate delight. "Was it nice, darling?" I heard her whisper. "Oh, Connie, just heavenly!" murmured Alice tenderly and with loving kisses. "Are you ready again, darling?" whispered Connie eagerly. "Yes! Yes!" replied Alice softly, beginning to agitate herself under Connie.

"Our mouths together this time, darling, eh!" whispered Connie excitedly. "Don't stop kissing me, darling!" she added tenderly as she responded to Alice's significant movements under her and set to work to rub her cunt against Alice's. Soon both girls were hard at work with their cunts squeezed against each other, slit to slit, clitoris against clitoris—Connie's bottom and hips swaying and oscillating voluptuously while Alice jerked herself up madly. With mouths glued to each other they plunged, curvetted, wriggled, squirmed, till the blissful ecstasy overtook them both simultaneously, when madly they bedewed each other with their love juice to the accompaniment of the most exquisite quiverings and thrillings, utterly absorbed in rapture!

With a deep-drawn sigh of intense satisfaction, Connie presently rose slowly off Alice, and tenderly contemplated her as she lay still fastened by her widely extended limbs to the four corners of the couch, her closed eyes and her involuntary tremors indicating that she was still tasting bliss. Then Connie turned to me and whispered rapturously: "Oh, Jack, she is sweet!" I kissed her lovingly and resting her on my knees, I sponged and dried her, then begged her to perform the same office to Alice, whose cunt was positively glistening with her own and Connie's spendings. As soon as Alice felt the sponge at work, she dreamily opened her eyes, and on recognizing me she made as if to rise: but when she found herself checked by her fastenings and realized that she was now to be fucked by me, she smiled somewhat uneasily as our eyes met—for often as she had tasted love's ecstasy in my arms, she had invariably been free; now she was tied down in such a way as to be absolutely helpless, and in this equivocal position, she had to accommodate herself to me and to satisfy my lustful passions and desires. But I smiled encouragingly back to her, seated myself by her side, and tenderly embracing her defenceless body, I whispered: "Darling, may I have you like this?"

Her eyes beamed gratefully on me, full of love; she was now perfectly happy because I had left it to her to say whether or not she would be fucked while tied down in the most shamelessly abandoned attitude that any girl could be placed in. So with love's own light in her shining eyes and with pretty blushes on her cheeks, Alice whispered back tenderly, "Yes, darling, yes!"

Promptly I got on her, took her in my arms, and gently drove my prick home up her cunt. "Do you like it like this, darling?" I murmured softly. "Shall I go on?" She nodded sweetly, our lips met, and I began to fuck her.

Tied down as she was, she was simply delicious! I had had first Fanny and then Connie in precisely the same attitude, but voluptuous as was the act of fucking them so, the pleasure fell short of what I was now tasting! To a certain extent both

Fanny and Connie were unwilling recipients of my erotic favours—Fanny was really ravished and Connie practically so, and their movements under me were the outcome of fright, shame, and even pain; but Alice was yielding herself sweetly to my caprices and was doing her best to accommodate her captive body to my movements. Perhaps this was the reason her little plump rounded figure suited the attitude better than the taller and more slender forms of Fanny and Connie—but whatever may have been the reason, the result was undeniable, and Alice fucked as a helpless captive was simply delicious! Her double spend under Connie made her usual quick response to love's demands arrive more slowly than was customary with her; and as this was my fourth course that afternoon, our fucking was protracted to a delicious extent, and I adopted every method and variation known to me to intensify our exquisite pleasure.

Commencing slowly, I fucked Alice with long strokes, drawing my prick nearly out of her cunt and then shoving it well home again, a procedure which always delighted her and which she welcomed with appreciative and warm kisses. Then I agitated myself more rapidly on her, shoving, pressing, thrusting, ramming, now fast, now slow, holding her so tightly clasped that her breasts were flattened against my chest—while she, panting and gasping, plunged, wriggled and heaved herself wildly under me, in her loyal endeavours to cooperate with me to bring about love's ecstasy. Presently she thrilled exquisitely under me! Fired by her delicious transports, I redoubled my efforts, as did she also—I began to feel my seminal resources respond to my demand on them; soon we both were overtaken by the tempestuous prelude to the blissful crisis—and then came the exquisite consummation of our wildly sexual desires! With a half-strangled, "Ah-h . . . Jack!" Alice spent in rapturous convulsions just as I madly shot into her my boiling tribute!

Oblivious to everything but the delicious satisfaction of our overwrought feelings, we lay as if in a trance! We were roused by Connie's gentle warning voice, "Alice! . . . Alice! . . . Alice, dear!" as she set to work to undo Alice's fastenings. Taking the hint, I rose after giving Alice a long lingering parting kiss, then we helped her to get up and Connie tenderly took her off at once to the girl's alcove, while I retired to mine—where Fanny deliciously attended to me, her eyes sparkling with gratified pleasure at the recollection of the voluptuous spectacle she had been permitted to witness through the peep-hole.

As it was getting late, we all dressed ourselves, and after a tender parting, I put Connie and Alice into a taxi and started them off home. On returning to my room, I found Fanny ready to depart. She was full of delighted gratitude to me for having managed that she should see all that went on and also have a share in the afternoon's proceedings; and when I slipped a couple of sovereigns into her hand, I had the greatest difficulty to make her accept them. Finally she did so, saying shyly and with pretty blushes: "You've only got to call me, Sir, and I'll come." I kissed her tenderly, put her into a hansom and sent her home; then wended my way to my Club, where in bumpers of champagne, I recruited exhausted nature and drank to the three sweet cunts I, that afternoon, had enjoyed, and their delicious owners, Alice, Connie, and Fanny!

The Three Chums: A Tale of London Everyday Life

by Anonymous

from *The Boudoir*

3

Mrs. Lovejoy and the Servants in Bloombury Square

It was nearly one a.m. when the boys got home to the Mortimer mansion in Bloomsbury Square.

"How late you are," said Mrs. Lovejoy, the housekeeper, opening the door to them, "and you have brought Master Charlie with you. I'm so glad to see him; your father has gone to bed hours ago, and I thought you would like a second course after your oyster supper at Scott's, so there's a little spread in my own room upstairs, only we mustn't keep it up too late."

"You're a brick," said Harry, "we'll go upstairs so quietly past dad's door, and kiss you when we see what you have got for us."

Mr. Mortimer père being a rather stout gentleman, who objected to many stairs, had his bedroom on the first floor; Harry and Frank's room was on the next flight, where their sisters also had their rooms when at home from school; the two servants and Mrs. Lovejoy located above them.

"There's my kiss," said Frank, as on entering Mrs. Lovejoy's cosy room he saw a game pie and bottle of Burgundy set out for their refreshment.

Harry and Charlie also in turn embraced the amorous housekeeper, who fairly shivered with emotion as she met the luscious kiss of the latter.

"He's only going to stay this one night, so it's no good taking a fancy to my cousin; besides, can't you be content with Frank and myself?" whispered Harry to her.

"But you are such unfaithful boys, and prefer Mary Anne or Maria to me at any time," she replied, pettishly.

"Yes, and Charlie is no better; he hasn't been in London one whole day yet without making up to the pretty Fanny at his lodgings; oh, she's a regular little fizzer, Mrs. Lovejoy."

The second supper was soon discussed, and Mrs. Lovejoy had placed hot water and spirits on the table just for them to take a night-cap as she called it, when there was a gentle tap at the room door, and a suppressed titter outside.

Harry, guessing who it was, called out "come in," when the two servant girls with broad grins on their faces walked into the room, only half dressed—in petticoats, stockings, and slippers, with necks and bosoms bare.

On perceiving Charlie they blushed scarlet, but Mary Anne, a regular bouncing brunette, immediately recovered her presence of mind, and said, "We beg your pardon, Mrs. Lovejoy, but we thought only Master Harry and his brother were here, and felt so thirsty we couldn't sleep, so ventured to beg a little something to cool our throats."

"We'll make a party of it now," said Frank; "this is only our cousin Charlie, so don't be bashful but come in and shut the door."

"Gentlemen don't generally admit ladies, especially when only half dressed, as we are," said Maria, a very pretty and finely developed young woman, with light brown hair, rosy cheeks, and such a pair of deep blue eyes, full of mischief, as they looked one through.

"No, but ladies admit gentlemen," put in Charlie; "don't mind me," getting up from his chair and drawing the last speaker onto his lap. "I guess we're in for some fun now."

The housekeeper looked awfully annoyed at this intrusion, but Harry laughingly kissed her, and whispered something which seemed to have a soothing effect, as she at once offered the two girls some lemonade and brandy. Hers was a very comfortable apartment, being furnished the same as a bachelor's bed and sitting room combined; the bed was in a recess, and there were two easy chairs besides a sofa, table, &c., in the room.

Harry secured the sofa, where he sat with Mrs. Lovejoy on his lap, and one of his hands inside the bosom of her dressing gown, whilst her hands, at least one of them, were God knows where, and very evidently gave him considerable pleasure, to judge by the sparkle of his eyes, and the way he caressed her, as well as the frequent kisses they interchanged.

Charlie was admiring and playing with the bosom of Maria, who kissed him warmly every now and then, giving the most unequivocal signs of her rising desires for closer acquaintance.

"We shall never be fit to get up in the morning if you keep us out of bed; let the girls go now," said Mrs. Lovejoy.

Each said "good night," and Harry, having something to say to the housekeeper, stayed behind. Frank and Mary Anne quickly vanished in the gloom of the outside corridor, and Charlie, at a loss where he was to sleep, asked Maria to show him to his room.

"You'll sleep with me, dear, if you can, and I won't keep you awake," she whispered, giving him a most luscious kiss; then taking his hand she led him into a very clean but plainly furnished bedroom.

"Mary Anne won't be back tonight, so you shall be my

bedfellow. I guess by this time Master Frank is being let into all her secrets," saying which she extinguished the candle, which had been left burning, and jumped into bed, Charlie following as quickly as he could get his things off.

"I've got a syringe, so I'm not afraid, although Harry and Frank will always put on those French letters. Do you think they're nice?" asked Maria, as she threw her arms around him, and drew him close to her palpitating bosom.

"Never used such a thing in my life," replied Charlie, "for my part anything of that sort spoils all the fun."

"Do you know," continued Maria, "Mary Anne and I lay thinking, talking, and cuddling one another, in fact we were so excited she proposed a game of what girls call flat c—, when we heard Mrs. Lovejoy take you to her room, and we made up our minds she should not have both Harry and Frank to herself, never thinking there was anyone else; and to think I have got such a darling as you!"

The girl fairly quivered with emotion as she lay on her side kissing and cuddling close to his body, but his previous encounters during the preceding twenty-four hours rendered him rather less impulsive, in fact he liked to enjoy the situation, which was such as none but those who have lain by the side of a loving expectant young wanton can thoroughly appreciate. Her hands roved everywhere, and she conducted one of his to that most sacred spot of all, which he found glowing like a furnace, and so sensitive to his touch, that she sighed, "Oh! Oh!" and almost jumped when she felt his tickling fingers, as they revelled in the luxuriant growth of silky hair, which almost barred the approach to the entrance of her bower of love. Charlie never had such a sleepless night in his life, for impatient of his long-delay in making a commencement, she threw a leg over his hip as a challenge, and, having his wand in her hand as fit as busy fingers could make it, she directed Mr. Warner so straight that he found not the least difficulty in exploring the very inmost recesses of her humid furbelow, which to judge from its overflowing state was a veritable fountain of butterine. How he rode the lively steed, till, exhausted by the rapidity of the pace, he fell off, only to find Maria had reversed positions, and there was no rest for him till seven o'clock in the morning, and at breakfast his looks only too plainly told the tale of the night's orgie, as Mr. Mortimer railled at all three young fellows of having had a rakish time of it, remarking that he hoped they would be more moderate in future, but it might be excusable for a first night in town.

Our hero was glad to stay in his own rooms and rest the next evening, and felt rather too used up to indulge in much more than a mild joke and a kiss with the pretty Fanny, who had a rather pouting expression on her face as she bid him good night after what she considered to be a decidedly languid kind of kiss.

"He isn't so fresh as when he arrived, but perhaps he will be more lively at breakfast time," she mused, going downstairs to the lower regions of the house. "I hope Mrs. Letsam won't get at him, that's all!"

Charlie was so done up that he went to bed by ten o'clock, and slept so soundly that he awoke quite early, feeling as frisky as a lark, and with the peculiar elevation of spirits which most healthy young fellows are subject to when they first open their eyes in the morning.

"J. T. is quite himself again," exclaimed Charlie, as he threw off the bed-clothes to survey the grand proportions of that part of his anatomy sacred to the service of the fair sex. Then looking at his watch by the aid of the lamp which he had left burning, "By Jove, how early; only half-past four. I'll look outside in the corridor in search of adventure, there is just a chance I might find Fanny's room, as this is the top story; she can't go higher up, and isn't likely to be lower down."

Quick as the idea flashed across his mind he stepped out of bed, and taking the little lamp in his hand opened his door very gently and stepped into the corridor, which was a long passage with three or four doors of rooms besides those of his own apartments. He listened at the first one, but hearing nothing passed on to the next, which was slightly ajar; hesitating for a moment he heard the loud stentorian breathing of a heavy sleeper, so shading the lamp with his hand he pushed the door gently open, when what should he see but his fat landlady, Mrs. Letsam, lying on her back in bed with her knees up and mouth open. Although so bulky Mrs. L. was what some would term a truly splendid woman, not more than forty, very pleasing face, and rich brown hair; whilst her open night dress displayed all the splendours of her mature bosom's magnificent orbs, as white as snow and ornamented by the most seductive strawberry nipples. In reality it was only a chemise, not a proper night dress, she was sleeping in, so that, as well as the bosom, a large but finely moulded arm was exposed to his searching gaze, and gave him such curious ideas as to the development of other unseen charms, that he resolved to satisfy his curiosity by a manual exploration under the bed-clothes. Turning down his lamp he put it outside the door in the corridor, then in the darkness knelt down by the bedside, and slowly insinuating his hand till he touched her thigh, rested till it got warm, then trembling all over with emotion he continued his investigations. His touches seemed marvellously to agitate the sleeper, for after one or two slight involuntary kind of starts, she stiffened her body out quite straight as she turned on her side with something very much like a deep sigh, and Charlie withdrew his impudent fingers, just as he felt the flow of bliss consequent on his exciting touches.

"She'll think it was a dream; most likely the old girl doesn't often feel like that;" laughed Charlie to himself as he sneaked out of the room, little guessing that Mrs. Letsam had been thoroughly awakened, and stepped out of bed the moment he was gone, peeping out into the corridor to see who it was.

"Ha, Mr. Warner, it's you, is it? It won't take me long to be even with you for this lark!" she said to herself as she got into bed again. "I wish the dear boy had got into bed though; his touches gave me most exquisite pleasure."

Meanwhile Charlie had got to a door at the furthest end of the corridor, which opened at once as he turned the handle, and sure enough it was Fanny's room, for there lay the object of his desires in a broken restless sleep, with nearly all the bed-clothes tossed off. What a sight for an impressionable youth! There she lay almost uncovered as it were, her right hand on the spot which so many men who scandalise the fair sex say they always protect instinctively with their hand whilst asleep for fear of being ravished unawares.

However that may be, Fanny's hand was there, and Charlie conjectured that it was not so much for protection as digitation, judging from the girl's agitated restless dreams; for she was softly murmuring,

"Don't! Pray, don't. You tease me so. Oh! Oh!"

He could see everything as he shaded his little lamp so as not to let the tight fall on her eyes—her lovely thighs and heaving mount of love, shaded by the softest golden-coloured down, whilst one finger was fairly hidden within the fair lips of the pinkest possible slit below the dewy moisture which glistened in the light.

"By heavens! What a chance!" said Charlie to himself. "Perhaps I can give her an agreeable surprise."

Quick as thought he extinguished his lamp, which he placed on a table, then in the dark groped towards the bed where the pretty Fanny lay quite unconscious of his presence.

The sleeper having tossed off most of the bed covering it was quite easy for him to lay himself by her side; he kissed the inviting globes of her firm plump bosom, but without awakening her, she simply moaned soft endearing words; as if she felt herself caressed by someone she loved so much. His right hand pushed hers aside and took possession of the tender cleft it had been guarding and pressing at the same time; then he gently placed one leg over hers, pressing his naked person close to her body. What thrills of delighted expectation shot through his whole frame, he quivered from head to foot. The temptation and the intensity of his feelings would stand no further delay. So, he glued his lips to hers in a long luscious kiss, whilst one arm held her firmly embraced, and the other was deliciously occupied in manual preliminaries for the attack on her virgin fortress below.

"Fanny," he whispered, as she unconsciously responded to his kissing. "It's me, darling; let me love you now?"

At first he thought she was going to scream, but he sealed her lips by the renewal of his fiery kisses, which seemed fairly to stop her breath. She did not speak but appeared awfully discomposed; deep, long drawn sighs came from her as her bosom heaved with excitement, and her hands feebly tried to push away his intrusive fingers. But desire evidently overcame modesty; her return of his willing kisses became more ardent, and her legs gradually gave way to his efforts to get between them, and instead of repulsing his advances her arms were entwined round his body.

"By Jove!" thought Charlie. "I'm not the first; she's too easy!" but to his delight he did not find the citadel of her chastity had been stormed before; the battering ram of love had to be vigorously applied before a breach was made sufficient to effect a lodgement. What sighs; what murmurs of love and endearment were mixed with her moans of pain.

"My pet, you are a woman now," he whispered, lovingly, at the conclusion of the first act, kissing her again and again.

"Oh, Charlie, what a darling; you have been so gentle with me. How I love you now; you will always love me, won't you, dearest? But you can't, you can't marry me, I know." Here she sobbed hysterically as that thought broke upon her mind. Our hero did all he could to comfort her, but found nothing so conducive to that end as drawing up the curtain for a second scene in the drama of love.

"I don't know what upset me so in my sleep; but dear, I went off thinking of you, and suppose I must have wanted you; your kissing has made me feel so uneasy and all-overish since you came to the house. No one ever upset me like that before," she confessed to him in her simplicity, as they lay toying and kissing till daylight.

Four o'clock, a.m., of a glorious sunny morning, as Charlie Warner opened his eyes to find himself lying in Fanny's arms, almost naked on his bed, the covering having evidently slipped off onto the floor during the amorous play of the preceding night; they were fast embraced, or rather locked together, his prick as stiff as possible, throbbing against the soft ivory skin of his companion's person, the curly hair of their organs of love mingling together in the close conjunction of their bodies.

Fanny's lips were slightly open, displaying a lovely set of small pearly teeth whilst her arms ever and anon clasped his form with a light nervous tremour, as if she was still dreaming of the delights of the past night.

"She f—d me as dry as a stick, last night," soliloquised

Charlie, "yet I feel brimming over with spunk again, and ready to spend over her navel."

"Wake up, Fanny, my love!" he softly whispered, putting two of his fingers into her still damp slit, and rubbing gently on her excited clitoris. "Wake up, sleeping beauty, I must have one quick. See how stiff he is. Look at your darling. Don't you know that this is the Queen's birthday, 24th May, 18—and, in honour of her Majesty, I mean to f—k as many girls as I can to-day, at least between now and to-morrow morning, and I mean to begin with you."

"You randy fellow, do you think I will oblige you after such a speech as that?" laughed Fanny, as she woke with a start. "I can't help myself this minute, because I've been dreaming of you all night. You seemed always in me, spending and spending till I seemed actually dissolving in love, and then you wake me up with a reference to having other girls during the day. Still I can't refuse this delicious morsel just now, but it will be different when you come home to-night, after your day's whoring. I shall look at you with disgust then."

"Oh, put it into me quick!" she ejaculated with a sigh, opening her legs, to receive the object of her desire.

It was a short hot affair, as most first f—ks in the morning are, when the blood is heated from wine, champagne, &c., imbibed over night.

He stroked her twice, to Fanny's infinite satisfaction, before he withdrew from the tight folds of her deliciously warm c—t.

Then they slept till nearly six o'clock, when Fanny had to get up for her daily work.

Our friend Charlie indulged in another two hours' snooze, till he was awakened by the sensation of feeling his p—k sucked by a delightfully warm mouth, and found Mrs. Letsam, his landlady, indulging in one of her erotic suckings, which usually gave him so much pleasure, and on this occasion the thought that she was cleaning his pego of all the dried-up spendings that Fanny had left on it, so excited his fancy that he came in a perfect frenzy of emission, till the spunk fairly frothed in her mouth and oozed from its corners, as she ravenously tried to swallow every drop.

After breakfast, Charlie again racked off Fanny's juice on the sofa, and then started to call upon Clara, in her little house at St. John's Wood.

Only Lena was at home with Clara, but they were overjoyed to see him so brimfull of spirits, and his p—k, as soon as he got into their company, was as rampant as ever.

The two girls were having a light breakfast, as they sat in their dressing gowns, fresh from the matutinal cold bath, their cheeks rosy with youthful health, stimulated by the cold douche, which, with the hard rubbing they had given each other, had roused all the warmth of their blood, till they were in that state of voluptuous readiness, so fit for the reception of a fine young fellow like Charlie.

Each pretty girl tipped him the velvet end of her tongue, as he kissed their cherry lips, Lena saying: "How nice of you to call so early, Mr. Warner; it is just in time to give each of us 'one of them,' before we go out for a drive round Regent's Park. Don't you know a f—k is truly delicious to a girl in the morning, just after she has had her cold bath, when she is all aglow, and the blood tingles through her veins from head to foot?"

"A cup of coffee, and then—" said Clara, pouring out one for their visitor.

"Without milk or sugar, if you please," replied Charlie. "I shall get all that as I gamahuche you both, and suck up your spendings."

Impatient for another go in, he soon led them into the bedroom, where there was a delicious and soft cool air from the open window of a small conservatory, which communicated with Clara's *chambre à caucher.*

They were soon as naked as Cupids, and Charlie, making them lean back on the bed, sucked each c—t in turn, till they writhed and spent on his active tongue, as its ravishing touches then rolled round their lascivious clitorises.

"This is Clara's house, so she is entitled to have the first put-in," said Lena, "and you shall suck as much honey as you can from my little buttercup fanny, whilst you f—k her."

"We'll show you a new position, Charlie dear," added Clara, as she extended herself on the bed. "Get between my legs and as soon as you are in—yes, that's it; now throw your left leg up over my loins, and put your right under my right leg, and then lay your body away from me, fork fashion, and gamahuche Lena, as she sits up and presents her fanny to your lips; isn't it awfully nice? Your cock goes into the exact corner of my q—m, and touches the very entrance to my womb! Ah, ah! Oh, oh! You do make me spend. I can't help it. Go on quicker, dear boy! Ah, Lena, it drives me mad. He seems to make me melt all over."

Charlie, on his part, was in ecstasies, and his delighted p—k was so sensitive to the clinging grip of Clara's lascivious fanny, that he was compelled to cry out he could not bear it any longer, as his hot spunk spurted into her c—t.

Lena was so randy that she took possession of Charlie's p—k the instant he withdrew, and, doubling her knees up towards her face, threw her legs over his shoulder, as he rammed it into her longing gap, whilst Clara lovingly kissed, sucked, and tongued his balls, bottom, and buttocks from behind, her busy fingers doing their best by handling his impetuous shaft, as it worked in and out of that foaming c—t, which was literally overflowing with their thick creamy emissions.

He kept himself back for a final spend, and so drew out the

length of that glorious f—k, that Lena craved in her unsatisfied lust, and fixed her teeth in his shoulders, till her lips were crimsoned in his blood.

Clara, the while, frigged herself with one hand, and at the finish, they rolled over together in a perfect fury of amorous frenzy.

After this, Charlie dressed himself, placed two sovereigns on the dressing table, although the dear girls protested they would not take his money as he had pleased them so, then, taking leave of them as they still lay on the bed, rang the bell for the servant to show him out.

Emma, the servant, was a pretty little brunette, about eighteen, and as the saying is, "fresh c—t, fresh courage," Charlie put half-a-crown in her hand, as he kissed her behind the door, and whispered, "My dear, I should just like to f—k you. You shall have half-a-sov if you run down and let me in at the area door, as I pretend to go out down the front steps."

Without speaking, she returned the kiss, and shut the door sharply behind him, so running down to the area, he was presently in the arms of another sweet randy girl.

His p—k stood in a moment, as he lifted her on to the kitchen table, and put his hands up her clothes, their lips meeting in luscious kisses and tongueings.

Emma was quite as hot as her mistress, and f—k'd with all the abandon of a true little whore, till he gave her c—t a warm douche of the elixir of life.

Her eyes were shut, and her head rested on his shoulder, as she whispered, "Oh, give me another before you go; it was such a beautiful f—k. I don't often get a treat like that. Oh, do, do! There's a dear!"

Luckily for him, just then, the upstairs bell rang, and he was able to effect a hasty retreat up the area steps.

Taking a cab, he called on his cousins to arrange for the

evening, after which he returned to his own rooms, and rested the remainder of the day.

About 10 p.m. found our three chums, arm in arm, elbowing their way down Regent Street, where the crowd became denser every moment, and at places was quite impassable, where the illuminations were more splendid than ordinary.

The groping for c—ks and c—ts seemed the proper thing to do; everyone in the crowd seemed to understand that, and the three friends had immense fun with a modest old lady and her daughter, who, although awfully indignant, were perfectly helpless, and were so teased and handled that they sighed and spent with desire, in spite of the shame that they felt.

Next a large closed furniture removal van which they were jammed against attracted their attention. It had portholes, like a ship, along the sides, and was lighted up inside.

Charlie mounted on one of the wheels, till he could peep inside, and found two old swells and several girls, nearly as naked as they could be, sporting their q—ms to amuse the old fellows, who had each got one of the nymphs of the pavement to frig him.

"Hullo!" shouted Charlie, forcing in the round glass, which acted on a pivot. "Don't you want some real f—k—g in there? We've got three good stiff p—ks out here, if you'll let us in."

"Eh! Egad! It wouldn't be amiss," said one of the old gents. "Let's have them in for a lark."

It was a matter of the greatest difficulty to effect an entrance by getting round to the rear of the van, and squeezing through the partially opened door.

"You look proper sparks," said one of their entertainers, opening a bottle of fizz. "Just a wet, by way of introduction, then the girls will soon take the stand out of you. Have you had some good gropes among the crowd?"

"Just what we wanted! They're three beauties," exclaimed

the girls, as they brought out the stiff p—ks of Charlie, Harry, and Frank.

There were six girls in all, and the three chums had all their work to do to give a f—k to each girl in turn. This, however, they did, much to the delight of the two jolly old cockolorums, who handled their fine firm pegos with unbounded delight, postillioning their bottoms, and licking their fingers with the greatest of gusto, after they had thrust them into the reeking q—ms of the girls, to see how the f—k—g was going on.

One of their hosts, in particular was ravenous to gamahuche and lick up all the spending from the swimming c—ts after each go in.

Little notice was taken of the illuminations as the lumbering van slowly forged its way through the surging crowd, which little suspected the lascivious orgie being enacted inside the sober looking van.

For three hours the game was kept up with spirit, till the three friends were so tired out, and overcome by the lots of champagne they had taken, that, when at length the van was driven into the grounds of a private house and stopped before the hall door, they were too stupid even to put on their clothes, and along with the girls were carried into the house by two or three flunkeys, who deposited the dissipated crew on some ottomans and sofas in a large and brilliantly lighted saloon.

Charlie was not quite so drunk but he had a dim recollection of curious liberties which the old gents took with his naked person, and for a day or two afterwards Frank and Harry as well as himself confessed to feeling rather stretched and sore, as if their rear virginity had been ravished when they were helpless to prevent what they afterwards felt quite disgusted at.

But it is anticipating the course of events. About five in the morning our hero quite recovered himself, and, waking from the short deep drunken sleep, found the sun streaming in through a window, so drawing aside the light lace curtains he found it looked onto a beautiful croquet ground surrounded by parterres of splendid flowers, and screened on every side by dense foliage of shrubs and trees.

Turning to the apartment, the two old gentlemen were fast asleep in armchairs, each with his trousers down, and a naked girl resting her head on his thigh, side by side with the languid p—k, which she had been in the act of gamahuching when they were all overcome by sleep.

Frank and Harry were lying mixed up with the other four girls on a very large and splendid catskin rug, all naked, forming a charming tableau, as the golden rays of the sun glanced on the warm flesh tints.

Just then a lovely young lady, wrapped in a dressing gown peeped into the room and Charlie, all naked as he was, bounded across from the window to meet her, but she putting her finger to her lips, signalled him to follow her as she withdrew from the room. He crossed the vestibule close behind her into a magnificent boudoir, the door was locked, and she threw herself into his arms, exclaiming "At least, I am sure you are not one of the filthy unnatural fellows my uncles usually bring here, I have not the least doubt you three have been tricked, made tipsy and outraged by them! Oh pity me, for I am a prisoner in this house—they have cheated me out of my father's immense fortune—and made me their lady housekeeper, where, just because I can't help myself, and the hope of some day succeeding to what they have cheated me out of, I have to shut my eyes and pretend not to see their horrible goings on, and even sometimes myself submit to their unnatural whims in my own person, without ever getting from them the satisfaction which a warm female nature requires. My case is like that of the lady you read of in the Arabian Nights, who although the jealous Genie kept her locked in a glass box, yet managed now and then to get a fresh lover, but very few suitable youths come to this house, they are mostly those debased men-women who prostitute themselves for money. Only four times in three years, have I had the delight to welcome to my boudoir such a one as I could surrender myself to. Do you know why you awoke first? It is because, when I looked over the lustful group asleep after their beastly orgie, you charmed my eye, so scattering some drops of a very somniferous essence over all the others, I applied reviving salts, &c., to your nostrils, and here you are my prize. We're safe for several hours!" she concluded, opening her dressing gown and throwing her lovely naked form upon his equally nude figure.

Receiving her in his arms, his p—k as rampant as ever (how could it be otherwise when thus challenged by such a lovely creature), taking her in his embrace, he carried her a few steps till she fell back upon a soft, wide couch.

Her delicate hand had already taken possession of his throbbing staff, and now at once applied its head to her burning notch, which was literally brimming over from a luscious anticipatory emission.

Drawing him upon her, her legs enlaced over his buttocks, she heaved up her bottom in enraptured delight, as the shaft slowly entered the well lubricated, yet tight sheath.

Then they paused for a moment or two, billing and kissing, tongue to tongue, as both evidently thoroughly enjoyed the sense of possession that they imparted to each other by mutual throbs and contractions, till, giving a long-drawn deep sigh of desire, she challenged him by her motions to ride on and complete her happiness.

Charlie literally trembled from excess of emotion, and the rapidity with which this bewildering and luscious adventure had fallen upon him. Her first few moves made him spend before he wished to, and in spite of his unsatisfied desires, his pego at once lost its stiffness, to the great chagrin of the lovers.

"Ah, I understand," she exclaimed; "it is over-excitement, after the enervating debauch of last night. Wait a moment, my dear, and we will soon be happy enough!"

Saying which, she ran to a cabinet for some Eau de Cologne, sprinkling a few drops over his excited face, then, pouring the rest of the bottle into a small china bowl with water, she sponged his limp p—k with it, then dried it on a soft handkerchief, and then kissed, sucked, and caressed the manly jewel with such marvellous endearment that she soon had him standing again in all his glory of ruby head and ivory shaft, the sight of which seemed quite to ravish her senses, for she threw herself on the sofa, and begged he would at once let her have the only thing that could possibly assuage her raging lasciviousness.

"Ah, I'm afraid you'll think me awfully lewd!" she sighed, blushing more crimson than ever.

This charming appeal was irresistible; he now charged her foaming fanny with such effect that she raved in ecstasies of delight, biting and kissing him by turns in her voluptuous frenzy, twisting, squirming her body, and throwing first over his loins, and then stiffening out straight in the dying ecstasies of spending, his p—k all the while revelling in the warmth and extraordinary lubricity of the tight grasping sheath, which held it so passionately that it stiffened more and more from excessive lust, that when he came it was quite a painful acme of delight. The tip of his pego was so tender that he positively could not bear the loving, sucking contractions of her womb, as it drank up every drop, which spurted up to her very heart.

After a while they renewed these delights, and kept it up, till prudence dictated his return to the saloon, where the sleepers were still unawakened; so Charlie, dressing himself, aroused Frank and Harry and assisted them to dress, then slipping away for a moment to his unknown inamorata took a loving leave, and by her advice they left the house leaving the two old gentlemen and the girls to wonder what had become of them whenever they might rouse themselves up.

It was almost 5 o'clock in the afternoon when our hero took leave of his cousins in Gower Street, sending them home to sleep off the effects of the long debauch; whilst he also made the mental resolve, to let this be the very last orgie for a long while to come, and content himself with the love of his little slavey, and the occasional erotic osculations of Mrs. Letsam, soliloquising to himself, as after a cup of tea, he lay on his own sofa, I mean to study and rise in my profession, so this of my sprees shall be . . .

from

GARDENS OF THE NIGHT

by Felicia Plessey

1

The girl in her long grey skirt and white blouse stood on the little balcony outside the hotel suite. Pressing her hands on the moulding of the rail, she watched the holiday scene below. At eighteen years old she was a pretty trim-waisted creature, still poised uncertainly between adolescence and womanhood. Debby possessed a neat prettiness of nose and chin, an appealing young face lightly sun-tanned with dark eyes and wide cheek-bones. The fullness of her mouth and the even line of her teeth appeared in a ready smile.

There was much about her that still hinted at childishness and subservience to others. Her golden-brown hair had not yet been put up in an elegant coiffure but was worn loose, combed back from her appealing young face so that its lightly waved tresses just overlapped her collar. As she looked at the scene below her, the silky hair fell forward a little in charming disorder.

Perhaps it was most of all her legs, bare from the knees downward, which showed a childish awkwardness of poise and bearing. Yet Debby's bottom and hips, even her thighs, also had the slight adolescent heaviness of the goose not yet become a swan.

It was late enough in the afternoon for the waves of the tranquil tide to burn silver in the sun's decline. Below the canopied balcony, the Sunday crowds were walking homeward through public gardens of tall camelias in blooming crimson and dark hedges of Monterey cypress. A pattern of small tables had been set out on the terrace, among the urns and balustrades where the casual café-music hung like warm perfume in the summer air.

The rain-drop pools of April
The apple-blossom bough . . .

A girl in a tailored suit sang to the ripple of a piano accompaniment in the interval of the tea-dance.

All that we did without last spring
Would make a summer now. . . .

Debby pressed upon the moulded rail as if there was a secret comfort in feeling its shape against her loins. She had the ready pleasant manner of one who serves others, the girl in the travel bureau with her quick and smiling answers for those planning their journeys. It was easy to see how she might give adoration to another. Round her right ankle she wore a white leather ring. Childish and yet womanly, it symbolised her fierce and willing bondage to the person she loved beyond all limit.

Yellow as a peach, the teatime sunlight patterned the white bulk of the tall hotel. Children's voices, high and frail as gull-calls, rose among salvoes of breakers on firm sand. Far out, where the sea darkened to a green horizon-band, a bird settled in a tiny feathering of spray.

At no time did Debby turn and try to open the French windows, to enter the hotel suite. Like a little girl dismissed by her elders, she was to remain on the balcony until they called her back. Yet the two men who were busy with the other young woman in the room made no attempt to draw the curtain across the glass nor to conceal from the girl what they were doing to the woman. Debby, ten years the junior, could only turn and look with an agony of love at Lesley during her humiliation.

The French windows had been locked but even had they not been, Debby knew better than to interrupt Anton and Mano in their dealings with Lesley. She stood at the glass, watching the men in the hotel suite, her pretty face and dark eyes following Lesley with desire and understanding.

The interior of the sitting-room had been furnished in a style of modernistic opulence. Deep-sided chairs and white drum-shaded lamps were arranged on a plain neutral carpeting. The muted tones of the luxuriously furnished suite reduced the marine light of the sky to a cool aqueous shimmer in the mirror-glass of the tables and the angular wall-mirrors bound in platinum.

The men, watching Lesley as she stood at their will by the fire-screen, were indifferent to the holiday world outside. In the closed room they were engaged in that most private and absorbing of rituals, the inspection of a slave-girl. It heightened their enjoyment to see that their victim was, by nature, a moody young woman with a dismissive manner towards the male sex. To subjugate such an emancipated female—and to see her own secret excitement in being subdued—was the most exquisite of pleasures.

It was Anton, a tall and golden-haired Apollo of thirty, who acted as the host. Mano, a distinguished patrician, already brushed with grey at the temples and Spanish or Italian in appearance, was the guest. To judge from the conversation, this was his first sight of Lesley. He talked of her without much addressing the girl herself, questioning Anton and advising him on his future treatment of her.

Lesley stood waiting at the centre of the room in a white short-sleeved singlet and a black coolie-suit, its jacket and trousers made of thin cotton. Her appearance revealed her for what she was, a spoilt and pampered young Englishwoman of the middle-class who indulged her own rights and privileges at the expense of others. As if to emphasise her equality with the male sex, her straight fair hair had been cropped perversely short in a plain pudding-basin cut. It hung to her jaw-line and her nape, lying in a long parted fringe on her forehead. Ironically, this plain boyish style excited perverse desires in her admirers.

Everything about her hinted at her upbringing as a wilful and indulged little girl, a demanding and promiscuous student at college; a young bride greedy for pleasure, but a young wife moody and resentful towards her husband and children. Below the level of her fringe, the blue eyes were disdainful and brooding. Her fair-skinned features were clear-cut and firm but there was a sullen weight in her jaw and a sulky line in her mouth. It was on this unlikely idol that Debby now gazed with such mute adoration from beyond the balcony door.

Mano laid down his cigarette in the brass ashtray.

"I should like to see her undressed a little," he said, "At least her trouser-suit and singlet must be removed."

As if it was beneath her contempt to question or resist such a demand, Lesley took off her black jacket and pulled off the white singlet over her head. The milk-whiteness of her back and shoulders contrasted with the black halter in which her taut young breasts were moulded. She shook her short-cut hair into place and began to unfasten the black trousers.

"Her breasts will be important," Mano said, "But the sort of men who will possess her will transfer their attentions below the waist. Her legs and her arse will interest them most of all."

Lesley pulled down the trousers and stepped out of them. From the waist down she wore only a white suspender-belt, a pair of golden-tan stockings drawn well up her pale thighs by the suspender straps, and tight-fitting black panties of a filmy translucent material to match her breast halter. Mano walked closer and looked at her.

"How old is she now?"

"Twenty-eight," Anton said.

"And how long was her marriage?"

"About seven years."

"She conceived her two children very early?"

Anton nodded and Mano seemed satisfied.

"I shall know how to deal with her when the time comes," he said, "She is tall enough and trim enough for her erotic maturity to be an advantage. There are things one would hesitate to do to a schoolgirl of fourteen, even to a nymph at nineteen or twenty. In the case of a young married woman like Lesley—seven years experience of her husband's penis in bed—one has no such qualms."

He walked round her then turned to Anton again. "You say she exercises? Bicycling perhaps? Her thighs are so long and trim. That is good. Her hips have a marginal broadening after her two children but that counts as an advantage too in such a case. How did the marriage end?"

Anton shrugged.

"Abruptly. She wanted to live with another man. Lesley's claim of being an emancipated young woman entitled her to choose who should penetrate her. One day, while her husband was at work and the children at school, she packed a suitcase and left to share her lover's bed."

Mano smiled.

"She was promiscuous during her marriage?"

"Quite often."

"Did she refuse her husband's penis?"

"When in her sullen moods. She sucked him only once, during the height of their honeymoon passion. In her infatuation she let her next lover use her mouth—but never, never her backside!"

Mano smiled again at this, trying to see the expression on Lesley's face as they talked about her. But she had lowered her head until her chin was almost buried in her breast.

"She was never whipped by her teachers or parents—or her lovers?"

"Never." Anton laughed at a sudden recollection, "Her young daughter was caned at school—ten strokes across her bottom—and you can scarcely imagine Lesley's outrage on behalf of injured womanhood!"

Mano now walked across to Lesley and stood in front of her. He ran his hand over the smooth whiteness of her skin, the slight proud curve of her belly. Then Mano slipped the hand into the front of her tight silky briefs, feeling her flinch back instinctively as he touched the soft fair hair on her pubic mound. He put his other hand at her bare waist to steady her. The fingers in her black diaphanous panties intruded between her legs, feeling the moist warmth of her softly-haired vaginal flesh.

"You like to play with yourself, don't you, Lesley?" he said quietly, "You do it quite often, I think."

She looked up suddenly, the blue eyes now startled out of their self-possession. Lesley seemed about to answer and then failed to find the words of denial.

"Yes you do," said Mano understandingly, "It asserts your belief in your right to use your own body as you choose—

even to be independent of the male sex. When did you last make love to yourself?"

She stared at him, as if unable to believe that he required a response. He moved his fingers further between her legs.

"Answer the question, Lesley," Anton said sharply.

"I d-d-don't know. . . . I c-c-can't remember. . . . " In her confusion she arched her hips back, as if to escape his fondling.

Mano smiled.

"She has had sex with other women?" he asked Anton.

"With several. The first while she was a student, just before her marriage. And now, of course, with Debby. At the Villa Rif she masturbated with Judith Terry, a girl of sixteen."

Mano drew his hand away.

"Turn around and show me your backside, Lesley," he said, teasing a little and yet demanding obedience.

She obeyed him awkwardly, standing with her back towards him but her legs and buttocks clumsily tightened in apprehension.

"Take your knickers off, Lesley," he said, "Then go and bend over the back of the sofa."

They watched as she hesitantly wriggled the briefs down her trim fair-skinned legs. In her suspender-belt and stockings she seemed aptly dressed for the inspection of those areas which most interested the men. At the front the triangle of fair hair on the base of her belly, and the tops of her thighs above her stockings, were bare. She turned her back to them and walked with careful steps of her stockinged feet towards the tan-coloured leather of the broad sofa. Her head was bowed like a child in disgrace and the short crop of her fair hair parted on the nape of her neck under its own weight. The two men watched the undulating movements of her hips and thighs as she walked. Her state of undress seemed, once again, designed to draw their attention to her backside as the area of their examination. The white elastic arch of the suspender-belt across the back of her waist, its straps drawn taut to the stocking tops at mid-thigh, the tops of the filmy gold stockings themselves, all seemed to act as a frame for the proud bare cheeks of Lesley's bottom as she walked.

Mano stopped her with a hand on her bare hip as she stood at the back of the sofa. He turned to Anton.

"She should stand against the sofa-back and then bend forward over it with her hands supporting her on the seat-cushions. She will be better that way. The leather back will support her under her belly and make it easier for her to endure the indignity of being examined by a mere man. There will be less temptation to try squirming free when she knows she can so easily be held down."

Lesley glanced back over her shoulder at Anton, the first hint of her uneasiness betrayed in the clear blue eyes. When he nodded at her, she lowered herself a little awkwardly, having to stand on tiptoe in order to bend over the leather back and reach the sofa cushions with the palms of her hands.

Mano spoke quietly to Anton.

"You should use your camera now. A supercilious young woman like this needs frequent lessons in subservience to her admirers. It will do her good to know that she must show herself not only to us but also to the men she most despises, who collect sets of such photographs."

Anton saw Lesley's thighs and buttocks tense together a little as he walked to the table and picked up the camera. Mano had previously arranged the sofa so that the full sunlight fell upon it.

"Turn your head and look into the camera, Lesley," said Anton impatiently. "The men who collect such photographs will want to see your face as well."

Mano shook his head.

"You have treated her too gently. She must be taught to show herself properly without being coaxed."

Lesley had turned her face to Anton and was looking at the camera with the moodiness still visible in her clear features. Mano stood behind her at the same time and began his examination of the young woman's body. He laid his hands on the smooth backs of her thighs where the pearly skin was bare above her stocking-tops. He pressed the firm surfaces apart a little and saw the lightly haired lips of her vagina from the rear.

"Keep your legs still, Lesley!" he said sharply as she tried to press them together. The camera recorded the sudden, widening dismay on her face as his hands enforced obedience while she bent. He cupped the fleecy softness in his palm as the young woman lay bottom-upwards over the sofa. "When did you last play with yourself?"

The camera shutter clicked again, and then again, recording the appealing confusion of her eyes and firm features under the long parted fringe of her gamine crop. Mano caressed the warm humid flesh between her thighs.

"When?" As he repeated the question more brusquely, he felt an involuntary shiver in her legs.

"Yesterday," Lesley bowed her head as if to muffle the reply in the sofa cushions, "Last night."

"Alone or with Debby?"

"Alone." Now the voice was begging for a respite from this interrogation.

Mano took his hand away and spoke to Anton.

"She should be photographed from this angle next. Make her part her legs a little wider."

This was done and the camera shutter clicked several times on this view of Lesley bending and straddling, looking back over her shoulder at the lens. Mano's hands now touched the cool pale mounds of the young wife's buttocks. Though an instinct of pride or modesty made her compress them, he held her firmly.

"A refusal, Lesley?" he asked gently, "A good whipping with a pony-lash would cure you of such reluctance. Is it that you still regard your body as your property to show or not to show as the mood takes you?"

She looked at him uncertainly but made no answer. Anton, as her master, made the decision for her.

"Do as Mano tells you," he said.

She turned her head away, bowing it until only the high crown of soft fair hair was visible to those behind her. Yet the moon-pale cheeks of her backside now relaxed. Mano pressed them apart and looked down into the stretched valley of Lesley's bottom-crack.

"So self-conscious about your arsehole, Lesley?" he asked, "Do you imagine you are made differently in that area to a thousand other girls who have bent over before their masters? You see? You flinch at the touch of a finger there! Ah, I think it is because you envisage what will be done to you in that part by the men who possess you!"

He held her in this spread posture while Anton clicked the camera shutter again. Then Mano was satisfied.

"Let her lie there like that," he said, drawing Anton aside, "The pictures should be added to the ones already taken of her and shown to men who may wish to enjoy her. Lesley is far from being your slave yet, however much she may whimper for your penis between her legs. I will give you my advice."

He sat on the arm of a chair and looked up at the younger man.

"First you should take her somewhere, a place where other people may walk or ride by. She must obey you in small things. In showing herself as you please to strangers. In submitting to be birched like an awkward pupil."

Mano lit a cigarette and then resumed.

"Then you must let her see how a girl who has accepted slavery is dealt with. You might choose Julie, or Maggie, of one of the others. Let her see them beaten."

"Her curiosity would get the better of her," Anton said with a laugh.

Mano nodded.

"Then she must submit to an ordeal. You should arrange for her to be taken somewhere where she must show her obedience through suffering without ever receiving pleasure. It could be done in a day or a night. Only after that can you tell whether she is the right woman to accompany you on the first stage of the journey into total submission."

"That is the hardest part for her," Anton said, smiling, "Look how she squirms at the mention of it. Lesley knows that there can be no return from such a journey as that. Her slavery would be as final and as complete as that of a girl in the most secure and perverse regime of a harem-master."

"And as exciting to her," said Mano sardonically, "See how fast the blood pulses in her veins at the mention of such horrors!"

"In ten days," Anton said, "In ten days I will take her riding and test her obedience in public."

They stood there, looking at the young woman who lay bottom-upward over the sofa-back, her long breaths audible in the warm room, her thighs touching and pressing, for all her aloof self-possession, like a schoolgirl of twelve or thirteen unable to control a thrilling of her nerves.

The two men watched her a moment longer. Beyond the glass, on the balcony of the tall hotel, Debby contemplated the scene, her dark softly-lashed eyes wide with innocent longing for the young woman lying over the sofa. With the fine prettiness of her features, the openness of her wide-boned face, the charming cut of her golden-brown hair in its pretty fringe and the coy brushing back to uncover her ears and neck, she had all those qualities which Lesley seemed to lack. Yet it was Lesley who possessed the urges of a mature young woman, some of which Debby could not yet comprehend.

Mano looked at Lesley for a moment longer.

"I will make a suggestion," he said presently, "I will find you a sadist when you put Lesley to her final test before beginning the long journey. Look at her. In order to show her liberation from marriage and children, to assert her equality with men, she cuts her hair almost like a boy. She wears a black trouser-suit or jeans. Very well, let her be taken to a place where her femininity will be disregarded."

"The prison-farm," Anton said.

Mano nodded.

"An institution whose warden is an unabashed sadist. Let her taste such equality by being treated as a delinquent youth. She will be punished as those lads are. Without pleasure and without pity. Since she cuts her hair like a boy, let her buttocks be bamboo'd while she sprawls bottom-upwards like a prison-farm boy over the warden's sofa. He makes such punishments last an hour or more. He will not care if she has the bottom-cheeks of a young married woman with two children of her own. Lesley may scream and squirm, but he will bamboo her until the cheeks of her arse are bruised and wealed."

"I know his reputation," Anton said softly, as much for the young woman's benefit as for Mano's, "He will not be checked by weals and bruises on Lesley's buttocks, nor a few trickles of blood. His practice is to cane all the harder when the culprit is in that state. She will cry out and scream, of course, but they are used to hearing such things in that place and no one will think it unusual."

"Then let it be her final proof before she submits to you absolutely," Mano said, "If she cannot do so after such an experience, it will still have checked her arrogance. She will be a curiosity to men—but to women most of all—an emancipated young woman who smuggled herself into such a place in order to be thrashed like an adolescent boy!"

They watched Lesley and saw that horror and excitement contended in her at the description of the ordeal they proposed.

The hour between the warm scented afternoons of the beaches and the more formal engagements of the evening was devoted to such secret pleasures and bondage as Anton or Mano inflicted upon Lesley and their other young woman. It was a time of yellow sunlight through wan curtaining, of naked thighs parting and yearning on silk or leather, of the girl's eyes imploring her master over the gag which widened her lips.

Later on, when dinner was over, the actors in these scenes appeared in a dress and a manner which would have made their private excitements the wonder of the world. Evening was a time of paved gardens among dark evergreens, of balustrades and the glass moons of lamps on their wrought-iron standards. Starlight shivered and splintered on a gently filling tide.

Such men as Mano and Anton led, with their women, lives of the greatest formality in this respect. Not for them the easy cadences of the café-song and the chatter of the little tables.

Lesley's thighs and hips were covered by a long skirt, her back and breasts by an ornate bodice. With her companions, she passed each evening in the gilt and plush of the recital rooms. More surely than Mano or Anton, the genius in the fingers of the pianist held the young woman in mute obedience to his mood. From the bland crescendoes of Chopin the minutes passed to the dark chords of Beethoven, waking drama from the tomb of silence. At each pause in the sonata's flow, girls sat meek as nuns in the warm velvet stirring of the piano's harmonies. Lamplight shone on bare shoulders in the still air. Presently the dark majesty of the instrument sounded the elegaic charm of Schumann, quietly reflective in the *Kinderscenen* or soaring in the exhilaration which concluded the *Etudes Symphoniques*.

After the summer evening recitals, the counterpart to the operas and concerts of the winter city, the men led the young women back to their rooms. Though Lesley and Debby were permitted to share a room, while Mano and Anton gave their attention to Kim or Trudi, the events of the afternoon had made Lesley seem indifferent to the girl's adoration of her.

They undressed in one another's sight, Debby taking off her red jacket and white blouse, her light grey skirt, without averting her gaze from Lesley for more than a moment. Lesley had chosen as her night attire a short top of translucent black silk and a pair of panties to match. Debby had imitated this style, though in pale blue.

Lesley had put on her diaphanous black top and was about to pull the panties up when Debby sighed and slid her arms about her. She was trying, as if in a child's game, to snatch the black silk briefs from the young woman's hand.

Hugging Lesley, the pretty girl of eighteen kissed the bare arms and murmured to her.

"Please," she whispered, "Please don't put them on. I want to love you. I want to love you so much. Please let me."

The older woman made no affectionate response to this beyond putting the briefs down on a chair and stretching herself on the bed. Debby, taking off her own panties, lay down beside her. Safe in one another's arms they kissed and petted each other with gentle sighs and lascivious little squirmings. Yet the difference between them was evident at once.

Lesley masturbated Debby first. She slipped her hand between the eagerly opened adolescent thighs and then did it quickly and expertly. Debby gave a shuddering little cry as her excitement began. She closed her wide innocent eyes. The pretty teeth worried her lower lip in her ecstasy. Alone among the clerks with whom she worked, the other girls of the travel bureau, Debby's lover was a woman. Lesley stroked the golden brown hair where it was cut back to show the neat whorls of her ears. She kissed the short level fringe on the girl's forehead.

Debby responded by little squeezing motions of her awkward thighs, as if in clumsy gratitude to the hand which rubbed her between them.

Lesley turned slowly and lay down so that her own face was level with Debby's thighs and the girl's mouth almost touching Lesley's tuft of pubic hair. Lesley kissed the moist feminine tract between the girl's legs and felt Debby respond in the same manner, though less certainly.

Far off a clock chimed midnight. They settled down to tongue and nuzzle one another in a passionate lovemaking which would be renewed with little interruption until two or three in the morning. With a half indifferent air to the girl's pleasure, Lesley brought Debby to orgasm by quick kissing and peremptory fondling of her roused vaginal flesh. A brief manipulation of the girl's clitoris was then enough to precipitate the crisis.

Debby, though less expert, grudged nothing to the older woman. Her lips had lavished their adoration on Lesley's face and the buds of her breasts. Now she ran her energetic tongue to and fro in the pubic slit, saluting the clitoris with gentle sucking kisses. She nuzzled Lesley's thighs and bottom-cheeks. Like Mano in the afternoon, she was insistent upon parting them and did not even hold back from imparting her kisses between them.

At last, by an unspoken agreement, their desire had been satisfied on both sides and they lay damp from their exertions in a light embrace. Only then could Debby bring herself to ask the question which had troubled her during the past hours.

"Will you truly let Anton beat you when you next go riding?"

Lesley paused before replying. Then she said, "Yes. If I must."

"But why?"

"Because he will be the master then and I his slave."

Debby drew one arm away.

"I don't understand," she said miserably, "I should hate to be beaten. I could not bear the pain of it."

Lesley touched her lightly.

"A beating is not something one understands at eighteen. Most women never understand at all. It only comes after a great many other experiences."

"If you go away with Anton," Debby asked suddenly, "will you be his slave for ever?"

"Yes, if I go. I may not go after all. If I do, I must be his slave for as long as he wants. If he gives me to another man I should be that other man's slave. That kind of slavery is final. The girls who submit to it go to places from which there is no return. No escape from the love of the man who owns them."

Debby seemed to understand and her pretty face relaxed something of its tension and anxiety. She kissed the side of Lesley's neck.

"If you were Anton's slave, would you let me be your slave?"

Lesley hugged her, as if reassuring a child.

"If I am Anton's slave, whatever is mine is his. You would not be my slave, love. We should both be his."

"But perhaps I could be with you," Debby whispered.

"Perhaps."

As if to end so awkward a conversation and such gentle interrogation, Lesley slipped her hand once more between the girl's legs, feeling the slipperiness and warmth of her earlier lubrication. The lovers' words grew hushed and formal in caution.

"Make love," she murmured, "Make love, Debby, and forget about such things. We shall talk about them later."

The girl began to fondle Lesley between the thighs. Then she stopped.

"When you next go riding with Anton, when your training begins, will you let me be there?"

Lesley kissed her.

"Anton must decide."

"Whatever happens," Debby said, "I want to be with you. If they beat you, I want to be there. Whatever happens. To be with you."

"Perhaps," Lesley said gently, "perhaps Anton will allow it. We shall see."

Then the young married woman and the girl of eighteen began to fondle and play with one another again. The first thin light had broken over the sea before they finally drew from each other and sank into the separate worlds of their dreams.

The Devil's Advocate

by Marcus van Heller

from *Seduced*

9

The woman began to search for her step-ins. She found them laid out neatly on the chair near her dressing table. 'Thank you, my dear girl,' she said with a smile. 'You make a marvellous lady's maid. In fact, you're so good that I'm reluctant to let . . . ' Her voice trailed off and her smile was replaced by a perplexed frown as she looked at Clara's obviously horror-stricken face. 'Whatever is the matter?' she asked. 'You look as though you've just seen a ghost. And you're pale enough to pass for a ghost yourself. Are you ill, child?'

'No, no, not at all,' said Clara with a thin tight-lipped smile. 'I'm just feeling a tiny bit faint. It's nothing to be alarmed about. You see, I haven't eaten any dinner. As a matter of fact, I haven't eaten since breakfast. But I've been drinking—and quite a bit more than usual, I'm afraid. I guess a large quantity of alcohol on an empty stomach will make almost anybody queasy. And it is a bit warm in here, don't you think?'

With this last sentence, Clara's voice assumed a voluptuousness that it had not contained before, and the woman looked at her thoughtfully. 'Yes,' she said, 'now that you mention it, it is rather warm in here. Strange that I didn't notice before. Well, I'll just dress quickly, and we can go for a stroll in the garden to cool off. After you have some dinner, that is. You know, my dear, you really need someone to look after you. Do you live with your family?'

'My parents died in an accident. I've no family at all. Except my sister, that is.'

'Oh, does your sister look after you?'

'No. Not any more. In fact, she seems to have been having some trouble looking after herself.'

'Oh, poor little . . . ' The woman broke off abruptly and laughed in an embarrassed fashion. 'My goodness,' she tittered, 'I don't even know your name.'

'Oh, do forgive me. It's Clara . . . Clara Morrow.'

'Clara. Spanish for "clear." Clear . . . pure. How very appropriate.'

The smile took the sting out of her sardonic tone. 'My name is Alice Burton. And I apologise for keeping you from your dinner. Do come and hook my brassiere for me, will you?"

She slipped her arms through the slender satin straps and turned her naked back towards Clara, who fumblingly hooked the garment's three hooks into its three eyes. Her fingers lightly brushed the woman's warm shoulders and, for an instant, rested there. Alice promptly turned, caught them in her hand and gave them a quick, affectionate squeeze.

The older woman now crossed the room and sat on the edge of the bed. Picking up the stockings Clara had chosen for her, she extended one. 'Here,' she said, 'put it on for me.'

Wordlessly, the girl took the stocking, drew it over Alice's tiny foot and carefully pulled it up over her thigh. Smoothing the silk, she then slipped a black satin garter into place over it. Alice prettily extended her other leg, and Clara repeated the performance.

As she drew the garter on, she stammered: 'I . . . I . . . don't think I got the seams straight. If you'll stand up, I'll . . .'

Alice didn't wait for her to finish the sentence. She rose gracefully and turned, spreading her legs slightly apart so that Clara could hold on to one of them for support as she adjusted the stocking on the other.

Somehow, as Clara fumbled with the seams, her face became pressed against Alice's thigh. She attempted to rise, but Alice's hand was planted firmly atop her head. She dropped back on her haunches. The older woman then lowered her hips back onto the bed and hugged Clara's head to her thigh. Clara remained in that position the better part of a minute, then suddenly pulled away.

'Was I mistaken?' mused Alice aloud.

'What do you mean "mistaken?" Clara asked in apparent confusion. 'About what? What do you want from me?'

'Don't you know?'

The girl shook her head.

Alice smiled and began stroking the girl's silky hair. 'Just a few moments ago,' she 'said very softly, 'you acted as though you knew. As if you wanted it, too.' She raised one thigh and gently brushed Clara's cheek with it. 'But I don't want to force you to do anything you don't want to do. Anything you do with me you must do because you want to; because you like me; and because I like you.'

At this, Clara lifted her head and smiled back. 'Be patient with me,' she said softly. 'Please . . . be patient.' She rubbed her chin against the softness of the woman's inner thigh and again offered a bitter-sweet smile.

Alice slowly drew the girl's head back into place between her legs. Clara's mouth pressed the lace fringe of the woman's panties, and she kissed first the broad expanse of thigh, then the warm, perfumed groin. 'Put out your tongue,' Alice whispered.

Clara touched her tongue to the softest part of the woman's thigh and ran it along the milk-white inner side. She fastened her fingers over the top of the panties to draw them down. Her lips, under the crotch of the wispy garment, touched a few curling hairs that escaped through the legholes. Her tongue dragged sideways over the perfumed petals of the woman's lotus-bud. She pushed the panty crotch to one side with her hand.

Suddenly Alice backed away. 'Get up now, dear,' she said sweetly. 'It's early yet. We have all evening.' She rose from the bed and swung one thigh across Clara's head to step free of her, then recommenced dressing as Clara, dishevelled and apparently distraught, got to her feet and started towards the door.

'Where are you going?' Alice asked, catching Clara's fleeing reflection in the mirror.

'To my room,' Clara answered. She lowered her eyes and added in a voice so low it was barely a whisper: 'To wash my face.'

Alice came to her side and took her wrist. 'No, you mustn't do that. I don't want you to wash your face.'

'But it makes me feel ashamed to stay this way.'

'Then that's all the more reason for staying that way. My goodness, child, if you've never been ashamed of yourself before, you must have been leading a terribly sheltered life. Shame is like wine to a woman; she grows drunk and wanton and glowing on it. How old are you? Twenty?'

Clara nodded.

'Twenty-years-old, and never drunk on shame; never crept to your room and bed feeling wonderfully dirty and used and degraded? My poor little Clara, you have a great deal to learn. So we'll call this your first lesson. You will not wash your face, Clara, any more than I will wash the stains of your lip rouge from my thighs. Those stains will stay there, do you understand? I want you to remember them and think of them every time you look at me tonight?'

She raised her dress to reveal the splotchy marks left by Clara's lips on her thighs. 'Shame wells up inside of you until you think you'll die of it,' she went on, 'but it never fails—all of a sudden the shame is gone and in its place is a wild exhilaration. You'll see, Clara, you'll see.' She paused and gazed at the girl tenderly, almost maternally. 'Don't wash up, but do straighten your dress and comb your hair. As soon as you're presentable, we'll go down-stairs and get you that dinner I've been promising you.'

In less than ten minutes, Clara was comfortably reclining on a lounge chair, a heaping plateful of steaming hot spaghetti and meat balls on a tray across her lap. On a small table at her side sat a basketful of warm garlic bread and a glass of red wine. Alice Burton, seated on the other side of the table, raised her own wine glass. 'To our love affair,' she smiled. 'And to shame.' She waited until Clara lifted her glass in apparent acknowledgement of the toast. Then both women drank.

The next hour passed quietly. The wine and food seemed to relax Clara, and she was soon chattering away with Alice Burton and a few other people who had joined them. She did not seem the least bit embarrassed—and, in fact, she had quite captivated the blasé little group with her native air. It was thus that John Webster found her, in the midst of four or five people, laughing animatedly, her cheeks flushed and her eyes sparkling. 'Here you are!' he beamed enthusiastically. 'I've been searching everywhere for you.' He took Clara's arm and helped her to her feet.

'But she belongs to me now,' Alice Burton objected.

'Then I'll see to it that she comes back to you,' he replied amiably.

'You'd better,' she warned coolly. 'I have plans for her.'

Webster led Clara down the terrace steps and off towards the garden. 'Where are you taking me?' the girl asked.

'To meet two friends of mine,' he said, hustling her past the sundial and into the darkness of an arbour with a cushioned double swing chair hanging between two great oaks. 'You seem to be such a great believer in marital "togetherness" I thought I'd show you a little sample of it.'

'What took you so long?' a woman's voice asked out of the shadows.

'I had a hard time finding her,' replied Webster.

'We almost didn't wait,' said a masculine voice. 'Look what happened.'

The couple was lying in the swing chair, their limbs intertwined. In the darkness it was impossible to fathom where the male left off and the female began.

Clara turned away. Webster tightened his grip on her forearm. 'Just where do you think you're going?'

'Back to the house. Can't you see that we're disturbing your friends.'

Peals of laughter greeted the comment. 'I told you she was naive!' said Webster triumphantly.

Turning to Clara he added: 'We're not disturbing them, honey. We're going to help them out. You know—entertain them a bit, inspire them.'

The three friends laughed again.

'Oh! Take me back to the house,' Clara begged. 'Please, Johnny.'

'Listen,' said Webster roughly. 'Don't start the innocent virgin bit again. It won't work. He lowered his voice and said softly into Clara's ear. 'Unless you do exactly what I tell you to, I'll strip you right down to the skin and take you back to the house like that . . . to Blanca!'

'I'm not afraid of her,' said Clara defiantly.

'You should be. Remember that I know things about you that she doesn't.' He felt her resistance lessening, and, interpreting this as a sign of acquiescence, said aloud: 'Sorry, folks. The little lady's still kind of shy. But she's got over it now, haven't you, baby?'

Clara nodded.

'Haven't you?' he repeated harshly.

'Yes,' said Clara. 'I've got over my shyness now.'

'And you don't mind undressing now, do you?'

'Undressing?' There was a note of incredulity in her voice as she echoed the word.

'Yeah. Undressing. You know—taking your clothes off.'

More laughter from the swing.

'Don't answer. Just strip,' said Webster.

The girl began to obey, taking her dress off slowly, as though she were in a trance. Next came her shoes and stockings, then her slip. Finally, with great hesitation, she removed her brassiere. Then she stood facing the swing, her arms crossed over her pretty, pink breasts.

Webster tugged at the waistband of her panties. 'I said to take off everything,' he commanded in a voice that brooked no argument. And then, in a gentler tone, he added: 'You've got a beautiful body, darling. Did I tell you that? You should be proud of it. You should want these people to see it. The way I want them to see it because I'm proud of it. Proud that it belongs to me. That I can do whatever I want with so much loveliness.' As if to prove his domination over her, he violently tugged the seat of the panties over her smooth, round buttocks. 'Take them off,' he snapped. 'Now.'

Clara began to cry softly, whispering. 'Oh, no,' over and over again, like a litany. But she obeyed.

Grinning lasciviously, Webster clutched her breasts and squeezed tightly. Then he manoeuvreed her hands onto his penis, which he had removed from his trousers and which now stood bravely and sturdily erect. 'Rub it between your legs,' he said.

Clara did so as a tiny gasp, which welled into a shriek, emanated from the swing, indicating that the couple ensconced there had not been paying full attention to the activities being staged ostensibly for their benefit. The shriek was followed by a duet of giggles, and suddenly the couple bounded off the swing. The man knelt at the base of one of the oaks and fumbled around for several seconds. Then he struck a match and with it lit a small kerosene torch. Carrying the torch, he sat beneath his partner on the grass, not two feet away from where Clara and Webster were standing. Promptly a second act of copulation was begun.

The tiny flame of the torch flicked and quivered, shedding a soft glow around the entangled couple. 'No, No, No, NO!' cried Clara, her voice rising hysterically. 'I can't bear her to look at it!'

Webster gripped her by the shoulders, his fingers digging into her flesh. 'Stop it,' he hissed. 'Just stop it.' The force of his grip and the authority in his voice seemed to have a tranquillising effect on the girl, for after a moment she relaxed visibly.

'All right, now?' asked Webster.

Clara nodded dumbly.

'Then forget the lamp. Just forget it. Pretend you're still in the dark. Just you and me. In the dark.' He had softened his voice, and he spoke the last words in an hypnotic sing-song. He held Clara almost tenderly, gently stroking her hair. When he felt the tension go out of her he again placed his organ in her hands. 'Rub,' he whispered.

She held the rigid device against her own hairiness, rubbing it between her palms and against the flesh of her groin.

'Spread your legs and rub it against your pussy,' Webster commanded.

She pressed the large bud of the swelling stalk between the soft petals of her dear little flower. She stood on the tips of her toes, rocking back and forth. Presently, dew covered the sweet petals—liquid from Webster's rigid watering can, and liquid which flowed out of Clara's little well.

Webster toyed with her buttocks and her breasts, bruising her nipples against the roughness of his jacket as he pressed her close to him. He curled his fingers and ran his nails lightly along her sides to her thighs.

'You tickle,' she said with a giggle.

Unsmiling, he told her to kneel in front of him.

When she complied, he said: 'Lick it. Lick the part you had between your legs.' He pushed her head close to his crotch, close to his swelling love instrument, and repeated his demand.

Clara dutifully obeyed him. She ran her tongue slowly up and down his organ, making it lurch stiffly. Then she curved her finger around it and held it firmly as she licked the sides and the bare tip.

'Good,' said Webster. 'But not good enough.'

She held it up and licked beneath it, up and down the underside where the rim of the head came together in the little slot at the tip. Webster's hands gripped her head tightly, holding her mouth fiercely to its task.

Suddenly the other woman sprang up and came to kneel beside Clara. Her naked thigh touched Clara's, her fingers slipped over the fingers which clasped Webster's shaft. Her voice whispered voluptuously into Clara's ear, 'Lick it with me, honey.' She then faced Clara, pressing her own cheek against Webster's thigh. Her full, sensual lips buried themselves in his groin. Then they touched Clara's lips, kissing them over the arc of Webster's maleness. Her tongue flickered out, wetting Clara's lips with its hot moisture, brushing across Webster's member, then returning to Clara's lips.

'Lick it with me,' the woman repeated urgently. Her tongue pressed more firmly against the side of the shaft, forcing it harder against Clara's mouth. She placed one arm around Clara, and feverishly stroked the girl's breast. Her own breast brushed Clara's other breast and their nipples kissed. Then she slipped her hand down to Clara's buttocks, avidly caressing their round fullness. She tried to push the head of Webster's swollen organ into Clara's mouth, but Clara slid her lips away and tucked her tongue under the head.

The woman's tongue covered Clara's, tickling it teasingly. Clara curled her tongue in the other direction; the woman's tongue followed, licking more insistently and firmly. At last the woman drew Clara's tongue into her mouth and sucked it, lipping Webster's manhood at the same time. Then she drew his weapon into her mouth, sucking it and Clara's tongue simultaneously. Her lips pressed the organ firmly against Clara's tongue, so that it was being licked by Clara and sucked by the other woman at the same time. Webster's hips began to plunge back and forth, back and forth, and Clara violently pulled her tongue free.

The other girl's mouth stopped working and she pulled her lips away with an audible pop. 'Don't you want to suck it too?' she asked.

'No!' gasped Clara. 'Oh, no.'

'Then lick it.'

She pushed Clara's face against Webster's groin. 'Lick!'

She waited for Clara to obey before she replaced the end of the organ in her mouth, compressing her lips tightly around it.

Then she slipped her hand through Webster's open legs and tickled the groove between his buttocks with one delicate finger. Meanwhile, Clara dutifully continued to rub the base of the shaft with the tip and blade of her tongue.

Suddenly, the older girl's face convulsed. Her lips grew wetter and she sucked more noisily than ever. Webster's hips were gyrating wildly, and his legs trembled and pressed more firmly against the girl's cheeks.

Webster suddenly pushed both women away, and stepped back. Clara's whole body drooped, and she closed her eyes, a relieved expression on her face. She remained there until she felt the man's member once again rubbing her lips. Even then she didn't open her eyes. She merely stuck out her tongue and resumed her former task. After awhile, she opened her eyes, raised her head . . . and gasped. It was not Webster who towered above her, but a stranger—the man who had just witnessed the little scene in which Clam had participated.

Clara's eyes widened, and she pulled away. The man quickly grabbed her body between his knees and placed his hands on her shoulders: The other girl, who had already begun to suck this new lollipop, also placed her arms around Clara.

'You're not going to stop now—after you've begun so well, are you?' the man queried mockingly.

'I didn't realise,' cried Clara. 'I didn't know . . . I don't know you . . . oh . . . please . . . '

'It isn't any different, honeychile,' the other woman said. When she spoke out loud, her voice carried the heavy langourousness of the deep South. 'You didn't even know the difference till you looked.

'But if it will make you feel any better, why, just pretend it's Johnny you're loving up.'

Clara appealed to Webster, now seated in a corner of the swing, watching dispassionately. 'Johnny,' she said, 'do I have to?'

'Yes, Clara, you have to.'

'Oh, please don't make me. Please take me back to the house.'

'When you've finished what you've started. This is a funny time to turn squeamish, don't you think? You've already licked one man. I can't see why you should object to licking another. Don't they all taste pretty much alike, Mary Lou?' he asked, addressing the other girl.

'Practically,' she laughed. 'Make her suck it if she doesn't want to lick it. Maybe it would be fun to see your virgin girl friend suck my husband. Arnold, darling, have you ever been sucked by a virgin?'

The man glared at her. 'Can it,' he said, 'and get back to work.'

The girl reached for her husband's love instrument and rubbed it against Clara's mouth, whispering in her ear as she did so.

Clara flushed. 'No!' she spat. 'That's disgusting! I'd never say such a thing.'

'Say it, or I'll have Johnny make you swallow Arnold's come.'

Clara lowered her eyes and said softly: 'I like licking men. I want to do it again.'

Arnold smiled and arched his hips forward. 'That's the spirit, kid,' he said. Clara resumed lipping his organ, rubbing her mouth up and down the sides of the penis as though she were playing a flute. She mouthed it up and down to the tip, finally nibbling on the tip itself. Mary Lou came in on the downstroke, and the two wet tongues played an andante up and down the length of the instrument. Then, when the jerking motions of his hips told the woman that her husband was about to reach his climax, she put the tip into her mouth and pressed forward until her lips almost reached his pubic hair.

Clara drew back as Mary Lou began sucking violently, driving her mouth up and down and shaking her head from side to side.

When she had finished, she rose and began to dress. Clara remained seated, as though she was too dazed to move. She remained there, squatting on the flagstones, until Webster touched her shoulders and silently held out her underwear. She then rose and stepped into her panties. She extended her arms and he slipped the straps of the brassiere over them. Then he hooked the hooks in the back and slipped her dress over her head.

Finally he handed her her evening purse, saying: 'I suggest you powder your face and put on lipstick. That is unless you want everybody to know what you've been doing for the past hour.'

Clara blanched and immediately withdrew her compact from the purse. When she had finished making herself as presentable as possible, Webster said: 'Come on, now, we're going back. After all, I did promise Alice I'd return you to her.'

Alice Burton dragged on her cigarette and sensually blew the smoke out through her nostrils. 'Aren't you drinking rather heavily?' she asked Clara, watching the girl down two straight shots of Hennessy Seven Star in as many gulps.

'I haven't had anything else to drink but the wine for dinner,' said Clara, reaching for a glass of ice water. For a moment she held it in her hand—a hand which trembled so much that Alice could hear the ice cubes tinkling against the glass. Then she lifted it to her lips, gulped down the contents thirstily, and poured herself another jigger of cognac.

Alice waited until the girl had put down the shot glass. Then she said softly: 'You've really been through the mill, haven't you? Would you like to tell me about it?'

Clara gulped. 'No! Oh NO! I *couldn't.* I don't even want to think about it again.'

'All right, dear. I won't force the issue. Shall we just go out on the terrace to clear our heads? The cigarette smoke is really dreadful in here, isn't it?'

'Yes. All right,' agreed Clara. She followed Alice out onto the terrace and sat opposite her in the same deck chair in which she had been sitting less than two hours before, amusing Alice's friends with her naive banter.

'It seems like two years,' she said suddenly.

'What seems like two years, Clara?'

'The time that's passed since the last time we sat here. I was so happy then. Silly little baby. Being cute for all the grownups. Making them laugh. Oh, I'm funny all right. A real laugh riot.' Her voice broke with a sob, and she buried her face in her hands.

Alice, who had been standing at the railing of the terrace, moved next to the girl, placing her arms around the shaking shoulders and lightly stroking the tousled hair. At last the sobs ceased and the shaking body grew still. Clara drew away from the warm shelter of Alice's arms and sat erect, drawing her knees up and hugging them to her chest. 'Thank you,' she said, in a barely audible voice, 'for being so good to me. I don't deserve it.'

'Don't be silly,' replied Alice sharply. 'I'm only being nice to you because I want you to like me. If I weren't interested in you, Clara, I wouldn't have ever suggested that you help me change clothes. I probably wouldn't even have been so nice about your spilling water on my dress.'

'Oh!' Clara opened her eyes very wide. 'I didn't realise . . . that is . . . I mean. I didn't think . . . I mean . . . Oh, dear, I'm so confused.'

Alice laughed softly and patted Clara's hand. 'I know, lovey, and that's what interests me about you: your innocent confusion. You know, Clara, you're not the type of girl one expects to find here. I've been wondering just what it is that makes you stay . . . ' She waited for Clara to say something, but the girl remained silent. 'If you don't enjoy yourself here,' Alice continued, 'you should go home. Where life is safe and sane. Where you won't see too much; where you won't scorch your pretty tinsel wings.'

'I don't understand what you mean.'

'And you won't understand until it's too late, I suppose. You know, you really have seen nothing terribly shocking yet. Don't you realise that? You think it's been like a nightmare, don't you? You think the things you've seen and done are utterly depraved. Well, my dear, you're wrong. Although I don't know exactly what you did tonight, I can take a pretty fair guess. I know John Webster and I know what his tastes are. That's why I let you go with him. Because I knew you'd be safe in his hands.'

'Safe?' Clara gasped. 'Safe?'

'Yes,' Alice smiled. 'Safe. You see. I told you you hadn't seen anything yet. Just listen, Clara, listen to the conversations around us. Listen carefully. . . .

The two women sat silently for a moment, and strange voices wafted through the night air.

' . . . sent his wife into their son's bedroom, naked, with two bottles of champagne. A kid of fifteen; never drank a drop before . . . '

' . . . a wonderful place. . . . Completely integrated . . . In a coffin, on top of a white woman—with black candles lit at both ends. Terribly dramatic. And perfectly discreet.'

' . . . an incestuous family, all five of them, including the grandfather. Charming people.'

' . . . but after she'd been to bed with him and then went to New Orleans and Switzerland, she couldn't think of anything better to do with her sixty thousand a year and her million dollar education and six languages but get the Doberman to make love to her while the Pekinese curled up underneath and lapped her—that's why they call them lap dogs, you know—at the same time . . . '

'I feel rather tired,' said Clara. 'I think I'll go to bed now.'

'Do you want me to take you back to your room?'

'Yes, please.'

The older woman helped the girl to her feet, put her arm around the slender waist and walked her into the house and up the staircase.

'Here it is,' said Clara, stopping in front of the door and fumbling in her purse for the key. At last she found it and placed it in the key hole.

The two women entered the room. Clara took the key from the lock, closed the door and replaced the key in the keyhole on the inside of the door. She paused for a moment, then locked herself and Alice in.

The woman stood quietly, watching, waiting for Clara to make the next move. But the girl seemed rooted to the spot, as though locking the door had sapped her of her last ounce of strength.

Alice went to her side and prodded her gently. 'Come to bed, dear. It's way past two a.m. and you're exhausted.'

Clara obeyed, moving towards the bed as though in a trance.

Alice switched on the small bedside lamp. 'Take off your dress,' she said, crossing the room to turn out the overhead light. 'And I'll take off mine in just a minute. Then I'll come back to you and we can make love. That is, if you really want to. If you don't, tell me now and I'll understand. But tell me now.'

She took the girl's continued silence for assent, and slipped her dress off and hung it neatly over the back of a chair.

Glancing at Clara, she saw that the girl was still fully clothed.

'Your dress, dear,' she said in the tone one uses with a recalcitrant six-year-old. 'Take it off.'

Clara obeyed, sitting up to do so. Then she fell back heavily on the bed as the dress slipped to the floor.

Now Alice returned to the bed and gently began stripping off Clara's underclothes, pausing occasionally to stroke and audibly admire the slender young body under her hands. As she stripped off Clara's stockings, she exclaimed: 'Why, your knee is badly scraped. But your stocking isn't even snagged. Now I'm beginning to understand. So John had you act out one of his little dramas, did he? He wasn't content with you as an audience, eh?' She paused. 'But why did you go along with it, Clara? *Why?* If you don't like these libertine excesses, why don't you leave here? You're free to go at any time, you know. Are you a masochist? Is that it? Is that why you stay here? Because you like to be hurt and humiliated? Tell me.' She bent over the girl, cupped the wan, heart-shaped face in her hand and gazed at the soft blue eyes. But she could read nothing in them.

'Please,' begged Clara, twisting her head away, 'I don't want to talk about it. Really I don't. Not now, anyway.' She sat up and put her arms around Alice, awkwardly unfastening the hooks of the black brassiere which, earlier in the evening, she herself had fastened. Then she slid her hands down to the slender waist and tugged gently at the waistband of the flimsy black step-ins. Alice arched her buttocks while Clara pushed the thin garment over her ample hips. She began to draw it down over the shapely legs when suddenly she stopped, and, with an exclamation, bent over the woman's mid-section. She put out one finger and tentatively touched the scorpion brand, as though she expected it to sting her. 'What's that?' she asked.

'So that's what startled you when you saw me nude earlier tonight,' she chuckled. 'It's a kind of tattooing.'

'But it's burned in. Didn't it hurt terribly? And why a scorpion? And in such a place?'

'One of my lovers put it there. He wanted a scorpion and he wanted it there, so that's why. And it didn't hurt when it was put on. He used an anaesthetic salve.'

'I didn't know there was such a thing. But then it seems like everything here is new to me, doesn't it?' Clara gave Alice a shamefaced smile. Then her face went serious again. 'But didn't your husband object?'

'Never mind about my husband and the scorpion,' said Alice. 'I don't like to talk about other lovers when I'm with you. Look! Your lipstick is still on my thighs. I told you I wouldn't remove it.' She took Clara's hand and guided it to the grotto where the now faded and smeared lip rouge obscured the smooth whiteness of her thighs.

'Have your thighs ever had lipstick on them?' she asked.

'No. I've never . . . been with a woman before,' said Clara.

'So. I'm the first, am I?' Clara nodded.

'Well, then, it's up to me to teach you the joys of lesbian love. If you don't enjoy this evening, it'll be all my fault.'

During the conversation, Alice had been rubbing Clara's nipples with the flat of her hand. Now the two bullet-like protuberances stood out sharply, and the older woman leaned over and delicately took one between her teeth and gnawed it lightly. Then she began tonguing it, moving in ever-increasing concentric circles which soon covered a good sized area of Clara's breast.

'Oh!' said Clara.'That feels nice!' She sounded surprised.

Alice lifted her head and smiled at the girl. 'I'll show you something else that's nice,' she said, and taking her own breasts in her hands, she rubbed the nipples against Clara's until they, too, grew hard, and began to tingle. Then she drew Clara to her and held her tightly. Their two bellies rubbed together, the strands of hair between their legs intertwined.

Alice gently forced Clara's thighs apart with one of her own, and began moving that thigh up and down against the mouth of Clara's treasure trove. 'Relax,' she whispered. 'Just let yourself go. Stop thinking. Let your mind merge with your senses. Feel, Clara, feel! Feel how nice it is, how warm. Very, very warm.' She spoke in a low monotone, almost as though she were trying to hypnotise the girl. And indeed, the words did seem to produce a hypnotic effect, for Clara's body relaxed, and the lines of tension on her normally smooth young face had vanished.

Alice continued to move her thigh up and down, up and down, feeling with satisfaction the warm moisture spreading out of the little girl's oven and onto her own flesh. 'Take my breasts in your hands,' she whispered. 'Excite me as I excite you.'

Clara complied, awkwardly crushing the woman's swelling globes in her moist palms. As she did so, Alice began to rub her own slit against one of Clara's legs. She was already quite excited, and she could feel Clara stiffen as the hot moisture spread over her thigh. But then the girl relaxed again and continued to toy with Alice's breasts.

'Put your hands on my buttocks now,' said Alice. 'But slowly. Work your way down. Explore me. Learn my body. Learn the things which excite me.'

Clara looked puzzled, and Alice smiled. 'Never mind, I'll explain all that later. Right now, I just want you to feel pleasure.'

Clara obediently but awkwardly ran her hands down Alice's body. Her awkwardness kindled a flame in the older woman, who began squirming and more insistently rubbing herself against the girl's leg. Clara then reached for the woman's buttocks and began patting them with one hand as, with one finger of the other, at Alice's instruction, she explored the valley between the two ripely swelling mounds. Suddenly

Alice gasped as Clara's finger slipped between the lips of her love nest.

'Oh, that's good!' she moaned. 'Keep it there! Don't take it away!' She pushed the girl onto her back and pressed her own delta firmly between Clara's legs. She began to push her hips back and forth so that the two plants which flowered between their legs rubbed petals. Alice began to bite and suck at Clara's nipples as she rocked back and forth, and was rewarded with another gasp from the young girl. 'Oh don't stop, Alice! Please don't stop!'

'I won't darling, I won't.'

And she didn't stop until she felt the spasm welling and breaking through the girl's body, until the girl herself went limp and whispered: 'I don't feel a thing any more.'

Alice would have smiled had she not been so excited. Instead, she rolled off Clara and onto her back spreading her legs wide. 'Do it to me, now, Clara. Do to me what I just did to you. I'll show, you how.' She pulled Clara between her legs. 'Make love to me, child. Love me with your sex, the way I loved you with mine. The way Johnny loved you tonight.'

'Oh!' Clara gasped. 'But he didn't . . . that is . . . I . . . oh please, he didn't make love to me and I don't want to think about it any more.'

'Tell me about it,' Alice commanded. 'Tell me about it while you make love to me, while you excite me and set me on fire. Tell me, Clara, what happened tonight?'

'I told you, I won't talk about it. You didn't want to talk about your lovers while you're with me. And I don't want to talk about mine.' Then, all traces of reluctance suddenly leaving her voice, she said quickly: 'But if you really want to know, tell me about the man who put the scorpion on your stomach and I'll tell you all about what I did with Johnny.'

'Touché,' laughed Alice, pressing herself ever closer against Clara and gently guiding the motions of the girl's body with motions of her own. 'But I pass for now. Let's make love, and we'll talk later.'

After a great deal of awkward experimentation on Clara's part, Alice reached a climax. Then she lay quietly at Clara's side, smoking a cigarette and idly stroking the girl's thighs and lower stomach. Suddenly she said. 'Clara. You told me Johnny didn't make love to you. That means he made you suck him, didn't he?'

'Oh, no. I'd never do that! Mary Lou sucked him while I licked.'

Alice suppressed a laugh. 'I see,' she said, as she stubbed out her cigarette. 'Would you like to lick me, Clara? While I lick you? Shall we lie here and lick each other?' She kissed Clara's hip and then the fleshy part of her inner thigh, brushing against the swelling Mount of Venus with her cheek.

'No!' cried Clara. 'Oh no! I just couldn't. You won't make me do it, will you?'

'Why, of course not, darling. I won't make you do anything you don't want to.' Inaudibly she added: 'Not tonight, anyway.' She continued in a normal voice. 'But you won't mind if I do it to you, will you?' Without waiting for an answer, she kissed Clara squarely between the legs. Then she extended her tongue and began exploring Clara's delightful rose bush.

'You've done this to a lot of girls, haven't you?'

'We're not going to talk about our sexual experiences any more this evening,' came the reply, the sound of Alice's voice muffled between Clara's thighs. She went back to her task with renewed ardour.

'It's you who should be ashamed now,' said Clara suddenly.

The woman again, stopped tonguing. 'Perhaps I am,' she said. 'But if I am, it's part of the thrill I get. I told you before, shame is like wine; it goes with a good meal, heightens the taste of it and makes you high.'

'And that's why the mark on your belly is there. It's a mark of shame, isn't it? Did you want it there so that every man who made love to you would know about all the terrible things you'd done?'

Alice laughed. 'Really, Clara. You have the most vivid imagination I've ever encountered. And I hate to disappoint you, but I haven't done all that many "terrible" things.' While she was speaking, Alice's fingers had replaced her tongue, busily exciting and inflaming the swelling petals of Clara's sweet bush. Now Alice bent once more again to tongue the flowerlets, as Clara's body tensed and began to move in response to the probing fingers.

'Rub inside,' Clara said, and the woman slipped her tongue deep into the warm, moist cavern. To Alice's surprise, Clara now slipped her finger inside Alice's well and began to move it vigorously up and down. Alice began to suck again, harder than ever.

'Oh, stop!' Clara cried. 'Stop!'

But Alice did not stop. She continued rubbing back and forth against Clara's finger, and sucking and licking the girl's love parts.

'Oh, I'm going to explode!' cried Clara as, suddenly, the woman's finger intruded between her buttocks and plunged violently in and out. She twisted and writhed around.

Now Alice moved so that her Mount of Venus was about an inch from Clara's face. The girl, thrashing wildly, turned towards the dripping wet grotto. She reached out her tongue, licked the tiny petals and began to suck them violently, as her hips gyrated ever faster.

Alice threw her head back and smacked her lips, then bent forward again and nipped the soft flesh of Clara's little pink lips.

Clara screamed. A violent spasm shook her. She opened her mouth, and Alice pressed against it harder than before.

Clara stuck her tongue into the gaping cavern of Alice's sex and reached a second climax.

Travel Light

by Michael Hemmingson

from *66 Chapters about 33 Women*

Here he was. He'd come here to be free. Now what did he do; what did he want?

—William T. Vollmann
The Rifles

34

LITTLE MISS FUCKY-SUCKY

"What I wanted most," Gene said to Nick at the bar, "was to fuck a wide variety of women—I mean internationally. I wanted to be global about it. So after I graduated from college, I did a little jaunt around the world."

"In search of pussy?" Nick said.

"Oh yeah," Gene said. "The logical first place to go was Thailand. I mean, I heard the stories about the whores. I wanted to go and see for myself. So I went. Just got on a flight, with a good deal of money I saved, and I went."

"Wow."

"Wow is what I said when I got there. I mean, I'm sure you've heard the stories."

"I've heard the stories."

"So you know."

"I kind of know."

"You've heard the stories," Gene said, "and I lived the stories. Or some of the stories."

"Like?" Nick said.

"These whores in Bangkok were so pretty, so sweet, so cute, so young," Gene said. "It breaks my heart just thinking about them. But they were also dirty little whores."

"I bet."

"You saw them everywhere, hanging off the arms of these fat and unattractive Europeans. And Americans. And then there were the GI's. And then there were regular guys, like me. I was just a regular guy, right?"

"Right."

"So I walk into this one bar, and a lot of these Thai girls were in there—bar girls—and they immediately come up to me and they go, 'You want for me to smoke you?' Smoke me? They meant sucking my dick. I see this guy getting his dick sucked right at the bar counter and so I go, 'Well, why not?' I see this very pretty very skinny little bar girl and I say, 'You and me fucky-sucky?'

"'That my name, Mr. American Man,' she goes, 'my name is Little Miss Fucky-Sucky.'"

35

LITTLE MISS FUCKY-SUCKY

"And was she ever," Gene continued. "She blew me there in the bar, I shot my load right down her gullet, and it was one of the best blow-jobs I'd ever had—at the time. And it only cost me like two dollars." Gene smiled, took a drink of his beer.

"No," Nick says. "No way."

"Hell yes way," Gene said. "The dollar gets you far in Thailand, or at least it did then: got you a lot of bhat for your buck. And more bang for your buck.

"Anyway, I took a liking to Little Miss Fucky-Sucky. I especially liked her little brown titties. Those were the kind of little brown titties I really liked.

"It cost me about twenty bucks to have Little Miss Fucky-Sucky spend the night with me, which is a pretty good rate, wouldn't you say?"

Nick said, "It's a great rate."

"We fuckied and suckied all night every way imaginable," Gene said, "and she liked it. I mean, she wasn't like some whores who just lay there and not make a sound."

"I wouldn't know."

"Never been with a whore?"

"No," Nick said.

"You should try it some time."

"Maybe I will."

"I mean, I was so impressed, in the morning, I asked her to stay. Another day. I said I'd pay her double. She was very happy about this. Maybe because she didn't have to go back to the bar. She went, 'Okay-dokay, Number One American Guy, I will be your wife for the weekend.'"

"Wife?"

Gene laughed. "Yeah. I said, 'I don't want a wife for the weekend.' 'Then I'll be your Number One Girlfriend for the weekend,' she said. And so she was."

36

LITTLE MISS PISSY-PISSY

"But then there was Little Miss Pissy-Pissy," Gene said, "and boy was she something else."

"These Thai girls sure had colorful names," Nick said.

"Well they went by Ha and La and Woo and Loo and Joy and Oy and whatever; but I liked it when they were, well, like Little Miss Pissy-Pissy. See, Fucky-Sucky did a lot of things but she wasn't into watersports or scat; and I wanted to get down and dirty and kinky so I had to look for a new girlfriend. I found her in another bar, a different bar, one of very many. I asked around, I told the bar girls what I wanted:

" 'I want a girl who'll drink my piss and who'll piss in my mouth in return.' What I really wanted was a drinker.

"So this little whore who was even younger than Fucky-Sucky said, 'I will drink your pissy-pissy, Mister.'

"'Can I call you Little Miss Pissy-Pissy then?' I ask her.

" 'She goes, 'Yes, sir.'"

"'So we negotiate a price. This cost me five, six dollars. I take her into the men's bathroom, which was a small smelly hole with a trawl. She gets on her knees and says, 'I am a toilet now.' I tell you, it was sexy."

"So?"

"So I pissed in her mouth and she drank it."

37

LITTLE MISS PISSY-PISSY

Gene said, "Of course, I wanted her for the night as well. So I took Little Miss Pissy-Pissy back to my hotel room where we had a great night of watersports fun."

"She piss on you?"

"Yeah. I just do it for the hell of it. I get off more pissing on a woman, especially in her mouth."

"You're one nasty motherfucker," Nick said.

"You don't know the extent of my nastiness," Gene said.

38

WIFEY-WIFEY

"I sampled a lot of the whores there in Thailand," Gene said, "going from one to another. But there was one in particular, I spent a whole three weeks with her, just her. She thought we were married. At least that's the game we played. She called herself my Wifey-Wifey. You know, there's some guys who there, and they actually do marry these girls for a few weeks, a few months, and then take off. It's really bizarre."

"But you didn't marry her?"

"Hell no. But she was my Wifey-Wife for a short while."

"Which meant?"

"Which meant she was my wife for a while," Gene said.

39

WIFEY-WIFEY

"She lived with me for those three weeks," he said. "She was very beautiful, and a lot more mature than the others. I mean, she wasn't a teenager."

"How old was she?"

"Maybe twenty. A great fuck."

"How great?"

"Very great."

"So what happened?"

"It was time to leave Thailand."

"I bet it was hard to leave," Nick said.

"It was very hard to leave," Gene said. "Wifey-Wifey just cried and cried. It hurt to see her like that. 'Will you come back?' she asked me. 'Yes,' I lied. But I had to go. I had to meet my old friend Abdellah in Morocco."

40

SHARONA

"Abdellah and I were dormmates in college," Gene said. "We were like brothers, or so he treated me. As did his family. I flew into Casablanca and got the red carpet treatment. It was great."

"Casablanca," Nick said, shaking his head.

"Yeah, all the connotations. It's a big city, a sprawl like any other. He took me out to some clubs. And he also introduced me to Sharona. She was from Algeria, and she was gorgeous."

"Describe her."

"Dark Arabic skin, large eyes, thick eyebrows, long legs. She was twenty-eight, I think. She's been to the States, and she spoke fairly good English. She was getting her Ph.D. in something—engineering or, I don't know. Something impressive. I was just impressed with the woman. We hit it off. Abdellah said I'd like her and he was right.

"The other thing I liked about her was that the only way she'd fuck was by getting fucked in the ass.

"Or the way she put it, 'Getting fucked by the ass.'"

41

SHARONA

Gene said, "It was a weird culture thing. She explained it to me. She was expected to marry an Arab man, and said one day she would. She was also expected to be a virgin for this husband. But many Arab girls found a way to get around this: by taking it up the ass, only. This way they were technically still virgins. And this was okay with the men. I don't know it was—maybe the cunt had to be pure, because that's where the children came out of. Who cared about an asshole?

"For me, this was a dream come true. I'm an assman, I love fucking women in the ass. And Sharona loved it. I spent two and a half weeks in Morocco, and every day I pounded it into Sharona's little dirty brown Arab ass. This way, that way, we did it every way and she couldn't get enough."

"You lucky bastard," Nick said.

"That's what I told myself every day when I was there. I think Abdellah knew. he kept saying, 'So you really like Sharona?'

"'Oh yeah,' I said.

"'You happy I bring you two to meet?' he said.

"'Oh yeah,' I said.

"'I fucked her too,' he said.

"'So I figured,' I said. "By the ass?' I said.

"'It's the only way with bitches like her,' he said."

42

VERONIQUE

"Speaking of bitches," Gene said, "I met a fine one when I was in Salzburg."

"Austria?"

"That's the place. I was at a party. I don't know how I got to this party, or why I was even there. But there I was. I met a young lady at said party, she was Belgian; her name, she said, was Veronique."

"She said?" Nick said. "You say that like you didn't believe her."

Gene said, "I think her name was Veronique. Maybe it was Dominique. I was kind of out of it. It was one of those type of parties."

"I see what you mean."

"Veronique, if that indeed was her name, was a knock-out brunette with a sexy little Belgian accent. How could I resist her? I couldn't. We were drawn together, or so I recall."

"What was she doing in Salzburg?"

"I'm not sure. She told me she had a VW bug."

"Yeah?"

"She wanted to know if I'd go for a ride with her," Gene said, "back to Belgium. How could I resist?"

"I don't know."

"So I said sure. So I left the party with this hot Belgian bitch and got into her VW bug and we left."

"Wait. What about your luggage?"

"What luggage? I travel light."

"How light?"

"Very light. It's the only way to do it. Why be bogged down by things?"

"True."

"We're driving, and she looks at me, and I see the devil in her eyes," Gene continued. "Veronique stops the bug and she gives me a blow-job as we're sitting there on the side of the road."

"Was it a good blow-job?"

"She was a pretty decent cocksucker."

43

VERONIQUE

"I spent a couple of pretty decent days in Belgium with Veronique. She had this tiny apartment. I didn't care. All we did was fuck, and then it was time to go."

"Where'd you go?"

"I was off to Japan."

"Traveling light."

"'Come back and see me some time,' Veronique said. I looked at her, and I could see traces of my dried come on the edges of her lip. All of the sudden she didn't seem so hot.

What did she look like? Like a used-fucked, fucked-out Belgian whore bitch. I was still a little amazed that I was just walking out her door and into a foreign country I didn't know. I didn't know where the fuck I was. But I made my way to the airport in Antwerp, and got on a flight that would take me to Tokyo."

44

COCKSUCKING JAPANESE GIRL

"Let me tell you about these places in Tokyo," Gene said. "They're called Pink Salons."

"Pink Salons?"

"They're whorehouses that specialize only in one thing: oral sex. The girls there are the world experts on giving head."

"Yeah?"

"Yeah. I heard about them when I got there, so I had to check them out. They're also the 'poor man's whorehouse' since they're cheaper than regular brothels. There are also group rates. See, a bunch of guys go into a room and stand in a circle. Inside the circle is a whore—she's naked or she's clothed— and one by one, she sucks off each guy in the circle."

"You saw this?"

"I was one of the guys in the circle."

"How many guys?"

"Seven. Two Americans, the rest were your typical Japanese businessman types."

"And she sucked all seven of you off?"

"She drank every last drop."

45

COCKSUCKING JAPANESE GIRL

"I had no idea what her name was," Gene said, "but I had to experience her mouth on my dick again. The next night I went back to the Pink Salon and requested a private party with her. Cost me more, but what the fuck did I care? I had her blow me three times in a row that night. What was that like. It was like Heaven."

from

JENNIFER

by D. M. Perkins

2

The helicopters drifted along the beach and darted into the waves, almost touching the water. They were like enormous dragonflies, and for a moment their appearance was so startling that Jennifer and Marina were transfixed. The rotation of the large blades that held the man-made birds aloft flattened the sand and threw it in their faces.

One by one they touched down, six of them. They weren't very large, and they were gaily painted. Unlike the workhorse Sikorsky helicopters Jennifer remembered from watching television news coverage of the war in Vietnam, these mechanical insects looked playful. The people who sat in them could afford expensive toys.

"Friends of yours, I suppose?" she asked Boyd Ransom.

"Yes, we play together," he said dryly. "My gang."

Then she was conscious that the people behind the tinted glass must be looking at her, and she had no clothes on. She felt her forehead grow hot, and she blushed. It was silly, she thought, but she did feel embarrassed. Maybe it was because she couldn't see their eyes, that it was like being on the blind side of a two-way mirror. Her body was her pride, but she was not an exhibitionist. At least not for strangers.

Marina must have had similar thoughts, because she reached into her capacious beach bag and pulled out the bottom half of her bikini. She got down on her knees to search for the missing top half.

"You wouldn't happen to have another one of those suits would you, 'Rina?" She had left her own suit in the car.

"Sorry, Sis. Every nudist for herself in this one."

"Would you like to come for a ride with me down the beach?" Boyd asked, cheerfully enjoying the sisters' discomfort. His deep baritone voice carried over the noise of the copiers and the surf behind them, but she had to shout to make herself understood.

"I WOULD LIKE TO GO WITH YOU BUT I DON'T LIKE RUNNING IN PACKS."

"I can take care of that."

He pumped his right arm in the air to signal the machines facing them, and one by one they hovered up and veered off into the blue sky. One remained, a gleaming black and yellow bird.

"Duck your heads," he warned the twins. The door slid open and a man dressed in a white uniform extended his arm to help Jennifer into the chopper. Marina followed, and then Boyd Ransom. They rose swiftly and headed in a straight line down the beach ten feet above the waves. Everything sparkled. It was a perfect June day, clear and fresh and blue.

They were sitting behind the pilots on a soft pad. Their host poured them drinks from the bottle of vodka he brought out of the small refrigerator in the rear of the aircraft.

"To chance encounters," he said, holding up his glass. The twins drank, and then Jennifer remembered that she was naked. Boyd's eyes had not left her body. They had remained frankly appreciative—as if he were studying a piece of art—so she felt no compunction to cover herself up. She enjoyed his attention.

"Make my next one lemonade," she said, handing him her glass, sure that he would have it. He did. The three of them sat with their legs crossed, knees almost touching. He smiled, but seemed in no great hurry to talk.

Jennifer looked out the window and watched the beach pass by under them, a white blanket with a few sunbathers scattered over it. How strange all of this was—like a dream! She was a bold young woman with an adventurous nature, but she'd never been in a situation like this before. One glance at her sister confirmed that Marina was also wondering what they were doing up in the air with a complete stranger.

Was it because she'd been daydreaming all morning about a strong man who would sweep her off her feet that she'd decided to get into the helicopter? Or was it really because she was hypnotized by Boyd Ransom's power and celebrity?

"You seem uncomfortable, Miss Sorel. If you like I can give you something to put on."

"You have a strange effect on me, Mr. Ransom. I don't think clothes are going to change anything between us."

Jennifer felt the pull of his magnetism when his knee touched hers. He leaned back to grab pillows for them and they stretched out on the pad.

Jennifer's photographic career had taken her all over the world. Her pictures had appeared in all the major news and fashion magazines in America and Europe. She'd had the opportunity to meet many famous men, and had generally been disappointed by her inability to get behind the surface they presented to her camera.

Even without knowing him, Boyd seemed different to her. It was as if he had nothing to hide from them. Despite his money and his power and his striking good looks, he wasn't wrapped up in himself. He was as interested in them as they were in him. He lacked vanity, because he was certain of himself—and that was interesting.

When his eyes caught hers she felt swallowed up by them. She also began to feel wet between her thighs, and a tingling ran up and down her legs. She saw that Marina was in the same condition, that her twin's darker nipples were swollen and she was licking her lips.

Jennifer had fought through her teen-age years against being a twin. Wanting to establish her own identity, she had taken advantage of every opportunity to distinguish herself from her sister. Now that she was a woman, being a twin was no longer a problem. Not everyone could see herself in reflection, walking, talking, even thinking like one half of a greater whole. It was a privilege to be a twin, except perhaps in a situation like this where they were potential competitors. Where the man was so exciting they couldn't simply draw straws.

It was as if Boyd guessed what was going through her mind, for he touched them both at the same time. Jennifer felt a charge of electricity go through her when his long, well-shaped fingers began stroking her thigh. She could not restrain an involuntary gasp. His touch was firm and sure. She shifted her legs to accommodate him.

"Oh, God," she heard Marina groan. She knew without looking that her sister was moving her head back and forth with her eyelids shut, and that Boyd's hand was at her sex now.

His touch released a dark flood of sensation in Jennifer. It coursed through her body and changed her from a rational, intelligent, career woman into someone else: a woman who would do anything—move to any primitive sexual level—when she was aroused.

She'd always had an active fantasy life. One of her earliest sexual scenarios was a daydream she'd embroidered through her adolescence of being kidnapped by a strong, ruthless man who would turn her insides into warm jelly and seduce her against her will into absolute sexual submission.

In addition to ruthless strength, this fantasy man also had to posses a dozen other qualities, among them gentleness, self-sufficiency, and a sense of humor. At the moment, Boyd Ransom looked like a good bet to fill this bill of particulars she had treasured for so long.

She turned toward him and placed her hand on his arm, entreating him to get closer to her, pulling him away from Marina. She didn't care about the etiquette of the situation, all she knew was that he moved before she had to do anything more, moved to bring his warm, full lips down on hers. His lips were slightly salty, but his breath was sweet, and his tongue moved boldly between her teeth and traveled sexily over her gums and her responsive tongue. It knew what it wanted, this insouciant male tongue; she tingled from its explorations. Minutes passed and nothing else existed beyond the passion of their kiss.

By the time he broke the connection at last, he had started a fire in her. She lay back with her eyes closed, waiting for him to touch her. She wasn't going to play games with this powerful man who'd hypnotized her.

But when she opened her eyes he was kissing Marina. Would he never come back to her? The minutes dragged by, and he was as absorbed in Marina as he had been with her. She had to do something. She didn't mind sharing—but she wanted a part of him. She took his free hand and began kissing the tips of his long square-tipped fingers.

She tried to be patient but she could feel the pressure building inside her. She moved his wet fingers over her sensitized breasts and soon they were rubbing her nipples. Teasing them. Circling them with liquid slowness so that her legs began trembling.

She decided to attack the problem straightforwardly. When she tugged at his nylon briefs he lifted his lean hips to help her. Then he was naked and she was rendered breathless, so she inhaled to focus her energy; then she placed her hands on his knees and ran them slowly up his thighs, stroking him with the soft pads of her fingertips and then with her nails, and then at last with the smooth palms of her hands. The deep breathing helped her to concentrate.

When he touched her breasts at last—grazing them with his knuckles—she leaned forward to deposit her flesh in his cupped hands.

He squeezed gently but with increasing pressure until his touch was almost painful for her to bear, and she thought she might cry out with the unexpected pleasure.

He switched again. *Damn!* Jennifer's nipples ached. Her own hands moved to pluck at the swollen tips of her breasts. She was deliberately rough, hoping to relieve the need she felt. As always when she fondled her breasts, she marveled at their softness, and how at the same time they were hard; she thought sometimes how nice it would be to be a man feeling them. Any woman could play with her own breasts, and in this respect no matter how poor she was, she could be a pampered queen; but a man always had to find a woman in order to—

He touched them again, weighing them in his palms, stroking their high undersides where the skin was most satiny. The sensations ran down her belly and activated the button between her thighs again. She'd once had an orgasm simply from a man's manipulation of her breasts. She poked them forward hopefully.

But no matter how much attention he paid to her breasts, he was kissing Marina, and his other hand was between Marina's thighs. Which one of them was he going to take first? She felt an urgency to find out, to welcome his flesh into her body and swallow it with her wet satin sheath. When she had him all the way inside herself, she would suck him with her vagina, milking him until he was forced to scream, until he was trembling and he wore a silly smile of ecstasy upon his face, and she pulled the most shattering orgasm of his life from him, pulled on the long, hot, milky thread of desire that now joined the three of them on the floor of a helicopter flying down a Long Island beach.

Jennifer's body lay twisted before Boyd, her ecstatic toes curling not five feet from the chairs in which the pilots sat. She rested on one thigh, her elbow on the floor, hand propping her cheek, staring at his uncircumcised penis. It rose like a tiger lily from his lap, so much more powerful than she might have hoped for. It rose to past his navel, but it wasn't *that* large. No. Size was not its prime characteristic. What it had that Jennifer found delectable was its flexibility. It swayed like a firm stem from side to side, rising magnificently from dark, tight pubic curls and the large double sac of his testicles.

(She corrected herself: they were not testicles, but *balls.* Her upbringing and education had conditioned her to wince at four letter words, but she was finding that they had been invented for good and necessary reasons. "Testicles" could in no way represent fairly the soft and silky skin or the heavy orbs that lay inside that soft skin. "Balls" was not really satisfactory, but at least it was brief and neutral.)

Her fingers lifted them away from his body, carefully, like a Swiss jeweler examining rare gems. She weighed the pair of them on her palm, shaping them and luxuriating in the textures under her fingers.

He moved to make himself more available to her touch. She was gratified at his recognition, but disappointed that he didn't break the kiss with Marina. Her competitive spirit was being stimulated.

Her golden-silvery hair was in her eyes, and her mouth felt dry-heated, like her vagina. It wanted to shape something with its tongue. Her hand grasped his penis, squeezing the soft thickness at its base, her fingertips brushing up the prominent vein to the sensitive cap on top, now engorged with blood. It was so hard that Jennifer gasped, imagining it being driven stroke by careful, loving stroke into her body. It seemed the perfectly appropriate extension of his desire for her, the vulnerable flower stalk of his erection; but recognizing that it was also a result of his desire for Marina, she didn't waste time exclaiming over his potency.

Instead she began licking upward in little circles from his knees. She made a detour and sucked each of his toes (after brushing the sand from them) and then returned to his thighs. His muscles were quivering. She tried to soothe them, but her wet, pink tongue was not a calming influence. She noted proudly that there was a hollow on his left inner thigh below his balls where a blood vessel was beating with the rhythm of his excited heart. She wanted to tease him, but her impatience was too great.

Her soft lips—which were silken caresses on the cheeks of friends and strangers alike—pressed against the soft, wiry hairs of his balls. Her nose brushed against his skin, inhaling the fragrance of a healthy male in a state of arousal. She sucked one of his oval balls into her mouth as gently as if she were blowing hummingbird eggs.

Her tongue rolled around its sphere. She released it with a very soft pop, and her lips began their inevitable advance up his hard flesh. Her mouth lingered for minutes on each inch, savoring his pleasure, which was still connected to her pleasure, still one circuit of a two-way current.

"Oh, *now,*" he called out, squirming a little as she filled her mouth with warm saliva and let her lips suck the bulbous tip of his sex along the liquid groove of her tongue, suck it deeper and deeper without the slightest hesitation, until she felt it in her throat. Her mouth was relaxed, and it allowed her to swallow him like a sword of flesh.

It allowed her to move her head up and down on his erection with the joy of a woman who is tingling somewhere inside herself beyond the physicality of sex. Her lips touched his pubic hair and pulled back to the tip, and then swallowed him again.

She pulled her head up at one point—deliberately forcing herself to forego the pleasure of his turgidity, his smells, the way he tried to escape from her mouth by wriggling his hips, his absolute vulnerability—and saw with some satisfaction that his eyes were upon her, although his slack mouth was still at Marina's breast. She felt his hand press approvingly upon her head; it was a sign of his pleasure and his absorption in her work.

She was causing him to lose control; she could always feel that loosening moment when a man was about to come apart—and she didn't know when to stop when it happened. When she felt herself falling, the man was signaling her that he was falling too. In her mind they held each other like the lovers in a Chagall mural and fell forever through the warp and woof of sexuality. Wherever their instincts took them was all right.

But there was his hard hand over her mouth, holding himself between two fingers and lightly brushing her lips and chin. What did he want? She was ready to surrender herself to him; anything he wanted was his, no questions asked.

He pulled away from her, his hips turning purposefully to provide Marina with the opportunity to use her mouth on him. The sisters looked at each other, speaking with their eyes just as they had as ten-year-old children conspiring over the family dinner table. Marina invited Jennifer to join her.

This man was incredible. The twins had never before been able to share a sexual experience with such totality of feeling. No jealousy, no competitiveness, simply a mutual drive to drain from this amazing man every drop of bubbling honey.

They joined heads over his swollen hardness, looking into the mirror of each other's eyes, taking turns sliding their heated, slick mouths over his penis, engulfing it in their wide-open throats.

Their hands met on his moistened stalk. Their tongues thrilled to the same texture.

At last he moved his body around—that lean, hard body—and lowered his face between Jennifer's legs. Like a king dispensing royal favors, his insistent lips and greedy tongue pressed into her humid, open slit.

Marina continued to suck him, but Jennifer fell into a trance. While his firm lips pursued their goal, she drifted off. It was, in a way, how she defended herself against the excitement of being taken into a man's hot mouth.

His hands pushed her legs into the air and his fingers played with the opening between the butter-soft cheeks of her ass. His tongue was as deep inside her as the sexual organs of many less adequate men had been.

She drifted off. Being sucked by a man—being eaten like a summer fruit, slowly and deliberately and juicily—turned everything on inside her. She remembered a boy who had insinuated himself into her pants when she was just sixteen, a boy who licked and sucked between her legs until his appetite had sent her into the throes of the deepest orgasm she'd ever had from cunnilingus.

His practiced tongue played among the folds of her gleaming vulva, outlining the moist rose lips and darting, every once in a while, into the tight wetness of her sex, the hot hole at the center of her being, the grasping emptiness at which his tongue made flirtatious passes before going farther, up to her clitoris.

She couldn't stand it at first when his mouth surrounded her throbbing button. His teeth were gentle, but they still nibbled at the quick of her being. Her clitoris was her property, the organ with which she gave herself pleasure when she was alone, and this stranger was claiming it with his tongue and his lips and even his fingers. And she was feeling so delightful. He was stealing from her.

For a moment she glanced up at reality. She saw the molded chairs the pilots sat in, and their discreet uniformed backs. She looked over at the windows and saw the blue sky passing by outside.

Then she relaxed and let Boyd steal from her again. His mouth was overwhelming, so gentle but insistent, as if he were eating a peach and letting the succulent juices run over his chin. It was obvious that he loved her sex as much as she loved his, that they were equal partners in the endeavor to bring each other to a brink from which they would leap, locked together.

She was confused when Marina stretched out in such a way that she completed their circle. Marina's mouth engulfed Boyd's penis and her body shook with the electricity of the connection that was made. What confused Jennifer was the sight of her sister's aroused pink sex, because it mirrored—as it slowly and almost imperceptibly blinked before her eyes, carrying its message of lust—her own state. She stared straight into her sister's small, pink perfect vagina and understood why men like Boyd Ransom—strong men who prided themselves on their self-sufficiency—would spend their lives searching for such beautiful flowers. For aesthetic reasons aside from sex, vaginas were worthy of worship.

For Jennifer her vagina was many things. It played many roles in her life. But with a man like Boyd it became an opening into the truest heart of her being.

Boyd's mouth felt so good that she couldn't stop herself from locking her thighs around his head, and as she did so his tongue stabbed into her sex. How did he do it? How did he send his tongue so deeply into her? Her buttocks twisted and squirmed. She couldn't keep still, but he stayed with her rolling hips, his fingers tracing the insides of her elbows.

It occurred to her that she had met her match, that she would have to be careful or she'd find herself falling in love.

He lifted his head and looked into her glazed eyes, savoring the gratification reflected in them. His face was wet with her juices.

"You taste wonderful," he told her. "I want you now."

Marina groaned her disappointment.

Jennifer held her arms out, and he moved up her body, sliding on the light perspiration that covered them. His lips found hers again, and his tongue played over her teeth. Then he entered her, pulling her legs under his arms and cupping her buttocks in his hands to force himself deeper into her.

He was like a flame burning into her. She gasped and couldn't stop to catch her breath, the feeling was so intense. Where had this man learned his stuff? Where had he learned to make love to a woman so that everything else ceased to exist except *them?*

He paused, deep inside her, his body rigid on hers, the muscles of his arms like steel bands—and then he began a slow, stroking movement that she relaxed into like the steady rhythm of competition swimming. She was able to take several deep breaths and look around her during this respite.

Marina was lying on her side watching them, her hand on Boyd's back. She winked at Jennifer.

"Time out," Boyd called, disconnecting himself from Jennifer and leaning back against a pillow. His face was flushed but otherwise he gave no sign of being tired. What was it? She purred inside, as if a small, powerful motor called libido was just clicking into high gear.

She had to have more of him. It was too soon for him to end it.

The twins looked at each other quizzically when he moved up to confer with his pilots. One of them handed him a package. When he sat back down with them he opened it and withdrew a clear plastic straw and a plastic bag fat with white powder.

"Our bodies are up in the air," he said. "Let's get our minds to join them."

"I'll pass," Marina said. "It just gives me a big old headache."

"It's been a long time for me," Jennifer said. "I'd like to try some."

She knew the wickedly sharp power of cocaine to intensify her thoughts and feelings, and she wanted to make love with that extra edge. Normally moderate in everything except sex, Jennifer had learned to use drugs sparingly, and to judge when the occasion was right.

She snorted two lines and felt a light bulb go off. Her heart had slowed down enough to let her mind catch up. Why was she so attracted to this man? Apparently her thoughts were visible on her face—or was he a mind-reader?—because the next thing he said was clairvoyant.

"You looked right then in the middle of wondering what you're doing here."

"I'm in a helicopter with my sister making love to a man I only know because I keep up with the news. It's like a bird swooped down out of the sky. There I was sunning myself on the beach, and now look at me. At both of us."

Her blond hair was tousled, she knew, because Marina's dark hair was. Her thighs were wet with her own juices. Her eyes were wide, their clear blue clouded with passion. For the first time she was truly aware of the noise of the helicopter, the stuttering rotation of the blades above them pulling the metal bird through the sky.

"Where are we?"

"Not far from where we met. We've just been flying up and down the beach. We turned awhile back, but you probably weren't aware of it." He smiled and leaned over to kiss Marina's cheek.

"I wasn't aware of anything. But—do you do this all the time?"

"I like to move around. When I'm staying at my place here there's so little to do. The people out here are so stuffy. So I call up some of my friends—my gang—and they come visit and go flying with me."

"And you patrol the beaches looking for women?"

The clarity of cocaine showed Jennifer how one of her fantasies—of being kidnapped by a strong, ruthless man—had led her into an adventure that she could take as far as she wanted.

She wasn't ready to test the limits yet, however. She wanted to finish what they'd started together.

But Marina felt the same way. "You know what?" she said. "It's my turn."

"But . . . " Jennifer protested. There was so much more she was looking forward to. She *couldn't* wait. She didn't care if she was being selfish or not.

"Jenny," her sister reminded her. "Sisters, remember? All for one and one for all?"

"Please?" Jennifer's will when she wanted something was invincible.

"Let's not leave *anyone* out," Boyd chuckled. "Let's see if three people together can build a better fire than two. Looking at the two of you, I want to discern differences, but try as I will, you look to me like perfect halves of the same being. One woman with two faces."

Jennifer and Marina were used to male speculation about the eroticism of twins, but they had always resisted sharing lovers, knowing that problems like this might arise if they did.

"Just wait," Jennifer said. "You'll get to know us."

"I think I would like to feel both of you."

In her imagination Jennifer saw the pleasure the two of them could give him and the pleasure they could receive in return, and she nodded. Marina looked at her and giggled like a naughty ten-year-old. They were co-conspirators, as they'd been since childhood.

Boyd moved to Marina, and when she raised her thighs, he opened her up with his fingers. His penis was erect—Jennifer didn't remember if it had ever gotten soft, but she thought it probably hadn't. It was red, not the dark purple that blood trapped for a long time in the spongy tissues produced, but red and moist at the slit. Ready for them. A challenge.

He reached for Jennifer at the same time he entered Marina, becoming a storm inside her.

This man can't get enough, Jennifer thought. *This won't be any problem. It will keep my mind free. I won't be emotional about him.*

Reassured by this thought, Jennifer felt her body begin to tremble at the touch of his hand on her breast. She would share him and increase her pleasure, she resolved to herself.

The cocaine was opening up all her senses.

She pushed her breasts into his hands and pressed her full

lips against his chest. There was a small patch of silky hair between his nipples that her tongue claimed when he turned onto his back, and Marina rode him, sitting straight above his thighs, her hands back on his slightly upturned knees.

If she expected him to be overwhelmed—and many men would have been, simply because the Allen twins were overwhelming by virtue of their beauty and intelligence and style—he was not about to reward her expectations. He remained a step ahead of her.

He was king. His eyes revealed his soul. Each movement of his body was a gesture that further eroticized the triangle they now shared. His limbs were hydraulic liquid, and his hips moved in a rhythm all his own. Marina swayed in the air, making small *ooh*ing noises with her half-opened lips, brushing her hair away from her wet forehead, a smile on her face that glowed with primal satisfaction.

He kept moving. Never still for a moment, his energy turned them on as much as his male beauty. Jennifer realized for the thousandth time how striking men's faces were when suffused with passion. His angular cheekbones and deep-set eyes poured electricity into the air because they were so set on what he was doing.

Jennifer wanted to get closer to him and took the only avenue she could see that was left to her.

It helped when Marina and Boyd rolled onto their sides, still connected; she insinuated herself between their sprawling legs and cupped her hands around their joined crotches. She caressed them both, her hands moving tightly over his balls and the round globes of Marina's ass. She pushed them together, helping them to tighten, and when Marina and Boyd were panting in unison, she offered her lips to both of their mouths. At least she wasn't denied the freedom to interject herself between them. Boyd did not object when her lips found his balls and tongued them down to the sensitive perineum that ran from behind his balls to the warm crack of his buttocks.

His ass was her goal. As he pressed himself into Marina, Jennifer's hand's first encouraged him with little slaps and then she began to insert her little finger into his tightly puckered anus. She wet her finger and persisted despite the resistance his rosebud offered. His buttocks were strong and hard and it was minutes before her finger really penetrated him. At the same time she was caressing his balls—the balls that banged against her sister's pubis—and playing with his nipples. His free hand moved up and down her body with a frenetic passion that excited her beyond human endurance.

She had to do more. Only a connection with his magic penis would satisfy her. The thought that he might erupt, that he might spill all the passion they'd built up in their previous encounter in one long geyser that Marina alone would enjoy stimulated her.

She would steal his orgasm, sister or no sister.

She pushed her face between their bodies and moved her tongue along the wetness between his wetness and her sister's slick groove. She tugged at the hair on his balls with her teeth and kept up with their excited movements, their passion.

She felt the reward of his kiss upon her cheek, and turned her face to feel his mouth clamp to hers with primitive force. His tongue sucked hers and his hands clawed desperately for her breasts and Marina's, and then just as Jennifer could feel the pressure in his hard flesh building to unbearable limits, just as she could feel that at last his orgasm was imminent and his whole body was concentrated on moving in and out of Marina, forcing himself into her—he slipped out. He tried frantically to return, but without success.

It was the moment Jennifer was waiting for. Her mouth

claimed him, and while Marina's thighs were waving in the air frantically trying to get back to where he was, Boyd exploded in wave after sensuous wave into Jennifer's eager mouth.

"Oh!" he cried, like a man riding a glider down the Grand Canyon. "Nothing can be this . . . *good!"* His body jerked with such electric force that Jennifer lost him and he plunged back into Marina and continued to pour forth his sperm.

The sisters looked at each other like they'd just endured a tornado together. They had never experienced anything like Boyd, or felt quite so at the mercy of pure sexuality.

They returned slowly to reality, like deep sea divers drifting up to the surface. Their arms and legs were tangled together. When Jennifer at last lifted her head to look out, she saw that they were back on the ground.

When had that happened?

"We're back at your blanket," he said. "I don't know what to say."

"Don't say anything," Jennifer told him.

"It's better if you don't," Marina agreed.

"Maybe it's the coke, but I'm not entirely certain I didn't just dream what happened between us."

"We'll come to your party—then you'll know you weren't dreaming."

He kissed them softly and lingeringly and said that he would call. The helicopter lifted him into the sky.

from

VIOLETTA

by Stan Kent

18

I might have splurged four grand on a business class seat, have leg and foot room to suit a jolly green giant, all the free booze I can knock back, brought to me by drippingly polite and always smiling flight attendants, and free movies in my own personal player, but I'm not at peace.

I'm not even comfortable, and it has nothing to do with my period being a week late or the ralphing I've endured. It has nothing to do with it being the Christmas season and who have I got to buy presents for. Ellen's in jail and the best present I can give her is to not fuck her life up anymore. No, that's not it. My unsettled feeling has little relationship to Crista's revelations or the panicked manner of my escape from New York, barely making it past the clutches of numerous law enforcement agencies who may or may not have been specifically after me for any one of a number of potential felony incidents. Using a passport and the identity of a dead woman to buy a ticket and leave the country didn't faze me in the least. Neither does the prospect of returning through immigration with bogus documents whenever I sort out all this curse shit and can come home a free woman.

Who knows? I may not come back, depending upon what I find out in Italy.

No, it's not these heavy thoughts that spoil my relaxed mood.

It's the fucking Italian lover boy gigolo sitting next to me who seems to think I've been placed in this seat for his personal pick-up pleasure.

I'ma not a gonna attempta to mimica da way he speaka da Englase. Anyone who's seen a Fellini flick knows.

He introduces himself as he sits down, even though I'm looking out the window to make sure there isn't a fleet of police cars belting down the runways to prevent the plane from leaving the gate.

"Hello gorgeous lady. I am Johnny—Johnny Gianni. I am Italian from Roma. I've been visiting my cousins in New York. We own art galleries in Roma and New York, either of which would be proud to display such a priceless treasure as you. And what do I call this vision of timeless beauty?"

I don't even turn around. I pretend to be asleep. He doesn't miss a beat. The guy would bother a corpse.

"Maybe you are nervous about flying? Not to worry. I am experienced traveler. You can hold my hand should you be scared."

He pats my hand. Okay, now I'm pissed.

"Touch me again, and I'll rip your balls off, Johnny Gianni, and stick 'em in your fucking gallery—a tender little piece called 'Annoying Man's Balls.' "

He doesn't flinch. His wide-eyed smile doesn't crack. I might as well have told him he was my dream boy.

"Ah, you are sad—" He glances at the boarding pass I stuck in the seatback pocket.

"—Nicola Anderson. I understand. Leaving perhaps your lover. Not to worry. Roma, she is the best balm for a broken heart, and I, Johnny Gianni, are the perfect surgeon to ease all your pains."

My mouth opens, but for a few moments I'm speechless. Just a few moments. I'm Violetta Valery Cutrero, Avenging Angel Sex Goddess, and I don't take this kind of crap from serial killers, let alone serial sleazes.

"Look, Johnny, you speak so much shit you have two assholes, and the one on your face needs wiping shut."

He smiles, cocks his head to one side and bats his eyes.

"I think I am in love with you."

"Oh fuck me."

"So forward, and we've only known each other mere moments, but I understand your desires. With pleasure. Maybe once we've taken off we could become members of the mile-high club?"

I figure it's time to quit this bullshit.

"Look, Johnny, I'm sure this line of crap works with some women, but right now I'm tired, and I need a rest. I don't want to fuck you. So please shut up and try picking up a stewardess. Leave me alone."

"I let you rest, but I shall not be fickle and waste my attentions on other women. And those stewardess—they butt-ugly."

This makes me laugh, which I think is a good way to end the conversation, so I turn to the window again and actually do doze off and stay that way all through take-off until a butt-ugly stewardess wakes me up with a hot towel. I take the warm, wet offering noticing Johnny is busy wiping his face. His eyes are closed. He isn't that bad looking for a guy. His face is thin and angular, but not skeletal. He's tanned with dark eyes and tousled midnight black hair to match. He wears a purple velvet shirt out of orange baggy silk trousers. He's got that Euro skinny boy look, and well, what can I say, his shoes are cool, and for me to say that about men's shoes is a big deal. Most men wear crap shoes with about as much thought and creativity put into the selection and style as they would put in to taking a crap. Johnny's shoes are purple suede cuban-heeled short-height boots with side zippers.

"You like what you see?"

He's finished his hot toweling and stares at me. Busted in the clocking mode, I regroup fast. Pretty damn fucking fast.

"Just glad that you finally wiped your asshole mouth clean of all that shit you been spouting."

"Ah, Nicola, you are the last of the great romantics."

I've had a bad day. My only relative, who I worked so hard to find, is probably in the slammer. I may be a fugitive. I'm pregnant and am heading to a foreign land where I know no one. The cellular growth in my womb is the incestuous product of a brotherly fuck. In Italy I might find out why this West Virginian soap opera is my destiny. What the fuck? I could do with something to take my mind off all this thinking.

"Fuck romance, Johnny. Let's just cut all this word dancing and have sex."

Johnny's eyebrows rocket up so fast they threaten to jump over the Moon. He's shocked. I'm relentless.

"What's the matter, Johnny? All talk and no action. Afraid to put your cock where your mouth is?"

"No, no, no, I was—"

"You have a condom, right."

"Of course."

"Then meet me in one of the bathrooms and bring your hard dick."

He makes to stand, placing his hands on the seat armrests,

ready to launch himself out of the chair. I push him back into his seat.

"I'll go first. You come by in a minute or so."

"How will I know which bathroom?"

"I'll lock the door when I go in. I'll open it for you after counting 60 seconds. Be quick to dash in, but if the coast ain't clear then I'll just go back in and wait. You tap on the door when everything is cool."

"You think of everything."

"Yeah, well, that's what happens when you have brains instead of balls."

"Are you a spy?"

"I'm whatever you want me to be, Johnny. You just be a good fuck."

"I will. You will be impressed with my dicky, Nikki. I am already hard just thinking of sliding this into your tight, wet pussy. Perhaps you should bring something to stuff into your mouth so you don't frighten the passengers with your screaming."

He adjusts himself in his seat. He's right. There's a lovely bulge in those loose silk pants.

"Oh, don't worry, Johnny, if I feel the need to muffle a scream I know just what to stick in my mouth."

I stand and slide past Johnny, careful to brush my ass across his body as I step over him. This toilet fucking will be much fun. I haven't had a dick since Tony, and thanks to the Cutrero Curse I don't have to worry about getting pregnant, although with a gigolo like Johnny he's still gonna wear a condom or he won't be invited into the pussy party. I don't know where he's been, but I know where he's going, and he'd better keep those cool cuban heels on all the while I fuck the ass off of him.

19

My legs are spread, my feet are bare, and I'm fucking naked. I'm propped up between the plane wall and the toilet. Thank the gods of fuckdom that I'm in good shape since I'm supporting myself by my arms on the sides of the john. Johnny is between my legs, which are balanced on his shoulders. His trousers are down around his ankles. His purple velvet shirt is unbuttoned, displaying his hairless, tanned chest, BB nipples, and flat stomach. His dick is hard, voluminous, and condomed. He's going in and out of me in spectacular fashion, the locomotioning aided by his thrusts and my body lifts. We're a fucking machine, pumping with well-lubed efficiency. We don't speak, all the earlier verbal play unnecessary now that we communicate in the timeless body language of sex.

Oh, and he's still got his cuban heels on, so if I sneak a shoefuck later, I'll be able to see what Johnny's thinking about while I fuck him senseless seven miles high above the big, wet Atlantic Ocean. That's the method to my sexual madness. I haven't simply gone dick crazy. Johnny is going to help me in Rome. He doesn't know it yet, but he is.

Irrespective of my ulterior motive, this is some of the best hetero sex I've ever creamed on. Admittedly, the only other dick fucks I've experienced—not counting the hundreds of shoesex dicks I've bucked, fucked, and sucked—were my virgin-buster fuck with Jimmy in the DNA alley in San Francisco, and Tony's half-brotherly lust in Oakland. Not the biggest dick-database, but combine it with my shoefucks and it's enough for me to know good from bad, and I moan without fear of contradiction that this Italian Johnny dude ain't bad.

Far from being uncomfortable and constrained by the confines of an airplane toilet, the fuck we enjoy is rich and expansive. Every little buffeting of the plane by whatever minor turbulence we encounter goes right through our bodies. Every shake and vibration thunders in my cunt. It's like the entire jumbo jet is super dildo-ing my pussy through Johnny's penis. The fucking plane even looks like a dick with that big bulbous head. Note: I'm enjoying myself so much I don't even make an oblique reference to the DK's Mister Perfection. No way, not me. I'm fun fucking in the airplane toilet. It's truly the best in-flight entertainment. Beats the shit out of movies and cocktails.

Johnny too is in sensory overload. Ever the narcissist I can tell he likes watching himself fuck me in the mirror. From my perspective he's getting an awesome peep show. He sees my tight naked body profiled for him, my cute face smiling, moaning, rolling from side-to-side. Every so often we make eye contact when he's not ogling my small tits, nipple hard and vibrating with every thrust. Tearing himself away from his "mirror, mirror on the wall" posing he stares at my pancake-flat belly undulating snakelike as I ripple around his dick, alternating his view back to the mirror to look at my leg muscles taut around his neck.

I can hardly wait to get in his shoes and see what he's seeing, know what he's thinking so I can put the next phase of my conquering Johnny plan into action. He won't be able to hide any secrets from my prying feet. Yum, yum, just the thought that I'll soon be able to do me the way I'm doing him gets me juicier than an overripe kumquat. I don't really know if an overripe kumquat is that juicy, but the name just sounds like it should be mop- and bucket-sex related, so what the fuck.

Johnny leans forward, kisses my hard nipples and this I major like. The gentle bouncing of the plane makes for mega-hot fumbles, where his nipple kisses slide away, sometimes pinching my tit with his teeth. Drippy making rough stuff.

This kind of titty torture I can stand. To show I dig his attentions, I arch into Johnny, using my runner's legs and sit-up strengthened abs to curl forward, throwing my arms around his neck so I'm anchored to his body, held aloft by his erection and his teeth on my tit. His cock slides into me to fill my cunt, and now that my mouth's close to his, he lets go of my tit and our tongues fuck, lips locked as tight as our genitals.

Johnny picks up the pistoning pace as he approaches his climax. His balls bang against my ass with each rapid-fire thrust. I feel the solid slap of his sac all wet from my cuntjuices. It's a rude feeling. Makes me think of two in-heat animals fucking in mud. I can't resist looking in the mirror at the way his balls swing like the gong in a bell. Fucking good analogy that cause Johnny sure is ringing my bell. This is my kind of nasty sex, and it's obvious Johnny likes delivering the goods.

He grabs me tight around the waist during his final few thrusts before coming. What a fucking awesome sight—skinny tanned-boy Johnny and my skinny whitey girl flesh melded together by gravity in such a perfect way we could be a Mapplethorpe photograph.

My butt nestles in Johnny's crotch. My thighs climb his stomach, over his chest, where my knees bend just below his shoulders and crest above that Adonis physique, anchoring me by my locked ankles and clasped hands behind Johnny's neck. My body bends forward to accomplish this feat, and yup, there's no unsightly bulge in the tummy. Not even any folds. At twenty-two I still have my girlish figure, and fuck does it feel good on the abs and pussy to be fucked in this gymnastic way. My stomach muscles burn, my pussy throbs, and my body feels on fire. Johnny holds my waist, lifting me up and down his arching shaft, milking his come from his swinging balls. Every time we complete a pumping, my clit grinds on Johnny's pubic bone. At just the right moment in our fucking

I release my grip around his neck and all my weight focuses on that tiny spot, rocketing many small orgasms from my pussy through every nerve in my body.

I defy anyone who fucks in this position, who knows the heroin-like rush of a threesome with Isaac Newton's wonderful sex toy—gravity, not the apple—to ever go back to the boring-ass missionary position or even doggy style. Okay, doing it this way requires some physical prowess, so it ain't for everyone, but if you want normal or relaxed sex, knock yourself out being mellow. Me, I want the kind of fucking only Olympic sexual athletes can attempt and enjoy, you know, like you know, err, "I saw the dick so I fucked it" ath-a-letes.

Judges, hold up your cards.

Five-point-zero. Five-point-zero. Five-point-zero.

A perfect score.

Fuck yeah, I'm banking on Johnny thinking so. I wanna give him a fuck that makes him not want any other pussy for a while. I need a place to stay in Rome, at least until I find out the secrets inside Carlotta's boots, and Johnny could be my home away from home. Not speaking the lingo I don't feel too comfortable walking the streets looking for the wop equivalent of the Providence. Yeah, I could also not wait to get to Rome to try on Carlotta's boots and who knows, maybe I'd know where to stay, but I don't like the risk of slipping them on in the plane's toilets. Who knows what kind of evil shit I'd unleash. No way do I want to be responsible for the crash of TWA flight 69 from New York to Rome. No, I'll stick to fucking a pretty boy in the toilet, thank you very much. This is time off for bad behavior, and it very well could lead to a place to stay for a while.

I don't so much as come as comes—whatever the term is for a swarm of orgasms—I have 'em in stampedes. Every up and down cunt cycle brings multiple releases, each pussy melting building upon the last. I know I'm moaning, and I don't fucking care if the entire planeload of passengers hears. Neither does Johnny as he explodes deep inside my pussy and moans something that sounds like Jeeeesus sweet Jesus, and I actually feel the swell of the condom as his spunk expands the covering to match the contours of my convulsing cunt. What a fucking neat feeling. Whoever said safe sex was boring needs to experience Johnny's dressed-up dick up an orifice.

As our climaxes subside our legs melt. We kiss and tumble backwards, my ass landing with a sweaty bang on the toilet seat. Johnny collapses to his knees at my feet, but we keep kissing as best as we can, his black mop fringe cascading down his face, strands of it messing with our tongue action. I chew on his hair until he brushes it aside and plants kisses down my throat, tracing a path to the space on my chest that passes for cleavage. He bounces from tit to tit, adding a delicious dessert to the main course of coming and coming and coming.

Not content to call it a fuck, Johnny continues kissing lower until he reaches my tenderized twat. This is a real test of his overall coital capability. Of all the sexual arts, cunnilingus separates the men from the slobs. He's clearly eaten enough pussy in his short time to know just the right pressure in exactly the right spot, and thank the fuck he doesn't blow on it. He knows the value of eye contact, looking up at me while he's tracing my labia with his tongue, zeroing in on my clit, where he plants a kiss that ripples a nice closing orgasm to our fuck.

But wait, there's more.

He doesn't stop as I cream all over his face and my legs threaten to pop his head like that overripe kumquat which keeps squelching into my mind. He kisses little pecks and nibbles down my thigh, bending like a man with only one bone in his body to tongue the back of my knee. Oh fuck, the orgasms keep dripping as he licks down my calf and oh man, he's going for my feet.

He starts his shrimping by nibbling my heel. The nibbles turns to bites and he's fuck near making a meal of my foot when he stops with the chewing and licks my sole. Oh fuck me pink, this is too much of a good thing. Thanks to my power my feet are my most sensitive sex organs, and it's as if Johnny knows this, because he sucks each toe and when he plunges them all in his mouth and runs his tongue in between them and bites down with his teeth I go into orgasmic seizure. My body arches and locks into position as if I'm turned to stone. My inactivity doesn't last long. Oh shit, I'm going to scream the fucking plane down or die. I'd give my left tit for a dick to suck, to stifle my impending shriek, but Johnny's too busy sucking on my foot, and there ain't another cock in reach so I stuff my fist in my mouth and draw blood as my body convulses.

Johnny doesn't stop despite my thrashing body. He suckles the other foot, and I'm on my way to fuck heaven. My body melts into a giant sloppy pool of girljuice as I come in tidal waves that shoot up from my feet and wash out my cunt, violent tremors ripping through my body with every blinding crescendo.

As I slow my shakings and my vision clears I see Johnny looking up at me from between my thighs. Sure looks like he belongs there, smiling the look of a satisfied man as he speaks the first intelligible words to have passed between us since we began our toilet tryst.

"That is just a taste of what I'll give you in Roma."

I high-five Johnny and yell "she shoots she scores."

20

Typical man Johnny falls asleep right after our toilet tryst. He's no sooner back in his seat than he kicks off his shoes, pulls a blanket over his well-fucked body, and kisses me goodnight. How fucking cute is that.

And how fucking convenient.

I score his shoes and step carefully over him. I'm back in the toilet faster that I can say shoefuck, thank you very much.

Two people, one body, that old, familiar feeling.

I'm in Johnny fucking me. Talk about ourselves as others see us. It's always a trip to be someone fucking me, and to experience it so soon after the real thing is fucking bizarre. I'm still wet from the real fucking, and here I go getting turned on, getting my hard dick up that crazy American chick. Wow, look at that skinny girl body. I am a hotty.

Oh shit.

Johnny thinks in Italian.

This is no fucking use.

Wait a minute. This is so fucking cool. He might be thinking in Italian, but I understand his thoughts. How, I have no fucking clue, but I know what he's thinking. This is the weirdest shoe-fuck—being inside someone whose native tongue isn't English makes for a more weird experience than the usual weirdness of being inside someone when they're fucking. Add that it's me that's the fuckee, and well pardon me for being an Alice in Wondershoefuckland. It's the Mad Fuckers Tea Party all right.

I try to figure out what the fuck's going down here. Maybe it's because I'm Italian-American and the lingo's in my genes. Maybe I understand Johnny's thoughts because it was me he fucked in the shoes, so somehow my power knows what went on and is interpreting and translating his thoughts. Very strange. One way to know for sure. I'll have to experiment when I get to Italy with fuckshoes in which I haven't been an active participant.

Hold the phone.

I have just such a pair in my bag, and I never even thought about the difficulty of foreign language fuckshoes. Here I was figuring I'd pop on Carlotta's boots once I got to a safe place in Rome and all the secrets of my power would be revealed. What did I expect? Subtitles? Maybe there was more of a reason for my fuck-in-the-sky with Italian speaking and fucking Johnny. Maybe this is my power's way of making sure I understand woppo-lingo before peering into the crystal ball of Carlotta's boots.

Fucking amazing. Not only do I have a hard, thick dick that I'm ramming in and out of me like a steam engine but I can speak a foreign language too.

No need of a dictionary when you have shoesex power.

I cannot believe my luck. Here I was just flirting. I had no idea she'd really want to fuck me, and yet Johnny man, here you are in the toilet giving this crazy American chick your dick. This is wild. She is wild. Look at her. She is an animal. When I tell Franco and Phillipo about this they will die with envy.

Look at her.

Feel her.

Tight pussylips sliding up and down my cock.

Tiny titties. Nipples so hard. They feel the best between my finger and thumb, rolling, twisting her titties into tiny cones. Sexy. I'm going to bite those and make her scream.

How many times has she done this? She knows all the tricks. Is she a pro? Her pussy is too tight to have fucked so much. She's just a natural. Gifted and so young. Maybe twenty at most. Shit. I hope she's legal.

Not too worry. I can lose her once we land. Roma is a big city.

Thinking too much, Johnny. There's something about her.

She's too into sex to be a problem child. I may not want to lose her in Rome. Gina will be gone for a few days visiting her relatives in Sicily. This little girl could just be my early Christmas present.

I like doing it in front of a mirror. I shall have to put one in my bedroom. Look at me. I am a stallion. Muscles so hard. Cock to match. I'm a fucking—

Ouch. Almost lost my balance there. I hope I didn't hurt her. Hah, she likes that. She likes it when I stick it in hard all the way. American girls—so horny. My cock fills her tight and tiny pussy to perfection. It's hypnotizing to watch her pussy lips slide so wet and glistening up and down my dick. Her clitty glows red and throbbing. The little sexbomb rubs it on me when my cock goes in all the way. This standing position is the best for fucking. I can't wait to try this out with Gina. Maybe my little sexbomb likes girls. Maybe I'll convince Gina to have a ménage à trois with her. Stop thinking with your big little head, Johnny, Gina, she's too jealous.

I wish I had a picture of little sexbomb and me making this hot love. She's like a gymnast on my pole. The Olympic cock trials. Oh that's funny. We would win the gold medal.

Working out is worth it. My body looks tight, good. No fat on me.

O-oh—she's watching me. Like what you see, honey? I smile. She smiles. She's a naughty girl. I bet she'd like Gina. So different. Gina's all curves and long, auburn, curly hair and big titties. These two women would look good together, legs wrapped around each other's necks, eating their pussies as I alternate sticking my cock into their just-licked holes.

What a beautiful face little sexbomb has. My adorable little fuck punk. Does she have a boyfriend? I hope not. No, she can't or she wouldn't be doing this in a bathroom with a stranger. How about a girlfriend? No, she likes dick too much.

Mamma mia, she could be bisexual. Maybe she just broke up with a boyfriend or girlfriend or both and needs a good fucking. Maybe I'll offer to show her around Rome. Maybe I'll fuck her again and again.

She's insatiable. She is a fucking athlete. A fucking devil too. There are things about this little minx that don't seem human. Moans so sexy. She's like a cat. I can't control myself. She sucks me in. I ram into her. Thinking about Gina and little sexbomb is too exciting. I'm going to come.

My balls are soaked from her juices. Strange how my balls slap against her ass. This position is amazing. I shall have to try it with Gina.

Ah, Gina, should I tell her? She can be so jealous. No, She must not know. I'll keep my little ménage à trois idea in my fantasies.

How shall I keep my little sexbomb fuckpunk a secret?

I can say she's my American cousin come to visit me.

An excellent story. Maybe she'll be gone by the time Gina returns, and if any of my friends mention anything I'll just say she was my little cousin from New York. And if she's still here. We'll see.

I can hope. I can dream. I can fantasize. A ménage à trois would be so wonderful. Imagine Gina kissing those tiny titties, rubbing her big breasts all over them. Hmmmm, let me kiss them, little sexbomb fuckpunk. First one nipple and then the other. Lick it, wrap my tongue around that tight little button. Bite it a little. Oh she likes—

Lost my balance again, pinching her nipple in my teeth. Should I say sorry. No, look at her face. She likes rough sex. She likes a little pain. Gina would get off on that. She liked it when I spanked her.

Look at little sexbomb's moaning mouth. Such kissable lips. Come to me. Let our tongues fuck. Gina could learn much from this little one. She kisses like she fucks. The way her tongue probes my mouth, thrusts into me, makes me thrust my cock into her harder. My balls swing solid into her ass like those things that destroy old buildings—wrecking balls. Too right, Johnny Gianni. The more I feel and hear my balls slap against her pussy-soaked skin, the more I will be wrecked.

What is she doing now?

I can't believe this. She's sliding her legs over my shoulders. Look at the contrast in our skins. Her thighs are hot and sweaty against my skin. Our bodies slide and slip with the turbulence. I'm not sure if the plane is making us bounce up and down or whether we're shaking the plane with our lovemaking. She swallows my cock further inside her with little wriggles and shimmies of her hips as we bounce. Her pussy squeezes and teases. She's shaking. Her pussy quivers. Look how sexy she is with her head lolling back like a sexbomb fuckpunk ragdoll.

I'm going to come. I feel it in my feet. Shooting up my legs. My balls, my balls, each slap and squash of them is exquisite, like the way Gina kneads them.

I don't want this beautiful sex to stop. I want to fuck my little sexbomb fuckpunk forever.

But—I can't—I can't—I can't—slow down.

Coming—coming—coming—oh Gina—Gina—Gina—"Gi—"—be careful "Jeeeeesus sweeeeet Jesus." Thank you God for saving my ass.

My coming doesn't stop. I keep pumping. It's exciting to feel my jism fill the condom. I hope it doesn't burst. My cock feels bigger than it ever has. I come longer than I ever have.

I want this little sexbomb fuckpunk for my own. She is—oh dear. My head's floating. I feel dizzy. I can't stand up anymore. I'm going down. We kiss as we topple, lips briefly separating.

Sexbomb lands on the toilet. I'm on my knees. Looking up from the floor at her legs spread, juices glistening, pussy lips splayed and drenched, bush tangled and wet, clitoris calling me to suck it, I can't resist her. I start on her mouth. I want her to know I know how to make love like a virtuoso.

My hair falls in between our kiss, but I don't mind. She nibbles on it as our lips fight through the black strands. I work my way lower, meandering a wet path through her sweat-dampened skin. Between her tiny titties I snap out of my lazy mood and kiss her nipples, moving my head from left to right so fast I make myself dizzy. She likes the speed of my attentions arching her body toward me. She wants me to eat her pussy, and I will, but I'll tease her some more, my kissing slowing to a crawl as I inch down the flatness of her belly, pausing to nibble on her come-soaked bush, tasting the sweet-sour of her juices.

Then I'm there, circling my tongue around her swollen clitoris, not too hard and not too light. Lingering not too long, I wind my tongue around her pussy lips, zeroing into her opening where I bury myself deep into her sex. Gina goes crazy when I do this to her, and my little sexbomb fuckpunk is no exception. Her thighs squeeze my head as she responds to my expert tonguing. She's strong, and I feel the blood rush to my head, but I don't stop and I'm rewarded with a fountaining of her juices into my mouth and across my face.

She relaxes, but I don't stop. I work my way down her thigh, kissing behind her knee I contort myself to lick down her calf until I reach her foot. It's cold and clammy from sweat, but I don't mind as I bite her heel, lifting up her leg to kiss the sole until I take her toes in my mouth and suck.

She arches into one elegant curve of rigid female flesh and stuffs her fist in her mouth to stifle a scream. She thrashes, but I don't stop. I switch to the other foot and work up to her pussy, where I look up at her admiring eyes. I think I'll invite her to join me in Rome.

"That is just a taste of what I'll give you in Roma."

The look on her face tells me she is mine to play with. She slaps my hands and screams something about shooting and scoring.

What the fuck does that mean?

"Can you suggest a place to stay?" I say as we sip on a glass of wine a few hours before landing.

Johnny smiles.

"Why stay in a hotel. I have plenty of room in my apartment."

"Don't you have a girlfriend?"

He hesitates.

"I have many."

"I don't want to cramp your style."

"You won't. You won't."

"I might even expand it. Do you know what I mean?"

"You already have."

"Have you ever fucked two women?"

"Of course."

Liar.

"Well, you've never fucked two women where one of them was me."

"Ah, that is true."

I slide my hand under the blanket, unzip Johnny's trousers and stroke his already steaming hard cock.

"Imagine Gina and me eating each other while you take turns fucking us."

The look on Johnny's face is priceless. His cock arches harder.

"How do you—"

Out comes my smokescreen.

"You talked in your sleep. You mentioned Gina's name. I guessed she wasn't your mother. The rest is my idea of a good fucking time."

"You amaze me."

"I'll do more than that, Johnny. Now why don't you tell me what you'd like for Christmas from your little sexbomb fuckpunk."

The look on Johnny's face is a mix of fear and wonder.

"You are the devil," he says as he comes into my hand.

from

The Autobiography of a Flea

by Anoymous

2

Curiosity to learn the sequel of an adventure in which I already felt so much interest, as well as a tender solicitude for the gentle and amiable Bella, constrained me to keep in her vicinity, and I, therefore, took care not to annoy her with any very decided attentions on my part, or to raise resistance by an illtimed attack at a moment when it was necessary to the success of my design to remain within range of that young lady's operations.

I shall not attempt to tell of the miserable period passed by my young protegee in the interval which elapsed between the shocking discovery made by the holy Father Confessor, and the hour assigned by him for the interview in the sacristy, which was to decide the fate of the unfortunate Bella.

With trembling steps and downcast eyes the frightened girl presented herself at the porch and knocked.

The door was opened and the Father appeared upon the threshold.

At a sign Bella entered and stood before the stately presence of the holy man.

An embarrassing silence of some seconds followed. Father Ambrose was the first to break the spell.

"You have done right, my daughter, to come to me so punctually; the ready obedience of the penitent is the first sign of the spirit within which obtains the Divine forgiveness."

At these gracious words Bella took courage, and already a load seemed to fall from her heart.

Father Ambrose continued, seating himself at the same time upon the long-cushioned seat which covered a huge oak chest:

"I have thought much, and prayed much on your account, my daughter. For some time there appeared no way in which I could absolve my conscience otherwise than to go to your natural protector and lay before him the dreadful secret of which I have become the unhappy possessor."

Here he paused, and Bella, who knew well the severe character of her uncle, on whom she was entirely dependent, trembled at his words.

Taking her hand in his, and gently drawing the girl to the same seat, so that she found herself kneeling before him, while his right hand pressed her rounded shoulder, he went on:

"But I am wounded to think of the dreadful results which would follow such a disclosure, and I have asked for assistance from the Blessed Virgin in my trouble. She has pointed out a way which, while it also serves the ends of our holy church, likely prevents the consequences of your offence from being known to your uncle. The first necessity which this course imposes is, however, implicit obedience."

Bella, only too rejoiced to hear of a way out of her trouble, readily promised the most blind obedience to the command of her spiritual Father.

The young girl was kneeling at his feet. Father Ambrose bent his large head over her recumbent figure. A warm tint lit his cheeks, a strange fire danced in his fierce eyes: his hands trembled slightly, as they rested upon the shoulders of his penitent, but his composure was otherwise unruffled. Doubtless his spirit was troubled at the conflict going on within him between the duty he had to fulfil and the tortuous path by which he hoped to avoid the awful exposure.

The holy Father then began a long lecture upon the virtue of obedience, and the absolute submissions to the guidance of the minister of holy church.

Bella reiterated her assurances of entire patience and obedience in all things.

Meanwhile it was evident to me that the priest was a victim to some confined, but rebellious spirit which rose within him, and at times almost broke out into complete possession in the flashing eyes and hot passionate lips.

Father Ambrose gently drew the beautiful penitent nearer and nearer, until her fair arms rested upon his knees, and her face bent downwards in holy resignation, sunk almost upon her hands.

"And now, my child," continued the holy man, "it is time that I should tell you the means vouschsafed to me by the Blessed Virgin by which alone I am absolved from exposing your offence. There are ministering spirits who have confided to them the relief of those passions and those exigencies which the servants of the church are forbidden openly to avow, but which, who can doubt, they have need to satisfy. These chosen few are mainly selected from among those who have already trodden the path of fleshly indulgence; to them is confined the solemn and holy duty of assuaging the earthly desires of our religious community in the strictest secrecy. To you," whispered the Father, his voice trembling with emotion, and his large hands passing by an easy transition from the shoulders of his penitent to her slender waist.

"To you, who have once already tasted the supreme pleasure

of copulation, it is competent to assume this holy office. Not only will your sin be thus effaced and pardoned, but it will be permitted you to taste legitimately those ecstatic delights, those overpowering sensations of rapturous enjoyment, which in the arms of her faithful servants you are at all times sure to find. You will swim in a sea of sensual pleasure, without incurring the penalties of illicit love. Your absolution will follow each occasion of your yielding your sweet body to the gratification on the church, through her ministers, and you will be rewarded and sustained in the pious work by witnessing—nay, Bella, by sharing fully those intense and fervent emotions, the delicious enjoyment of your beautiful person must provoke."

Bella listened to this insidious proposal with mingled feelings of surprise and pleasure.

The wild and lewd impulses of her warm nature were at once awakened by the picture now presented to her fervid imagination—how could she hesitate?

The pious priest drew her yielding from towards him, and printed a long hot kiss upon her rosy lips.

"Holy Mother," murmured Bella, whose sexual instincts were each moment becoming more fully roused. "This is too much for me to bear—I long—I wonder—I know not what!"

"Sweet innocent, it will be for me to instruct you. In my person you will find your best and fittest preceptor in those exercices you will henceforth have to fulfil."

Father Ambrose slightly shifted his position. It was then that Bella noticed for the first time the heated look of sensuality which now almost frightened her.

It was now also that she became aware of the enormous protuberance of the front of the holy Father's silk cassock.

The excited priest hardly cared any longer to conceal either his condition or his designs.

Catching the beautiful child to his arms he kissed her long and passionately. He pressed her sweet body to his burly person, and rudely threw himself forward into closer contact with her graceful form.

At length the consuming lust with which he was burning carried him beyond all bounds, and partly releasing Bella from the constraint of his ardent embrace, he opened the front of his cassock, and exposed, without a blush, to the astonished eyes of his young penitent, a member the gigantic proportions of which, no less than its stiffness and rigidity completely confounded her.

It is impossible to describe the sensations produced upon the gentle Bella by the sudden display of this formidable instrument.

Her eyes was instantly rivetted upon it, while the Father, noticing her astonishment, but detecting rightly that there was nothing mingled with it of alarm or apprehension, coolly placed it into her hands, It was then that Bella became wildly excited with the muscular contact of this tremendous thing.

Only having seen the very moderate proportions displayed by Charlie, she found her lewdest sensations quickly awakened by so remarkable a phenomenon, and glasping the huge object as well as she could in her soft little hands, she sank down beside it in an ectasy of sensual delight.

"Holy Mother, this is already heaven!" murmured Bella. "Oh! Father, who would have believed I could have been selected for such pleasure!"

This was too much for Father Ambrose. He was delighted at the lubricity of his fair penitent, and the success of his infamous trick (for he had planned the whole, and had been instrumental in bringing the two young lovers together and affording them an opportunity of indulging their warm temperaments, unknown to all save himself, as, hidden close by, with flaming eyes, he watched the amatory combat).

Hastily rising, he caught up the light figure of the young Bella, and placing her upon the cushioned seat on which he had lately been sitting, he threw up her plump legs and separating to the utmost her willing thighs, he beheld for an instant the delicious pinky slit which appeared at the bottom of her white belly. Then, without a word, he plunged his face towards it, and thrusting his lecherous tongue up the moist sheath as far as he could, he sucked it so deliciously that Bella, in a shuddering ecstasy of passion, her young body writhing in spasmodic contortions of pleasure, have down a plentiful emission, which the holy man swallowed like a custard.

For a few moments there was calm.

Bella lay on her back, her arms extended on either side, and her head thrown back in an attitude of delicious exhaustion, succeeding the wild emotions so lately occasioned by the lewd proceedings of the reverend Father.

Her bosom yet palpitated with the violence of her transports and her beautiful eyes remained half closed in languid repose.

Father Ambrose was one of the few who, under circumstances such as the present, was able to keep the instincts of passion under command. Long habits of patience in the attainment of his object, a general doggedness of manner and the conventious caution of his order, had not been lost upon his fiery nature, and although by nature unfitted for his holy calling, and a prey to desires as violent as they were irregular, he had taught himself to school his passions even to mortification.

It is time to lift the veil from the real character of this man. I do so with respect, but the truth must be told.

Father Ambrose was the living personification of lust. His mind was in reality devoted to its pursuit, and his grossly animal instincts, his ardent and vigorous constitution, no less than his hard unbending nature made him resemble in body, as in mind, the Satyr of old.

But Bella only knew him as the holy Father who had not only pardoned her offence, but who had opened to her the path by which she might, as she supposed, legitimately enjoy those pleasures which had already wrought so strongly on her young imagination.

The bold priest, singularly charmed, not only at the success of his stratagem which had given into his hands so luscious a victim, but also at the extraordinary sensuality of her constitution, and the evident delight with which she lent herself to his desires, now set himself leisurely to reap the fruits of his trickery, and revel to the utmost in the enjoyment which the possession of all the delicate charms of Bella could procure to appease his frightful lust.

She was his at last, and as he rose from her quivering body, his lips yet reeking with the plentiful evidence of her participation in his pleasures, his member became yet more fearfully hard and swollen, and the dull red head shone with the bursting strain of blood and muscle beneath.

No sooner did the young Bella find herself released from the attack of her confessor upon the sensitive part of her person already described, and raised her head from the recumbent position into which it had fallen, than her eyes fell for the second time upon the big truncheon which the Father kept impudently exposed.

Bella noted the long and thick white shaft, and the curling mass of black hair out of which it rose, stiffly inclined upwards, and protruding from its end was the egg-shaped head, skinned and ruddy, and seeming to invite the contact of her hand.

Bella beheld this thickened muscular mass of stiffened flesh, and unable to resist the inclination, flew once more to seize it in her grasp.

She squeezed it,—she pressed it—she drew back the folding skin, and watched the broad nut, as it inclined towards her. She saw with wonder the small slit-like hole at its extremity and taking both her hands, she held it throbbing close to her face.

"Oh! Father, what a beautiful thing," exclaimed Bella, "what an immense one, too. Oh! Please, dear Father Ambrose, do tell me what I must do to relieve you of those feelings which you say give our holy ministers of religion so much pain and uneasiness."

Father Ambrose was almost too excited to reply, but taking her hand in his, he showed the innocent girl how to move her white fingers up and down upon the shoulders of his huge affair.

His pleasure was intense, and that of Bella was hardly less.

She continued to rub his limb with her soft palms and, looking up innocently to his face, asked softly—

"If that gave him pleasure, and was nice, and whether she might go on, as she was doing."

Meanwhile the reverend Father felt his big penis grow harder and even stiffer under the exciting titillations of the young girl.

"Stay a moment; if you continue to rub it so I shall spend," softly said he. "It will be better to defer it a little. "

"Spend, my Father," asked Bella, eagerly, "what is that?"

"Oh, sweet girl, charming alike in your beauty and your innocence; how divinely you fulfil your divine mission," exclaimed Ambrose delighted to outrage and debase the evident inexperience of his young penitent.

"To spend is to complete the act whereby the full pleasure of venery is enjoyed, and then a rich quantity of thick white fluid escapes from the thing you now hold in your hand, and rushing forth, gives equal pleasure to him who ejects it and to the person who, in some manner or other, receives it."

Bella remembered Charlie and his ecstasy, and knew immediately what was meant.

"Would this outpouring give you relief, my Father?"

"Undoubtedly, my daughter; it is that fervent relief I have in view, offering you the opportunity of taking from me the blissful sacrifice of one of the humblest servants of the church."

"How delicious," murmured Bella; "by my means this rich stream is to flow, and all for me the holy man proposes this end of his pleasure—how happy I am to be able to give him so much pleasure."

As she half pondered, half uttered these thoughts she bent head down; a faint, but exquisitely sensual perfume rose from the object of her adoration. She pressed her moist lips upon its top, she covered the little slitlike hole with her lovely mouth, and imprinted upon the glowing member a fervent kiss.

"What is this fluid called?" asked Bella, once more raising her pretty face.

"It has various names," replied the holy man, "according to the status of the person employing them; but between you and me, my daughter, we shall call it spunk."

"Spunk!" repeated Bella, innocently, making the erotic word fall from her sweet lips with an unction which was natural under the circumstances.

"Yes, my, daughter, spunk is the word I wish you to understand it by, and you shall presently have a plentiful bedewal of the precious essence."

"How must I receive it?" enquired Bella, thinking of Charlie, and the tremendous difference relatively between his instrument and the gigantic and swollen penis in her presence now.

"There are, various ways, all of which you will have to learn, but at present we have only slight accomodation for the principal act of reverential venery, of that permitted copulation of which I have already spoken. We must, therefore, supply another and easier method, and instead of my discharging the essence called spunk into your body, where the extreme tightness of that little slit of yours would doubtless cause it to flow very abundantly, we will commence by the friction of your obedient fingers, until the time when I feel the approach of those spasms which accompany the emission. You shall then, at a signal from me, place as much as you can of the head of this affair between your lips, and there suffer me to disgorge the trickling spunk, until the last drop being expended I shall retire satisfied, at least for the time."

Bella, whose jealous instincts led her to enjoy the description which her confessor offered, and who was quite as eager as himself for the completion of this outrageous programme, readily expressed her willingness to comply.

Ambrose once more placed his large penis in Bella's fair hands.

Excited alike by the sight and touch of so remarkable an object, which both her hands now grasped with delight, the girl set herself to work to tickle, rub and press the huge and stiff affair in a way which gave the licentious priest the keenest enjoyment.

Not content with the friction of her delicate fingers, Bella, uttering words of devotion and satisfaction, now placed the foaming head upon her rosy lips and allowing it to slip in as far as it could, hoping by her touches, no less than by the gliding movements of her tongue, to provoke the delicious ejaculation of which she was in want.

This was almost beyond the anticipation of the holy priest, who had hardly supposed he should find so ready a disciple in the irregular attack he proposed; and his feelings being roused to the utmost by the delicious titillation he was now experiencing, prepared himself to flood the young girl's mouth and throat with the full stream of his powerful discharge.

Ambrose began to feel he could no last long without letting fly his roe, and thereby ending his pleasure.

He was one of those extraordinary men, the abundance of whose seminal ejaculation is far beyond that of ordinary beings. Not only had he the singular gift of repeatedly performing the veneral act with but very short respite, but the quantity with which he ended his pleasure was as tremendous as it was unusual. The superfluity seemed to come from him in proportion as his animal passions were aroused, and as his libidinous desires were intense and large, so also were the outpourings which relieved them.

It was under these circumstances that the gentle Bella undertook to release the pent-up torrents of this man's lust. It was her sweet mouth which was to be the recipient of those thick and slippery volumes of which she had had as yet not experience, and, all ignorant as she was of the effect of the relief she was so anxious to administer, the beautiful maid desired the consummation of her labour and the overflow of that spunk of which the good Father had told her.

Harder and hotter grew the rampant member as Bella's exciting lips pressed its large head and her tongue played around the little opening. Her two white hands bore back the soft skin from its shoulders and alternately tickled the lower extremity.

Twice Ambrose, unable to bear without spending the delicious contact, drew back the tip from her rosy lips.

At length Bella, impatient of delay, and apparently bent on perfecting her task, pressed forward with more energy than ever upon the stiff shaft.

Instantly there was a stiffening of the limbs of the good priest. His legs spread wide on either side of his penitent. His hand grasped convulsively at the cushions, his body was thrust forward and straightened out.

"Oh, holy Christ! I am going to spend!" he exclaimed, as with parted lips and glazing eyes he looked his last upon his innocent victim. Then he shivered perceptibly, and with low moans and short, hysteric cries, his penis, in obedience to the provocation of the young lady, began to jet forth its volumes of thick and glutinous fluid.

Bella, sensible of the gushes, which now came slopping jet, after jet, into her mouth, and ran in streams down her throat, hearing the cries of her companion, and perceiving with ready intuition that he was enjoying to the utmost the effect she had brought about, continued her rubbings and compression until gorged with the slimy discharge, and half choked by its abundance, she was compelled to let go of this human syringe, which continued to spout out its gushes in her face.

"Holy mother!" exclaimed Bella, whose lips and face were reeking with the Father's spunk. "Holy Mother? What pleasure I have had—and you, my Father, have I not given the precious relief you coveted?"

Father Ambrose, too agitated to reply, raised the gentle girl in his arms, and pressing her streaming mouth to his, sucked humid kisses of gratitude and pleasure.

A quarter of an hour passed in tranquil repose uninterrupted by any signs of disturbance from without.

The door was fast, and the holy Father had well chosen his time.

Meanwhile Bella, whose desires had been fearfully excited by the scene we have attempted to describe, had conceived an extravagant longing to have the same operation performed upon her with the rigid member of Ambrose that she had suffered from the moderately proportioned weapon of Charlie.

Throwing her arms round the burly neck of her confessor, she whispered low words of invitation, watching, as she did so the effect in the already stiffening instrument between his legs.

"You told me that the tightness of this little slit," and here

Bella placed his large hand upon it with a gentle pressure, "would make you discharge abundantly of the spunk you possess. What would I not give, my Father, to feel it poured into my body from the top of this red thing?"

It was evident how much the beauty of the young Bella, no less than the innocence and "naivete" of her character, inflamed the sensual nature of the priest. The knowledge of his triumph—of her utter helplessness in his hands—of her delicacy and refinement, all conspired to work to the extreme of lecherous desires of his fierce and wanton instincts. She was his. His to enjoy as he wished—his to break to every caprice of his horrid lust, and to bend to the indulgence of the most outrageous and unbridled sensuality.

"Ah, by heaven! it is too much," exclaimed Ambrose, whose lust, already rekindling, now rose violently into activity at this sollicitation. "Sweet girl, you don't know what you ask; the disproportion is terrible, and you would suffer much in the attempt."

"I would suffer all," replied Bella, "so that I could feel that fierce thing in my belly, and taste the gushes of its spunk up in me to the quick."

"Holy Mother of God! It is too much—you shall have it, Bella, you shall know the full measure of this stiffened machine, and, sweet girl, you shall wallow in an ocean of warm spunk."

"Oh, my Father, what heavenly bliss!"

"Strip, Bella, remove everything that can interfere with our movements, which I promise you will be violent enough."

Thus ordered, Bella was soon divested of her clothing, and finding her Confessor appeared charmed at the display of her beauty, and that his member swelled and lengthened in proportion as she exhibited her nudity, she parted with the last vestige of drapery, and stood as naked as she was born.

Father Ambrose was astonished at the charms which now faced him. The full hips, the budding breasts, the skin as white as snow and soft as satin, the rounded buttocks and swelling thighs, the flat white belly and lovely mont covered only with the thinnest down; and above all the charming pinky slit which now showed itself at the bottom of the mount, now hid timorously away between the plump thighs and with a snort of rampant lust he fell upon his victim.

Ambrose glasped her in his arms. He pressed her soft and glowing form to his burly front. He covered her with his salacious kisses, and giving his lewd tongue full licence, promised the young girl all the joys of Paradise by the introduction of his big machine within her slit and belly.

Bella met him with a little cry of ecstasy, and as the excited ravisher bore her backwards to the couch, already felt the broad and glowing head of the gigantic penis pressing against the warm moist lips of her almost virgin orifice.

And now, the holy man finding delight in the contact of his penis with the warm lips of Bella's slit, began pushing it in between with all his energy until the big nut was covered with the moisture which the sensitive little sheath exuded.

Bella's passions were at fever height. The efforts of Father Ambrose to lodge the head of his member within the moist lips of her little slit, so far from deterring her, spurred her to madness until, with another faint cry, she fell prone and gushed down the slippery tribute of her lascivious temperament.

This was exactly what the bold priest wanted, and as the sweet warm emission bedewed his fiercely distended penis, he drove resolutely in, and at one bound sheathed half its ponderous length in the beautiful child.

No sooner did Bella feel the stiff entry of the terrible member within her tender body, than she lost all the little control of herself she had, and setting aside all thought of the pain she was enduring, she wound her legs about his loins, and entreated her huge assaillant not to spare her.

"My sweet and delicious child," whispered the salaclous priest, "my arms are round you, my weapon is already half way up your tight little belly. The joys of Paradise will be yours presently."

"Oh, I know it; I feel it, do not draw back, give me the delicious thing as far as you can."

"There, then, I push, I press, but I am far too largely made to enter you easily. I shall burst you, possibly; but it is now too late. I must have you—or die."

Bella's parts relaxed a little, and Ambrose pushed in another inch. His throbbing member lay skinned and soaking, pushed half way into the little girl's belly. His pleasure was most intense, and the head of his instrument was compressed deliciously by Bella's slit.

"Go on, dear Father, I am waiting for the spunk you promised me."

It little needed this stimulant to induce the confessor to an exercise of his tremendous powers of copulation. He pushed frantically forward; he plunged his hot penis still further and further at each effort, and then with one huge stroke buried himself to the balls in Bella's light little person.

It was then that the furious plunge of the brutal priest became more than his sweet victim, sustained as she had been by her own advanced desires, could endure.

With a faint shriek of physical anguish, Bella felt that her ravisher had burst through all the resistance which her youth had opposed to the entry of his member, and the torture of the forcible insertion of such a mass bore down the prurient sensations with which she had commenced to support the attack.

Ambrose cried aloud in rapture, he looked down upon the fair thing his serpent had stung. He gloated over the victim now impaled with the full rigour of his huge rammer. He felt the maddening contact with inexpressible delight. He saw her quivering with the anguish of his forcible entry. His brutal nature was fully aroused. Come what might he would enjoy to his utmost, so he wound his arms about the beautiful girl and treated her to the full measure of his burly member.

"My beauty! you are indeed exciting, you must also enjoy. I will give you the spunk I spoke of, but I must first work up my nature by this luscious titillation. Kiss me, Bella, then you shall have it, and while the hot spunk leaves me and enters your young parts, you shall be sensible of the throbbing joys I also am experiencing. Press, Bella, let me push, so, my child, now it enters again. Oh! oh!"

Ambrose raised himself a moment, and noted the immense shaft round which the pretty slit of Bella was now intensely stretched.

Firmly embedded in his luscious sheath, and keenly relishing the exceeding tightness of the warm folds of youthful flesh which now encased him, he pushed on, unmindful of the pain his tormenting member was producing, and only anxious to secure as much enjoyment to himself as he could. He was not a man to be deterred by any false notions of pity in such a case, and now pressed himself inwards to his utmost, while his hot lips sucked delicious kisses from the open and quivering lips of the poor Bella.

For some minutes nothing now was heard but the jerking blows with which the lascivious priest continued his enjoyment, and the cluck, cluck of his huge penis, as it alternately entered and retreated in the belly of the beautiful penitent.

It was not to be supposed that such a man as Ambrose was ignorant of the tremendous powers of enjoyment his member could rouse within one of the opposite sex, and that with its size and disgorging capabilities of such a nature as to enlist the most powerful emotions in the young girl in whom he was operating.

But Nature was asserting herself in the person of the young Bella. The agony of the stretching was fast being swallowed up in the intense sensations of pleasure produced by the vigorous weapon of the holy man, and it was not long before the low moans and sobs of the pretty child became mingled with expressions, half choked in the depth of her feelings, expressive of delight.

"Oh, my Father! Oh, my dear, generous Father! Now, now push. Oh! push. I can bear—I wish for it. I am in heaven! The blessed instrument is so hot in its head. Oh! my heart. Oh! my—oh! Holy Mother, what is this I feel?"

Ambrose saw the effect he was producing. His own pleasure advanced apace. He drove steadily in and out, treating Bella to the long hard shaft of his member up to the crisp hair which covered his big balls, at each forward thrust.

At length Bella broke down, and treated the electrified and ravished man with a warm emission which ran all over his stiff affair.

It is impossible to describe the lustful frenzy which now took possession of the young and charming Bella. She clung with desperate tenacity to the burly figure of the priest, who bestowed upon the heaving and voluptuous body the full force and vigour of his manly thrust. She held him in her tight and slippery sheath to his balls.

But in her ecstasy Bella never lost sight of the promised perfection of the enjoyment. The holy man was to spend his spunk in her as Charlie had done, and the thought added fuel to her lustful fire.

When, therefore, Father Ambrose, throwing his arms close round her taper waist, drove up his stallion penis to the very hairs in Bella's slit, and sobbing, whispered that the "spunk" was coming at last, the excited girl straightway opening her legs to the utmost, with positive shrieks of pleasure let him send his pent-up fluid in showers into her very vitals.

Thus he lay for full two minutes, while at each hot and forcible injection of the slippery semen, Bella gave plentiful evidence by her writhings and cries of ecstasy the powerful discharge was producing.

A Victim of his Passions

by Michael Perkins

from *Burn*

27

STUDIO VISIT

The studio was filled with the rich odor of roses. Nicholas Wilde stood at a large open window gazing out a the immensity of the Atlantic. It was the morning of his fifty-first birthday, and he was considering a challenge he had set himself during another sleepless night. It was a dreamy, half-hallucinatory consideration, blackly edged with self-doubt. The challenge was to paint like a madman through the summer months, burning sun and salt into each canvas. It would require concentration, luck, and an indefinable element he compared to the alchemy of fire.

It would also require him to find models willing to pose in erotic tableaux of his devising. He wasn't sure he was equal to the challenge. It might be easier to swim across to Spain, he thought, watching the surf roll up on the beach below. Anyone approaching over the high dune would find him framed by his studio window, as he sometimes posed people for portraits—slightly off-center and larger than life.

Behind him stood a huge, battered easel, made from his own design years before. The roses sat on a long, equally battered workbench crowded with coffee cans bristling with paint brushes, crushed tubes of paint and the other occult tools of his art. Canvases were stacked in rows behind the dilapidated leather couch where he'd spent the night. A precariously balanced stack of art magazines stood anchored by a piece of driftwood in one corner. One of these magazines, *The Blue Rider*, had persuaded him to grant an interview to a free-lance critic about the new direction in his work. The exhibition of his series of erotic paintings of Rose Selavy at the Museum of Current Art had indeed put a spot light on him, as Gavin had predicted. Assured he'd have the cover of the magazine, he agreed.

Now he was regretting his decision. The effort of talking about his work—and, no doubt, having to defend its direction—would wring him out. He would lose a day of valuable studio time.

But it was his birthday, and it was a fine morning on the Cape, so he tried to relax. He mused about his visitor.

The critic's name was Natalie Wray. She'd made a reputation for herself by writing a book about fetishism in nineteenth-century painting, and followed that up with a critique of Camille Paglia that earned her the title of intellectual bad girl of the month.

He hoped that despite this reputation, she would be intelligent, and that her questions would surprise him by attempting to explore his work rather than his psyche. Above all, he wanted her to be attractive; but he supposed she would probably be middle-aged, academic, and sexually and aesthetically challenged. Dry and literal and androgynously breastless and hipless like so many of her ilk: no juice.

Therefore he was more than pleasantly surprised to see,

coming over the dune toward his studio, a deeply tanned young woman in a straw hat, gray V-necked T-shirt, and white linen shorts. Seeing him at the window, she moved rapidly toward him on strong legs, stepping purposefully up on his deck and striding barefoot across it. Her eyes were hidden by sunglasses. Her hair was jet black, falling over her shoulders like a raven's wings.

She extended her hand through the window. "I'm Natalie. Sorry I'm late, but despite your excellent directions, I got lost in the woods. So I parked in the public lot and walked up the beach."

Her smile was dazzling. Her handshake was firm. He was overwhelmed with this birthday present. She excited him.

She removed her sunglasses, and the blackness of her eyes surprised him. They conveyed a challenge—to what? Her mouth was full and sensual, and the only flaw in the beauty of her features was a gap in her white teeth.

She entered the studio and put her beach bag down, taking in the room at a glance and walking straight toward the only art on display, a tattered postcard pinned to the wall of Courbet's "Origin of the World." She looked inquiringly over her shoulder at him, catching him openly admiring the way her behind filled out her shorts.

He shrugged. "It's kind of a touchstone for me."

She smiled, saying nothing, and went to her bag. He watched as she placed a tiny tape recorder on a coffee table next to an overflowing ash tray and an empty coffee cup. They sat across from each other. He liked the fact that she didn't make nervous small talk, but jumped right into the interview.

"Have you always sought to provoke in your work? I mean, your show at the Recent Museum has become a focus of controversy."

He watched the gap in her teeth as she spoke so that he

wouldn't appear to be staring at the pronounced shape of her breasts under the T-shirt. She didn't seem to need a brassiere.

"There are different kinds of provocation," he said. "The nature of my work—before I painted my first nude—has been against the grain: it has been figurative and expressionistic, and that direction made me anti-establishment. My subject is not paint, but people."

He knew this sounded stiff, but he'd wanted to be prepared.

"But this new emphasis on explicit sex. Did you deliberately set out to draw more attention to your work?"

"My celebrity portraits brought me attention—*and* sales, if that's where you're going." His gaze went to her breasts.

"But this show, and your attack on your most important collector—the publicity from both of them have made you famous."

"If you can't get them in the door to look, they won't see."

"And if they don't see it, you can't sell it?"

"Well, of course. Every artist wants his work to be seen by as many eyes as possible."

Now as he spoke he stared boldly at her breasts, willing her nipples to pop forth.

"Unlike Courbet, when you paint female genitals, they look violated."

"Don't you mean *wet*?" he shot back. "Excitement is not violation."

"They're more than wet. It's like there's semen oozing from them." She looked down at her breasts. He had willed her nipples forth.

"Perhaps the woman has just made love."

"Frankly, the effect is pornographic."

"You don't believe that."

She shook her head, looked at her nipples, and blushed at last.

"No, I don't. But the question comes up in every story about you. Pornography or erotica? Which do you do?"

"I do realistic paintings of people having sex."

"Not making love, then, but having sex."

"It's in the eye of the observer. Love is subjective, but sex is observable. I'm a painter. Sex is my latest subject. I used to do landscapes and still lifes, before portraits. Many artists have taken sex for their subject. Look at Rauschenberg in the late sixties, taking photographs of his friends fucking and then painting from them. Look at. . . . "

"You don't have to lecture me. I'm aware of the history of erotic art. I've even written a book about fetishism."

She was defensive. They were flirting. He continued to stare openly at her breasts.

"I have a question about your models."

"Most people do." *Here it comes*, he thought.

"You seem to be able to *become* them—as if they are your own self-portraits—do you know what I mean?"

She was referring to his series of paintings of Rose Selavy.

"I work with certain women for a long time, or sometimes only a short time. I take their photograph hundreds of times. I draw them from life. We become intimate, perhaps. That's the best scenario. Then they express me as I paint them."

"You were lovers with Rose Selavy, then?"

"We were lovers, yes." *It always came down to the personal.*

"Do you want to talk about her importance in your work?"

"I think that's obvious." Now he was uncomfortable. Stalemate.

"Why don't we stop here?" she suggested, leaning forward to turn off the machine. He was grateful to stop talking about himself, but he wondered why she had stopped so abruptly: her discomfort, or his own?

"Let me buy you lunch," he said. "We can talk more later."

After oysters at a cafe on the Bay, artist and critic were more relaxed with each other. Back in his studio, Nick found himself trying to seduce her with words—specifically, his ruminations on the direction his work was taking. Somehow, as they sat together, he thought she understood when she asked him about voyeurism.

"But that is one of the effects of all art," he said, pacing as she listened. "If you look at an interior by Vermeer, you're peeking into someone's intimate life. But that is acceptable, just so long as you don't show people getting it on. It's ridiculous for the artist to censor himself and say certain human activities are off limits."

He didn't feel defensive with her, as he'd anticipated, and as the hours passed he noticed that she was looking at him differently. It was the way her eyes followed him as he paced, explaining or pursuing some point. It was how her hand brushed against his, accepting a glass of wine from him. It was late afternoon when they agreed to stop. A tension had built between them. A change of scene was in order.

"Let's go for a walk on the beach," he suggested. He could see that she wanted to, but she hesitated. "Afraid to cross the line?" he teased, pointedly staring at her breasts again.

"I don't know what to do." Her voice was small and soft.

When she confessed her indecision, he realized that the issue of his age and her youth hadn't come up all day. "Is it because I'm twice your age?"

She nodded. "And your reputation for going after younger women. I don't like it when things get messy. I like to be in control."

"Look—you've flirted with me. We've had a good time talking. Age? You're not some college student. You're old enough to handle taking a walk on the beach. I won't molest you."

She was persuaded, and they kicked through the sand to the water's edge, jumping back when the tide rushed in and sitting to watch the waves. He didn't speak, or look at her. He was thinking about Rose, and remembering how charged up he'd been by her, while with Natalie, despite her beauty, intelligence, and youth, what he felt was a kind of benign, indifferent lust. A lust he could easily ignore, if she said no.

He wondered, idly, what she thought of him.

Had she flirted with him just so he would open up? Did she understand how serious he was about his views? Did she sense how crazy he was? Did she think him too old? Obviously.

He felt like an adolescent too shy to take his date's hand—but only for a passing moment. Then he surrendered to his indifferent passions and reached for her. She allowed him to stroke her arm, but when he moved closer to her she stood up, shaking her head. "I just can't," she said. "I'm sorry."

To his surprise, he was relieved.

28

A NEW PORTRAIT OF ROSE

At every new corner the artist turns in his work, he encounters a possible version of himself. Each one beckons seductively. Each one is part of a puzzle that derives as much from mythology as psychology; but he does not know which. When he finds out, it's too late.

Or so I told myself as I worked daily on a new portrait of Rose that was drawn from memory and from what I'd learned about her. Each night I tore up what I'd done and fell on my studio couch exhausted. It was no longer me drawing, but *him*—and he was confused. He was unable to turn the next corner. He realized he was avoiding the challenge he'd set for himself, to work all summer on a series of erotic paintings that would bring the wrath of the gods down on him. He would then be Prometheus, not Tantalus. Potent. Rebellious.

Meanwhile, the truth was, I needed to get laid. I tried to tell him that, but he wouldn't listen. He had taken Natalie's rejection to heart. He was too old to turn the next corner.

So I called Midge from my studio by the sea and asked her to pack Lola in her old Mercedes and come for a visit.

Perhaps he could not paint a new portrait of Rose until he could see Rose in all women.

29

"JUST TELL ME WHAT YOU WANT"

He'd rented the studio near Wellfleet so he could escape Midge, as well as the flack over his exhibition at the Museum of Recent Art. Midge had made a deal with Boz Skeffington to show Boz's drawings in her gallery, she had Manfred Damien cunt-crazy again, and she'd taken on Lola as a house pet; she should have been happy with her good fortune, but she wanted him more than ever. And more than ever, he evaded her.

Seeing that I couldn't shake her, I decided to put her in the middle of things, like the irritant in the oyster. She was pleased, and so agreeable with my directions to bring along a camcorder and a couple of her best cameras, that I knew she had something up her sleeve.

He found out what that was when the old blue Mercedes pulled up in the sandy driveway. Manfred Damien bounded out of the passenger seat to hold the rear door for Lola. Manfred had dyed his spiky punk hair pink, and wore what Nick could only think of as German hot pants. Lola, by contrast, wore a full-length beach dress. Midge wore a blouse and slacks appropriate for an office on the day the I.R.S. visits. Nick welcomed them with the misgivings a terminally ill patient might have for the figure of Death as Assisted Suicide.

"Midge," he said to her when they kissed hello, "I asked you to bring Lola to model for me. Not Manfred the butcher boy."

"Well, Manfred I brought along for me, Nick. Since—" She gave him one of her reproachful looks, dropping her gaze to his crotch.

"All right, all right. Come on in." He greeted Manfred with a wave and offered to carry Lola's bags. Lola, he was glad to see, no longer seemed pouty. Indeed, she looked pleased with herself. The three of them had settled into a suite in a Provincetown guest house, tucked into a good lunch, and were ready for an afternoon at the beach.

After they'd inspected his studio, Midge and Manfred changed into beachwear. Lola sat on his couch watching him with murky anticipation. It made him nervous because it turned him on.

"We're going out to inspect the ocean, Nick. Maybe we'll even get some sand in our crevices. I've already given Lola her instructions. She'll do anything you say." She waggled her prominent eyebrows like Groucho Marx. "She knows that if she's not a *good* girl, she won't get the spanking she wants."

Off they went, leaving him to set the tone for a working relationship that would last all summer and meet the challenge he'd set himself: to create erotic paintings to hang next to those of the masters.

It was a hot day at the beach. The air was still. Except for the distant crash of breakers, there was only the buzz of a fly to disturb the silence. Nick thought for a moment about what to say to his model.

He stood behind her, so she had to turn her head to see him. “You’re a lucky girl, Lola,” he began, adopting a *faux* fatherly tone with the twenty-something brunette. “I’m going to make you famous. All you have to do is exactly what I tell you. If you have any limits, let me know now.”

She shook her head. “Midge told me what you need.”

“Well, Midge thinks she knows what I need,” he said with more irritation in his voice than he felt. “Even I don’t know what I need until it happens. I’m going to take pictures, I’m going to draw you and paint you. What we do together will evolve naturally, I hope.”

She looked ready, even eager. Midge had indeed prepared her. (What more could an artist ask of a wife?)

“You understand, don’t you, that I’m going to be painting what most people think of as dirty pictures of you.”

“I love it. You’ll see,” she assured him.

“In a sense, I’ll be painting with my penis.”

She giggled. “Whatever turns you on. You don’t have to convince me, Nick.”

“Of course, I’ll pay you well.”

“Just tell me what you want, and I’ll do it.”

He cleared his throat. Lola’s willingness had given him an erection so swollen it was painful.

“Take off your dress.”

Lola stood up and slipped out of her dress, She was naked underneath, full copper-tipped breasts swaying, shaved bush a smudge at the bottom of her belly. She turned so he could see her generously proportioned ass. “I’m your slave,” she said.

The artist debated with the man where to start. The power of her submission was such that it forced him to reach deeply into himself for his own submission to passion. He unzipped and showed her his penis. They watched each other, waiting for the next move. He could hear her quickened breathing. He began to masturbate himself, and her hand went to her crotch, two fingers slipping inside her sex.

"Bend over the couch so I can see your ass," he ordered. When she complied, he spread her cheeks and spat on her anus. Without warning, he shoved himself inside the tight ring. She cried out. But she adjusted quickly as he started to fuck her, bringing her hand around behind her so she could circle his penis with two wettened fingers, increasing his pleasure as he came inside her. He didn't withdraw, but held the moment while he thought about how to draw it.

30

ARTISTS AND MODELS

Painters as diverse as Utamaro, Toulouse-Lautrec, and George Grosz have turned to whores as models in their art. While not placing myself in their company, I can attest to the importance of Lola in the creation of the paintings I did on the Cape. If one might say that Rose awakened my passions and Veronique Aury educated me in how to submit to them, one might also say that Lola was the vehicle for my success. I'd challenged myself to create, over the summer, paintings etched with sun and sea about the varieties of love. Feverishly, I followed my passions, inventing with Lola an entire vocabulary of physical love. My lines were bold and my use of color was even bolder.

I came to respect Lola not only for her willingness and her ability to submit to the passions we were enacting for my camera and brush, but for her native shrewdness about sexuality. Her naive ambition to be an "artist" seemed to me a denial of her own innate artistry of love.

By Labor Day our work was finished, the lease on the

studio was up, and I shipped twelve large incendiary paintings to Max at the Boatwright Gallery.

31

A DIAMOND IN THE ROUGH

The exhibition Max mounted looked great, and the advance publicity could not have been better. A cover story in *The Blue Rider* by Natalie Wray created a sensation—well, at least a tempest in a teapot—in the art world of Manhattan. In her profile of me, Natalie had been confessional. She described the sexual tension between us, and—to my relief and amazement—credited it with having given her an insight into my work she might not have had otherwise. She made an argument for me that would set the agenda for all the articles that followed. She said, essentially, "Here is a male artist who loves women and their sexuality. He is reclaiming territory long claimed by artists from Pompeii to Picasso." It was hyperbole, of course, but I was very grateful in retrospect that nothing had happened between us on the beach. her focus was on the paintings.

Max took a chance on my exhibition, because I insisted that none of them be sold. I wanted to freeze out the collectors and wait for my prices to rise and museums to come knocking at the Boatwright door. After all, now I was famous. Or notorious.

I thought fame was something I wanted until I had a taste of it. Max had warned me that I would be branded a pornographer, but neither of us expected my work to arouse such fury in the right-wing tabloids that speak for the worst in the public mind. The brand on my ass was a symbol for me of my inner development. The brand on my work made me feel even more like a defiant pariah in the art world.

I hid in my studio, unable to work, unable to sleep. I turned down all interviews. I seldom visited Midge in her new *ménage à trois* with Manfred and Lola, but I was coming home from an evening with them late one night when I saw Rose on the street.

I stopped in the middle of the crosswalk at Broadway and Houston, near my studio. She was standing in the service station on the corner there, leaning into a car window. It looked like she was selling something.

My heart leapt. I felt dizzy, but I made it the rest of the way across the street and grabbed onto a lamp post for support. I watched as she shrugged, and turned to walk off east on Houston Street.

I had to force my legs to move. I staggered, then set off after her as she hurried into the darkness of the East Village. I was able to stay close enough to her to confirm what I at first couldn't believe: she was dressed like a cheap streetwalker, in a short, tight skirt and red vinyl jacket. She'd dyed her hair blonde, but I knew that it was Rose when she walked into the light and I saw the fire around her. The flames of hell couldn't have been brighter.

She stopped at Allen Street and crossed Houston into hooker heaven, a park that crack whores used; but without stopping she continued walking south, wobbling tiredly on her high heels. She was headed for a dark building that looked abandoned, and as I watched from across the street, she disappeared into it.

Soon a light flared, and then another. She was lighting candles. Through a dirty broken window the mounting glow was like a fire. I saw her burning herself alive, as she did in my nightmares. I saw her in her smoking grave.

I ran into the building and fumbled for a match to allow me

to climb the rotting stairs of the abandoned tenement. On what I thought was the right floor I banged on one door and then the one next to it.

"What do you want, motherfucker? Don't you think I know you've been following my ass? Get away from my door."

Her voice was high-pitched, roughened by fear.

It wasn't Rose's voice. Maybe she was with someone.

"Rose?"

"Nobody by that name here. Go away, I said."

"Rose, it's me, Nick. I won't hurt you. I just want to talk." My pleading worked. She opened the door and stood half in the shadow, the glow of candlelight behind her.

It wasn't Rose. I saw that immediately. This woman was Rose's age, but her face had been shellacked by street life. Her eyes were swollen and inky blue, not emerald. There was a small scar on her nose. I could smell beer on her breath. We stared at each other.

"I'm sorry. . . . " I mumbled to her. I was about to turn, to leave her alone, when I saw the nimbus of flame about her head.

She started to close the door, but I stopped her.

"What do you want?"

"Just to talk."

"That's not what I do."

"I'll give you money." I pulled out my wallet and let her see how well padded it was. Her greedy look was a For Sale sign.

"You want to fuck me? You want some good pussy? I'll give you the best you ever had, baby. Or maybe you want my asshole? You can have that, too. Jesus, yes. My asshole is incredible, guys say. Even dudes with real big dicks say they're amazed at how much I can take . . . "

I put my hand up, holding a twenty. "Let me in, okay?"

She backed into the room, tucking the bill into her jacket pocket. I closed the door behind me.

"So you're a hooker?"

"What does it look like, baby? I ain't no call girl, am I? I'm just squatting here till I can get some money and then I'm out of here."

She spoke rapidly with what he thought was a Queens accent.

"What's your name?" he asked, when she paused for breath.

"Call me anything you like, baby. You want to call me Rose, that's hunky-dory by me."

"No. I want to know your name."

"Okay. My name is Jewel. That's because I'm a diamond in the rough, everybody says."

He looked around the scarred room. Fallen plaster and broken boards, candles on the floor. A nest of newspapers and old blankets in one corner. Jewel lived like a rat. He thought of Rose's immaculate loft, with its white piano. Could he have summoned up another incarnation of Rose through his portraits of her? Was Jewel the punishment for his pursuit of a ghost? The resemblance was uncanny.

He made up his mind. "Jewel, I want you to come to my place with me."

She was suspicious. "Uh huh. No thanks. You want my pussy, have it right here." Pulling up her skirt, she showed him that she wasn't wearing underpants.

"I'll pay you to come home with me."

"How much?"

"Hundred now, hundred when we get there. If you do what I want, I'll give you a lot more."

"What kind of kinky are you?"

"I want to paint you."

32

A MOTH TO FLAME

When he saw Jewel naked, standing in his shower washing her hair, he trembled with excitement and recognition. Her breasts were larger, but her nipples were as pink; her flanks were longer, her hips wider, her pubic thatch blonde and thick; but if he blinked, it was Rose's body that glistened with soap. She moaned with pleasure as the hot water stung her skin with its needles. She even grinned at him sitting on the toilet seat, holding a towel, watching her like a father bathing his grown-up daughter—and embarrassed by the awkwardness of the situation.

"Hey, Pops," she called to him. "What's your thing? You like golden showers, maybe?" He shook his head and handed her the bath towel he'd been holding. "You like to watch girls in the shower, then? I mean, man, if that's it, I'll take all the showers you want. I like to be clean!" She wiggled herself as she dried off.

"That's a start," he said dourly, wounded by her calling him "Pops." He suddenly felt old and dirty, and—handing her a fresh toothbrush—he left, closing the door behind him.

He made tea for them, but when she emerged, looking younger, her features softer, she laughed at the tea pot and cups he'd put out. Her body made his old bathrobe beautifully bumpy.

She snickered with the contempt only the young can summon up for the ceremonies they consider irrelevant. "No, no, no, Pops. I don't hold up my pinky and drink tea. Don't you have something *real*? I mean, like something a little stronger?"

He poured her a glass of tequila.

"Don't call me 'Pops,' okay?"

He said it through clenched teeth, and sipped his tea, watching her big eyes flare up as she downed the strong liquor.

"Okay. No Pops. What should I call you, baby? And what am I doing here? Isn't it about time we cut a deal?"

"You can call me Nick. I am a painter. I want you to model for me."

"Now, tell me, why is that? I'm a banged-up scuzz bucket, frankly, Nick. Nobody wants a picture of *that*."

"You look like somebody I used to know. Somebody I used to paint."

It sounded feeble, and she looked puzzled.

"All kinds of people look like all kinds of people. That's show business. But you know what? I'm a whore. That is spelled w-h-o-r-e, you know?"

"I'll pay you better than you've ever been paid."

"To do what?"

"To stay here, while I paint you. I'll take care of you."

"Shit. I can take care of myself. Always have, always will."

She looked around my loft, stuffed with markers of the past.

"I'll make you up a bed. We can start in the morning."

"You got a television?"

"Does it look like it? You didn't have a television in that rat hole I found you in."

"You got a cigarette, then?" He lit one for her and she squinted at him through the smoke just as Rose had. "Okay. Two hundred a day, and you get me a television. I can't sit still without nothing to watch. I'd be twittering like Tweety Bird after a day."

"Deal. But I want you to dye your hair. Red."

"What the hell for? Red's not my color. How about blue?"

"Red."

"Right." She blew a smoke ring at him. He sipped his tea.

"How old are you?" she asked suddenly.

"Fifty-one. Does that bother you?"

"Nah. I like it. Young guys are idiotic. Old foxes like you know how to take care of a girl's needs."

"How old are you?"

"Old enough to know better, but I'm bound for hell anyhow. Don't worry, I'm legal."

"How long have you been on the street?"

"This time? I guess it's been about a month since I got locked out of my crib in Queens."

"Is that where you're from?"

"There, here, everywhere. I get around. I've even been to Los Angeles." She blew more smoke rings, then straightened up and pulled open the robe, revealing her breasts. "Don't you like me?"

"Oh, I like you very much." The dirty old man licked his dry lips.

"Then why don't you want to fuck me? Hey, you're not weird or anything, are you? Because if you are, our deal's off. I need a good hard screwing on a regular basis. I guess I'm just a nympho, but I can't get enough dick in me. You know what I mean? Guess that's why I'm not very good at my profession. I like to give it away."

He cleared his throat, feeling like he was about to dive into a very deep, black well. His voice was thick when he spoke.

"What do you want me to do?"

"I want you to eat me, old man."

She squirmed on her chair and spread her legs wide, reaching between them to hold her wet pink lips open for him.

He stuck his tongue inside and flickered it, his nose tight against the big button of her clitoris, inhaling and licking her juices, straining to get his tongue as deep in her as he could.

"Bite me! Bite my pussy!" He sucked and used his teeth, reaching up to cup her breasts and squeeze them. "That's good, that's good!" she moaned. "Squeeze my tits. I'm going to come in your mouth, you dirty old man!"

When he got to his feet she was still coming. She grabbed her breasts and twisted them, dropping her head so she could chew on her own nipples. He stuck three fingers inside her and fucked her that way until she stopped him. "Show me your big fat dick!"

Licking his lips, he unzipped and pulled his penis free. It was so painfully rigid it was throbbing. He pulled at it frenziedly. His nose ran with her secretions. The power in her eyes was that of an insatiable goddess, a pitiless queen of lust.

"Oooh," she gurgled. "It's so big! I think it's too big for my baby pussy." She teased him with whore talk. "It's too big for my asshole—it might split me in two. Maybe you want to put it in my mouth? I'll bet you want to do something dirty like that—choke me with that horse cock."

She used her teeth to scrape him, but it wasn't hard enough. Her mouth was smaller than Rose's. She bobbed her head expertly, taking half the length of his shaft in and chewing on it, then using her fingernails to scratch his testicles, fingers squeezing with increasing pressure.

She might bite his penis off, and he didn't care, he was so lost in his submission to the passion she aroused. It was as if she knew exactly how far gone he was. She spat on the purple head of his penis, and with a smooth motion, took him into her throat for a minute of intense pleasure before pulling him out and putting him between her breasts. Enveloped by those firm pillows, he ejaculated up onto her chin and into her open mouth.

"You taste bitter," she told him, sticking her tongue out. It was milky with his semen. "We're going to have to sweeten you up."

The Twins

by Lisabet Sarai

from *Incognito*

2

The master summoned me to the library just after tea. "Come in, Mary," he called in response to my shy knock. I could not help but wonder what he wanted with me, merely a downstairs maid, the least of his great household.

"You asked to see me, sir?" I curtseyed as gracefully as I could.

"Yes, Mary." He did not rise from his armchair by the hearth. "Come here, Mary, and stand before me."

I did as he bid me, trembling a little, for his voice was cold and severe. He looked me up and down, as I stood there with my eyes on the figured carpet.

"Mary," he said at last, "are you happy here?"

"Oh, yes, sir," I exclaimed. "Very happy."

"Then why do you steal from me?" he asked sternly.

"Steal from you, Sir! Nay, I would never do such a thing!" I dared to look at him, and saw a strange light burning in his eyes.

"Cook tells me that you have been rifling the pantry while the house is asleep, stealing the choicest delicacies and hiding them in your room."

"What, Sir? Why would I steal food? The provisions here are far better than I've had in any other house, wholesome and plentiful." Indignant in my innocence, I held his gaze. "To be honest Sir, I believe that Cook is envious of me, though why she should be so I cannot tell. Always she gives me the most unpleasant tasks, and never does she have a kind word for me."

"Hmmm," he said, stroking his beard. "I almost believe you. You are quite sure, Mary, that you are not telling me falsehoods to save your skin?"

"Of course not, Sir! You and the Mistress have been very good to me since I entered your service two months hence. I would never lie to you."

"Still, Mary, I must punish you. If I do not, Cook will be so grouchy that she will poison us all with lumpy soups and undercooked roasts. I believe you, Mary, but nevertheless you must be punished."

He reached behind the chair and retrieved a wicked-looking bundle of birch switches. "Turn around, lift your skirts, and take down your drawers," he said in an odd, strained voice.

"Please, Sir, no! T'is not fair!" Tears streamed down my face, but even at my young age, I knew there was no fairness for one such as I. There were the highborn and the low, that was the nature of things, and if one of the high had a fancy to beat one of my standing, it did not matter whether the supposed culprit was guilty or not. Silent and reluctant, I obeyed his instructions. I blushed as I let my linens drop to the floor, baring my hind parts to his scrutiny. Surely this was improper, I thought, hoping wildly that my Mistress would knock on the library door and interrupt this scene. Then I remembered that she was taking tea with her mother in Knightsbridge, and my heart sank.

"Kneel on the edge of the chair," he commanded. I knew he meant the matching armchair on the other side of the hearth. "Bend over and hold tightly to the back of the chair."

I disposed myself as he dictated. Looking over my shoulder, I attempted one last appeal. "Please, Sir, I beg you, do not birch me. I will do whatever you wish, but do not punish me unjustly."

"I have no choice, Mary," he said, almost sadly. "However, if you take your whipping well, I will do something nice for you afterwards."

I crossed my arms on the back of the chair, and buried my face in them. I waited for the first sharp cut. Something seemed to delay him, though. For several minutes, there was no sound but the crackling from the hearth. A draft swept between my naked thighs, and I shivered a little, from suspense as much as cold.

Finally he spoke, almost in a whisper. "You have a lovely bum, Mary," he said, and then the switches slashed across my bare bottom.

I cried out loud. "Hush, Mary, hush," said the Master. "We cannot have you rousing the whole staff. This is a private matter, between you and me." I wondered at this, given his insistence that my punishment was required to preserve household peace. Still, ever dutiful and observant, I bit my lip and struggled to obey.

It was indeed painful, but not as bad as I had expected. I could feel each flexible rod lay a stinging track across my skin, sharp and bright like little needles. Afterwards, though, a kind of glow came over me, as if I were warming my poor bottom at a nice fire.

Nevertheless, I could not help but jerk and squirm with each of his strokes. This seemed to inflame him, for he rained blows upon me, faster and harder, the more I moved.

All my nether parts were on fire. They pulsed hot and raw, but I blush to admit that I did not wish him to stop. There was something strangely exciting about the circumstances, my cheeks exposed and open to his gaze, my now-willing adherence to his bizarre instructions. I will be the perfect servant, I thought to myself, a little giddy. I will do what my Master bids, no matter how strange it may seem.

At last he stopped. I could hear him breathing heavily, as if from great exertion. Then I jumped, for I felt his hands stroking my bare arse.

"Good, Mary. You are a very good girl." He lightly brushed his fingers over the welts that I knew crisscrossed my nakedness. "I believe that you are innocent of any wrong doing, and I apologize for beating you." Another surprise assaulted my senses; my master had knelt behind me and was tracing my stripes with his rough, wet tongue.

I would be untruthful if I claimed that this was unwelcome to me. For indeed, his mouth on my scored flesh was wonderfully soothing, and more. It set up that aching hungriness that I sometimes feel between my legs, late at night when I am in my bed. Then I turn over on my stomach and push my palms against that secret, furred place, pressing through my nightdress until I find some relief, while Priscilla, the upstairs maid, snores beside me.

It was the same now, but much stronger. I sighed softly, and without realising what I was doing, pushed my hips back toward my master. He seemed to understand that he had succeeded in exciting my passion.

"Ah, Mary, you enjoy that, don't you?" I was silent, blushing with shame. "Do not worry, my dear, I will not hurt you. I told you that I would do something nice for you, and I shall."

Before I could protest or reply, he pulled the globes of my buttocks apart, and thrust his tongue deep into my cunny. I thought I would faint with delight. He flicked his tongue rapidly in and out, almost like a serpent (as I thought later). Then he fastened his whole mouth on that dark, moist crevice, lapping and sucking until I lost all control. As I spent myself, he licked greedily, as if my juices were the most delicious of wines. I sank exhausted onto the leather upholstery, my skirts tangled around me. After a moment, the Master raised me up, his hand under my chin. "You are special," he told me, his voice kind. "You are obedient and good, but you also have a voluptuous spirit." My cheeks burned and I hung my head. "No, my dear, do not be ashamed. Be grateful, for you will have a better life than your proper and virtuous sisters."

"Now, I have one more service to require of you. I trust that you will not find it too distasteful." I watched, horrified, as he unfastened the buttons on his britches. "As you can see, administering to your carnal needs has left me quite aroused." He spoke the truth. His member sprang from his clothing, rigid and flushed with blood. "I must ask your assistance in allaying this unseemly desire, before my dear wife returns from her afternoon jaunt."

I am sure he read the fear in my eyes. I knew of too many maidservants undone, cast out of doors alone and in shame, bearing their master's unborn child. "Fear not, sweet Mary," he said, smiling. "I shall not get you with child, nor will I take your virginity, if you have it still."

"Undo your waist and your corset, so that I may see your breasts." I did as he requested, not completely unwilling. I know that I have pretty titties. "Lovely," he murmured, stroking his hand up and down his swelling tool. "Now, back on the chair. I will not pierce your maidenhood, my sweet, but by Heaven, I will spend myself in your tight little arse."

* * *

A knock on her office door brought Miranda back to the here and now. She had been lost, uncharacteristically, in the manuscript, a classic piece from the collection of the British Museum. There were no annotations, no commentary, on the photocopied pages. Her laptop, neglected, had turned itself off to save power. She sighed and shook her head as if to clear away the lascivious images.

"Come in," she called, wondering who it could be. She often worked on Saturdays, precisely because the department was deserted and she could read and write undisturbed.

The grizzled head of Harold Scofield poked through the door. "Hello, Miranda. I am sorry to intrude, but I have someone to whom I would like to introduce you." Miranda smiled to herself; her genial thesis advisor always sounded like a grammar textbook. The gray-bearded figure in suspenders bustled in, followed by an attractive young man in dark-framed eyeglasses.

"Miranda, I would like to present Mark Anderson, our new lecturer. Mark will be handling the Dickens course for the summer session."

"Mark, this is Miranda Cahill, my most promising graduate student." Miranda blushed, and Dr. Scofield's eyes twinkled. "Miranda has chosen a rather controversial topic for her thesis: a new interpretation of the corpus of Victorian erotica."

The newcomer's polite smile expanded to a grin. "Really! That's fascinating. Sounds far more—stimulating—than my dissertation on the metaphorical significance of orphans in Dickens and his contemporaries."

Miranda's blush deepened as she noted the double entendre. She met his teasing gaze, almost defiantly. "Yes, it is an intriguing topic, and I believe one of considerable literary and social significance, as well." He had thick, dark hair, slightly tousled. His eyes behind the glasses were velvety brown with glints of gold. In his face, she saw intelligence, energy, and humor.

"Miranda has championed an unusual theory: that the explosion of sexually-oriented writing during the latter half of the nineteenth century was a reflection of actual practices, rather than a reaction against repressive public morals." Her advisor appeared to be enjoying the role of agent provocateur. "She believes that the detailed accounts of sexual adventure and aberration published during the era chronicled real experiences, not merely fantasies."

"Hmm." Their bespectacled companion looked both amused and interested. "What evidence do you have to support this proposition?"

"Well, to begin with," said Miranda, automatically adopting an academic tone, "a significant fraction of these writings are first person accounts. And a surprising number are related from a woman's perspective. If this were primarily a literature of fantasy and titillation, I would expect a male point-of-view to dominate, as it does in modern pornography." Miranda was encouraged to see that her audience listened attentively and gave due consideration to her points.

"Secondly, these tales are full of real-world details and commentary that would be superfluous and even distracting in fictional erotica. The protagonists discuss social issues such as poverty, child abuse, oppression of the lower classes, things that can only detract from a work intended as escapist fantasy. Even a hack pornographer knows better than to mention the unpleasant or the mundane: illegitimate pregnancies, unpaid bills, rising damp. Yet references to such items are common in the corpus.

"Finally, I find in many of these writings a thoughtfulness that conflicts with the conventions of the pornographic genre. The narrators are engaged in a wide variety of sexual activities, which are described in vivid and provocative detail. At the same time, in many cases, they reflect on their own desires and behaviors, sometimes justifying themselves in the face of the official morality, sometimes castigating themselves for weakness and sinfulness. Either way, there is a psychological depth that would be redundant in fictional erotica."

"So, what you are saying," interposed Mark with a grin, "is that a fictional character would simply go ahead and bugger his maid, whereas an individual writing a clandestine diary would spend some time and effort wondering why he wanted to bugger his maid, before he got around to actually doing it?"

"No, no, that's not it at all!" Miranda, embarrassed and flustered, wondered if the new instructor had been reading her manuscript over her shoulder. Her eyes flashed. "You're not willing to take me seriously, any more than the submission review committee for the Association for Modern Literature!"

"Now, Miranda," soothed her advisor. "Mark was just teasing you." Looking again at the attractive stranger, Miranda saw that Scofield was telling the truth.

"Sorry, I really didn't mean to offend you, Miranda." Mark held out his hand like a peace offering. "I really am delighted to meet you. I think your theory is unconventional and provocative, but who knows, it might actually be true." His skin was cool and dry, the pressure of his fingers firm and confident. "Let me take you out for coffee, and you can tell me more about what your research has turned up thus far." As he released her hand, he brushed his fingers lightly against her palm.

The secret, sensual gesture terrified her. Miranda found herself reacting as she so often did in the presence of a man who desired her. She felt herself tense, contract, her fears and uncertainties condensing into a dense, cold knot under her solar plexus. Her face was stiff and wooden as she tried to smile. "Thank you, but I can't right now. I have an incredible amount of work to get done."

"Diligent, industrious Miranda!" her advisor scolded her lightly. "You need to take more time for yourself. It is Saturday, after all."

"Thanks, but I need to work harder. I need more evidence to support my theory. Deeper study, of a larger number of texts."

"Please . . . ," Mark began, disappointment plain in his voice. Then he saw clearly that she would not be swayed. "Well, another time, perhaps." He smiled so warmly that the icy knot thawed slightly. "I definitely would like to get to know you better, Miranda."

After they left, Miranda sank back into her chair and put her face in her hands. She did not understand her own reactions. On the one hand, she nervously rejected the attentions of an attractive, educated, appealing man like Anderson. And on the other—she could not bring herself to review the events of the previous night, but she was acutely and uncomfortably aware that she had acted outrageously. She had coupled like an animal, unthinking and uncontrolled, with a stranger who had no face. Then she had run away, stealing someone else's coat to cover her nakedness, not even ashamed.

She had awakened the next morning, forgetful at first. Only as she stood in the shower, the hot stream coursing over her body, did she begin to recall the night's adventures. Her vagina was tender and sore. The water made her buttocks sting; looking around, she found that her skin was marked with the red traces of fingernails. When she emerged and saw the trench coat draped over the chair, the full memory assaulted her.

For a moment, it was if she were back again in the alcove, blind, sweaty, moaning, impaled upon the exquisite hardness of her unknown companion. She sank down on the bed, her eyes closed, panting, dizzy. Then, she pushed the images away, too disturbed to consider their implications. She rifled through the pockets of the raincoat, seeking some clue as to the identify of its owner. All she found was an enigmatic business card.

It was expensive, textured stock, with crimson text printed on a black background. "The Fantasy Factory," it read, in flowing, modern script, with a telephone number below. That was all. No name, no address. Only the number, with a local city code.

She had packed up the coat and sent it back to the disco by courier, with an anonymous, apologetic note. Hopefully, the coat's owner would inquire at the club and have the garment returned to him. Or to her. Miranda realized that the garment was equally appropriate for either sex. She found herself wondering about this individual, this stranger with whom her life had obliquely intersected.

She had kept the card.

Miranda tried to return to her reading, but she could not concentrate. She kept hearing Mark Anderson's voice, affectionate and mocking. At last she gave up, shoveled her books, notes and computer into her backpack, and headed across the river to Beacon Hill. I'll read some more tonight, she told herself, but right now I need a break.

She decided to drop her heavy bag off at the apartment she and Lucy shared. There was a message from her roommate on the answering machine.

"Hey, Miranda. I just wanted you to know I'm fine, and that you shouldn't worry about me. I'm here at Ray's place, and he is taking very good care of me . . ." Lucy's voice trailed off into giggles, as if she were being tickled by an unseen companion, then composed itself again. "See you in a few days. By the way, help yourself to anything of mine you want to wear. You looked sensational last night." There were more giggles. "Bye!" She hung up abruptly.

Miranda felt a bit envious. She wished, sometimes, that she had Lucy's casual, comfortable attitude toward sex. Still, she was glad that she would have the apartment to herself for a while. She needed some time to sort out her feelings before telling Lucy about her experiences in the disco.

Miranda's tomcat, Heathcliff, lay curled on her bed, a compact mass of ginger fur. He opened one eye reproachfully as she dumped her backpack on the coverlet, annoyed at being disturbed, but he quickly settled back into purring repose when she scratched him behind his ears. She left him on guard while she went out for a walk.

Miranda felt delightfully free as she strolled down Charles Street, enjoying the afternoon. It was only May, but already the trees were in full leaf, dappling the brick sidewalks with patterns of shadow. Girls passed her in tank tops and shorts, legs and arms bare and already burnished with sun. She felt warm in her long-sleeved pullover and overalls.

She loved this district, with its historic buildings and narrow lanes. Most of the townhouses dated from the middle of the previous century. They offered a delightful jumble of architectural detail: wrought-iron balconies, fanlight transoms, stained glass, mullioned windows, Corinthian columns. Many of the brick-fronted buildings were draped with ivy. Some were traversed by aged trunks as thick as her wrist, twining around doors up to the many-chimneyed roofs. The tall windows offered glimpses of chandeliers, Oriental carpets, Siamese cats, and bookshelves that stretched floor to ceiling.

In Beacon Hill, gas lamps lined all the streets, burning day and night. Her own apartment looked out on a private alley, flanked by ivy-hung brick walls and lit by gas lights. Miranda appreciated the irony of her living in an environment that dated from the same period as her research. Perhaps, she sometimes thought playfully, I had a previous life as a Victorian matron.

Most of Beacon Hill was entirely residential, but Charles Street was lined with shops and cafes. There were many vendors of books and antiquities; Miranda loved to rummage through the crowded, chaotic shops, savoring the atmosphere of the past, although she rarely made a purchase.

She entered one of these places now, a dim, comfortable space half below street level. She had to duck her head as she entered. A silvery bell tinkled to announce her arrival.

The proprietor, an energetic, fussy old man with wire spectacles, knew her by sight. "Hello, hello," he said as he emerged from a back room. "Can I help you find anything today?"

Miranda smiled. "No, thank you. I am just browsing at the moment."

"Well, if I can be of any assistance, please let me know."

Miranda wandered happily through the shop. It was much larger than it first appeared, with several rooms stretching backward into the building. The front room, near the street, was crowded with furniture of obsolete categories, armoires, commodes, carved dressing tables surmounted by triple mirrors. There were other rooms with porcelain, jewelry, cutlery, iron fittings, tarnished brass. Finally, Miranda found herself in the book room.

Books were piled everywhere, in boxes, on shelves, in pillars that reached up from the middle of the floor. Although most were in English, Miranda noticed volumes in French, Russian, and Arabic. The room was veiled in dust, but Miranda did not mind. She loved the rich smell of the leather bindings, the tarnished gold embossing, the fragile texture of the old paper.

Rummaging through a box of miscellaneous tomes, she made her find. It was a leather-bound diary, about the size of a modern paperback book. There was a brass lock, crusted with verdigris, but it was broken. The leather strap that had sealed the diary shut now flapped about ineffectually.

The paper was wonderful, thick and ivory-toned. Miranda rifled through the heavy pages, which turned lazily under her fingers. She found no sign that the diary had ever been used.

Miranda wondered about the age of the volume. She held it to her nose, smelled oiled leather but no mildew. The cover was plain, save for a manufacturer's imprint too small for her to read in the dim shop.

She wanted it, suddenly, knew that she had to have it no matter what the cost. She made her way back to the front of the shop, where the proprietor sat behind his desk.

"How much are you asking for this?" she asked, trying to sound offhand.

The little man took the diary and turned it over and over in his hands. "One hundred dollars," he finally said.

Miranda knew she would pay that, if she had to, but something made her object. "One hundred? That's outrageous! There's no text, so it has no historical value."

The shop owner pursed his lips firmly. "It dates from the eighteen-eighties," he said. "This is a real antique."

"The lock is broken," Miranda insisted. "And corroded. I'll give you fifty dollars."

The watery blue eyes behind the wire frames looked at her fixedly. She stared back, unfazed. Finally, he shrugged. "All right, fifty dollars. It has been in my collection for years; it is about time that I got rid of it."

Miranda felt inordinately pleased with herself as she took her prize back to her apartment.

She put the diary on her bedstand and sat down at her desk, determined to work. She felt somehow uncomfortable returning to the text from *A Maid's Tale,* so instead she started reviewing and organizing her notes on other manuscripts. For several hours, she doggedly tried to make progress, but her thoughts were scattered.

Heathcliff sat on the corner of her desk as he often did when was working, his owl-like eyes unblinking as he watched her shuffle papers and scribble notations. Normally he did not distract her, but now she found his curiosity and intensity unsettling.

Restless, she prowled around the apartment. Dusk was falling. Her senses felt stretched, amplified. She could hear a dog bark half a block away, smell the garlic being fried by her Vietnamese neighbors upstairs. She threw open the window to the alley and leaned out, breathing the soft, fragrant spring air. Spring fever, she thought, but she knew this was a fever of another kind.

Finally, she gave in, picked up the card she had found in the raincoat, and dialed the number. She held her breath while the line rang once, twice, three times. She was about to put down the receiver, almost with a sense of relief, when the line was picked up.

It was a recorded message, a melodious, controlled female voice. "Welcome to the Fantasy Factory, where you can build adventures from your dreams. We offer an exciting, safe environment where adults can explore, and fulfill, their fantasies." Miranda listened, learned that Wednesdays were fetish nights, Fridays for couples only, Saturdays and Sundays open to all. She noted the address, in an industrial area on the fringes of the city, then hung up. She was breathing heavily.

Almost as if she were sleepwalking, she drifted into Lucy's room, and opened her closet.

* * *

Just after nine P.M., she emerged from a taxi in front of a massive brick building, lit by spotlights at each corner. The rest of the neighborhood appeared to be derelict, abandoned warehouses and chain link fences. "American Tool and Die Company," read the huge faded letters just below the roof. Much smaller, in purple neon above the old loading dock, she read: The Fantasy Factory.

The loading dock door was hung with strips of rubber. She made her way through and found herself in a red-lit anteroom. An exquisite Asian woman with hair to her waist sat behind a chrome desk. The woman wore a mask; when she spoke, Miranda heard traces of an accent.

"Welcome to the Fantasy Factory," she said, "where everything is permitted, and anything is possible. Is this your first visit with us?"

Miranda nodded nervously. The woman handed her a mask, and kissed her on the cheek. "You will enjoy yourself," she said softly, her lips just inches from Miranda's ear.

"Why the masks?" asked Miranda.

"Anonymity," the hostess replied. "Privacy. But that is not all. Donning a mask can free you, to be someone else, or perhaps more truly, to be yourself."

"Now," she said, holding aside a velvet curtain, "enter, and enjoy."

Miranda pulled on the black silk domino and stepped through the archway, at once eager and reluctant.

She found herself in a cavernous space, three or four stories high. The décor was industrial chic. A network of huge steel beams crisscrossed the ceiling; hung from the beams on heavy chains were several massive chandeliers that appeared to be fashioned of old tires. Flickering red bulbs embedded in the rubber lit the scene with a rosy, irregular glow. The far reaches of the room remained in shadow. There was music, something electronic; synthesizers swelled from throbbing lows to ethereal highs.

Miranda took another hesitant step forward. The room was occupied by perhaps a hundred people: women, men, and individuals of indeterminate gender. Some danced, some embraced, some lounged on low couches that lined one wall. Some were clothed, often in elegant evening dress, but many were naked, or effectively so. Miranda watched a lovely woman with long platinum hair glide past, wearing only her mask and a transparent black veil knotted around her neck. A burly man in a leather jockstrap met the blonde in the middle of the floor. Laughing, he flung her over his shoulder and headed for one of the couches.

Miranda felt a little thrill at this interaction. Still, this was only one of the erotic tableaux displayed before her. The light was dim, but even with the shadows she could see the voluptuous form of a woman stretched out on a low table a dozen feet away. She lay on her back, thighs eagerly clasping a giant of a man who was pounding her with his cock. Meanwhile, another, slighter male figure straddled her face, offering his pulsing erection to her hungry mouth. Even as she arched her back to bury one man's cock more deeply inside her cunt, she dug her fingernails into the other's buttocks, seeking to swallow more of his flesh.

A wave of vertigo swept over Miranda, as if she teetered on the edge of a precipice. She tried without success to look away, while the three strained toward their climax. As if they were one animal, they bucked and shuddered, groaned and clawed at each other's limbs. Finally, their frenzy peaked. The two men cried out. The woman arched and opened herself to their ultimate thrusts. For a moment, they lay quiet and exhausted. Semen dribbled from the woman's slack mouth. Still, Miranda was transfixed. The penetrator knelt between his lady's legs and kissed her deeply there, triggering moans of delight. Then, unexpectedly, he rose, circled around her, and pressed his mouth to that of his well-fellated comrade. With blunt fingertips, he fondled the other man's muscular buttocks, clearly marked by the tracks of the woman's nails.

Miranda was somehow more fascinated than shocked. The trio rearranged itself. The slender man lay atop the woman, his penis firmly planted in her cleft. The heavier man positioned himself behind his slighter companion. Miranda flushed hot with guilt and desire as she watched his thick rod of flesh disappear ever so slowly into the darkness between those smooth cheeks. Despite his mask, she could read ecstasy on the younger man's face, his mouth slack, his eyes screwed shut, his hands gripping the shoulders of the woman beneath him, plowing her as he was plowed.

"Lovely," sighed a cultured feminine voice, close to her ear. "Don't you agree?"

Miranda whirled round, startled and embarrassed. She had not realized that she had companions in her blatant voyeurism.

They were young, close to her own age, and enough alike in stature and demeanor that they could have been siblings. Both had thick brunette hair. His was brushed back from his brow, while she wore hers in a bob with blunt bangs. They were clad in black spandex jumpsuits that highlighted every curve and swelling of their slender, athletic forms. Prominent nipples capped her small breasts, clearly visible through the clinging fabric. His half-engorged organ was equally obvious.

They were masked, of course. Brown eyes gleamed behind their dominoes. It was their mouths, though, that captured Miranda's attention, their ripe perfect lips: inviting, sensuous, bowed in the perpetual promise of a smile.

Miranda ached to kiss those mouths, to trace their luscious curves with the tip of her tongue. She felt the ache in her throat, in her chest, in her painfully taut nipples, in the damp, hungry recesses of her womb. Her palms ached to glide over those smooth thighs, those flat bellies. She wanted them, both of them, craved them in a visceral way that was totally new to her.

She stifled a moan, and took the hand the woman extended.

"I'm Marla," the other woman said, her voice melodious and a bit husky. "And this is Marcus." The young man smiled mysteriously but said nothing. "We were admiring your costume."

It took Miranda a moment to recall the red velvet jumpsuit that she had chosen from Lucy's wardrobe. It was defiantly flamboyant, clinging to her body like a sensuous second skin. A gold-colored zipper ran from the scoop neck down to her navel. Matching zippers adorned her wrists and ankles. She knew that the color suited her, contrasted with the hair spilling over her shoulders like a river of jet. She also knew how obvious it was that she was naked underneath the velvet. Not a shy garment, thought Miranda, but perhaps just right for tonight.

Choked with desire, she found it difficult to speak. "Thank you," she managed, finally. "I like your outfits also." (What an understatement, she thought to herself.) "Are you twins?"

They gave identical, musical laughs. "Not exactly," said the one called Marcus. "But we enjoy pretending."

His voice was vaguely familiar. However, Miranda was too occupied with other concerns to wonder at this.

"Don't you?" asked Marla, searching Miranda's face.

The question was serious, and stopped her short. She did not know how to answer. Was she pretending, now? Never had she felt sensations so compelling, so real.

Marla still grasped her hand. "Come play with us," she said sweetly, pulling Miranda toward one of the walls lined with couches.

Miranda felt sudden panic. Much as she desired them, she

did not believe that she could bring herself to couple publicly like that threesome. Not now, not yet. Marla led her past the sofas and cushions, however, through a curtained doorway into a small, private space. Marcus followed. As they entered, Miranda felt his hands, molding her hips, cupping her buttocks. It was delightful but too brief, a flirtation, a promise.

The translucent drapery fell back into place. The three of them were alone. For a long moment they stood motionless, facing each other. What am I doing? thought Miranda, wondering at the thud of her heart against her ribs and the swollen heat of her sex.

Then all her awkwardness and uncertainty dropped away. With her right hand, she reached for Marla, her fingers seeking the hard little nubs pushing through the spandex. With her left, she drew Marcus to her, reveling in the sensation of his tumescence pressed against her thigh. Marla's breast cupped in one hand, Marcus' scrotum in the other, Miranda kissed them in turn.

Their mouths were surprisingly different. Marla's kiss was soft, almost tentative, though she readily opened her ripe lips to the probing of Miranda's tongue. She tasted faintly of cloves, sharp and sweet.

Marcus kissed with a fury that robbed Miranda of breath. At the touch of her lips, his opened, and he seemed to inhale her, sucking her tongue into his mouth and tangling it with his own. Meanwhile, his arm encircled her hip and pulled her more tightly against him. He ground his bulging crotch against her velvet-clad thigh, setting up sympathetic tremors in her sex.

If Marla's kiss was a gentle invitation, Marcus' was a challenge. Once again, a fleeting impression of familiarity rose in Miranda's consciousness, then slipped away as hands and lips expanded and complicated the three-way caress.

Marla broke away first. Without speaking, she pulled the

jumpsuit off her shoulders and wriggled out of it, somehow managing to look charming rather than clumsy.

Marla was slender, but far from boyish. Miranda could not take her eyes from the dusky rose nipples that pertly tipped the girl's palm-sized breasts. Her skin was golden all over with a light tan; there were no pale patches. Marla's hips swelled invitingly from a narrow waist, then down to firm, straight thighs. At their meeting point, her neatly trimmed triangle of brunette curls left Miranda feeling weak and confused.

I've never been attracted to women before, thought Miranda. What's happening to me? Then an image from her past flooded her inner vision. High school, Rebecca—the minister's wild daughter, long blonde locks flying, laughing as she danced at a party, while a younger Miranda watched from a corner, overwhelmed by a craving she could not name. So, thought Miranda, beginning to understand how little she knew her real self.

Marla raised her arms behind her head, stretching luxuriously as she lifted her thick locks away from her neck. Miranda helplessly admired Marla's elevated and accentuated breasts, the faint, symmetrical trace of her ribs, the slight indentations of taut muscle on either side of her dimpled navel. Then Marla took hold of her own nipples, rolling them between her finger and thumb, so that they lengthened and hardened. Her eyes behind the domino were locked on Miranda's. "Do you like what you see, darling?" she asked. "Can you see how much I want you?"

She relinquished one of her nipples and brought her palm down to brush ever so lightly over her bush. Electric shivers tingled in Miranda's sex as she watched and imagined the other woman's sensations. Now Marla pressed the heel of her hand against her pubis and slid her middle finger in among the curls. Miranda could clearly see its quick, oscillating movements as it teased the woman's hidden clit. Marla's eyes were half-closed, her ripe mouth half-open as her breathing grew more ragged.

Miranda moaned in sympathetic arousal. Then suddenly there was a hand squeezing her tit through the velvet, and another making lazy swirls across her sex, while hot lips nibbled at the sensitive spot where her neck met her shoulder. "Marcus!" she gasped, writhing against the hard body behind her.

"At your service." His voice was almost a whisper, close to her ear, but Miranda still caught the tone of amusement. She reached behind her, felt his warm, dry, naked skin. While she had been focused on Marla's performance, Marcus had apparently removed his jumpsuit.

"Do you like my little sister?" He drummed his fingers against her velvet-sheathed pubis in a maddening, thrilling tattoo.

In fact his attentions distracted Miranda from his supposed sibling. He rubbed three fingers firmly back and forth across her mound, intruding ever so slightly into the space between her thighs. Almost automatically, Miranda spread her legs, allowing, inviting greater access.

Being touched through the taut fabric was both exciting and frustrating. It felt dirty and clandestine, as if she stood still while someone groped her private parts on the subway. The velvet transmitted pressure, heat, urgency. It dampened under his fingertips; she knew he could not fail to notice. The deepest touches were foiled by the stretchy barrier, though she thrust herself shamelessly against his knowing hand. She craved the bareness of his flesh on hers.

As if he eavesdropped on her thoughts, Marcus stopped playing with her. Still behind her, he grasped the zipper tongue. "It is not really fair," he said, "for you to remain dressed when we have disrobed." One pull, and the jumpsuit sprang open to her navel. Her breasts bobbed as they were freed from confinement. Deftly Marcus caught her left nipple with one hand. The other he plunged down into the hungry wetness of her sex, stretching the fabric now from the inside.

Miranda knees weakened at the sudden, delicious penetration. Marcus held her up with one strong arm, pulling her against his chest while he continued to delve into the juicy space between her thighs with his other hand. She closed her eyes and allowed herself to be supported, explored, ravished.

She was being drawn ever closer to the edge, her whole body trembling in concert with the throbbing in her cunt. Her masked partner played the instrument of her flesh with a virtuosity that would have astonished her, had she been less muddled by lust. He touched her in a thousand distinct and delightful ways, coaxed her toward climax then backed off, barely in contact. Her arousal smoldered, flared, subsided to burn ever hotter in the next cycle of caresses.

Amid the flood of stimulation, Miranda was startled by a new touch. Soft wetness enveloped her taut and aching nipples. She opened her eyes to see a sleek cap of dark locks. Marla half-knelt, half-crouched before her, licking and sucking at her breasts with sweet abandon. The sight, the realization, as much as the sensation, pushed Miranda past the final barrier. She clutched Marla's shoulders, crushing the girl to her breasts as Marcus thrust all four fingers deep into her vagina and spread them wide. Sandwiched between the lascivious twins, Miranda lost all control, and for a long instant, self-consciousness, letting her body speak in its own ancient language.

When she was next aware, she was lying nude on a pile of cushions. Marla's gentle hands brushed her tangled hair from her face. The brown eyes behind the mask held a look of concerned affection. "Are you all right, darling?" the other woman asked.

"Wonderful," sighed Miranda. "Just a bit overwhelmed by the two of you." She reached up impulsively, and kissed the ripe lips below the black silk mask. "Thank you."

"What about me?" Marcus leaned forward, and she threw her arms around his neck, kissing him fiercely. Thank you, she thought, for seeing through my veil, for giving me what I really wanted.

After a long moment she released him. He stroked her breast idly with one hand; with the other he toyed with Marla's pubic curls. He looked at her, a bit of challenge in his eyes. "You know, we still don't know your name."

The question caught Miranda off-guard. A twinge of something, fear, caution, embarrassment, sang through her, holding her silent for a moment. "Randi," she said finally, grimacing inwardly as she noted the unintentional pun. "You can call me Randi."

"Randi, we are more than pleased to make your acquaintance," said Marcus with a grin. His fingers ventured deeper into the tangle between Marla's legs. She wriggled in delight and opened her thighs to his expert touch. Miranda swallowed hard at the sight of the girl's rosy folds, swollen and glistening with the juices of lust. Her own cunt was just as wet; she fought an urge to sink her fingers into those moist depths.

As Marcus continued his probing, Marla pressed her pelvis against him, twisting and moaning. "You see how much you've pleased my little sister." Suddenly he withdrew his hand from Marla's sex, and held it to Miranda's lips. She breathed deep, filling her nostrils with Marla's sharp female scent. It made her dizzy. Without thought, she took Marcus' fingers in her mouth, sucking and running her tongue over the salty, ocean-flavored skin.

"Ah, you like that!" Marcus smiled and sat back on his

heels, giving Miranda a better view of his sister's luscious body spread-eagled on the cushions. "Why don't you taste the source? I'm sure that Marla would enjoy that."

Something tightened inside Miranda's chest, stopping her short. I'm not ready for that, she thought, and I don't know what to do. Marcus sensed her discomfort. He cupped her chin in his hand and kissed her briefly. "Allow me to give you a demonstration, Randi," he said, and knelt between his sibling's welcoming thighs.

Marla had responded enthusiastically to his manual ministrations; she became delirious as his tongue began to dance inside her sex. "Oh, Marcus, darling, more, more!" She grabbed his head and mashed his mouth into her crotch. "Eat me, baby, oh yes, please, harder . . . !" Her exhortations trailed off into inarticulate moans as her brother brought her closer and closer to the edge.

Miranda shifted so that she could watch the changing expressions on Marla's face. The other woman's breath came in gasps. One instant her features would contort in response to some ecstatic pain; the next, a simple grin bowed her lips. Are they really brother and sister? Miranda wondered, excited by the perversity of the thought. If they are, how far do they go?

Without a conscious decision, she began to finger herself, lightly massaging the swollen knot of her clit through the damp mat of black fur that covered her pubis. Soon this was not enough; Marla's whimpers inflamed her. Miranda raised one knee, spreading her lower lips wide. With her thumb she rocked the hard knob of pleasure back and forth, while she plunged her fingers as deeply as she could into her vagina. Marcus looked up briefly, catching his breath, and smiled at the sight.

Marla's breathing was harsh and labored; her body flailed wildly against her sibling's busy mouth. Miranda was a heartbeat or two behind in the climb to climax, and gaining.

Suddenly, the brunette gave a wail and her whole body convulsed. As she shuddered in the throes of orgasm her eyes flew open, and fixed themselves on Miranda.

Raw lust blazed in those eyes, shocking and pure. Miranda saw, understood, felt her own lust answering. She tumbled into her climax, felt her muscles constricting her fingers as she drove them as deep as she could. No thoughts, no questions, only the unarguable truth of her own carnal nature.

When the last shudders had faded away, Miranda's eyelids fluttered open. A new tableau confronted her, rekindling the heat between her thighs.

Marcus reclined on the cushions now, more or less in the position previously occupied by his sister. His arms were folded behind his head, his eyes were shut, and a broad smile decorated his lips. Marla knelt gracefully on one side of him. Her slender fingers danced up and down the length of his cock, which rose magnificently from his belly. The pale skin stretched taut over the swollen member, silky and inviting. In contrast, the bulb was spongy, shiny, almost purple. Marla grasped him with thumb and ring finger, just under the head, then ran her forefinger across the tip, smearing the droplet of moisture that trickled from the eye. Marcus stirred slightly, then relaxed into her hands.

Marla alternated her strokes with a skill that belied her apparent youth. First she would trace with the barest touch the pulsing veins that decorated his massive shaft. Then she would wrap her whole hand around him, squeezing until Marcus groaned aloud. While one hand worked his penis briskly, the other teased the underside of his balls, fingertips brushing lightly over the tender, wrinkled skin. In response, his rod grew still fatter and longer. He was clay in her hands, and she was the master sculptor, molding him into the perfect effigy of lust.

"I thought that Marcus deserved some attention," said

Marla softly, without interrupting her ministrations. "After he was so nice to both of us."

"Let me help," said Miranda, moving to kneel on the other side of Marcus' torso. He opened his eyes briefly when he sensed her presence and grinned, then settled back into happy passivity.

"Of course," purred Marla. She was stroking him more energetically than before, and he was starting to jerk his hips in time with her motions. His rampant organ rose proudly, angled toward his chest. Flushed skin stretched taut, it seemed ready to burst. The knob was wet with pre-come. Miranda eyed it hungrily for a moment. Then she bent and encircled the swollen flesh with her mouth.

"Ooh. . . ." Miranda thrilled at the sound of Marcus' involuntary response. His skin was exquisitely soft against her lips. The steely hardness underneath was a delicious, exciting contrast. He tasted sharp, musky, a little salty. Acting on instinct, she sucked strongly, pulling more of him into her mouth,

"Yes, that's just right," advised Marla huskily. "He loves to be deep-throated. Suck him hard. Take in all you can." The other woman leaned close. Miranda caught a whiff of her woman-scent and understood that Marla was both voyeur and exhibitionist. "Oh, Randi, that's so good," she sighed. "Oh, yes!" Miranda felt a fluttering against her lips and realized that Marla had joined her in her sensual repast.

Try as she would, Miranda could not swallow the full length of Marcus' cock. Marla turned her attention to the few inches at the root that remained outside the warm wetness of Miranda's mouth. She licked at the shaft, then lightly grazed the velvety hardness with her teeth. Marcus moaned and trembled slightly. Miranda felt a ripple of tension traveling up through the rigid flesh and backed off, freeing more of him for Marla to devour.

The two women worked together, bringing Marcus ever closer to his peak. Miranda felt Marla's lips often on her own. Their saliva mingled as they alternated positions, one swallowing the head, the other teasing the root. Though they were focused on their companion and his pleasure, they could not help but touch each other. Each brush of Marla's nakedness against her own increased Miranda's fever. Each shudder that shook Marcus' frame made her hotter and hungrier.

Suddenly Marcus' hands were on their shoulders, gently pushing them away from his cock. "You're both fantastic," he said, "and I am extremely tempted to give one of you a mouthful of my come. But that would be selfish, wouldn't it?"

"Besides, you have such a hot mouth, Randi, I can only dream what it will be like to fuck your wet, horny cunt."

His crudeness made Miranda weak. She sank back on her heels, watching Marla, who was smoothing a condom down over her sibling's rigid flesh. He wriggled playfully. "That feels so good, Marla," he sighed.

"But not as good as this," she said, giving his hardness a squeeze. "Come on, Randi. He's more than ready for you."

Miranda needed no further invitation. On her knees, she straddled Marcus' prone form. Marla, behind her, reached down and pulled Miranda's labia apart, holding her open. The other woman's touch brought Miranda to the very edge of orgasm. The sensation of Marcus' engorged penis sliding into her swollen folds pushed her over.

She heard someone scream, and realized that it was her own voice. Her form convulsed. She fell forward against her partner's body, jerking lewdly, grinding her cunt against him to call back echoes of her pleasure.

Her first conscious reaction was embarrassment. How selfish, how unsophisticated of her, to climax so quickly. She climbed off of Marcus' penis, blushing and suddenly shy.

Then she saw that her twin lovers were both smiling indulgently. They know I am a hopeless, helpless slut, she thought, and they don't mind. That's what they were looking for. Still, she felt the urge to apologize.

"I'm sorry," she said. "I didn't realize . . . " Marla silenced her with a kiss. When their tongues disengaged, Marla reached into a tote bag on the floor and extracted an object that, even in her state of arousal, made Miranda blush.

It was a strap-on dildo, a thick prong of hard, pink rubber nestled in a leather and elastic harness. Miranda swallowed hard. She had heard that women used such articles to penetrate their female lovers. However, Marla did not don the infernal contraption herself. Instead, she fastened the straps around Marcus' hips, so that the base of the phallus rested on his pubis, just above his own rampant cock. "You see?" said Marla with a devilish smile, and, horrified and titillated, Miranda did.

"Now we can all have some fun," said Marla. "Climb on, Randi."

Miranda's face burned, but that was nothing compared to the heat between her legs. Without hesitation, she positioned herself over the pink shaft, spread herself wide with her fingers, and sank down until it was buried deep inside. The juices from her recent orgasm were more than sufficient lubrication. The artificially smooth surface of the dong slid over her sensitive inner folds, still quivering from her last climax.

It felt nothing at all like a human cock. Yet it was tremendously exciting: both the sensation, and the thought of what she was doing. She had almost total control. By angling her pelvis in one direction or another, she could stimulate regions of her internal anatomy that she had not known existed. Marcus lay mostly passive, but occasionally he would give an involuntary jerk, driving the artificial phallus deeper than she would have believed possible.

She moved slowly and deliberately, willing herself not to hurry after her last, precipitous climax. Marcus watched her as she humped him, eyes smoldering behind his mask. He appeared to be enjoying this as much as she was.

A stir in the air, the sensation of heat behind her: with a sigh of delight, Marla settled herself on her twin's sheathed penis. Miranda felt the other woman's warm breath on her neck, heard her whispers. She's doing it, Miranda thought wildly, almost unbelieving. She's fucking her own brother. Then sensation overwhelmed her, and Miranda stopped thinking.

"Oh, Randi dear, isn't it lovely? We've been looking for someone like you for such a long time . . ." Now there was silence, only groans and exclamations, as Marcus arched his back and thrust hard into both their depths.

They had found their rhythm now, the three of them, riding together toward ecstasy. Miranda felt Marla's rigid nipples brush against her back. She reached behind her with one hand, seeking the heart of the other woman's pleasure amidst the wet curls. She felt a surge of triumph as she found it, the slippery little button buried there, and heard Marla's gasp of pleasure. In answer, Marla reached around and secured Miranda's nipple between her fingers. As Miranda rubbed Marla's clit against the hard shaft buried between her legs, Marla answered with a pinch that caused Miranda to cry out.

They were one being, like the triad in the hall outside, thrusting and answering, teasing and tormenting each other, each pulling the others along on the upward climb. The curtained room smelled of sweat and sex; it was hot, and close, but no one noticed. Miranda worked Marla's clit with one hand, squeezed the base of Marcus' penis with other. Marla's finger slid provocatively between the wet cheeks of Miranda's buttocks, a mere suggestion, but enough to send Miranda into a frenzy of fear and desire. Marcus had two fingers inside

Miranda, alongside the dildo, stretching her to the edge of pain and over into pleasure. Unable to help herself, she climaxed again, urged on by Marcus' surging hips and his sister's sweet wails.

They finally lay together, sticky, sated and exhausted, covering each other's flesh with languid kisses. Miranda's mind was working again, and she struggled with conflicting emotions.

"Will you give us your phone number, Randi?" asked Marla softly, tracing the line of Miranda's shoulder with her tongue. "We would so love to see you again."

"I—I don't think so," Miranda began, feeling selfish and ungrateful, but terrified at the thought of them becoming a part of her life.

"Here, take ours, then." Marla extracted a card from her bag. Miranda took it without looking at it. "This has my cell phone number. You can call me anytime."

"And perhaps we will see you again here at the Fantasy Factory," said Marcus smoothly, delicately mouthing one of her still-throbbing nipples.

Miranda wriggled in involuntary pleasure, and pushed her mind back into the background. "Perhaps," she said. Deep down, though, she knew she was lying. If she were to encounter them again, she would be cold and unresponsive. Because now, they were no longer strangers.